BLISS

BLISS

A Novel

Danyel Smith

Crown Publishers New York

Published in the United States by Crown Publishers, an imprint of the
Crown Publishing Group, a division of Random House, Inc., New York.
www.crownpublishing.com

Crown is a trademark and the Crown colophon is a registered trademark
of Random House, Inc.

Library of Congress Cataloging-in-Publication Data
Smith, Danyel.
     Bliss : a novel / Danyel Smith.—1st ed.
   1. Americans—Bahamas—Fiction.   2. Sound recordng industry—Fiction.
3. Pregnant women—Fiction.   4. Single women—Fiction.   5. Music trade—
Fiction.   6. Abortion—Fiction.   7. Bahamas—Fiction.   I. Title.
     PS3619.M575B58   2005
     813'.6—dc22   2004029302

ISBN 1-4000-4642-4

Printed in the United States of America

DESIGN BY BARBARA STURMAN

10 9 8 7 6 5 4 3 2 1

First Edition

For

Parker

and

Hunter

and

for

Elliott

Hail, happy saint, on thine immortal throne,
Possest of glory, life, and bliss unknown;
We hear no more the music of thy tongue,
Thy wonted auditories cease to throng.
Thy sermons in unequall'd accents flow'd,
And ev'ry bosom with devotion glow'd,
Thou didst in strains of eloquence refin'd
Inflame the heart, and captivate the mind.
Unhappy we the setting sun deplore,
So glorious once, but ah! It shines no more.

—PHILLIS WHEATLEY, 1770

BLISS

leek and pinned-back as a ballerina, Eva strode through the Great Hall of Waters, efficiently hiding hurt. She was a living ad for sexiness and blithe self-sufficiency, an earthbound overlord of sun and stars. Eva was at the Lost City Resort on Paradise Island in the Bahamas, and Eva had to pee.

She clicked past a casino's smoked windows and stepped into a lobby restroom of the Coral Towers. In a mirror, Eva checked her quick grimace for smudges, then, from the knot at her nape, deftly pulled bangs across half one eyebrow and fully over the other.

I look good. It's all about singularity, attitude, and lotsa panache. Plus the sit-ups. And the Tuscan pollen face cream with olive oil.

Eva took a long glance at the doors guarding toilets. She tightened up, decided to hold it. Decided the tension would keep her on her toes.

Her cell chirped. A 206 number flashed on the caller ID.

Home calling.

Eva's father.

She watched the number until it faded. Eva's new phone fit in her palm like a secret, and she could reach out and be reached wherever she was in the world. Absently, she ran her thumb over the phone's buttons. Eva believed the cell tripled her productivity and her freedom.

She walked through the Corals toward The Lagoon Bar & Grill, which had been closed to the public for the night to house Showcase Savoir Faire. Eva wasn't one to sweat promptness. It wasn't a priority in the music industry. But on this night, she was desperate to get to a show, and with its bright lights, The Lagoon shone like a sanctuary. Eva felt thin-skinned and distracted by the independence of her insides. But if she could get to the showcase in time to handle what she was supposed to as associate general manager of Roadshow Records, and get there looking flawless, it might matter less that she was probably pregnant.

In the Coral Lounge Atrium Lobby, Eva's cell rang again and she quickly answered the familiar 212 number. "It's Eva," she said airily, like the caller should be lucky for the connection.

"All on track?" It was Eva's boss, Judeo-Spanish Sebastian, calling from New York. Judeo-Spanish was the first thing that came to mind about Sebastian because he always talked about Judeo-Spanish history and how, among other honors, Judeo-Spanishness should have a month of its own. He was raised in Arizona, spoke fluent Español. He went to mass on Easter Sunday and Christmas Eve, and demanded a kosher town house at the same time he demanded ebony vertical blinds. He loved to turn cocktail conversation into an homily about how he was a true Sephardic, a *converso*, a *sabatista* descended from Jews forced to convert to Catholicism and flee Spain way back in Columbus's time.

God bless him, Eva often thought. *But it's old.*

"Yep," Eva said to him, "all on track."

"Sunny's hype? And you're sure about these changes to the show, this—"

"I'm sure." *Don't say "hype," when you've never been, in your life. You hired me to oversee the so-called urban acts so you wouldn't have to attend Showcase Savoir Faires. Let me do my thing.* Sunny was Roadshow's barefoot, yoga-preaching, tie-dyed, incense-burning superstar singer. Sunny was Eva's responsibility.

"I don't have to tell *you* how much rides on this," Sebastian said. "It's not just the money, though it is that . . . it's Sunny . . . she could . . . you know her contract situation better than I do."

Don't patronize. "It's all going to work out. I'm sure of it." *Almost.*

"Everybody's contracts are about up—yours . . . mine."

Yours pays you out in the millions. Mine— "It's fine, Seb, all fine. I need to—"

"Go, go! We're pulling for you back here, Evey. You're the money-maker."

My name is Eva. The *tink-tinkle* of a nearby fountain caused Eva to tighten up again. But to pee would stab her with the fact that she should be taking the pregnancy test she had in her suite. It would put her in warm wet touch with a life-and-death decision. She walked past another restroom.

"See you when?" Sebastian broke the silence. "Day after tomorrow? Evey?"

"Yes, Seb, for sure." Eva hated Sebastian's wheedle. *Why wheedle from a position of power?*

"You're my girl," he said atypically, like she might confirm her loyalty. "You know that. My ace."

"I'm at the venue," Eva said. He'd set off an alarm in her brain. She thought he might be overcompensating for something, or that he'd somehow peeped her weakness.

Plus, Eva was actually in front of a store at the Crystal Court: duty-free shopping, local stoneware, and lavishly printed Bahamian picture books. She stared through the window with her jaw tight. Eva heard Sebastian say, "Hit me back later," as she took in the store's main display—a basket stuffed with two magnums of champagne, and a tray of chocolates big as a briefcase. The shrink-wrapped basket sat above a sign: THE ULTIMATE GIFT: PURE INDULGENCE.

Eva had one on the vanity in her suite. Card signed, RON.

Dead cell still at her ear, Eva stared at the package.

That lazy motherfucker.

I got your ultimate gift.

The showcase had begun. Almost everyone attending the Vince the Voice Urban Music Takes Over the World: International Marketing for the Millennium convention was packed into a pergola surrounded by a moat filled with real sharks and stingrays. Mostly there were middle-aged eastern and midwestern radio executives at The Lagoon—hometown heroes just town-bound enough to relish Paradise Island for its medley of mock and real splendor. Beneath a ceiling painted to look watery and filled with things thalassic, they drank and ate freely and for free, celebrating year-end bonuses and the heaven of a seventy-five-degree December evening.

At the bar, there were major and minor executives from major and minor record labels. These people had not only shopped for Prada and Zegna at stateside stores, they'd trudged Milan's Via Spiga lugging ribbon-tied bags and stopping for risotto at trattorias mentioned in magazines. These were Eva's cronies, and most were notorious either for having seen a project to multiplatinum fruition, or for having run it, burning, into the ground. The ones accorded the most deference had lucratively brought an artist back from the hushed hell of irrelevance. Eva'd done it twice in her career. It was a mission that required an array of exaggerated expressions (including a steadfast poker face), plus experience, contacts, timing, dirt done (and so markers on call), providence, perceived and real power, and luck. Plus the ability to persuade, counsel, negotiate, and straight-out lie—all while seeming to tipsily shoot the breeze.

She was on the brink of a less colossal exercise, but Eva was fighting industry talk of Sunny's burnout, of Sunny's disenchantment with Roadshow, and of Sunny's lack of appreciation for her mostly black fan base. Industry talk had a way of seeping out to the record-buying public, so Eva had been charged—by herself and, to a lesser degree, by Sebastian—with the mission of bringing Sunny back to black. How Eva would articulate such a skill on her résumé she'd work out when the time came. But she had a plan and it was about to go into effect at Showcase Savoir Faire.

Out of respect, Eva'd sent personal invitations for Sunny's show-case to influential execs from other labels, and she was gratified to see her occasional mentor, Meri "Ms. Exception" Heath, duck in. There were also programmers there from MTV and BET, and columnists, mostly from the trades. Sunny secretly loved being interviewed and written about, dissected, and pseudo-psychoanalyzed, so at Roadshow's expense, a few high-ranking consumer magazine editors had been flown down. It was a recoupable expense for her company, which meant Sunny was paying for them.

Eva had slaved in artists and repertoire, in marketing, and in radio promotions. She'd worked in Los Angeles, New York, Washington, D.C., and Chicago. Her current position at Roadshow afforded her a bland, professionally decorated three-bedroom on Manhattan's Riverside Drive, as well as a duplex in Santa Monica, where Eva had installed a stone-trimmed fireplace far too big for her gleaming living room. Eva'd barely been at either place since she'd signed Sunny. There was always another business trip she could take, something more she could be doing for her salary of $531,000 a year, and her "points" on Sunny's albums. For every CD sold, and in addition to her salary, Eva made a couple of cents. In addition to managing a small staff, and being responsible for a hefty portion of Roadshow's profit margin, what Eva did for this money, when it came down to it, was attend to Sunny. Eva was quite clear on the fact that any labels' self-depiction—that it was a genuine sponsor for its artists—was bogus, and that the only fair payments record companies made were to those acts who had the means to coerce accountability.

Eva looked up at the slaty clouds and placed her hand briefly over her navel. *Sunny*, Eva thought, *has the means.*

So Eva was able to look Sunny in her face, most of the time, with some ease.

In a wraparound white silk jersey dress, Eva stood at The Lagoon's bar on four inches of stiletto. Across her foot, where her toes began, was a white kid braid. Another, with the help of a tiny gold buckle, fastened above her ankle. Nicks decorated Eva's shins—trophies from long-ago softball afternoons. Each of her ears was pierced once, but her skin was otherwise pure; not so much as a strawberry mark, or a ladybug of a mole. Her neckline plunged, but Eva had on a reliable,

Swiss-lace, half-cup bra. *Lifts 'em up round and high. Shows everything but itself. These younger chicks, even the ones with a check—still wearing dresses from mall stores and Playtex brassieres.* Eva was as comfortable in her outfit as she was in a jogging suit. She strode and stood in her teetery sandals like they were rubber-soled. *Been doing this a long time.*

In walked Ron. Eva liked that Ron was gruff and clever and that he didn't care that people knew he was a sneak. Eva liked his wide, firm body. He was president of urban music at one of the major record labels. Properly late and properly dapper, Ron had his palm on the back of a former MC, a pretty girl who'd had one regional hit and then faded from the public eye, but not completely from Ron's. That she was his choice for the Bahamas made sense, as the girl was from nearby Tampa. Eva'd heard the girl was teaching elementary school, and a recent Where-Are-They-Now?-type radio show had mentioned that the Tampa teacher had "renounced music and the business that was killing it."

Yeah, Eva thought. *Right. More like mad that her singles never hit outside of Florida.*

Tampa homegirl was thick and pretty. Hair pinned in an elegant bun, she had on an ill-fitting, expensive orange dress.

Blocky sandals, probably from Macy's. Nails done by Koreans. Tacky.

Ron guided his date to a choice table. She wore the tetchy face of a sister who'd be happier laid up in front of a movie on her suite's pay-per-view.

A bartender was trying to catch Eva's eye. She knew he wanted to offer her something special.

Ron nodded sharply at Eva, face tight because he knew the situation called for it. Once Tampa MC's face was turned, Ron glanced at Eva conspiratorially.

No doubt, Eva thought. *I'm in on it.*

Ron walked to Eva at the bar, ordered a cognac and a champagne cocktail. "You got the stuff?"

"Stuff."

"Don't fuck with me." He was breezy, watching his drinks being made. "That champagne basket. For later."

"You look busy, sweets. Doing the most, as usual."

"Huh? She's been here. Got her over at the Hurricane Club. Away from all this bullshit."

"Away from me." It was a slipup and Eva felt it, like she'd tumbled off her heels.

"You? Oh I know you don't trip off . . . me . . . girls, women, whatever. I'm talking about . . . all these people. She hates it."

"She thinks it's fake." Now Eva wanted her something special. "She's real."

Ron picked up his cocktails, turned to walk back to his table. "She don't understand it."

And she doesn't want to. Eva finally looked directly at the bartender. "What you got for me?" She toyed with the snarl of yarn and bead bracelets on her left wrist.

"Little gin with coco water," the man said, smiling. "Good for you."

Eva shook her head. "You got a nice single malt?"

"He's got whatever you want," Hakeem said, knuckle suddenly, softly on the outside of her thigh. "And pour me a vanilla rum. Same as before." Hakeem was a consultant, an old-school music impresario, and Eva's boy from way back.

Six years ago, Hakeem had been accused of mishandling funds and was asked to resign. He retained boisterous lawyers, and went to the urban and the white press screaming about "the plantation system," and the "Jim Crow setup" in the record business. He detailed salary discrepancies between the "pop" and the "urban" departments for jobs with the same titles and tasks. Until he was called on the carpet, Hakeem had never complained. So his own staff only vaguely supported him when he went Al Sharpton. The theory everyone operated from was that Hakeem was sitting on $15 million. It was 1998, though, and he still wore linen like the DRY-CLEAN-ONLY status symbol it had been for brothers in the eighties—stiffly pressed to a sheen.

"Where you been?"

"Looking for you," Hakeem said. "Smoke with me."

Unsmiling, the bartender put both drinks on the bar.

"Evey! Baby!" Myra strolled up, laughing. A tiny tape recorder dangled from a rhinestone strap at her wrist. Sunny's brother D'Artagnan was with her, and it looked like he was holding blood in his mouth.

Dart seemed taller. Less heavy. Eva hadn't seen him in four months. She talked to him on the phone all the time, business, but their curt conversations had revealed nothing of his transformation. The last time she'd seen him—*In Toronto,* Eva thought, *for some meeting with some producers*—he'd been his usual bulging self, in decent sprits, but always watching the door, or for a gap in conversation, anything through which he could escape his job as Sunny's manager.

Fixed to Dart's slab of a back was a tangerine shirt, wet and glued to a wetter sleeveless white undershirt. Sweat wept at his temples. Sweat dripped from the top of his flat nose.

Crybaby, Eva thought. *Control yourself.*

"I've been searching all over for you," Myra said, wagging her recorder at Eva like it was finger. "D'Artagnan's trying to get me drunk! Ha! He don't know the blocks I been around."

"Miss *Myra,*" Eva said with open arms. "Queen of All. In the house to see my girl set shit off." Myra'd been running her own so-called marketing company for eleven years. But she didn't have clients. Mostly she hosted cocktails—little in-things at which attendance was required in order to gain her good graces. Her clout rested in a gossipy, preachy weekly column—"Square Biz"—mass-faxed to everyone in urban music. Myra had long-standing associations with the United Negro College Fund, *Soul Train,* and the Congressional Black Caucus. She was petted and patronized and often paid as a consultant by casting directors and potential corporate sponsors. Myra led them toward trendily yet completely clothed artists who lamented in interviews about the state of the youth and the injurious, embarrassing nature of gangsta rap. Myra's faves publicly craved "positivity" for the Community, so, after Chevrolet or Budweiser phoned Myra for a high sign, Chevy or Bud called the artist's manager: *You want to be a part of our concert tour? We'd like to use a song of yours in a commercial for our new sedan.* Then glasses clinked. Myra clocked her dollars and her power points. Eva would sit back at these buttery post-contract-signing lunches and calculate how much authenticity her artist was trading. She'd figure out from which pile her own money would be made.

At the showcase, Myra was sparkly and important. "Yes, *sweetums*. Here strictly for Sunny. And my expectations are high-high-*high*." Myra gave a little cackle, and then looked at Eva more directly. "I know you're not nervous."

"Never that," Eva said. Eva liked Myra, but hadn't trusted her for years.

"You all right? You look fabulous as usual."

Eva squared her shoulders, resurrected her game face, and showily hitched up her already high breasts. "I am fine, sister. I know you know how *I* do."

Dart slid up to the bar next to Eva. Got the bartender's attention, asked for tonic with lime. Dart looked at Eva with hazy interest. She was the busty cover of a how-to he'd half-read.

"*Good* boy," Eva said to him after a sweet wink good-bye to Myra. "Keeping your mind on the job."

"What job?" Dart said.

"Taking care of Sun." Eva took a swallow of Scotch as Hakeem and Myra discussed the details of their earlier weed purchase. "If you'd ever do it."

"This ain't the place to discuss." Then Dart pressed Eva's wrist, as if to convey that what came next was an authentic request, apart from the mise-en-scène. "Talk with me about my so-called job," D'Artagnan said, "later."

Eva finished her drink. *I'm probably giving the baby defects.* She looked again to the bartender. "Tall glass of still water, please?"

Ron came up behind Eva, put a bearish hand on her back, and reached out the other to shake Dart's. "How's Sun?" Ron said as greeting. It was usually the first thing people said to Dart.

"She's doing her thing," he said. "Like always." Dart returned Ron's handshake in the robotic way it had been offered. Dart watched Ron move his hand to the top of Eva's ass, watched as Eva, seemingly untouched, looked with weary eyes into the door-size mirror over the bar. Dart pushed Eva her water, looked at her with his brows in a frown.

In the mirror, Eva saw a huddle of young guys hustle up to seersuckered Ron, urging him to go with them.

The looks on their faces, Eva thought. *They want to be him so badly they'd eat shit. They are eating shit. But at least they're eating it in the Bahamas.*

After a meaningful pinch to Eva's waist, Ron made his way, hand-shaking all the time, backstage. He kissed Myra grandly, full on the lips. Hugged Hakeem like he was a long-lost cousin. Ron was to go onstage, introduce his already successful new act, and talk about his plans for them.

It was also time for Eva to check on Sunny. As Eva rose, Dart said, "I'ma stay with Myra for a minute."

Myra turned when she heard her name. "Yes, *babeee,* see me to my table. I know Sunny's got me someplace *nice.*"

Eva zigzagged through the crowd with as few Hollywood hugs as she could manage, and it still took fifteen minutes. Amid the jump and jabber of backstage, Sunny spoke to Eva from behind a paper screen attached to the ceiling. "Yes, I'm dressed," Sunny said, annoyed with the rough setup. "Yes, I'm ready."

Eva hated that Sunny could hear the loud applause for Ron's group as they left the stage. His trio shouted out Tupac Shakur and the Notorious B.I.G., "We all gotta come *together* now. We gotta do it for hip hop!"

How about we all gotta be not quite so wack? How about we all gotta stop biting 'Pac's style? How about we gotta realize—just like jazz, just like grunge, just like punk, just like what fools still call "rock"—hip hop is over, dead, finished, and we're still in costume, in denial?

Then Myra and Dart came backstage. And Hakeem. And then Ron was nearby, backslapping. Eva barely heard him, but she heard him mutter to someone, "Tie-dye . . . rose petals, yoga. Same . . . barefoot Sunny shit. Played out."

Fuck him. I got his tie-dye.

"This is gonna work, right?" Sunny asked. Before Eva could answer, Sun said exactly what Eva would have: "These fools, they'll see."

So Eva left Sunny's side to boss the crew's placement of the yoga stuff. It was Sunny's thing—to do, and to command audiences to stretch into yoga positions from the stage. In her heels and white dress, Eva rearranged ropes and rolled mats. Pushed forward the microphone stand. Dart was spacey, as he could be sometime. *But he could at least help me make sure the set is right. Is this what it is to be associate GM?* It was all Eva knew: to do. To overdo. To keep her bat high and her eye on every ball in the vicinity. She dusted her hands on the back of her outfit.

Sun's small band trudged onstage, bulky and uncomfortable look-ing in baggy black pants and huge work shirts. For the giant cones of incense Sunny usually burned, tall white urns were placed onstage. All this was done, purposefully, with the stage lights up.

The convention chairman came over and told Eva it was time. He was a spry eighty and owned a tiny, trendsetting soul station outside Cleveland. Eva looked at Dart. He got it, and with his biggest voice, began to clear backstage.

"*EVERYBODY* out." Dart was even louder than usual. In his regular tones he said to Eva, "Giving it my best 'cause it's my last time around."

But Eva barely acknowledged Dart's usual escape plans because her ears were tuned to Myra's voice. "Drama queen Sunny," Myra cooed to a colleague. "Behind that paper like the Queen of Sheba."

"Sunny needs backstage *CLEAR. NOW.*" The audience could hear Dart, which was a large part of the point. His bottomless voice was such that even Myra and Hakeem scuttled off.

Sunny's band silenced their tune-up when Eva stepped onstage to catcalls. It took only two flashing camera bulbs to get her mind right.

"Ladies and gentlemen," Eva said coolly into the microphone, "I give you Roadshow Records' number one artist for the last two years in a row. I give you one of the best singer-songwriters of our time. I give you a two-time Grammy winner. I give you a two-time *Soul Train* Award winner. I give you an American Music Award win-ner, and an MTV Music Video Award winner." Swingy and confident, Eva delivered her spiel like the pro she'd become after thirteen years in the record business. Plus she'd seen her father perfect pitches for everything from juicers to desert real estate. *Don't convince anyone of anything,* he used to say. *Say it like you're saying grass is green. Say it half-exasperated, but like you're gracious enough to remind them of the obvious. Then they're indebted.* "I give you an artist," Eva continued after a contrived sigh, "grateful to all her friends at urban and Top Forty radio, grateful to MTV and BET, grateful to the urban press and the pop press." Eva took a big, exaggerated breath. *"Ladies* and *gentle*men, I give you the woman who showed you the way to a *Bliss Unknown.* Who introduced you to *Poems on Various Subjects.* A young woman, who, after a debut that remained in the number one slot for fourteen weeks, remained in the top ten for another *forty-three.* A singer-songwriter who has sold *thirty-seven million* albums world-wide. Ladies and gentlemen of radio, I give you a—"

"Um, Eva?" There was some satisfied laughter from the audience. "You're going on," Dart said, "kind of long." Rumbling from the public address system, his tones were otherworldly. People clapped and hooted. No one could see Dart, but they knew his voice. Knew his role as Sunny's protector. Had heard that he took no cut of Sunny's money. People operated on the theory that Dart and Eva were still having an affair. The music industry was performance on all levels, so Eva and Dart were the show within the show.

"Oh, am I?" Eva put a hand on a hip. Shtick all the way for deto-nating trade magazine flashbulbs. Eva stretched her mouth, tried to show every tooth she had. It was the way to look genuinely enthusi-astic. A photographer'd told Eva that long ago, and it was the kind of tip she held onto. "Well then, Dart—*honey,*" she said. "I guess you better take on over."

He waited a beat. Then: "I thought so."

People started to laugh more loudly—the beautiful Evil Eva had been *put in her place.* Then the lights were black. The crowd startled into sudden, short silence. The lights hadn't gone to *complete* black all night. Eva dashed offstage. All was going to plan.

Dart's voice boomed again from the PA. "There's no worry about the *dark* when we've got our *own light.* MY SISTER . . ."—he started speaking more slowly, and more like a professional announcer—"the SUN . . . is about to . . . RISE!"

The lights went up. And amid the yoga clutter stood Sunny in a pale yellow georgette dress. The Empire waist hid her hips and not-quite-flat belly. The dress was cut just off her lustrous shoulders, and beads winked from her bodice. A layered skirt split in front to display a shimmering gold sheath underneath, hem bent against the floor. Sunny wore her hair tight off her face and bursting from the back of her head in a pouf of dangling tendrils. Gone was the puffy ponytail. Gone were the faded overalls and tie-dyed tank. Eva thought for a second that people might not even know it was Sunny.

The keyboardist hit one chord and the band stood.

He hit another and they yanked off the work shirts to reveal tuxedo jackets and bow ties.

Drama!

One more chord and the band took a slow bow. They started at the same time, stopped, and came back up. In unison. The crowd, especially for an industry crowd, went wild.

Damn! We love it when things happen in unison. We love a goddamn talent show.

The keyboardist banged another rich chord and the lights went dark again. There were gasps.

Eva smiled in the darkness, and this time it wasn't so wide, but was far more true. Lights up again, and the stage crew ran out and removed all the yoga stuff. They placed long-stemmed white lilies in the urns. This took seven seconds. The audience was enthralled.

"All right, Sunny, you better work it out!" Someone shouted it from near the front, and claps popped off like firecrackers.

Then Dart walked onstage and slipped on his sister's wrist a corsage of miniature lilies. Sun looked like a prom queen. Dart gave her a kiss on her cheek, and then a little bow. As he walked off, Dart handed Myra a lily from the stage. The whole plot was Eva's idea.

Put that in your goddamn column, Myra. Headline: SUN SHINES!

The house was dark again, except for a soft spot on Sunny.

No more incense. No tired rose petals. Now what, assholes? Now what?

The band played the first bars of a classic early eighties slow jam from an R & B group honed long ago in a Memphis studio. Sunny began to sing. No microphone.

At the chorus, an older guy walked on stage to a standing ovation.

It was a brother who'd been part of the popular Memphis group. During the mid-eighties, he'd gone solo to worldwide acclaim. The guy did two concerts a year: one free outdoor show in his rural hometown, and another in Vegas, at $300 a seat.

Don't call it a comeback, Eva thought, in L.L. Cool J's fadeless words. *I been here for years.*

The star and Sun picked up mikes and sang together. Sunny's band picked up the pace and pumped up the volume. She'd pretty much recomposed the song—modified it harmonically, added bass, left out the synthesized strings and the sax bridge. The older guy raised his brows in places, startled by Sun's stuttered phrasings in the last chorus, but by the last soaring notes, the man was smiling. His eyes wet, face shiny, and artist's soul flattered: Sun had taken his song seriously, treated it with creativity and respect.

Eva was elated. *So much could've gone wrong. It's not a new trick, taking it back to the old school, but it can still work.*

In his too-tight suit, the tenor took a bow, waved graciously, then went to a table in the front near Myra and Hakeem and Dart. By staying for the rest of the show, the singer blessed Sunny. There was stomping from the audience, and barking.

"Lilies ev-er-ee-where," Sunny cooed. People quieted quickly, eager, after the extreme makeover, for a bit of Original Sunny, conveyor of arcane, vaguely mystical knowledge. The speech was important. Eva had written it after she and Sun came up with the lily idea together. Sunny had practiced it down to the pauses between sentences, just as they'd choreographed every inch of the performance. Eva thought the speech would ward off naysayers who'd claim Sun had sold out in a chiffon dress. Forgotten herself. It was the main trick required of successful entertainers—no matter how much money you made or how differently you felt or how differently people treated you, you could never not be the same person you were when you were searching for a deal. Even if you hated that person, she was the core of the story fans fell in love with. The rule—for purveyors of soul and realness—was to not sell out, even when everyone was buying you. "Unplanted by human hands, lilies appear on graves of people executed for crimes they didn't even commit. Lilies protect gardens from evil spirits. To dream of lilies in spring foretells marriage, happiness, and prosperity." And then with a small laugh, she said, "And the Romans cured calluses with the juice from lily bulbs—so you know I like lilies!"

Eva'd nixed some of the other lily myths. *Legend tells that the lily sprang from Eve's tears, when upon being expelled from Eden she learned she was pregnant. In China, the daylily is the emblem for motherhood.*

The folks down front were delighted.

There were shouts of "Where's your feet, Sun?"

"You got shoes on with that dress?

"Sunny, show your toes! Even if they got corns!"

Backstage, Ron looked at Eva like he was bored. Then, with mock affection, he embraced a minor rap duo—DJ Victorious and MC Swansong—now too old to ever even go gold. They'd devolved into almost pure hangers-on, and Vic, especially, hung on to Sunny whenever she called him.

So Eva looked at Ron like he was boring. Then her attention went back to Sunny. All her new songs were covers of liquid seventies and eighties ballads, and her medley struck a chord with this group. They were pleased Sun had shown respect for what came before her. By recording songs written by artists who'd peaked back when Michael Jackson was the only black singer selling tens of millions of albums, Sunny was making old heroes some new money. Plus, the radio execs at The Lagoon would go home and program Sun's covers because they'd want to hear the songs they'd grown up listening to.

Finally, Sunny sang her own "Imagination." It was the first song Eva had heard Sunny sing, and her biggest hit. It was about an outsider lonely child's journey toward her authentic self and the tainted loves she imagines she'll have along the way. By the last verse, the lonely child loves herself and that love opens the door for a true, lasting love relationship built on respect and passion and acceptance. Sunny put the mike down and blew it out like she liked to, with no music behind her at all. Sunny sang "Imagination" because the crowd always wanted it, and the reason people wanted it was because Sunny sang the song like it would die inside her without liberation. Heads nodded slowly. Hands rested on forgotten cocktails. Eva felt privileged to watch and hear Sunny, overcome by the fact that she was a part of bringing Sunny to the world.

As she closed the last soft notes of her theme song, sweat glowed on her forehead, and Sunny lifted, like a princess about to ascend a staircase, the front hem of her dress to her knees.

On cue.

Sunny's feet were bare. Like always.

Where is the line? Between authenticity and act? Is this a pure moment? Or is it corrupt and fake because of the choreography, the plan?

Please, stand, people! My life will be so much easier if I'm not pregnant, and if you all just stand up.

The crowd leaped to a standing ovation.

Eva laughed loud and big and no one could hear her over the applause and shout-outs.

"Love you, Sunny!"

"We love you!"

"Sun, rise! Sun, rise! Sun, rise!"

Sunny basked in the chant until it almost faded, then she faced her palms to the crowd. "Thank you all. A special thanks to my friend—" she held her hand out to the Memphis star, who stood and kissed it. Sun put her hand over her heart like she would die of the beauty. "I'd like to thank my brother Dart, of course, and Roadshow. I'd like to thank all of you at radio for—"

"You got it, Sunny!"

"Straight to number one!"

"We'll be rocking you in Chi-Town, Sunny!"

"Birmingham's been down since day one!"

Eva felt Ron in the wings beside her. She looked at him, and he gave her a clandestine thumbs-up. Eva pressed down in herself the urge to kiss his face.

"There's another person I want to thank," Sunny said. "You all know Eva."

Eva's heart beat fast. She loved money, no question. Money was important. Money was security and freedom and fun. But it was for the Showcase Savoir Faires that she worked so hard: lots of times, the planning paid off. The traveling, the cajoling, the budgeting—the work *worked*. And when it did, there was this praise. This feeling of accomplishment and appreciation. There was a thumbs-up from Ron. Eva's pulse thumped in her throat. On a night like this, she'd do it all gladly and for free.

"Eva, come out here."

Okay, Sun's not one to call people onstage with her. I had to crawl over thumbtacks to get her ass to agree to the duet.

"Go on out, Eva," Ron said. "Sun's in a good mood."

Eva walked out aflutter, and Sunny hugged her tight. "Thank you," she said, pulling back and looking Eva in her eyes. "For opening me up to new things, for caring about me and my music."

Eva placed her palms together like she was praying, put the tips of her index fingers to her lips, and bowed her head. Tears in her eyes, there were no clouds higher that Eva could walk on. Validation surged in her calves and thighs, and it rolled her hips as she strode offstage to cheers.

"A-plus for you," Ron said. "Gold stars." His eyes drooped with admiration and competition and the want to have Eva under him, way off her heels, her eyes closed as usual to the depth of their rendezvous.

"Just one more thing," Sunny said, addressing the audience again. "If I could impose on your patience."

She's going to sing another song? Ron's right. Sun is in a great mood.

"This convention is about new music?" Sunny said. "Am I right?"

"Yeah!"

"Goddamn right!"

Eva had no idea what Sunny was going to do. This wasn't rehearsed.

"I seen you in that dress before," Ron said in Eva's ear. "In Miami, at the Rap Symposium. Some zero from L.A. all in your chest."

"So," she said with a quick, interested look away from the stage. "You were checking me."

"Checking you right now. Got something I want to show you in my room. A video. I want your opinion."

"You want my opinion." Eva watched the stage. Sunny was taking accolade after accolade. They wouldn't let her finish her speech.

"I want you in my room," Ron said, pressing up on her. "And I want your opinion. On a few things."

"Go on," Eva said, shrugging him off. It seemed he was distracting her on purpose.

Ron held out a Lost City plastic key card like it was hers and he was returning it.

Eva swatted at it. "What makes you think I want to go to your room?" Eva was irritated, thinking about Ron's Tampa MC, over at the Hurricane Club. And Sunny was trying to say her piece. "There ain't shit for me in your room."

"That's not," Ron told her, "what you said earlier." He reached and pinched Eva's breast hard, through the white fabric, near her right nipple. "I said I got something to show you." He cupped his dick with his hand.

Eva could've bit him. *So fucking ignorant and wannabe.* But then she heard Sunny's voice.

"*You* all decide what's hot and what's not," Sunny said to the finally quiet crowd. "So I'm gonna . . . I've created my own label—Sonrisa, that's 'smile' in Spanish—and these guys are signed to it. We're looking for some radio play! They're just going to do one number, but you're going to want them to do more."

No.

Imitating Eva's introduction, Sunny said, "Ladies and gentlemen, I give you the future of hip hop—DJ Victorious and the extremely talented MC Swansong."

The wind knocked from her, Eva felt like she was going to pee on herself. Her breast throbbed where Ron had bruised it.

Eva turned to walk away and Ron grabbed her wrist.

She yanked it from him without looking back. Eva felt like she was going to trip, but she didn't.

hat's not what you said earlier.

Earlier.

Before the showcase . . .

. . . On the terrace of Ron's penthouse. Pink petals shot from bursts of greens. Two open champagne bottles sat on a glass-topped table near a carafe of clear rum. On an avocado omelet, flies rested like fat raisins. Eva identified with the insects. Accustomed to excess, they'd lost their intensity.

Ron opened his hotel room door. "I knew you'd be up here," he said. Then, as if against his will: "Your hair looks nice."

"You like?" Eva stepped closer to the open sliding glass, where the sun would show off her highlights. "Got a perm and a little color—Cherry Cordial, it's called—about . . . a week ago."

"Just take the compliment. Leave some shit to the imagination." Ron pulled off his shirt and walked into the bathroom. Water sprayed, and then hit tiles in a steady rhythm.

Through the open doors, Eva heard him pee. As his body split the strum of the shower, she heard him groan. Eva raised one nostril high.

It was difficult for Eva to get her arms around Ron. He ate skirt steak and vodka sauce and fried veal chops and brulées, but he worked out all the time, so lots of him, even though he was stout, wasn't soft. Eva'd gone out with Ron, on and off, for almost six years.

Theory was fact in the record business, and the prevailing theory was that Ron had $4 or $5 million, mostly cash. For eight years, he'd managed a respected, increasingly platinum trio from East New York. The relationship had ended in a fireball of lawsuits and threats of blackballing and bodily harm. But Ron bounced to a label job, and also became a not-so-silent partner in a consulting firm that coached companies through what was being called the "urban" marketplace. His company acted as interpreter, translating "inner-city" trends. The business plan mentioned the "articulation of ethnic style points" in boldface.

When *Rolling Stone* asked Ron why he didn't "retire," play golf with Tiger Woods, and travel the world, Ron, thirty-five, said that he already played golf with Michael Jordan, and that he'd been around the world so many times, he was tired of looking at it. Ron had been to many capitals, but Eva knew that most of what he'd seen were small, ugly hotel rooms and big, beautiful ones. Ragged two-bit venues and fabulous forums. Eva and Ron had a broad-yet-blind worldview in common. Eva believed that on their best nights, she and Ron learned important things from each other.

They rarely talked about Roadshow, or the label where Ron worked, and Eva didn't miss it. Really, they were competitors. Sunny and her younger brother, D'Artagnan, had self-produced a folksy, bluesy song that had become a local hit in San Diego in 1995. By the time stations in L.A. started playing it, four labels were bidding for Sunny, including Ron's. At the last moment, Sunny went with Roadshow. To Ron, making records had little to do with the labels or the conglomerates. He understood spreadsheets and profit-and-loss statements, but according to Ron, the record business was a business of personalities, and even paid as he was, it bothered him that his hadn't won Sunny over.

Eva poured herself a glass of warm champagne. It still had bubbles. *If I'm pregnant*, she thought, *it's got to be better for me than rum.*

Eva figured the record business to be like fencing—choreographed but bloody, and bound by archaic rules. She wasn't always the fastest, but Eva'd had her share of laughing last. When she won Sunny, Eva's saber had been sharp, no button on the tip of her blade. As soon as the signing was announced, people whispered, loudly, that Eva had boned D'Artagnan.

She's a slut. Only reason she got This is 'cause she did That.
I feel sorry for Eva. It's just how she is.
That bitch fights for shit like a man.
Shit, she fucks like a man.

Messengers Eva wanted to murder brought her bits of these bites, and they scratched a bare part of her. When Eva was still smoking, *You fight like a man* made her flick ashes in slow motion, hold the cig for a long minute with her thumb on the filter. The comments caused her to stretch her inhale.

But she always had something for the judgmental assholes who called her out. Later, after the mesh masks had been put away.

It was how her father did business, how he lived his life. Eva'd learned a lot from her dad. He'd told her many times that men could get thrown off by sex, or even the prospect of it. Told Eva one afternoon, when she was with her parents for the summer, and glowering over the end of a romance with a deejay, that she needed to realize some things early. "Every boy," he said, "ain't your boyfriend."

Eva's father was a tidy man with ice-white teeth, a crane's neck, and graying hair dyed black as licorice. They were on a ferry from Cape May, New Jersey, to Delaware for his mother-in-law's funeral. He leaned over the railing, watched the stern slice bay water. "You're a good-looking girl. This isn't coming from your father right now, it's coming from a man. Save yourself the bullshit." Eva's father turned to face her. "Love can be done without. More easily than people think." Eva was seventeen, and already done with her first year of college. Her stepmother was belowdecks, weepy and eating. "It's a whitewash, this love madness. A beautiful whitewash, but a whitewash just the same."

On deck with the dog people and first-timers and cigarette smokers, in a cold summer breeze, Eva's dad said, "You better know who you are. What you have to offer." He smoothed blowing hair from her face. "I have *never* seen you look this ugly. You're not going to be falling out over every man you sleep with." He swept his palms against each other. "I *know* that. I'm not saying some men won't be more important to you than others. What I'm saying is—there's nothing wrong with a little pussy between friends."

He stood straight, looked at her with a mix of pity and affection, and with irritation. His only daughter was wasting time. "Over some pissant," he said to Eva, chastely rubbing her back. "Men'll cry over *you*. Maybe this is good, though, how you feel. It'll get your mind right."

---

hat's not what you said earlier.
Before the showcase . . .

. . . Eva finished half a bottle of champagne. Baked in the Bahamian beams. She laughed in her head as Ron moaned about having forgot his mango-mint shaving cream.

"You like hot bubbly?" he said. "Come get in the bed."

"Don't have time for all this." Eva walked in the room. Stepped from her glittering sandals. Ron sat on the unmade bed, naked. On his right pec, there was an angry skull with an idea bulb bright yellow above. On his right bicep, a Chinese symbol for "peace." Around his left forearm, the words FOR LOVE IS WAR AND THERE IS HATRED IN IT were raised in a bleeding, calligraphic scar.

"Quiet with the bullshit." He waved at her bathing suit. "Off. Beautiful."

She liked to hear it like that. "That's what you want?" She untied the top of her suit and the back of it.

"Sit on my lap."

His belly came out far enough that there wasn't much lap to sit on. She stood in front of him and he pulled down the brief bottom of her bikini. Held her by her hips and kissed her stomach admiringly. Slow, mute kisses. Took a breast in each hand, pulled them down to his mouth. Sucked for a long time, until Eva's knees locked. He wasn't handling them roughly, but he was still hurting her breasts with his teeth, with the sucking and wringing. He was gorging himself. *As usual.* Eva was wobbly and wet. He knew how to do it.

Ron took a breath. Ran his palms up and down her torso. "This here keeps me coming back."

He took a nipple between each thumb and index finger. Pulled her like that, toward him. He had done it before, and Eva had pulled away from him, to lengthen the tug. But this time the pain had too fine an edge, like paper cutting into her flesh. Eva yelped, fell forward on him, and they both fell back on the bed. Ron laughed from his gut as he slapped around for a condom, then searched around for his dick, and then put it into her.

"You're my baby," Eva said.

"Say it for me again."

"You heard me," she said, stretching into him. "You're my baby."

Ron made it last. He could from his back. They both knew that.

Ron slept loudly. Eva put on her suit. It felt grimy, damp, and used. She tied her skirt around her in a plain knot. On the terrace for her beach bag, Eva smelled rum getting warm with the day. It was noon. With a last searching glance at the floor and other spare surfaces of the room, Eva was gone and back in her own room, a wing and three floors away. Room-service trays still stood in her corridor.

While in her bath, Eva watched the clock. Though Sunny was on the resort's premises, Eva heard and ignored her room's phone. She dried and lotioned and perfumed herself, then slipped into a white silk jersey dress, the best one in her bag. Eva didn't know where the afternoon had gone. Time had lost its usual texture. The clock flipped minutes and hours, but Eva was counting weeks. Counting the steps between herself and the pregnancy test in her nightstand drawer. Eva applied pale gold eyeliner to her lids and shimmery powder to her shoulders and three coats of mascara. It was soundcheck time for Showcase Savoir Faire.

But first she listened to her hotel voice mail.

```
. . . gone like a thief in the fucking night.
That's why we hang. You roll like a dude.
You know who this is. You got something
nice coming your way . . .
```

When she opened the door to leave, Eva startled a bellman. He stood there with a big basket of booze and sweets. "The gentleman says to mention he created it especially for you," the uniformed man said, looking past her. He set the gift on Eva's vanity, as flustered by Eva's glowy appearance as if she'd appeared in nothing but panties. "The gentleman wanted that fact impressed." Eva tipped the bellman $10 as he left. Right before she walked out the door herself, Eva smoothed a stray hair back into her tight chignon. She glanced at the packed basket, and then looked a final time in the mirror. Eva was glittery.

Yes, she thought, untangling the frayed bracelets at her wrist, and noting the gleam of the karat-and-a-half diamond studs she never removed from her ears. *I look very natural.*

D J Victorious and MC Swansong performed and they were faux thuggy and terrible, but Eva didn't see them. She left as the duo was getting started, and she was far from the only one. The after-parties had already started, and people farthest from the stage had been filtering out since Sunny started talking about lilies. Eva paced the grounds of the hotel, which suddenly seemed devoid of bathrooms. Eva really, really had to pee.

Plus, she knew the routine. Swan and Vic would perform badly, but folks would gas Sunny up and drive her to the top again, eventually lure her to their chitlin' circuit towns for Summer Jam concerts and Quiet Storm Extravaganzas. They'd also have the pleasure of watching Sun's new duo embarrass themselves. The radio-industry people would feel virtuous about blowing Sun up while at the same time tee-heeing because the sideshow was so amusing. This was the fun house Eva lived in. Support was iffy. Compliments were strategic. Competition was cutthroat. Emotions were product. Cliques were combustible. Jewelry was language. Generations grated. And friendships lasted as long as the mutual back-scratch. Friendships were futile, Eva thought, a vestige from the actual world, and existed in the music industry only to give it some infrastructure aside from levels of stardom and corporate job titles.

Numb from Sun's power move, Eva finally saw a well-lit hut. On the door was a triangle with a circle on top—so Eva heaved it open, hitched up her dress, and finally sat down. She felt guilty generally, but on the toilet in the bleachy bathroom she felt criminal, like she was flushing data, proof of probable life, down the toilet. Then, in the hut's bright mirror, Eva gave slight shifts or tugs to her bra straps, hem, ankle straps, and bangs.

I should go to my room, have a Scotch, drink three glasses of water, take the damn test, bathe, and fall asleep relieved, or stay up all night knowing my fate.

But I'm not.

She walked to an after-party at an economy room in the Coral Towers where neophytes—resourceful singers and MCs and producers, raring assistants, road managers, and radio jocks with overnight slots—stood hooded and high. MCs mumbled rhymes between dry finger snaps, trumpeted affiliations—towns, neighborhoods, record labels, crews—or adamantly, mostly misleadingly, told each other (and told probable sex partners) who they were, what they did, and, like verbal caterpillars, murmured about what would happen when they emerged, monarchlike, from the Studio. Neophytes said the Studio in the clubby yet reverential way sous chefs say the Kitchen.

I'ma bring it like you never heard. It was the theme phrase of all music studios, everywhere. Those pungent electrical places Eva loved with the rows of black levers and blue lights and hoop games on pause. The roti or the *pernil* or the pizzas get ravaged and crews egg on the one under the mike, each frantically happy to have landed in the Studio, but listening fearfully lest they hear genius, hear something real or perfect or daringly conventional enough to be a hit—because if they did hear it, what would they be but a sideman, hype-guy, the one on TV years later talking about monies never paid, about other shit stains on the dream. Eva had fallen in lust many times in the Studio—with MCs mostly, but with singers, too. Had fallen in love with herself and her job again during lulls in production schedules, during dips in her confidence.

At the Coral Towers party in 1998, the Studio boys didn't dance with the girls in snug jeans with strong bellies behind their snug shirts. The boys stood in ciphers like it was 1991, clung to beats like they sensed, as Eva did, even more betrayal. It wasn't just that Tupac Shakur was dead, or Biggie Smalls. It was that they were dead and the world kept spinning. The game hadn't been called on account of rain. The interns who'd rushed Ron at the showcase offered Eva purple marijuana and warm beer. Weak tributes. It wasn't what Eva wanted.

"You look right as hell," said a sweaty boy with nails bitten so low Eva didn't understand how dirt could be under them. "To have been in the game so long."

Girls peeked with envy at her superior dress and shoes and crossed bare legs. Girls decided then and there that they'd be home with kids or at least with a man at a fly-ass spot by the time they were as old as Eva. Definitely not, they thought disdainfully, getting put on a pedestal by grimy wannabes. Even the most ambitious girls thought these things, as they exchanged inky new business cards and dates of self-improvement seminars. They thought they'd be the same as Eva, except totally different from her, when they had Eva's kind of job and responsibility and dough.

Girls wanting to be large in the game. Girls wanting to make a loud statement with their look, to serve up prettiness and power. Eva could feel the hot, anxious, hating vibe.

Hmmmm, Eva thought to herself. *I am the vibe.*

So she left the smoky room and walked, still solo, to Ron's penthouse for the party with everything that everybody had seen one time on *Lifestyles of the Rich and Famous,* the things that must mean rich and famous or else why would it be a cliché? The green bottles of champagne, caviar on the tiny pancakes, giant striped shrimp, and the coke on the table in the back bathroom where the biggest wigs sniffed while talking about how they'd stopped last year for a few months because shit was getting out of control. Eva moved easily among huddles and sprawls of people she knew and people she knew of. The same men always, the same women always, and always a new bale of girls whose reps centered on a few choice video frames, a new crew of boys who swore they were the Berry Gordy of St. Louis or the Quincy Jones of St. Paul. Eva wandered through swamps of intoxicated industry couples, each with the wistful look of being enclosed in a thin bubble—her turn, now, to look on people with envy and pity: *One step*

*beyond the weak morals and morale of this business, and your relation-
ships'll end in a fire of truth and consequences. When it isn't about how
you can help each other move on up, when it's about just you two, and
your life, and a kid*—for Eva, for a change, Ron's party was stifling,
and his bar too crowded and too far away.

She saw no sign of Sunny, or Vic, or Swan. Usually, after a big
night, Sunny loved to sit in a corner and bless people with her presence. *She must really like Vic, if she's laying up with him alone, missing
out on glory.*

On a beeline for a drink, Eva breezed by Min-Hee, a former per-
former she'd toured with once who now worked for a cosmetics company. Min-Hee with her tatts hidden now; Min-Hee who hooked safe
pop stars like Sunny up with eye shadow endorsement deals.

Then Eva saw Lois, who was from a hip hop trio Eva used to work
with. Lois was chatting up Myra. Lois had been the only one of her
crew to save money. She'd started a hip publicity company, and the theory was that Lois had been paying one former partner's rent for two
years, and that she paid the other a salary for coming in daily to a modest office and saying, *Trix Public Relations—how may I direct your call?*
After a cheek-to-cheek air kiss-kiss for Myra, Eva surprised herself, Lois,
and Myra by embracing Lois tightly and telling her she looked beautiful.

Eva stood back a step. Lois had found something else to do. Had
become somebody else, and had the calm, bright-eyed face of a person who'd found the right place on the way to someplace different.
Eva felt good giving the sincere compliment, felt open, and kind of
square, for feeling anything.

"You feel good, Eva?" Lois searched Eva's face for evidence of
joy. "Sun did real good."

"She did," Eva said flatly, wanting to escape Lois suddenly.
"Thanks. And good luck to you." Eva gave Lois a last quick hug. "Anything I can do, *ever*, let me know." Then Eva walked toward the long
balcony with a flushed face.

Dart saw her through the doorway and stepped out. "You look
tired," he said.

"That's what I like to hear. Where's Sunny."

"Sunny's grown." He was holding a bottle of water.

"What are you doing here?"

"It's dark in my room."

"Turn on the goddamn lights."

"I see. You're in this"—he took a glance around the party—"kind of mood."

There was no dancing in this room, either, weighted down as it was by melted butter and heavy-bottomed bottles. Like stock vases at a florist's, *Make use of me*, the bottles seemed to say, and the response was long kisses and caresses to glass necks from open-shirted hip hop execs, double-breasted pretenders, queens requesting Prince, dykes in business-lady drag, and wise chicks like Eva held together with earned sweat, $100 pressed powder, and the kind of masochism necessary to undergo Brazilian bikini waxes. The various factions, more apt to explode among themselves than in an integrated group, churned to a mild froth. Eva knew the currents. She knew the rocks, and the fallen trees, too. Eva wondered if she'd ever have the babies she'd aborted. If, somehow, some part of them had remained. She'd seen a pale-brown baby with pretty lips at Miami International. The infant was in a pink jumper. It had been sleepy and pouting. Eva had smiled at the baby and it looked at her blankly, like Eva was benign, but alien.

"Can you get me a drink?"

"Tell Ron to get you a drink."

"Dart. Can you get me a Scotch, please." Eva needed a sting on her lips. That hot menthol on her throat.

"Yeah, *Dart*," Ron said as they trudged by each other. "Can you get her a Scotch, *please*." He dangled a green bottle by the neck like a chicken he'd killed. Ron no longer had the bodyguards that had attended him for a few years. As hip hop had moved from the political eruptions of bands like Public Enemy and Poor Righteous Teachers and Arrested Development and Boogie Down Productions, there were fewer ideological reprisals. People still got stomped, but the beatdowns—which in the past had seemed more spontaneous and emotional—weren't over message as much as they were over money. With the exceptions of the murders of Biggie and Tupac, even the newer, more financially planned brawls were sporadic. Gangsta and dance rap was keeping everybody paid and much more chill.

"Don't," Eva said to Ron, "start."

The fact that he was king of the room wasn't enough. Ron was jealous of what he imagined to be a metaphysical bond between Eva and Dart, and he was mad that Eva had swung Sun's bright night. Almost drunk, Ron fell back on mockery. "Congratulations, Evey! Sunny blew up the spot tonight." His eyes were damp and angry as a hungry baby's. "You had that shit down to a *science*, didn't let *nothin'* get out beforehand. And then"—he crouched a little—"just when everybody thought the show couldn't get any better, you had your boys come out with that *boomin'*-ass set—" Ron's eyes were sour and laughing at the fiascoes he saw in Eva's future. Dart returned and handed Eva her Scotch.

"Can you walk me to my room?" she said to him.

"You got fools walking you to your room now?" Ron shook like he was amused, but no laughter came out. He tilted the champagne to his lips.

Eva walked toward the door of the suite, thinking Dart was behind her.

"Keep fucking with me," Dart said, still near Ron. His voice thundered under the party buzz like a bass line.

"Walk Eva to her room. That's what she told you to do." The three of them were back in the suite, in front of everyone.

"You think I won't fight." It was more a realization from Dart, than a question. "I don't need to fight you. You're killing yourself. Smell like doom."

"Fight me." Ron snorted. "Wow." He watched Dart's face. The champagne bottle went from dangling between Ron's fingers to being enclosed in his fist. He was flushed more with fear, though, than liquor. "You don't wanna do that."

There was no puzzled or uneasy halt to the partying. There were those, like Min-Hee, who baldly watched, others who looked on with an irritated hopefulness, wondering why Ron and Dart couldn't enjoy the party or take their beef elsewhere. There were the oblivious, too, but mostly people were calculating the potential brawl, adding and subtracting with quantities based on what they knew of the neighborhoods Ron and Dart were raised in. Factored in was race, as well as whether either of them had ever been arrested, as well as to what degree Ron and Dart were more than normally (for the record business) egomaniacal. People calculated how much either man had to gain or lose in terms of being sued by the other, and in terms of reputation. They gauged each man's history of viciousness, diagrammed in algebraic detail the business dealings between Ron and Dart, and, of course, the women they had in common. The calculations happened so instantaneously, and so subconsciously, the partiers had no idea they were doing math. In a blink, sums were considered. To a person, it was decided that the worst case would be shoving and cursing.

"Dart."

"Momma's calling," Ron said.

"Ron," Eva said with a death glare. "Shut. Up." She looked at him like he should feel lucky he was at his own party.

Dart looked past Ron's bulk at Eva. Wary, his intensity cracked. Eva seemed to be on his side.

The instinct to go over, get between them, was the kind Eva could resist. She knew Ron was radiating belligerence to give the impression that he was not down, let alone out.

Ron knew, as most did, that Dart was impulsive, and Ron wanted Dart to embarrass himself—and so Eva and Sunny as well.

Eva didn't get in between the two of them because she'd busted up enough fights at parties. Been called every bitch possible.

"Go on, Dar-tan-*yan*," Ron said, sounding almost authentically hard-core. "'Fore you get your nose broke."

And with another shift of his eyes and a surge of his shoulders, Dart was back in the scrap. Ron stood fast. He had to in front of the room, and in front of Eva.

"What y'all doin' over here? What's the tension, children? Jeeeezus. Jeezus, Mary, and Joseph!" Myra tipped over on the balls of her feet, grabbed Ron's wrists in her hands and swung them. "Somebody peed in the sandbox? Ron, come with me, baby. Your Myra needs some more of this good wine you got up in here. Where's your people?

Have 'em call for some more of those fritters and things. Ev*aaaaa*," she sang out, "take Dart."

Myra was sure she knew who Eva was. And Myra liked her. Eva was renowned for liking sex. She had her own cash. Any observable need for a man's guidance and support, Eva'd have to manufacture and work to maintain. Eva could and did fuck men in the same set. She seemed to snicker at the contempt of women and men who judged her. Myra's educated guess was that Eva's fantasy included marrying someone who was paid. Maybe the guy would be in love with Eva, but maybe not. They'd have a friendship, though, a partnership through which they'd have one child. Eva and her husband would divorce when things got tough or boring, or when one of them, high hopes in a new, truer love, yearned to marry another. The only thing Myra envied of Eva was youth. Myra had been beautiful herself. And in the *Oprah*-sanctioned adventure that was her middle age, Myra thirsted for her thirties like she did for bourbon.

At Ron's party, Myra, flat-footed, turned to Eva—eyes clear with compassion. She thought the girl folks called Evil Eva was a throwback to a time when women and men had sensible expectations. Still holding Ron, Myra wasn't as drunk as she seemed. "I said take him and *go-go-go*, sweetums," came Myra's trill. Merrily, she swung Ron's champagne jug. "Put Dart to bed."

Walking back to her suite, Eva was working a problem at her own blackboard. Just when what Ron needed was to mark himself a clear winner in at least one Lost City battle, the spat he started had been stopped by a referee, and a woman—and scandalmonger Myra, at that. So even with the splotch of Vic and Swan, the convention was almost over, and back in the world, the phoenixlike rise of Sunny would be the only tale worth telling. Eva knew Ron wouldn't sleep until he could chalk himself up, in some way, as one of the night's champions.

va met Sunny in Monterey, California, at a
music festival on Cannery Row called Innovative Music for Innovators.
Two hundred miles north of Los Angeles, right on the peninsula. Eva
swooped down the Row in her leased SUV, bumping old Niggas With
Attitude so loud the dash trembled. It was 1994.

She wore cargo pants to the event, some work boots, and a short,
sheer shirt. Along with a web of rubber bands and dollar bangles
at her wrist, Eva wore what she thought of as her hippie-dippy sterling
and garnet jewelry. Except for the diamond studs—near colorless, set
in platinum—she sported no real jewels to alienate the hippie-dippy
crowd. No bright gold to give the targeted artist a clue to her newly
acquired tastes for glittery, affirming bangles. And, so as to seem extra
down-to-earth, Eva left her designer tote under the seat of the car. She
tied a black hoodie around her waist, figuring no one would know it
was cashmere.

Mostly lightweight freaks here, she thought, *smoking way too much
weed.* Lugging army-green canvas knapsacks. *And not using quite
enough of that crystal deodorant rock.* Eva was in familiar territory.
While she was in the fourth and fifth grades, Eva's parents had rented
a groundskeeper's bungalow in Carmel, a few miles north of Monterey.
Vehicle neatly parked, Eva hopped out and began walking toward the
pier. She tapped her pants pockets for credit cards and passport and
beeper, and the unfussy, mannish gesture made Eva feel free. Monterey, Eva remembered with a tremble, was where her father made
her mom go for better grocery deals.

Eva was also unsettled because she'd only just heard about Sunny. *I'm losing it. Losing my ear, losing my connections.* Eva'd been locked down in the Bronx, in an ancient producer-DJ's state-of-the-art basement studio, trying to revive the career of Miz Novymber, a woman who'd been a so-so success as an MC. In the late eighties, the girl had rapped over an atomic bass line about loving the black man, about loving oneself, about buying black, and about not calling people "bitches" or "niggas." Miz Novymber rose to the top in fluorescent fatigues while Eva—who'd believed completely in the lyrics and the music—zealously assisted the A & R guy who okayed the fatigues and plotted the charge. When he moved back to Charleston to open a restaurant with his point money, Eva'd stepped into his shoes like they'd been hers all along.

But by 1994, the girl MC's ghostwriter boyfriend was writing dick raps with titles like "Sweet Rock in the Honey." It's not like Eva had anything against dick raps or against dicks themselves, she just wanted the music to make her feel something.

Scare me, shit. Make me hot, offend me, something. Just don't be half-assed. Don't be weak.

Eva'd been deep in love with late-eighties hip hop—Public Enemy, Eric B. & Rakim, Salt 'n' Pepa, Doug E. Fresh. Back then, hip hop had the thick limbs of an infant the village was trying to raise, and possibilities for big change seemed endless. The music was all grown up by 1994—Nas's ill *Illmatic*, Biggie's *Ready to Die*, Snoop's "Gin & Juice"—husky and loud with the love of those who'd stood up and cared for it early on. But Eva thought rap could die at any moment. It was too vulnerable to execs and artists shearing luscious roughness off songs and beats, and too much a pawn of wannabe moguls still in the dope and/or extortion game. By the mid-nineties, hip hop had been seduced by America itself. The U.S. pop machine inhaled the music, then exhaled the smoke in which kids swayed and jumped with the gusto of those aware of but detached from the forensic files of the crimes that set hip hop in motion.

Eva's reaction to the world's newfound love of the music was split. It was great: the money, the acceptance, the pride-by-proxy of invention. It was terrible: the exploitation, the watering down, the idea that hip hop was being enjoyed by people who had only a tangential way of relating to it. People wanted to touch parts of it, love parts of it—people who didn't know anything about hip hop before Run-D.M.C. In the eighties, Eva believed you had to know where you're from to know where you're at. Had to know about obscured African-American firsts and slave revolts not mentioned in high school history books and about the financial rape of black musicians by the ever-strong cartel of Whites in Charge of Money and Music and Information Dissemination. Had to *fervently* know all of it and more, or you didn't have the right to love hip hop, let alone be *in* it. Things became more complicated when hip hop won, though, was no longer the underdog, and had gotten Eva and lots of other people crazily paid. It became more complicated for Eva when she could imagine the end of it more clearly than she could recall the beginnings.

But rhythm and blues, on the other hand, had been around for so long, Eva was certain it would be around forever. Eva was certain that by trying to find a singer, she was on her way back to the future.

So, as she'd done with rappers, Eva paid attention only to a pre-selected group of singers. She listened to no unsolicited demos—paid attention mostly to phone calls from her company's regional radio reps. Some of them had side businesses as showcase promoters. These neighborhood treasure hunters booked nightclubs or community centers. They charged singers a fee to perform, and charged admission. Folks paid good money to be swept up in a young person's desire to be found and celebrated for the part of themselves they believed most golden.

Some regionals paid their mortgages with showcase profits. Others, on a religious mission to get a pre-superstar signed, went broke trying to interest towns deafened to raw talent by local radio station playlists and national video channels. This was the kind of ardent regional rep Eva had been. Down to her last $100—in Chicago, and again in Fresno—Eva stayed at it because to be the anointing angel, the one with "an ear," to become the manager of a still-grateful artist, or to be in A & R and bring songs to life, was a dream as specific and seductive as an artist's own.

Even the regionals I trust to bring me news of someone making waves in a good-size city have been bringing me bullshit. By the time she got to Cannery Row, Eva needed more than just a singer. She needed a maniac—someone consumed with succeeding. An obsessive who'd reneged on debts and alienated family with dreamy talk and dead-end jobs and the audacity to press up his own discs and sell them at swap meets. Eva needed a new R & B singer with the heart of an old-school MC.

And it was on a hellish cell connection from that basement Bronx studio that she first heard about Sunny. Tired of Zapp-y samples blasting from the tiny, mighty speakers, Eva was damn near begging, trying to convince an older but still starry R & B star to release a bar of his from an ancient slow jam about making love last forever and ever. The old song had been a regional hit, and Eva was fiending for some old-school, underived bounce.

The Memphis star said no in the end, but teased Eva about Sunny. He scolded Eva for being "old" and "late," and for not being up on this new California sensation, this chick flattening crowds for free in city parks. "Blowing minds is what's she's doing," the old star said. "Singing from her gut while you sit on your ass. I love money like the next nigga, but your little—what? Forty grand?—for some rap that's not even gonna hit? Gon' make me look like I *need* money? Where's your head, anyway? Need to be in Cali is where you need to be."

All Eva could do was say, "I hear you," and press off. She was twenty-nine, and feeling like a senior citizen in hip hop.

I'll show a motherfucker "late."

Eva could buy clothes, and she always had her passport on her. She called her assistant to arrange a ticket. And the traffic from the Bronx to JFK International hadn't been bad at all.

On the pier off Cannery Row, Hakeem leaned against bleachers set up in front of a restaurant called Bubba Gump Shrimp Company Restaurant & Market. He drank red wine from a plastic cup.

"Looky here," Hakeem said. "Eve arrives in Eden." Eva and Hakeem had spent two room-serviced weekends together during the early nineties while working on an album that only they believed in until it spawned three number one singles and a Best New Artist Grammy. Hakeem mostly remembered the way Eva's mouth felt. Took some pride in the fact that while everyone else took in her body, he could look at her lips and feel his joint jump in his pants.

"And I got your apple, too," Eva said.

Hakeem smiled. He was pleased, as always, to be in the heat of Eva's snappy attitude. She proved to him that the music business was where the top girls migrated. The hardest, fiercest, strongest girls. Whether ugly or okay or bizarrely attractive, they were mission-minded and liked glamour, which made them unsuitable for marriage and unlikely to want it until their uteruses had damn near scaled over from a lack of babies. Hakeem had to respect that. *Tough,* he thought, *to be a chick in this game.* Hakeem waved his arm toward the food and souvenir stands. "All-natural everything, baby," he said, bullshitting, like he'd arranged it that way, to her special tastes. "Wine's organic. Just for *you.*"

"As fucking if. Unless they got some organic Scotch. Who you here to see?"

"There's just Sunny worth the drive. But play coy. It's cute on you."

Hakeem and Eva walked along the pier mall, ended up before a creaky bandstand, and then walked to the left edge of the rapt crowd.

Sunny sat on a stool onstage, guitar on an improvised stand next to her. A long, bushy braid hung over each breast. *Overalls over a tie-dyed tank top. Feet filthy and bare. Toe rings. Jeez. Take a bath.* From where Eva stood, Sunny's left arm seemed painted in fresco with reds, golds, and blues. Then Sunny got to a rising part of the last chorus, pushed patchy bangs from her eyes, and stepped away from her seat. She belted notes a cappella, and minus a mike, like it was the first time she'd sung the words. Like it would be the only time.

Eva thought that folks could probably hear Sunny in Spain.

She had never heard anything so full and sweet. *Like boiled-down sap from a tall, thick tree. Like that crystallized-to-amber rock candy. Sun's voice surging soft at first, then hard, and certain of her volume and range. The girl takes bottomless breaths. No worry—not before the highest or the lowest note. Heart's on her sleeve, too. Her whole body's heart. I feel it, so they'll feel it—feel like they're living.*

Thump fucking thump-thump-thump.

Happy-ass critics'll reach for words and they'll come up with Crucial. They'll say her shows are Sticky, warm as blood. Sunny. Dirty bare feet and all.

Eva was glad she could hear Sunny because she knew that no matter how loud and clear Sunny sang, not all on the pier could hear. No matter how healthy their eardrums.

Eva knew you were deaf to Sunny unless you were young enough to romanticize soft rape. Deaf unless you still craved being blindfolded, kidnapped, and persuaded in 4/4 time of your waning conviction that love is real/love is pain/love is all/love is nothing. Couldn't hear Sun unless you still had the heart strength of brightly dressed poor folks yelling, "These. Are. The. Good. Times," while paying $6 for a short bottle of German beer. Stone-deaf to Sunny unless through closed eyes you could see your lover's face in the low, moaned verses of another

For Eva, Sunny was a pealing bell. *Thank God,* she thought. *Thank God,* she felt—a slight shudder through her back and thighs, a desire to stretch her limbs, to think lonely thoughts, and to dance. *I was almost dead. Should've known somebody would bring me back. Music* does not *fail. Somebody's song always comes up from the cracks.*

Eva'd been in the music business for what seemed 101 years, seen too many artists chase speedballs of fame and fear with coke and cognac and quaaludes and crank. Seen artists piss away cash so plentiful it seemed as pink and yellow as Monopoly money.

This is work. I'm at work. I can hear her, though. On the pier, Eva swayed only barely to Sun's sound, keeping her excitement in check.

Every week, since bands were white and hairsprayed and named after cities, Eva'd perused music trade magazines, burned her irises searching for bullets next to charting singles and watching for bullets in makeshift discos. She worked for people whose son's tuition and wife's new Jaguar depended on how much sadness or glee or anger Eva could milk in the studio and market to colleagues over cocktails. Eva's own retirement and supersoft Italian boots depended on what MTV did with the video and what mix-tape DJs did with the B-side and what the urban black press did with the sex and "negativity" and what the mainstream white press did with the previous arrests. Eva was tired, had grown up and gotten wise enough to know that unless you were still open to at least the idea of purity, there was only silence from Sunny's mouth, even as it stretched into a long and long-lasting O.

Eva was grateful, if only for ten or twelve seconds, to be among the lucky ones for whom Sunny bellowed the note. Sunny's eyes were closed, head tilted to the left like she was listening to her painted shoulder. Like Sunny's body whispered messages to her soul for interpretation. Fingers curled loosely at her sides, her thick contralto bent the tail end of phrases like petals. Her knees bent slightly. Sunny sang.

Then she collapsed to the floor.

The crowd gasped. Hundreds of necks stretched cobra-curious, hypnotized.

After ten seconds, Sunny got to her knees smoothly and sat on her heels. "Imagination," Sunny said solemnly. "Imagination! Who can sing your force?" Her face was raspberry-flushed and grime-striped. "Or describe the swiftness of your course?"

Eva didn't realize then that Sunny was paraphrasing Phillis Wheatley. Sunny was fascinated and inspired by the poet, and within a year, Sunny's love for Wheatley would be a part of a list of quirks chronicled in newspapers and music magazines, a literary inspiration bolded in the label bio and whispered to reporters before interviews. That Wheatley was Sunny's muse sparked renewed interest in the poet and branded Sunny as deep and thoughtful and more interesting than more conventional nineties bare-midriffed R & B singers. Sunny would come to be considered, especially by the white press, the kind of guitar-toting black eccentric they could comfortably chat with. And due to Sunny's early vocal rawness, her songwriting ability, and the intellectual value placed on that by the rock music critics that dominate pop journalism, Sunny would be deemed a more light, "pretty," MTV-friendly version of Tracy Chapman—and so as much artist as product. To the black music establishment and to most African-American critics (before the embrace of her by the mainstream was complete, and so by definition, suspicious), Sunny was regarded as earthy and positive and obviously light-skinned enough to be chosen as special by editors and photographers and fashion designers.

Still on her knees in Monterey, Sunny bent forward and put her forehead on the boards. Then she swept her arms over the floor of the stage and behind her, palms upturned.

On the pier's planks, many in the audience hurried to copy Sunny. They folded themselves into *balasana*, the Child's Pose. The most submissive yoga position of all.

They'll say it, and they'll be right—they'll say Sunny is the Real Thing.

"Close your mouth, girl." Hakeem ran a knuckle down the back of Eva's neck.

Eva had been standing there with her mouth open. The crowd was multiracial, young. College kids and street kids. Parents with pre-teens. At least half of the spectators were down, foreheads on the pier.

When Sunny rose, Eva came out of her daze. Whoops and applause came from people still on their knees.

Time to work. "Clearly you know the deal," Eva said to Hakeem.

"Your boy Ron's here," Hakeem said. "Throwing money, sending Sunny all this macrobiotic food. And he sent her a limo that burns natural gas."

"She doesn't seem the type to be impressed by all that." *Ron's not my boy.*

"She'll be impressed by *you*," Hakeem said, animated. "*Young* sister! Getting it *done* in the business world! Little Miss Eva Executive. You and Sunny can take over the music business together. Make it a better place!"

"What is she?" Though it made her feel good, Eva had no time for Hakeem's rigmarole.

"She's black, stupid. They're from Louisiana. Her people, I mean. Her brother's brown-skinned."

"She's twenty-nine?" Eva had done some research. *A bit older than ideal, but doable.*

"On her birth certificate." Hakeem leaned his butt against the pier railing. "These white boys is sweating her hard. They're all here. In fucking Monterey. We need to do this."

"I'm about to."

Hakeem read her pronoun usage. He had no worries, though. He knew Eva would need him, or at least feel she did at some point, and would call him then. Hakeem knew Eva's strength was her weakness and her weakness her strength: She always felt like she was falling off, so she worked like a demon. Eva acted the student when it was wise, but calculated people's motivations like a physics professor. She fired her looks like warning shots, used sex like tuition and thermometer. But occasionally she surprised with wildly spontaneous moves. And Eva almost always succeeded. "Make this yours, Evey," Hakeem taunted her. "Be ahead. Be on some new shit."

"Why are you here, anyway?" *Had he heard Sunny sing? Heard her, for real?*

Hakeem had gotten himself more organic wine. He had money and the time that came with it. "Waiting on you, sweetheart, as always. Trying to get on *your* train."

Eva began walking toward whatever ragged backstage existed.

"I know her," Hakeem called out, still leaning on the pier railing. "And her manager. Told 'em I had someone they should meet. The *right* person, person who'd make Sunny the kind of star she's supposed to be."

"You said that?" *You could've said those things to Sunny—except about Ron. You could've said all that you've been saying to me—to Ron.*

"Yes, Pretty Girl. Something like it," he said with a bit of lust.

Eva kept walking. Hakeem was cute, but he talked too much.

Hakeem said, "What you smell like today, Evey?"

From twenty feet away, Hakeem leaned a bit in Eva's direction. People who knew Eva, or who'd slept with her, or danced with her, often leaned in to catch her scent. She never wore enough to perfume the air around her, but as Eva straightened an arm, or turned her head, pungent tuberose was released, or lilac. As the nineties rushed toward their midpoint, and the perfumes at the glassy counters became more gastronomic, Hakeem would lean in to catch sweet basil, or ripe fig, or apricot. The scents reminded him of an almost forgotten song, or at least a long ago voice. Reminded him that Eva was not so preternaturally perfect, that she gilded the lily.

"You won't know nothin' about that, ever again," she said with a big smile. Eva had turned to face him.

"Biding my time."

Go home, Eva wanted to say to Hakeem. *I can wrap this on my own.* But she waved at him to join her. At least for minute. *Just for the introductions.*

In her suite at the Lost City after the after-parties, Eva sat her drink on the vanity next to the ultimate gift Ron had sent earlier. There was a recent urn of lilies, too—card signed with a ballpoint-sketched sun.

Then she went to the bathroom, slid out of her silk jersey dress, and put on a robe. Eva called out, "Didn't you say you wanted to talk to me? Tonight at the showcase. Dart. You said, 'Talk to you about it later.'"

"Not tryin' to talk now." Dart's was in the bathroom with her, his hands under her bra pushing her nipples in, hard, in the exact way she hated her breasts to be touched. He was trying to distort them, and she let him do it because it seemed like he needed to.

It's not like he's brand-new to me, and he keeps condoms always.

Dart was on his knees trying to eat her out. Eva's feet were cold on the floor and the edge of the sink was pressing into her butt. She put her hands under his arms, and he was soaking wet there, but still Eva pulled at him to get up, and he did.

She tied the belt of her robe, walked into the room, sat down, and sipped the Scotch. She thought she might talk to Dart about what the hell Sunny had pulled with Vic and Swan. Hoped that Dart, whose attention span was short, would then settle for sleep. Eva had two beds. She thought it would be nice to hear him breathing.

But Dart picked her up from the bed. Eva let him do it. He cradled her in his arms and carried her. As an adult, Eva hadn't been lifted from her feet and carried. Even in the robe, she felt exposed and light-headed. She didn't squirm.

"Put me down," she said. *He is bizarre.*

"I will. When we get"—he placed her, like a rolled rug, on a cushioned chaise on her balcony—"here." Then Dart pulled his undershirt over his head. Eva liked the way the band of his shorts sat comfortably on his waist. His chest with its tight tufts. And night in the Bahamas, at Lost City, was balmy and sheer as day. Eva's feeling of exposure increased, and she was excited.

D'Artagnan kissed her, and after a few seconds, Eva kissed him back with force because he wasn't pressing her breasts in. She relaxed and got warm—the drink had helped, and Dart's new shoulders were like some big, padded dam. His new body seemed produced to hold things back. Hold things in. Break shit to pieces.

He could have taken Ron, easily.

She did her best to touch Dart's face and neck in a loverlike way. She figured if it weren't for his mottled back, she'd have sex with him more often. Dart's neglected back freaked Eva out. She wanted him to take care of it, take care of himself, but she forgot about his scars as Dart lay on top of her and started pumping like he was trying to find a cliff inside her high enough from which to jump.

It feels good. Hit single, Tony! Toni! Toné!, from their 1990 album *The Revival.* Midsong rap from Mo-cedes, supposedly Tupac Shakur's cousin. T!T!T!—Oakland, California, boys—Tim, Dwayne, Rafael—all three. *One or two of them related to Larry Graham of Graham Central Station. Graham, who'd played bass guitar for Sly "I-wanna-take-you-higher" Stone.* Eva's mind went *click-click-click.* Bass-drum-vocals. Date-album-artist. *If it really feels good to you, baby, let me hear you sing.* A snatch from "It Feels Good" tapped for the Notorious B.I.G.'s verse for the '96 remix of 112's "Only You." Big had a 1997 song called "Notorious Thugs." That's how Eva felt—the way the midwestern rappers on Biggie's album rap-sang it: No-tor-ee-us. It felt good.

Eva got caught up enough that she squirmed, flipped herself on top of him, and did the canal-tightening tricks she'd perfected, and Dart finished without any command from her. He put his face in her neck, and Eva gently pushed him away. She got up and went back into the room, got in the shower, and came back to find Dart in his clothes, on a bed. She slid Shakur's first album into the nightstand disc player. Forwarded past "Brenda's Got a Baby" to "Part-Time Mutha."

"Gonna go sleep in my room," he said. "I'll see you, I guess, in the morning."

"Mmmhmm." Eva finished her paled cocktail. She opened the small refrigerator, pulled out a tiny bottle, poured.

When you need it most—trapped on a plane, dissed in a hotel room— they give you toy bottles to drink.

"You understand how much respect I have . . . for you, but you act like—"

"Dude," she said shortly, as if on court to a teammate. "I'll see you at the gospel brunch. Sunny needs to be there, and you need to shake some hands."

Dart nodded his head slowly. Spoke with pauses between his words. "About to get my head together for that now."

"Glad I could be of service." Eva was chipper. Shakur raged.

"You're a trip," Dart told her.

"I'm a trip." She waved him off, angry at feeling hurt. "I'm tired."

"Not too tired to wash me off." Dart stood and buttoned his shirt. Right at the door, with a swing of his forearm, he pushed an urn from a table. With barely a thump it landed on the water-resistant carpet.

Eva jumped under her skin. It was an accident, but Dart didn't look back.

Lilies splayed in a puddle. Dart tried to slam the door on his way out, but the doors at Lost City drag as they reach the frame and shut with a haunting, assuring click-lock. Eva got up behind him, flipped the dead bolt, and then clicked on the television. She sipped at her drink, then got up and made herself another. She was at four now, for the night. Two on the rocks, two straight-up.

There was a show on cable about "the return of chain gangs" in Alabama. On another channel, a cult was about to disintegrate. Eva flipped to the resort's internal channel. *Come explore the mystery and grandeur of Lost City.* Eva looked at her legs, crossed at the ankles. They were shapely, waxed smooth. She thought they looked good. That anyone was lucky to get between them.

This ancient civilization has risen up from the sea.
Inspiration and adventure.
Six-story Mayan temple waterslide. Marine habitats. Casino.
Imagination.
Who can sway you from your course?

Swoosh!
The malicious machine spit softballs at forty miles per hour.
Fastball.
The Monterey air smelled like crushed grass and harshly of kelp. Eva was thirteen, and had on her pocked batters' helmet, sweatpants, last year's cleats, and a ripped practice jersey she thought made her look casually winning. She and her father were enclosed in a batting cage. Eva was an athletic girl, of the generation for whom the benefits of Title IX were ordinary. Her father signed her up for track and softball—no ballet or chorus or, God forbid, drama. It wasn't that Eva's father wished Eva were a boy, it was that he was dead set on creating a girl who moved through the world with the self-assurance and independence he felt the best boys took for granted.

"You closed your eyes, Eva," he said.

"I didn't."

"Here it comes a—"

Swoosh!

Fastball.

Eva had a forceful swing. She could throw far, and she could run fast, but she had trouble hitting the ball, and trouble catching it.

"You did it again," her father said. He felt Eva's troubles could be fixed.

"It's going too fast for me to see," she shouted.

"You're scared of the ball. I see it now. Your swing is fine. Here it—"

Swoosh!

Slider.

Eva swung violently. Her hand sweat in her batting glove, and she tightened the Velcro strap.

"Look at the ball," her father yelled. "Watch it come at you!"

"Watch it come at me?" To Eva this seemed beyond the rules of logic.

More prone to playing dominoes than a game of two-on-two, Eva's father believed sport to be the key to winning at life. He was sure that his late realization of sport as philosophy is what kept him slouching back to Amway meetings.

"Do what I say. Here—"

Swoosh!

Fastball.

"Dad, it almost hit me!"

"If you had your eye on it, you could get out the way instead of jerking around like a girl. Watch—"

Swoosh!

Curve.

"Once, Eva. For your*self*." Her father's eyes were brown and packed tight as the dirt he stood on. "Lock your eyes. You want a hit, don't you?" He stood fast behind the pitching machine. He'd watched enough interviews with athletes to know that if there was a ball involved in the game, the first step toward mastering the game was to keep the ball large in your eye. Eva's father had decided that there was a ball in any game that mattered.

Eva was contrite. She wiped her cheek with her shoulder. Scratched her left ankle with her right foot.

"You want to control the ball? Or you want the ball to control—"

Swoosh!

Slider.

Eva swung so hard she hit her shoulder blade with the wooden bat. She bit into her tongue. She rolled her shoulders backward a few times. Raised her bat again to position and swallowed a little blood.

"Okay," her father said, warmer now. "You didn't close your eyes. But you've got to look at it, Eva. I ain't raised no incompetent. Look—"

Swoosh!

Fastball.

Crack!

"See. Now. Do it again. If you can hit it—"

Eva glared at the flapped hole from which the ball shot.

Swoosh!

Then she watched the ball.

Eva would not disappoint her father. Teachers were faceless and satisfied with cooperation. Eva and her father had lived in three states in six years, so her friends were blurry and had vague, common teenage goals—they wanted to be "a lawyer," "a vet," "married," "a singer." Eva was not to the point of articulating it, but she wanted to know the world. She wanted to be around music. And she believed in mastery. Being the best was important. The win. She also wanted the means to leave wherever she was for someplace else whenever she wanted to— with no advice or permission from anyone.

Assess the situation, her father often said, *quietly get a plan, and lead the way.* In his brisk, cruel way, Mr. Glenn encouraged Eva's ideas and aspirations. He was uneasily envious of the opportunities that lay before his daughter due to the year in which she was born, but felt it his duty to prepare Eva for championship and riches. Eva wanted to be "a DJ" on some days, "a scriptwriter" on others, or to be in "computer science." Her father repeated often that to be a doctor or a teacher was fine, but to excel in a "cutting-edge" business—*now that was a life. That was the Future.* That was what *his* daughter would do, who she would be. So Eva caught fly balls like they were wafting wads of cotton. She bat fourth, brought runners in. She wasn't scared of a hard, white sphere. Eva was a team player when it was required, but mostly she looked out, as her father coached her, for Number One.

Slider.

Crack!

"Dad!" Eva was excited. Felt a rush through her body. She raised her bat again.

"You like it, don't you? It comes at you like it wants you, like it could kill you. But if you—"

Swoosh!

Fastball.

Crack!

"That's my girl! And if you can hit it, you can catch it."

Swoosh!

Eva watched it. The ball seemed to move through clear gelatin.

Curve.

Her eyes followed. The ball was a swelling globe of light.

This is easy, Eva thought. *Make up your mind to be unafraid. Keep your eye on the ball. The control rests with me.*

Crack!

"Dad, I'm doing it!" *Discipline works. Work, works.* Eva was all happiness. "That one's going home! I can't believe! Does everyone know this? That all you have to do is watch the—"

Swoosh!

"Eva, bat up. Pay attention."

"I'm just saying—"

Swoosh!

"Bat up!"

"Dad, it's what? A trick? A rule?"

"Shut up, Eva. Raise your bat."

The words bit into her now. *I'll shut up, and then one day I'll tell you to shut up.* Eva tightened her grip, feet spread just past her shoulders, toes slightly pointed in, knees bent, hands away from her body and back, just around her shoulder. Bat up like it was attached to a banner: I'LL DO IT AND WHEN I DO IT YOU BETTER FUCKING BE PLEASED.

Swoosh!

Slider.

She imagined it big as a bowling ball, slowly rolling toward her on a waist-high table. She'd sweep the bat across the table, make contact, and finish high with her swing.

Knock the shit out the goddamned park. Cage or no cage.

Crack.

"You learn this, you learn everything," Eva's father said curtly. "You got another forty minutes."

Swoosh!

Curve.

Crack.

Crack.

Crack.

Crack.

Eva's body jerked again. Then fingers tapped on her suite door. She didn't know if an hour had passed since Dart left, or a minute.

Eva waited. Tightened her robe around her. The taps came again.

"Who—"

"Who you think?"

Eva opened the door, and Ron stepped in like he was crossing a creek. He'd changed from his suit into a soft athletic ensemble and leather slides. Between the whiskey, the sudden bigness of Ron, the lingering whiffs of D'Artagnan, and the white flowers on the white rug, Eva needed to sit down.

"Looks like a party in here. Boyfriend mad?"

"Dart's not my boyfriend."

Ron sat on a chair, kicked off his shoes. He always sat in a room like it was his. "Homeboy's got problems. Real ones. Myra said—"

"Myra said."

"Pour me one, too. Myra said Dart's on meds. For his brain."

"So are you," Eva said, handing him a toy bottle and no glass. "So am I."

"Why was he all up on me tonight, then?"

"He's gallant." She swallowed half her drink. *Who's counting. Maybe the baby.*

"He's hostile." Ron sat back, geared up and pleased to talk about himself. "I have my problems . . . expressing emotions other than anger—sometimes. And I've seen somebody for that shit. I'm talking about a chemical imbalance—as far as Sun's brother. That's what Myra said."

"It's the lead for her next column?"

"Your boy's moods swing. He's known for that. On top of just being weird as fuck." Ron couldn't leave it at that. "Him and his sister."

"Your shindig must be over." Eva took another hard swallow. *Who's counting?*

"My shindig starts now." Ron would have no unfilled moment in his day. Eva wondered, for the first time since she'd known him, what Ron dreamed when he slept. She wondered, for the hundredth time, if he saw her when he looked.

"Go home," she said. "Or wherever. Don't you have a white girl you could be putting through this drama?" *Don't you have your Tampa MC over at the Hurricane Club?*

Ron ignored her. Eva's question was old between them, and had been rhetorical since their beginnings. "Put those shoes back on for me," he said. "The ones you had on."

"This is not the night." Eva was spinning high. Hot around the eyes. She pressed the back of her hand against her neck. *Who's counting?* It's what her mind shouted at her.

"You didn't like my present? Why you not drinking what I sent? You don't want me to go." He unzipped his jacket. "For what? 'Cause you were just with homeboy? I care about *that* fool? You need me now, after that creepy shit. I'm sure it was creepy, right, Eva? It was creepy."

Eva pulled the bedspread over her legs. *Maybe the baby.*

"I know how you do, Evey. Clean as a whistle. Condom queen. HIV monitoring. You just out the shower right now. I smell the soap, sweetheart. Come talk to Big Ron, baby. Feel nice."

Eva looked at him walleyed, her brain awhirl in her skull.

"I know you saved some for me." Ron got up, poured Eva another drink. "Best for last." He knew she'd had a lot but felt she was choosing to act drunk. Ron had seen Eva run shows and close deals after having had more.

"You have some other shit," Eva said slowly, "you could be doing."

"Put them shoes on for me." Ron returned to his chair. "Showing all that ass, all that leg tonight. Put the shoes on, Evey. Put 'em on. Show Daddy your talent, baby. Come on."

Eva took tiny sips of the drink he'd prepared for her. *He can make himself sound tender, saying the ridiculous things he says.* She reveled in the familiarity of her and Ron's situation.

The shoes were right by the bed. She could already see her toes spread in them—nails lacquered a near-white pink, a shiny amplification of their natural state. Strap around the ankle, dainty-looking but resilient. It was how Eva liked to think of herself, or, more exactly, the merge of those qualities was something Eva admired in other women. In her woozy mind Eva saw her legs lengthened by the mile-high heels, ass set up high and hung, it would seem when she had the shoes on, like a halved plum from her lower back. Quads tight, hams loose, knees locked. Soles of her breasts brushing her ribs, but still firm enough to *bounce—*

Yeah . . . Rock . . . Skate . . . Name of song??? Can't remember. Can't remember group or album or date of release. I am . . . gone. I am happy I am sad. I want to dance I want to lay down.

Eva was drunk.

There's a difference between high and drunk and I'm high.

She touched the strap of one shoe, and then paused. *Ask me some more.*

"Don't stop, Eva. Stand up when you put 'em on. With your back to me. Don't bend your knees. Don't mess up my picture."

Eva almost fell over. *Roll . . . Bounce . . .*

Heated through and wobbly, she gloried in doing what she was told. Eva walked over with the short terry robe open, and their bash began. From her knees they kissed, each pickled mouth opening wide, then wider. Ron stopped mauling Eva's body long enough to hold out a bracelet. A black leather cord drawn through a wooden plaque the size of a paper clip. The inches between Ron and Eva were already humid and fragrant with the successful sex they always had.

The bracelet stopped Eva. She dropped back, sat on her butt, and looked at it. On one side, half an orange sun against a minuscule rosy blue sky. On the other side, another half-sun, the tiny skies darkly maroon.

"Where'd you find it? I mean. Thank you."

"I found it is all you need to worry about."

Eva slid the bracelet on her wrist. *It's personal,* she thought with relief, *to me.* Her damp bath towel already on the floor, she quickly spread it. Down near the spilled flowers Ron tried to push Eva through the floor. She clawed at the towel, relished the pressure of Ron's weight, smashing her flatter and flatter.

"You know I hate you." Eva said it like she was telling him she wanted him to stay inside her for hours.

Ron's raised himself up and locked his elbows. He kept moving inside her to the slow march tempo that could often make her come. "Don't hate me." His words were slurred.

"But I do."

"Just love me," he said all lushy, then bent his arms and lowered his mouth to her ear. "Love me, Princess Eva, for a change."

Her elbows burned against the magic carpet. She raked her nails through it. It was flying, she was flying through a balmy never-never land where there was no need, no desire to embrace or be embraced, coo or be cooed at, no need to utter anything except satisfying, sentence-long tantrums that masqueraded magnificently as praise. Eva loved drunken sex. The act was intensified, the weak spots glossed over, and the words strong and without meaning.

I wanna sex you up. Color Me Badd, soundtrack to the motion picture *New Jack City,* 1991. Eva's brain was cranking back up. It happened when her buzz faded even a little bit.

Back-to-back, Eva sexed up Dart and Ron. No-*tor*-ee-us.

Eva pulsed. She and Ron were getting to the place they both wanted to go.

Yes. There it is.

Then, Ron.

Eva's body, rocked.

Her mind, fucked.

For the thousandth time she'd demonstrated her ability to rise to the occasion, to perform through inner crisis. And for that she got what she truly craved. It was just like the people had shouted to Sunny at the showcase: *Go 'head* or *Work it out!* or *You better do your thing!*

Same thing as *Stroke me sweetie, Bring it on home, I love the way you feel, You better fuck me like you know how. Like you need me. Show me. Your talent.*

Alcohol woke Eva up. She didn't have to look to know Ron was long gone. She glanced at her travel clock.

Six-twenty?

It took Eva some minutes to realize she might vomit. When she felt it behind her nostrils, Eva ran to the bathroom. Almost everything from the day and night before came up.

Eva leaned against the sinks. Waited. When Eva vomited, there was always a weak round one, then a powerful, all-cleansing round two. She straightened up and wiped her mouth with a hand towel, then held it to her throat, bunched at the center like a giant handkerchief. Warmth rushed her body. Her underarms and cleavage were clammy. Eva waited.

Never had morning sickness. When I was pregnant before. Has to be the Scotch. Drank a lot last night.

Six-twenty.

I was drinking two hours ago.

When was I throwing up all the time? Not for a while. Maybe when I was twenty-two, new to the game and drinking White Russians.

Even if I am pregnant, how pregnant could I be? No one has morning sickness when they're two weeks pregnant. If I'm pregnant.

Eva took shaky, deep breaths. She twisted a faucet, watched food-less vomit trail down the sink, and thought about when she was pregnant by a boy named Michael who everybody called Mix because he was a DJ. Mix was twenty, and when Eva called to tell him she was pregnant, he was honest about his fear and confusion, and he told Eva not to worry. She heard Alexander O'Neal in his background. *I can't go a day without my sunshine.* Eva loved that song, loved the name of the label he was signed to: Tabu. Eva was eighteen.

"I'm right here for you," Mix said.

She called him the next day and got his machine and then got his machine and got his machine for about nine weeks. That's how Eva counted time when she was pregnant. It's how everyone counts time when they're pregnant. Eva was counting, and it was nine weeks, and Mix went to college not fifty miles from where she went to college, so she could have gotten out there, but even in the midst of the nausea, she had an inch of pride. Eva knew Mix was getting those messages. And so Eva told her stepmother she was ten weeks pregnant, and told her boss at her on-campus employment, and they both advised abortion.

"You have so much ahead of you," they both said, in different ways, and, truth be told, Eva did.

Eva made the appointment, and the night before the appointment, Mix called.

"I spoke to Lynn," he said. "Day before yesterday." Lynn was Eva's boss. Mix was friends with her, too. Eva didn't have the energy to be angry with Lynn for telling Mix whatever she'd told him. "She told me you decided."

"I had to decide. It's tomorrow morning."

"Can I pick you up and drive you there?"

"Yeah. Don't be late."

Mix arrived at six o'clock in the morning in his Fiat sedan with the tore-up clutch and drove her over to a place where they made Mix sit in a room with magazines on tables and commuter news television, and they took Eva to a small room to watch a video about the procedure. They did an ultrasound, and then told Eva without batting an eye that there were twins in there. And so Eva said to herself, *Here's your big moment. Here is your time to make your own decision with no advice from anyone.*

I'm not ready, said the flush that burned, then dampened her.

Eva's body was screeching, trying to convince her mind. *Don't want a baby. Don't want an abortion. This is real. It's bad. It's sick. It's wrong.*

Eva said to the two technicians, and she had the clear jelly on her stomach and it was cold, she was cold within and without, and she was pregnant with twins and her belly was still flat at eleven weeks because that's how she was counting time, and Eva said, "Maybe I should say something to my boyfriend."

One of the techs, who didn't even look her way this time, said, "It's up to you, miss."

So Miss Eva asked for Mix, but word came back from the receptionist that Mix had been told he could go, and to come back in four hours, and so, really, it was up to Eva.

"I'm cool," she said to the tech. Eva was shivering.

"You're cool?"

"With going ahead," Eva said.

It was 11:01 when she got the IV in her left hand and went into the surgery room, and the doctor said, "Count backward from ten," so Eva counted weeks backward and when she woke up it was 11:07.

"How long is it gonna take?" Eva asked the nurse, who wasn't actually a nurse but an aide or a junior nurse or whoever wore pink or flowered scrubs in place of white. Wore fake gingham prints and soft clogs and loose ponytails. The doctor wore sneakers and a mask: was just big blue eyes and a smooth forehead. *How're you this morning?* All in the course of a sure-footed, red-Nike day. *You won't miss a step, Eva. You'll make your finals, no problem.* Those words would come later, from a nurse practitioner. Less than a doctor, more than a nurse. Eva was frustrated with the gradations. Who was a nurse, anyway? One who looked like one who nursed? Where was she?

"It's over. You're done. Rest."

Eva felt no pain. She was hazy, and in her haze, Eva wondered why they'd told Mix four whole hours, but then she woke up at 2:17 and they gave her pads to bleed onto and gave her salty chicken broth made from a foil-wrapped cube, and crumbly Lorna Doone cookies and saltines, and Eva sat at a round table with four other girls. The five of them like giant first graders in smocks and with their snacks, talking about how boys don't share. About how boys play, but then they want to play rough.

Eva had been going with Mix for a year and a half. He was the sixth boy she'd had sex with, although she'd told him he was the second. He was the first boy she gave head to, and for Eva and her school girlfriends of the time it was a womanly milestone, a graceless grab at new levels of fun and negotiation and, for girls raised to be all they could be, a quenching dip into surrender.

On her eighteenth birthday, Mix had taken Eva bicycling at Santa Monica beach. At around eleven that night, they went to a party at what people were calling an "underground" club, and Mix had told the DJ to say, "There's a birthday girl in the house! Happy happy to Eva!"

And people yelled it and clapped, and Eva and her man danced for song after thumping song. Then the DJ said, "This next song goes out to Eva, from Mix," and it was Keith Sweat's insistent "I Want Her," and for Eva there had never been such intense intimacy iced with public appreciation. *I want I want I want I want I want her.* There had never been such bliss.

When Mix came back in four hours to the clinic, she told him, as he tenderly helped her in the car, that it had been twins. Eva's movements were small. Once seated, she clenched everything. She hoped his clutch was fixed. She wasn't in the mood for a jolt.

"Twins?" Mix walked around back of the car, got in the driver's seat. He put his hands in the air, fists clenched, winner-and-still-champion. "That's my super sperm."

In her Lost City bathroom, a chill rolled through Eva's body. Skin rose in bumps. She leaned her face deep in the marble basin and retched over and over.

Whatever was still in her, Eva wanted out.

At a bit past seven-thirty, Eva picked up a brown woven bag packed before she'd dressed. In it was her passport; glutinous, glass-bottled oil of coconut; a boar-bristled hairbrush; ginger lip gloss;

and four fat fashion magazines. She wanted to lie by the pool before the hotel's throng emerged at around nine, before her convention mates descended, bloated and burping postmidnight antics.

No I didn't fuck him. Yes I sucked his dick.

They won't impeach Clinton.

Somebody stole my weed right from my goddamn purse.

Look, if my boy does the remix, it's fifty up front plus points.

Snoop did the dog thing already. DMX doesn't know that?

If O.J. did it, he should go on TV, admit it. Fuck everybody's head up with the double jeopardy.

Don't know why I didn't send promo CDs down to the Million Woman March.

Get off 'Pac's dick. He's dead. For real. Get with the new.

Eva wasn't in the mood. She was tense, and she had to pee.

The lobby chandelier dripped giant glass tears, was as big as a living room. Her sandals alternately clicked on marble and sunk into red-and-gold carpet. Small potted Christmas trees lit the concierge's desk. A gardener, who she also recognized as the bartender from Showcase Savoir Faire, sprayed plants with water and with something acrid from a dented metal can.

"Show your teeth," he said, smile brighter than his eyes.

Eva gave him the courtesy of a glance. She could see the pools and the beach beyond through the lobby's glass walls. *Same old slippers,* went a verse she remembered from one of her high schools, *same old rice.*

Same old glimpse of paradise. Eva didn't tug at her tiny skirt, a sheer silk orange scarf tied with flourish at one hip, even as she felt the man's eyes on her ass.

"Eva! Evillene!" Evillene was the name of the Wicked Witch of the West in *The Wiz.*

Don't nobody bring me no bad news. That was the witch's theme song. *Words and music by Charlie Smalls,* went the mainframe in Eva's head. *Performed originally on Broadway by Mabel King. Show opened 1975.* Evillene. People thought Eva didn't mind the tag.

As cheerfully as she could, Eva called out, "Hey, ladies." But she skirted the trio of older radio women curved over a clutch of lipstick-stained cups. Eva didn't have it in her to rehash the showcase. She barely had it in her to get to the family pool. It was called Ripples, but the water sat platter flat. Eva was still queasy.

But at least she was lying in real sun. As the pool filled with kids, Eva looked at them and couldn't imagine being responsible for one of them not drowning. She sat on the pool steps just as she'd sat in the pool closest to the lobby the afternoon before, except the afternoon before she'd been talking to her convention mates and talking to her assistant back in New York on her tiny cell phone. Eva had been drinking vanilla rum and listening to a Latin jazz band. Eva had been jovial yesterday afternoon. Yesterday she'd been thirteen days late for her period.

Today she was thinking about family, so she watched a man of about forty-five rub suntan lotion into his wife's arms. He wasn't a part of the second annual Vince the Voice Urban Music Takes Over the World: International Marketing for the Millennium convention. The man rubbed lotion into his wife's arms from where the short sleeves of her tee ended to the backs and palms of her hands. He tucked in a towel around her legs, from hip to toe, and fixed an umbrella so his wife was in the most possible shade.

Damn. How sweet.

Then the man walked around to the deep side of the pool and cannonballed in. He swam underwater until he got back to the shallow, then floated on his back, his hairy belly rising from the water like a giant coconut.

Eva eased herself down another step, so the water buoyed her breasts. She noticed a wheelchair by the wife's chaise. And then Eva saw that the woman's hand rested on her terry-covered thigh like a dead bird. That the woman's sapphire ring twinkled like a living eye in the sunlight.

The woman looked at Eva, and Eva didn't look away. The husband sighed loudly and got out of the water. He'd been talking to his teenage daughter, who was lolling on a blue raft, staring up at the blue sky, which was the brightest blue possible, the only blue that mattered, even in battle with the bottle-blue pool water, the teal blue of the sea, and the blue of the daughter's bathing suit, which was dyed the hostile kind of turquoise blue that only a sixteen-year-old Miamian with a springy body would wear.

The man walked over to his wife. His chubby body gleamed bronze, and water ran from his red trunks and pasted down the hairs on his legs. He reached in a sodden pocket and then did something to his wife's face that Eva couldn't see. His arm moved roughly. The wife's bird hand twitched.

The husband stepped from in front of her, and Eva saw him twist a cap back on something. The wife pressed and rubbed her lips together; it was that white zinc stuff, and it was all around the outside of her mouth. The husband leaned over and made the ointment sit perfectly on her lips. Like maybe another time they could have been going out and the zinc could have been lipstick he fixed for her and she would've been wearing shoes bare enough to be sexy but comfortable enough to dance in. The wife smiled at her husband in a grateful way, and the blue daughter looked at her father like she hated him, like he was an asshole.

Then the man moved his wife's hands the tiniest millimeter. Adjusted whatever discomfort the twitch might have caused. Eva baldly stared. She tightened her bladder, overwhelmed by the tenderness. Eva gulped back a sharp desire to care and be cared for. Then pee leaked from her body. It warmed the tepid water around her hips green. The daughter looked into Eva's eyes, then rolled off her raft, paddled to the other side, and clutched the pool's edge, disgusted.

Stiff and embarrassed, Eva rose from the steps and gathered her things. She felt even more queasy. Her body was out of control and rebelling in response to rotten treatment. Telling her it was tired and not to be counted on for its usual behavior. The family at the pool had come all the way from someplace else, had wheeled Mom out, folded and unfolded the wheelchair, got to and from airports. And then the husband had hauled himself from the pool to fix up his wife. Eva wiped at herself with a towel like she was contaminated.

He didn't have to do any of that. He didn't have to be here.

Eva felt dead to the world. Felt like she'd done too much, sold too much, been touched too much.

She lay back on the plastic slats of the lounge chair, unfastened her bikini top, and left the stretchy triangles covering half her breasts.

No show. No thrill. Sunlight was like the force of voices bearing down on her.

It's my right to do what I've done. Thank God it's my right because I didn't want those kids. Wasn't ready. Ain't ready now. It's my body. I get that. I want the decision to be mine. But, shit: I want candy. I want certain people to fall off the Manhattan Bridge. Just because you can do something, just because it's legal, doesn't make the shit all right. I'm not trying to overturn the law, but I hate freedom sometimes. Free to abort. Free to put out bitch-ho-kill records. Free to put out corny records. Free to lie. People's parents free to break out on kids already here. I'm free to weasel fools out of their dough. And you and me are free to be you and me.

Eva wanted a tall bottle of water. She wished she still smoked cigarettes. *I am so burned. Cuticles ragged, polish chipped. Haven't combed or curled my hair. Have on a cheap leather bracelet with a stupid sunrise-sunset design.* Eva thought of an old country song:

> *Single girl . . .*
> *She goes to the store and buys.*
> *Married girl . . .*
> *She rocks the cradle and cries.*
> *Single girl . . .*
> *She's going where she please.*
> *Married girl . . .*
> *A baby on her knees.*

From the twenties, Eva thought. *They were crooning that in the goddamn 1920s. And I don't care what anyone says, or what money girls have, the shit is still the same right now.*

She had her hand on her flat belly.

I got to be able to get up and go when I'm ready to get up and go.

A light palm that communicates, and checks, and protects.

"Eva! You incognito?" Sunny plopped down next to Eva at Ripples. "You look fucked up."

"Sick is what I am," Eva said. Her hand moved easily from her belly to her side. "Faded."

"Say it: *still drunk*. So am I." Sun leaned back in her chair, pleased for the moment with decisions made, with conquering performance, with morning heat on her face. Starting her own label was vanity, and a strategic pledge of allegiance to Sebastian. There'd been stacks of papers to sign, and an office space on a quiet floor of Roadshow's modest building in which to move furniture. Sunny wanted Eva to work at Sonrisa/Roadshow, needed Eva to sign artists and build it into something important. It had been her plan to shock Eva, though. Manipulating a melodrama in which Eva was the fool made Sunny feel strong and wise. "When I first got in this business," Sunny said, "somebody told me there were two bad ways it could go. Said women either get fat because of all the free food, or turn into alcoholics because of the free liquor—"

"Why didn't you say something?" Impatient with the new self-reliant Sunny, Eva wanted to slap back her star's shine. "To me, about Sonrisa."

Sunny shrugged. "Thought Hawk would've told. Or Ron. That's your man."

"Ron knew?" Eva said this dumbly. She didn't have it together enough to bite back.

Sun shook her head. "You actually like Ron," she said. "Why? He's smart, God knows. But he's an ass."

"You should have signed with him back in Carmel, then," Eva said. "Asses get the job done."

"He seemed to know everybody." Sunny shrugged again, her default gesture. "Seemed like a good guide for all this."

"And then here comes effervescent Eva."

"Yeah. My savior!" Sun put her arms straight in front and clapped her palms hard. Eva thought of a trained seal. "That night in Carmel—"

Sunny hugged herself with the memory. "You, me, and Dart were gonna go to the movies. I wanted to stay at the hotel, soak in that *giant* tub."

"So me and Dart left." *The story's old,* Eva thought. *And been told.*

"Ron beeped me, though," Sunny said, dropping new info casually, "talking about meeting them in the lobby—"

"Who's 'them'?" Any other time, Eva would have hidden her ignorance of the details. Figured out a way to let Sunny fill her in.

"You don't know? It was him and *Hawk*," Sunny said. She focused on the middle distance like she could see her beginnings there in 3-D. "They wanted to buy me a drink. 'Just come down,' Ron was saying. 'They got mineral water by the bucket.'" Sunny looked directly at Eva, and spoke dreamily. "You'd been so nice that day, though. Talking to me about my *style*, what I was trying to *do*. Talked about your mom. *Listened* when I told you about Wheatley, why I like her poems, why I wanted to name an album after her. Plus, you and Dart got along. You got us those rooms . . . at that place . . . by the ocean. I was curious, though—"

"I want to know what Ron was saying."

Sun got matter-of-fact. "That you were dope, but you didn't have the connections he has. That he has relationships with everybody—from the CEO of This to the CEO of That, to the guys who pay the PDs to program the songs at the big radio stations. Even the truck drivers who get the CDs to the stores."

Eva reached for her water. *Sounds like him.*

"He said that what I could really count on you for—"

"—was I'd fuck who I had to, to make your shit hit." *And what? He says* that *to me. Though he knows sex don't work quid pro quo. It's a stupid way to even try and do business. Sex is for . . . depends on who's it's with, what sex is for.* "You're telling me this now, why?"

Sun wasn't surprised by Eva's knowledge, but by her candor. It softened Sunny, momentarily. "Ron talks about you behind your back."

"If I started x-ing out people for talking about me, I'd be talking to no one at all." *I talk bad about him, too.*

"Hawk didn't defend you," Sunny said. She was hardened and hopeful again, about presenting a scenario Eva hadn't considered.

"He was supposed to?"

"Yeah he was *supposed to*, Eva. Jesus. For five seconds you sounded like a human being—"

"As opposed to?" Eva liked her rhyme—*supposed to* and *opposed to*.

"A bitter bitch." Sunny said this without smiling and without looking at Eva.

"You like that bitch when she's riding for you."

"You got me clocked, Evey." Sun faced Eva now. "Feel like you know me. What's funny is I thought I was going to love you like a sister. And you knew it. But it's cool. I'm not stupid anymore."

Eva didn't like to hear Sun call herself stupid. She didn't like it when any woman said that about herself. "You weren't stupid, Sun." *You were innocent.*

"Maybe not stupid. But new enough to fall for old tricks." Sunny began to taunt. "I didn't see back then how you *know* so much about everyone. Know each and every move people make. What their agendas are. You *know* the game 'cause you've been *in* the game. Whatever anyone does was already seen by you from a mile away. That night in Carmel, I thought you had more of a good spirit."

Eva tilted the bottle back, took gulps of cold water. "A guide for all this doesn't usually come with a good spirit."

"You didn't guide me to Sonrisa. I asked Ron and Seb and them for their little input. But don't get it twisted—*I* did Sonrisa."

"Their little input." Eva chuckled, angry.

"Because even a little from you is negative. In terms of real stuff. Beyond the next single. The next video."

"I'm negative," Eva said like she was noting the nature of characters in a skit. "And you're funny." Eva said *funny* like she was saying *not worth this conversation.*

"I was real funny when I mentioned Sonrisa to you like six months ago. Remember what I said? Remember what you said?"

Eva took more slow swallows of water. She'd no recollection.

Sun lifted her feet from the lounge chair and placed them on the smooth cement. She leaned toward the associate general manager of Roadshow and spoke like she was spitting. "You said, *Eva*, for me to concentrate on the *here* and *now*. Said to keep my eye on the ball and the future would take care of itself. You told me to write the arrangements for the cover songs. I hate covers. I hate this album. If it sells twenty million, I hate this album."

"No," Eva said, unfazed. "You won't."

"It was you who told me that, a long time ago, anyway. You told me in Carmel."

"Told you what?"

Sunny bloomed cool red. She wanted to know Eva better, to trust her more, and to team up. Sun didn't have many girls from which to choose her friends, and she had the celebrity craving to be near those who'd known her when she wasn't. "Told me to choose liquor, Eva. Go onstage fat, you said, and people are disgusted. Go onstage drunk, and people stay to see what you're gonna do." Sunny was angry with Eva and she was empathetic and Sunny wanted to shake her.

Eva was about to say, *And I was right*, but her cell rang. It was Eva's assistant, Piper.

"It's Eva," she answered. Then she said, as if they hadn't been arguing, "Sun, give me just a minute, please."

Sun placed her feet back on the lounge.

"There's other stuff," Piper said through the phone, "but on the personal tip, your mom called. Oh, and your girl Pritz called. Said she was in transit and would find you."

Stepmom. "What else?" Eva got up from her chair, walked fifteen paces from Sunny. Eva was hotter than the morning sun would have her, and she felt a little vertigo.

"Just interoffice," Piper said, chirpy as usual, and officious as Eva required. "Except, are you still coming here tomorrow? Your ticket says to L.A., but Seb was saying—"

So it's "Seb" now. "Sebastian don't know my plans. I'll call you tonight with those. Tell me how it's moving with Sonrisa. Sunny have everything she needs?"

"I'm, um, I'm not working on that."

"But you know about it."

Beat. "Yeah."

Eva said, "Do I know about it?"

"It . . . seems like you do. You're asking me about it."

"Did I know yesterday?"

"I don't know," Piper said.

"Did you know yesterday?"

"I knew a little bit. I—"

"Did I know a little bit? Yesterday?"

"I thought you—"

"What did you think?" Eva was pissed, and wondered if she was truly pissed or just absolutely sure that she ought to be. If there were instincts at play that she could override. The doubt made her angrier. The doubt was new.

"Why're you mad?" Piper whined. "I know I'm supposed to tell you everything that happens—"

"Everything you hear, everything you see, everything you know. What's changed?"

"*Nothing's* changed. You haven't been here. You don't know what it's like."

"What's changed?"

"It's just—"

"You know I don't like the word *just* in an answer. Trivializes anything that comes after it."

Eva could feel Piper trying to get her mind steely, her voice tight. Eva could feel Piper trying to be more like Eva. Piper huffed, then said, "I thought—"

"That you think whatever it is you're about to say is implied by you saying it." *But you ain't me, Piper. Not yet.*

"I tell you everything. I—"

"Just handle my travel, my flights and shit. My phones, give to an intern. I can't trust you to have my back."

"That's not true, Eva." Piper's voice broke. "Why're you saying that? Eva—"

"Little sister, what's changed?" Eva was patronizing. "Why am I out here in the Bahamas hearing shit I should've heard from you? Hearing it for the first time in front of a crowd of people?"

"Eva, Eva, I'm sorry. One second, hold on. Seb's buzzing me. Hold—"

Hold on? Hold on?!? Eva pressed OFF.

She looked up, and hated Piper, literally, out of the blue. Hated her keenly, and because Eva didn't imagine Piper's life to be anything but ingenue-perfect, Piper's uterus anything but hollow and unscratched, Piper's day and future days anything but filled with opportunity and loud sex and expensive shoes worn only in the season in which they were new. Eva had liked Piper from the first interview, thought Piper bright and organized and driven and gorgeous. It was why Eva had chosen her. Piper had reminded Eva of herself.

From behind a wide desk cluttered with CDs that bored her, digital audiotapes she'd not listened to, promotional stickers still on their peel-off backs, glossy invitations to which she'd not responded, and inch-thick stacks of memos, Eva should have seen it when young Piper shook her hand to seal the hire. Though it had been 1995, and hip hop was cresting—Tupac and Biggie quietly becoming the artists who would create the albums and personas that would transform and then obliterate the landscape—Eva felt, as she shivered in the Bahamian sunshine, that she should have been wise enough then to see the beginning of the end.

"Eva!"

Stop calling me, Gayle.

"Awake?"

"If I wasn't, I would be now." *It's 1989,* clicked Eva's mind to an inner blare of brand-new Public Enemy. *Another summer. I hear the sound of the funky drummer.*

Eva's stepmother stepped into the room stuffed with the queen-size bed. Eva was sitting on the edge of it, had just hung up the phone with an airline. "Made Cream o' Wheat," Gayle said.

I'm up. I'm out. I'm twenty-three. I'm grown.

"And," Gayle said brightly, "you're not going *any*where. They won't miss you one more day."

"Was off yesterday, and the day before. I have stuff—"

"Yeah, stuff." Gayle leaned in the doorframe. "Stuff envelopes. Type phone numbers, run around for folks' lunches."

"I got a flight." *I'm about to feel strong again. It's only two hours from Portland to Los Angeles.* It was Portland this year, but had been Silver Spring, Maryland, for Eva's dad and Gayle for eighteen months before that. On the plane from L.A., Eva'd felt glad for their proximity, thought she needed support after the procedure. But she didn't need it. She didn't feel like a murderer, but she did feel like an unprincipled, selfish slut, and there was no outside help for that. Eva wished she'd stayed in her own apartment, in her own head, so she could work and do the things that reminded her who she was and why she'd so quickly and firmly made her decision. *I have,* Eva said to herself as Gayle looked on kindly, *a life. The choices I make are the choices I make.*

"You'll need a ride to the airport," Gayle said like she wasn't about to give it.

Don't make me ask. Because Dad'll take me. And I know you don't want him to come back in before your hair is combed. Eva's stepmother had married Eva's father because he encouraged her consoling ways. Gayle got her jollies, and made friends easily, telling people how things would work out fine, especially when it was clear that things wouldn't. It's what she'd chanted like a new Buddhist to Eva's father, when he was suddenly single again. On the rare days Gayle was sad, being embarrassed about it made her sadder—and Eva's father didn't tolerate moping. But he and Gayle got along well.

"You like all this . . . with the music. Working at that place."

"I understand it. I have responsibilities." Eva was a radio promotions assistant at Warner Bros. Records and was about to be upgraded to coordinator. She'd interned at Warner Bros. while at UC-Santa Barbara. Her grades were Cs because she worked so hard for the label (driving back and forth fifty miles to Los Angeles three times a week) and at UCSB's radio station. Eva partied and worked so much, she had to quit the track team and intramural softball. She graduated, but skipped the oceanfront ceremony so as to work advance promotion for the southern leg of the Fresh Fest tour.

Gayle took a brush from a bureau and methodically pulled her hair back from her forehead. "What do you understand?"

"That people like music. Want to buy it. Somebody has to make it." *It's everything to me, you weirdo. It's all I hear. Have you even seen* Do the Right Thing*?*

"Manufacture it. That's the side you're on."

"Manufacture, make, whatever. Get it out there." *Me and the other low-levels are basically an in-house focus group. Look at this album cover, look at this video. Did you see the clothes they're taking to the shoot? Is it what the kids'll wear? The higher-ups, so desperate and trying so hard not to show it. I see the mistakes they can't help but make. Always thinking of the fans as one big stupid swarm. I'm not gonna be like that. I'll put out music that's real.*

"You've got to get back," Gayle said as Eva slipped into her Reeboks. "Or the place'll crumble."

"I won't have others blocking my moves," Eva said plainly. "I'm on my way to being a professional person. In *hip hop*. That's what I represent. Make my *own* money. Get fired if I'm wack, get promoted when I'm hot. Do you even know how that feels? It's going to be my living. Dad likes it for me. Ask him." *Go hard or go home. That's my motto. And I won't be coming home. Bad enough I had to be here now.*

Taken aback by Eva's intense eye contact, Gayle said, "I know what your father likes, thank you." She put the brush down.

Eva jammed sweats in her carry-on.

"You're going to take it easy, though, Eva," Gayle said delicately. "Going to be more careful."

Condom came off, Gayle. And even if it wasn't my fault, it's my fault, and I dealt with it. Eva said nothing.

"It's not just the procedure," Gayle pressed. "It's the stuff that's out there now. You know about it."

"I read," Eva said. *Why'd I come here? Dad all half disappointed and half approving, mumbling about Future this and Future that while I'm padding around in pajamas, holding my gut like it might fall out my body. And he says nothing directly to me. Pawns all direct conversation off on Gayle. Why does she bring me broth when I'm supposed to be gearing back up? Heard Dad in the kitchen with Gayle talking about, "Why not T-bones, put some iron in her blood? Coffee and purple grapes, get her system moving." He's right. I got to get moving.*

Eva slipped her passport in her back pocket, put her bag on her shoulder, and then followed her stepmother, who snatched up her keys and pocketbook, through the front door of the house and into the car. Eva stared out the windshield, pulled her hood over her long braid.

"You need your passport to fly to L.A.?"

"I always use my passport," Eva said without looking at Gayle, "in any situation. Supreme form of ID. There's no questioning it."

"People question your driver's license?"

Why is this broad all up in my business? "My passport is here, right?" Eva laid it on her lap, flipped it open, and then closed it. "In this little clear plastic thing. Little clear plastic thing's got pockets. In the pockets—driver's license, insurance card, things like that. Anything anybody needs to know about me."

"Is there a note in there explaining to all and sundry why you're so darned huffy?"

"Do I not have a reason, *Gayle*, to be the tiniest bit huffy *today?*"

Eva's stepmother set her lips tightly. And then in her more usual, chastened manner, Gayle murmured, "Twice isn't bad," as they clicked behind belts in the old, clean sedan.

Eva checked her bag for her Walkman and for her advance cassette of PeaceLove&War. She placed the cased tape with the handwritten song list in the zipper pocket of her bag, feeling privileged to have early notice of such a legendary group's new music. The advance tape was one of many secret badges of Eva's membership in hip hop. A talking amulet that proved she was damn near a corporal in what was still the few and the proud. She slipped her passport in her jacket pocket and kept her hand in there on top of it.

Mr. Glenn stood with a neighbor on the tiny lawn, Trail Blazers brim pulled down against the drizzly rain. He looked at his daughter, put skinny fingers to his lips for a long moment, and lifted them. It was his best kiss. Eva looked away, and then up, to keep water from rolling down her cheeks.

"Don't want you to think twice is bad," Gayle went on as she pulled onto the gloomy, glistening street. "It would be you, anyway, dealing with the afteraffects. The responsibility. Twice is okay."

I've wasted three lives now. Those twins and now this. Three chances is what?

E va!"
  "What?" Eva was standing next to a trash can so clean it could have been sterilized. Near a short palm so waxy and perfect, she wanted to tear off the leaves. Eva's teeth were in her tongue. She was trying to figure out when she'd lost it, and how she could get it back.

The list in her head went like this: Sunny had started Sonrisa. Sunny was down with Vic, who was probably telling Sunny what an asshole Eva was. Piper was keeping stuff from Eva. Piper was probably fucking Sebastian, had maybe been fucking Sebastian, just as Eva had fucked Sebastian off and on for a year before he hired her at Roadshow. Eva was trying to engineer a comeback for Sunny, and Sunny was creeping off.

Teeth scoring her tongue even deeper, Eva thought about Ron and Dart and how she kept coming back to them, and they to her. Eva felt throttled standing there by the clean trash can, throttled and thirsty and like she'd been assigned lustiness and fearlessness at a meeting she missed. But she embraced the traits because bravery and decision making came easily. And sex could be fun—as numbing or mood altering as any five drinks. Thinking about sex brought Eva right back to thinking about the baby, and that she must in fact be pregnant, because she was vomiting and dizzy, and it had to be the baby throwing her around. Messing her up. Distracting her. It was already in her life, changing her program, weighing her down.

"Why you way over there?" Sunny said. "Come with me up to

Dart's room." She'd relaxed. Had overheard parts of Eva's conversation with Piper.

Eva drank the last of her water.

In saucer-size sunglasses and a lime caftan, Sunny padded through the plastic pasture of bare chairs and tables.

Eva got her stuff and strolled toward Sunny. Eva wouldn't trot. That wouldn't do.

The lobby bar in the Great Hall of Waters trembled with a thick line of early birds.

"I'll rescue you," Sunny said with a tug at Eva's elbow, "in fifteen."

"Ten," Eva said, eyeing the gauntlet. But Sunny was on her way to the elevator bank. A few people stared at her, but Eva couldn't tell if it was because of Sun's billowing aura or because Sun was recognized.

Eva made her way over to the bar.

The O'Jays clicked her brain, and her stride moved to an inner beat.

Nineteen seventy-five, from the album Survival. *Sampled by Gang Starr for a lame album cut. Sampled by Devin the Dude and EPMD and Keith Murray. And more.*

The searing song in her head, and the idea that she knew everything there was to know about it, geared Eva up to face what she suddenly saw as a chain of fools. Backstabbers. Smiling faces that tell lies.

Got to give the people, went the O'Jays' classic jam, *give the people what they want.*

va walked over and kissed at chunky men clustered around chunky glasses, women with flutes poised over cheeses and pastries. Eva scorned women who ate doughnuts and cakes. It was cowardly, Eva believed, to maintain the shelter of a plump face and dimpled thighs. She thought them cows scared to go head-up with Naomi and Tyra, afraid to beat the famed white girls at their rangy, long-waisted games.

Special Ed's MC voice rattled in Eva's head: *I . . . am the magnificent. Supa-dope*, yelled the voice. *Outta sight.*

"Eva! Miss Everything! Come, *sweetness*, join us for a little pre-cocktail cocktail!"

Smile ablaze, Eva waved at Myra ecstatically. Eva wanted out of the Vince the Voice convention, away from the bar with its blueberry-stuffed French toast and hard curls of peppered bacon. Eva identified with the righteous smugness of the breakfast eaters. The feeling of having finally what was deserved, what was past due for past injustices to past players. The feeling of victory—for taking over rock's hold on pop culture with a coup d'état that began with the candle bomb of Run-D.M.C. and Aerosmith's 1986 "Walk This Way." The single looked accidental, and it was a skyrocket around which a zillion circumstances had conspired, but the rap song had been consciously lit by the grungy guitar Rick Rubin and Russell Simmons tagged all over Run-D.M.C.'s third album. Any lingering remains of the rock era were cremated five years later, when *Billboard*'s charts went computerized, and N.W.A's *Niggaz4Life* emerged as the album most purchased and stayed number one for week after incendiary week. Eva still remembered that first week of Soundscan charts with a thrill of vindication.

Yes, it's glorious. We're glorious. But we killed it. Biggie and Tupac are gone, and Kirk Franklin and his gospel family are at the top of the charts. It's like we can't even see the connection. Choirs sing at funerals.

"How about *you*, this morning, Eva?" Myra sang out. "How's Miss Queen of Doin' Thangs?"

"Working, woman. Getting my head together for the day. What about you?"

"What you *need* to be doing, darling, is telling those Roadshow white folks that Sunny needs to be around some more black people. Do some community stuff."

Eva sat down with Hakeem and Myra and pecked at a bowl of peanuts.

"Talk about how these Roadshow folks are bitter," Hakeem said. "How they can't actually *make* the music, so they gotta dictate every-thing else."

Eva rolled her eyes until they stopped on the liquor shelves to her left.

A waitress walked up with two drinks on a tray.

"Myra, can I have yours?" Eva took a glass of whiskey before the startled waitress could sit it down, and sipped it before Myra could an-swer. *In ev'ry job that must be done / There is an element of fun / You find the fun and snap! / The job's a game.* Eva took another sip. *The spoken intro to "A Spoonful of Sugar (Helps the Medicine Go Down)." From the soundtrack to 1964's* Mary Poppins. *Sung by Julie Andrews.* Eva wanted to leave. To talk more with Sunny, get things straight between them, and to see what was so important in Dart's room.

Hakeem handed Myra his drink, then asked the waitress for an-other. The three of them sat in silence and waited on Hakeem's drink like it would help their chat move in a most delightful way.

Eva'd tried to convince Sun to refurbish a recreation center in a housing project in San Diego, had spoken to her about being on the honorary boards of various safety-net-type organizations. These were things that needed to be done, the price of grounding legitimacy as a black pop artist. Sun had talked one time about starting an arts camp, and Eva'd made sure Sun's offhand idea had shown up in her bio and press materials. But Sun was about inner peace and poetry and the privilege of indulging passions that came with her success.

This only alienated her from the older set who prided themselves on talking about reaching back a hand, the set who felt they'd kissed white ass for years, and who'd been paid less money for doing more work. At a radio convention like Vince the Voice's, it was older black execs who'd been the first investigated for payola when they'd accepted or paid out the least. Who'd fought on principle, as well as for personal gain, for more airplay for black artists. This older set—Myra's contemporaries, and the super-old hands who'd put people like Hakeem on—they'd sons and nieces with Sun posters in their bedrooms and thought her too selfish, too quick to embrace the white pop aura.

But the showcase was a success. Fuck Myra. So why don't I get out of here?

Myra swept her hand through the air over the table—barspeak for another round.

Eva sipped the last of her first drink, glanced toward the golden front doors of the hotel. *I'm not pregnant. There's no way.* She looked fifty feet up at the ceiling. A dome lined with gold shells. Eva's mind filled the looming space with her father, with Ron, with a vision of herself free of work and hating the freedom. Then Eva looked toward the elevators, for Sun.

"She'll be here, baby," Hakeem said. He reached over, pushed a piece of hair behind Eva's ear, and stroked the curve of it. Eva let him. "Something I want you to do for me."

Eva thought if it thrilled him to touch her, and helped him to feel less threatened by her, then fine. The less threatened he felt, the more he was up to assist.

"Myra hasn't heard your speech about Boyz II Men, Evey," Hakeem said.

"She hasn't heard someone else give it?" Eva looked at Myra. The Boyz II Men homily was common as the N.W.A lecture. Most colored people in the business could deliver it.

"No one says it like you. You know dates and exact sales and all the fun facts. Come on, now," Hakeem said. "Bring the drama."

Me. Tell you about boys to men. "Abbreviated version, only," Eva said, and she stood.

Myra was suddenly an aunt pleased by a wayward niece's display of we-are-family. A few other convention attendees turned to watch and listen.

"In 1992," Eva began, in the tone of an infomercial hostess, "a harmonizing black boy group's single about the 'end of the road' bumped a white hero's single about cruelty from its slot as the longest running number one single in the so-called rock era. And the twelve-week record—for Elvis Presley's 'Don't Be Cruel'—had stood since 1956! After Whitney Houston tied Boyz II Men's record in 1995 with her rendition of the Dolly Parton–penned 'I Will Always Love You,' Boyz II Men broke the record again! For fourteen weeks their 'I'll Make Love to You' was the most popular song in America! Then, in 1996, Boyz II Men—in a quintet with Mariah Carey—stayed at number one for sixteen weeks with 'One Sweet Day.' Sweet! Before Boyz II Men proved it could be done, before hip hop music—and that includes acts like Jodeci and En Vogue and Mary J. Blige—became the nucleus of youth culture, even an artist who was a superstar among blacks had few hopes—with the exception of Michael Jackson—of selling the numbers of an artist popular among whites." Eva curtsied, finished. But she added, at her chirpiest, "The confluence of hip hop, Boyz II Men, and Soundscan marked the beginning of a new era in pop music." And then sat back down. A few people clapped. Myra and Hakeem were charmed. Eva was tired.

She rarely put the Boyz on the stereo anymore. She appreciated the foursome, though. Boyz II Men's accidental politics had given Eva's jobs the feel of a mission.

I thought since hip hop changed my world, it would change the world.

Eva wished Sunny would walk in. The conversation was turning to what it always did: the Grind.

Black and black-identified Latino personnel—vice presidents, directors of sales, managers of promotions, assistants to senior directors—worked colored rappers and singers at colored venues and colored radio stations and colored magazines until the act went—if it went—

"pop." The marker was usually one million albums sold—aka "platinum."

Then the artist moved over to the regular or pop side—the white side—of the label. There the white staff that worked for the white president worked the artist—who was now "mainstream" and so would benefit from being worked by people with "mainstream"/white press and white/"pop" video and Top Forty radio contacts.

Once platinum, the black artist (sadly, ecstatically, or in a quandary) left the colored side.

Some colored employees tearfully waved the artist off, as if it were a graduation.

Some bitched.

Got thrown juicy little bones.

Occasionally, an artist stomped feet in order to have a favored colored exec still active on a project, even as he or she became more super than star.

But the artist went over.

He or she had to in order to be considered, within the particular label, a real artist.

Real pop acts made real money.

Colored label employees got sick of the separate but unequal setup. Along with the rise of hip hop, resentments that had festered for years in urban music departments oozed at last. Eva was a part of that ooze.

I'ma get more / 'Cause I'm financially secure and I'm sure / So I don't need your tips or advice.

Special Ed, born Edward Archer in Brooklyn. Debuted in 1989 at sixteen with Youngest in Charge.

"Eva. Check in, please," Hakeem said.

Eva wouldn't be pulled from her brooding. She didn't want to be with Hakeem or Myra, and she was getting sick of paradise.

Before Rolling Stone *began putting iced-out, accommodating-ass MCs on its cover, before MTV started covering and playing hip hop to a larger extent and with more creativity than BET, before rap music became the pop rule instead of the maligned exception, before hip hop started accounting, with every passing quarter, for more and more major label profits, us "urban" execs accepted our second-best status as a tax on the money we make.*

We accept it as an uncomfortable but profitable cross to bear.

Eva was dirty with the knowledge that but for icons like Russell Simmons, Meri Heath, and Puffy Combs and a few low-profile bigwigs who wielded big sticks, for the most part the situation at the labels remained intact, if not so obvious in terms of job titles. "Urban," aka "black," departments began to merge with "pop" departments not in the interest of fairness, but because it had come to the point where whites in the pop departments had next to no "rock" to promote for their salaries. And, when departments did merge, and people had to be let go, some whites were fired, but like as not, it was colored people who were granted two months' severance and best wishes for their future endeavors.

It's life. It's reality. That's what I say. That's what we all say.

The unfairness was clear and verifiable. There was an occasional stink, a rare suit. But the money to be made was too much, the parties too fierce, the expense accounts too boundless, the discriminatory ways of corporate America too embedded in the psyches and habits of whites and nonwhites alike. Hip hop had changed everything—and not much, at all.

We all would do most anything just to be in hip hop, to be large in it.

And like those boys rushing Ron, we've eaten shit willingly.

And there is no doubt, Eva thought, *I am in on it.*

"What I'm saying is, there's no loyalty anymore! Eva? You hear me."

"You want me to talk about artists staying loyal?" Eva snapped at him. "Talk about how I convinced lazy-ass promoters to sell wack MCs to wack chitlin' radio when the MC was still Willie Lunchmeat from Queens? Broke-Ass Brenda from Flint? Shit—Sunny Addison from San Diego? That's what you want me to talk about, for the eight millionth time?"

Hakeem was amused by her anger. "Yes, love. Indulge me. Break down how we all came up in this."

In this business, in this life, *somebody always trying to make you prove your origins. Your hometown, yeah, but truly, your* origins. *Want you to tell them, in one way or another, that you identify. Want you to state that you're happy but not too happy with the size of your check and the options it grants. Let's sit up here and remind each other of the contracts signed, fondle the songs created and re-created, songs marketed and promoted and shipped. Let's relive parties planned and attended, deals cut, cornballs cut out, sex had, children inconveniently born, fans surprised or delighted or disappointed but still spending fifteen dollars on a disc you thought up or helped name or approved the budget for, something you knew was genius or truth or crap—who cared, the shit was hot. And everybody got paid. Everybody in your circle, anyway. Your cool-ass compadres. The fans, if they're broke, or desperate, or manipulated, what then? The music soothes them, hypes them, serves them. This is a business. Those mufuckers make their own decisions. God bless 'em, but shit: we're all grown.*

And here's Hakeem, talking about, Remind me, Miss Eva, Miss Sister-of-Mine, Sister Love, Sister-Who-Is-Down-for-the-Cause. Remind me that you still know who you are, Evey. Indulge me. We walk this road together. Sing that song.

Eva demanded them herself, the fissile pledges of solidarity. At Lost City, as she went along to get along, Eva hated it. But she turned herself up. Turned it on. She knew how to do that.

Got to give the people what they want. "You," Eva said, smiling like a hoochie, like a tough girl still ready to please. "You who was high rollin' before you had a roll? Who flew into town pimpy and shot callin', new AmEx hot off the press?" Today she'd take the easy way, prove her history by telling his.

"Yes, love! My first corporate card. Talk about it!"

"That super-fun pass. Magic—separate from your own fucked-up credit."

"Yes, Eva!"

"You with Chicago *and* Baltimore *and* Brooklyn stains still on your shirt!" Her laugh was crispy at the edges.

"I let fools know, though! However I looked!"

Myra wouldn't be left out. All she needed was her hand over her heart. "*I* let 'em know who Hawk *really* is," she piped in. "These negroes and negresses with their big heads, I remind 'em—Hawk bought you a burger and put you up at the biggest Holiday Inn you ever saw, didn't he? Hawk saw money in you when your nails were still bent back and bleeding from the clawing you did to get in this game."

Oh yes, Eva thought, *go picturesque on us, Myra. Bring it to life!* "What do you tell 'em when they say, 'So what?' What do you tell 'em then, Myra?"

"I say, big deal you had had a local following, a college radio hit. So *what.* When you were working at Kinko's so you could design and copy fliers for free, Hawk came through with a contract."

"Hawk don't care about no one but himself," Eva said. "As long as the liner notes say, 'Last but not least, I want to thank my man Hawk, for giving me a chance.' That's all he cares about."

"Exactly," Hakeem said like he was locking a door. "That, and a check. As long as the love comes with a goddamned check."

If you hate yourself, you should say it out loud. Hakeem Marcus Watkins, born 1958 on the South Side of Chicago, Illinois, he understood self-hatred, and he believed in it. It was normal. But to mull over it, to be distracted by it—*Check in, Eva*—was an insult to the greater discontent. A pause in Eva's beeline made Hakeem take pause, which would make Myra take pause, and so on and so on, and then how much work would get done? Hakeem refused to fall with Eva into thoughts outside of the music business, outside the dome in which the living seemed easy. What Hakeem cared about was points, period. Once Eva made associate general manager, Hakeem told her that's all she should care about. The title itself, he'd told her way before Paradise Island, didn't mean shit. "All the race music Roadshow puts out?" Hakeem often called it *race music,* like folks had in the old days. He wasn't old enough to have ever used the language when it was popular, but he called singles "sides," too, sometimes. For Hakeem it was a kind of homage, and a reminder. "All the niggas Roadshow's robbed? They need a black girl up there. To deflect all that. To monitor the negroes. Get your points, Eva. Shit. Get paid." Eva had taken Hakeem at his word.

I n the lobby bar, Hakeem said, "Relax your little body." In his ambiguous capacity as consultant, Hakeem made money off Sunny's back end. "Your cash cow," he said, "will stomp in here any minute."

"We gotta *use* your power, Eva." Myra was talking, almost to herself. All she needed was a fan to flutter at her face. "'Cause you *know* you got it. You can make this industry different. Help black people get the money and *respect* they deserve."

"Sun's not a cash cow," Eva said. "Don't call her that." Eva had called Sunny a cash cow so many times she couldn't count.

"You're the only black person even working Sunny's project," Myra said. "They got them others doing her marketing, her promotion—"

"I do her marketing, Myra," Eva said coldly. "I supervise her whole everything."

"I know, miss, I know. Don't get touchy. I'm your friend. Look out for you even though you never come to our Square Biz soirees. But I'm talking about the *real* marketing, sweetums. I know you handle what they *let* you handle. I know you're doing a lot, but I'm talking about her pop marketing—"

"Because you know all about that," Eva said. "Because you're an expert."

"—what those white boys talk about at the meetings Miss Eva isn't invited to." Myra paused. "Ron's in those kind of meetings, where he works."

Fuck you. "Ron's Ron. I win with Sun. Everybody else," Eva said, looking firmly at Myra, "waits for her to fall." *Waits for me to fall.*

"Of course folks is waiting on a fall!" Hakeem was still amped. He slammed his glass on the table, disturbing peanuts. "The bitch sold nineteen million with *Poems.* Out the gate! Where's she at now," Hakeem asked, "with . . . what's the name of that shit?"

"You know exactly," Eva said, turning her glare on him. "Nine million. With *Bliss Unknown.*"

"And it's a double CD." Hakeem shook his head. He weighed peanuts in his hand like they were gold pieces.

Myra tut-tutted. "Do it right, Evey, and Sunny's here for the long haul."

"Myra. Sip your whiskey. No one's here for the long haul." He put a finger on the inch of bare belly showing between Eva's sheer pullover and her wraparound skirt. "Eva's thinking about what's next, who's next." He rubbed the stripe of skin and Eva let him. Eva frowned at Myra as Hakeem said, "I can see it in Evey's little eyebrows . . . all scrunched up . . . Evey's thinking. Figuring out who she's gonna make happen when the Sun goes down."

Legs crossed at the knee, Eva pulled a strand of hair stuck in her lip gloss.

Nobody has this gloss but me. Got it in London. At a boutique. Sunny doesn't even know about it.

Eva looked again at the front doors of the hotel. *People with real lives,* she thought. *Coming and going.*

Going.

Eva turned back toward Hakeem to find him looking at her. She felt caught, and tried to put a nonchalant expression on her face.

But Eva felt certain Hakeem and Myra were laughing at her.

Sunny answered her suite door sleepily.

"What the hell," Eva said. "I was waiting for you. At the bar."

"You know I can't stand Myra's ass. And fuck Hawk, too."

Eva walked through the door, but Sunny pushed her out. "No. You're going to Dart's."

When they got to Dart's door, Sunny started to hand Eva a key card. "Wait," Sunny said, holding Eva's fingers. Sun's mouth turned down, confused. "So you got the bracelet."

"You spoke to Ron? This morning?" All Eva could think was how many thousands of miles she was off her game. So Sun and Ron were talking now. And about her. Sunny was probably going to leave her, go to Ron. *There's a trick to this. A trick I can play to make this right. Some blinder I have on that I have to lift.*

"Ron?" Sunny scrunched her nose, gave a quick, flustered shake of her head, then tugged the bracelet with a finger, as if to make sure it was real. "Speak to Ron? For what? Go in. See Dart." Sunny pressed the key card hard in Eva's palm.

"What's the setup, Sun? What am I walking into?" *Maybe I can just lay down.*

"Nothing," Sunny said in the too-enlightened, yoga-instructor cadence she often used onstage. "You are paranoid. Go."

In Dart's sunlit room, lamps were hot, too.

Water crashed into the bath. Clothes were splayed on the unmade beds, on the floor, on toppled chairs.

"Where's Sun?" he said.

"I guess in her room." Eva perched on the one tight bed corner.

Dart dashed around folding clothes, stacking them in a tower on a tall dresser. He was in a sleeveless T-shirt, and hair burst from his damp pits bushy. Dart's room smelled like Dart, distilled.

Eva walked to the balcony door and slid it open. Then she perched on a littered chair just inside the bright room. Breeze hit her directly.

"Not gonna manage Sun anymore," Dart said, puffing. "It's not me. Never was, but she's my sister, so there you go."

"You need to watch that water."

"I'm 'bout to get in there." He tore through drawers, then crashed his arm through closet shelves. He bulldozed chairs to see the floor beneath them, yanked a bureau from its place against the wall.

Eva got up and kept moving so he was always in front of her.

"I'm leaving this whole shit," he huffed. "Need to be in a situation where my best isn't always called for." Dart hurled back blankets. Then got on his knees and shoved his arm, to the shoulder, under the bed.

The spigot splash was tough to talk over. "You need to check that water."

In front of the open glass door he stopped abruptly. Behind him, the sea hung like a fresh painting. "Why did you come up here?" His voice was suddenly paced, as if to a metronome. The draft carried his sour-sweetness through the room.

"Sunny asked me to." *And because you've been my port in a storm before.*

He shook his head. "I'm not doing what Sun asks anymore." Then Dart snorted, on his click-beat. "What anyone asks. I am bigger than this industry. I am better than this. So are you."

Eva's words fell to the level beat of his syllables. Measured. Reg-u-lar. "You should try to chill."

"CHILL," he said, commando style. "It means, act like what you feel ain't real."

"It means relax." *Don't be crazy. I need to relax.*

He pulled his shirt away from his body, put his nose behind the neckline, inhaled, and then breathed out pendulum-weighted words from behind his pall. "You use this shit—work, Sunny, sex—like a Band-Aid."

"Work . . . art. Love. What else does a girl need."

"I said," he roared at her, but down into his own chest, face still behind his shirt, "you use it like a *tourniquet.*"

He looked like a bandit. A fuming Robin Hood. Eva was used to Dart's odd behavior, but he was making her jumpy. Bathwater thundered. Dart was in a mood to define things, shout things, find things. So Eva decided not to touch anything his. Dart moved fast again, *darted,* even, and refolded clothes as messily as they'd been folded in the first place. Eva wanted to bolt, but felt bolted to the chair, bound by his odor and voice and fascinated by his motions.

"Been thinking I could live," he said, "doing what I've *been doing.* Be like *you.* But I'm about to get . . . natural. Feel things that matter." His voice was low now, and full of dreamy commitment.

"Dart," Eva got it together to say. "Can you please turn off that water?"

"I TOLD you I was about to GET IN, Eva." Dart's voice almost pushed her. "Hotel tubs DON'T OVERFLOW. How many hotels have you BEEN IN, Eva? Would the world end if my bath LEAKED, Eva, if my floor got wet?"

Eva took long steps to the bathroom, Dart at her back. Water trembled thickly below the tub's wide lip.

"You got it under control?" Dart said. "You see for yourself?"

Eva was shamed, and overcome. She tasted Dart in her throat. Reflexively, her palm went to her belly. *I need,* Eva thought, *to calm down. I need for this baby not to be true. I need for Dart to say something that makes some sense to me.*

He stepped back into his room. She faced him from the bathroom doorway. Cramming clothes into a duffel, Dart paused, felt around, then pulled out a small brownish jar. He set it atop the television and looked at it for a few seconds, to remember he'd placed it there.

Eva was naked and soaking in the tub when Dart came back to the bathroom. Like it had been slit, her right wrist hung limply over the rim.

The bathroom was muggy.

"You're wearing the bracelet," he said, surprised.

Eva was relaxed in the water. She could reach the faucets easily. Turn them back on if she wanted, or turn them off.

"I didn't see it before."

"What?" Eva said, facing him. "You like it?"

Dart peeled off his clothes. "I'm not having sex," he said, tone conversational now. "You treat it like it's nothing."

He stepped in. Water sloshed. Dart sat crosswise, at Eva's feet, his knees bent, facing the door. He couldn't be more folded.

"You're comfortable like that?"

"Are *you* comfortable," Dart said, "the way *you* are? I got that bracelet for you because of what you told me in Carmel. About your mom. Your real mom. I saw it at a stand in the airport in Miami. It was . . . serendipitous."

Eva looked at the bracelet. *Dart got me this?*

Steam rose stinking of dried apricots.

That's what it is.

A metallic, sugar-vinegar smell of damp drying fruit. The bathroom transformed into a windowless roomful. In his cramped position, Dart was perfectly still.

"Walk out of here," he said. "With me."

His words were a soft siren, the story in all her private songs.

Hey baby, let's get away, go someplace far.

Let me take you on an escapade.

Down icy lanes, under a glass blue sky—this is living.

This is living.

"Not to a physical place," Dart said. "A real, true mental one. We can *live.* Get away from this madness. It's dying anyway. Hip hop's over. Pop is a joke. We get out before it sucks us down. See who we are without it."

I got two tickets to paradise.

Eva hated talk about searches for self; hated searches for self, period, felt they were detours from what one ought to be doing—which was working for a living. *It's what depressed people do. Imagine there's some parallel life being played out in which they are the hero. The superstar. The free and good one. They search for it around every corner. What you do is regulate what goes on within, and that what goes on without is to be responded to, dealt with, endured, accepted.* The top of Eva's head felt thin and hot. Her mind screeched. *Pick something, do it, and keep it moving.*

Make a decision, with no advice from anyone.

She wanted to tell Dart that she wasn't into daydreaming or disenchantment or restlessness. She wanted to make him understand that staring at the horizon, trying to ascertain one's place in the world, was vanity. But instead, Eva reached for a loofah. It would be waste of time to explain to him that she wasn't going anyplace but back to work, back to figuring out what to do about Sunny, and back to deciding what to do about possibly being pregnant.

Eva washed herself and found solace, as usual, in proactivity.

Dart unfolded himself, turned so he was between her legs, his back tight against her chest. The skin on his back was mottled, and Eva was nauseated. She let herself think that Dart's craziness made him talk about the bracelet. So she felt sorry for him. But then Eva remembered that Sunny had noticed it, too. Her hand twitched, and the bracelet shifted on her wrist.

"We're *meant*," Dart said, pressing his back even more tightly against her. "You found the bracelet. I didn't think anyone would steal it, hanging from the doorknob. Not like it's worth anything. Except to you."

Eva pushed him forward a bit, then lifted her hand in front of him. "You left this on the door?" A weak cuff, it dangled from her wrist sunrise side up.

He sneered ugly for a second, but it faded. "I got it for you because the bracelet has the feel of the Out Islands, Eva. Cat Island is where we should go."

When Dart started in with Cat Island details, it was clear to Eva. The bracelet hadn't been Ron's to give.

" . . . Obeah bottles strung from branches," Dart said. "Dangling bottles filled with graveyard dirt and hair and fingernails, protecting folks' property from thieves. We can find a healer. For me, and for . . . you."

Ron had given Eva nothing, as her real mother had liked to say, but a hard time.

" . . . we'll see goats," Dart said dreamily. "We can climb—or walk, it's really just a walk—up Mount Alvernia."

The bath had cooled. The water seemed suddenly stagnant. Eva pushed Dart far forward.

"Don't be typical of yourself," he said sharply. Dart ran a soapless cloth over his face and under his arms and stepped from the big tub. "Don't you need a relationship? A man? Even for a week?"

Eva climbed from the tub, shivering. He handed her his damp towel. She held it in her fingers.

"Not a buncha niggas," Dart said boldly. "One. This one."

"The choice between fucking one and fucking a buncha is the choice between one roller coaster and another." Eva's skin rose in goose bumps.

"You're already riding this one." He took his towel from her. "You found the bracelet. You think I'm so foul, but you have it on." He grabbed a fluffy clean towel from the shelf above the toilet and pushed it at her.

"I have to go to the gospel brunch," Eva said. She toweled her body crossly and way past dry.

Dart bellowed like there was a score of skeptics in the room. "Given how you DIS everything not in your everyday sphere, I shouldn't even SAY what I'm about to say." He looked hard at Eva, like maybe she was worthy of special information. He pointed at her like a quirky person on the street calling out a stranger. An eccentric, disheveled person who haunts you because of the copper connection crazy people often have to the truth.

Eva felt ignorant of her own body. Something inside her was speaking up, and she didn't know if it was her conscience or a baby or if those were the same thing. The not knowing was loud and strong, and even wrapped in the long towel, Eva was abnormally uncomfortable to be naked. Eva wanted Dart to say what he had to say so she could put her clothes back on and get away from him and take care of her personal business. Her breasts ached like a few veins were all that kept iron spheres from falling through her skin and to the floor.

They get sore, though, right before I start my period.

Dart mistook her discomfort for disdain. It was an error people made about Eva, whether she was pregnant or not.

"Just because it's the name of a SONG," Dart said, still pointing, and starting to perspire. "What I'm about to say is NOT automatically stupid."

"Okay." *I need a bra on right now. I need to be in my own bathroom.*

"DON'T patronize," he said in his booming voice. "Don't."

"I'm not." But she'd crossed her arms under her breasts.

"In my estimation, and in the estimation of a lot of other people—"

"Spit it out, Dart. I'm not really desperate for background."

"—the Age of Aquarius officially began last January, 1997. It was the end of the Age of Pisces. This heralds the beginning of the End Times. Some think it's the beginning of a New World Order. Opinions differ, but—"

He is crazy. But she listened.

"—the fact is, things are changing, and I need to be where I can contemplate that. Come with, Eva. Don't look at it like a spiritual thing. I know that freaks you out. Look at it like this: Cat Island's your type of spot—attached to nothing, in the middle of a treacherous ocean, happy to be pretty."

His voice was coming from far away.

"I know," he said solemnly, "there's more to you than what you let everybody see."

Eva ran the hand with the bracelet over her long belly.

Dart lunged toward Eva, pulled her hand away from her stomach, and kissed her knuckles. He fell to his knees and looked up, her hands in his. Dart's eyes had dark circles and the circles shone like he was tired of seeing things differently. Eva was overwhelmed and she was convinced.

I'm 'bout to go see my future. Leave my worries behind.

va, back in her room, glad that it was made up and brand-new.

Eva dressed, on her bed, sitting by the nightstand.

Can't keep staring at it. Two pink lines on a stick.

Phone book's right here. Someone has to confirm this. Have to speak to a professional.

Nassau Family Planning Association. Right nearby.

Dial the number.

"'Tis Malinda. How can I help you today?"

State the situation. That you took the test. That there are two pink lines. Like welts on a tiny palm.

"There's been mornin' sickness, then?"

"Yeah."

"Sleepiness?"

"I don't know. I've been working, so—"

Radio in Malinda's background. Buzzy as a shortwave in a war movie.

"The possibility, ma'am, is that you could be more pregnant than you think. First day of your last period?"

Period. Yes. Count. What's that song on her radio? It's one of Ron's groups? Or that other, sad one that Myra pumps all the time?

"Ma'am?"

"Forty-four days ago."

"Forty—"

"Little over six weeks."

"T'was normal?"

"Yeah, I think." Eva hated her answers to Malinda's questions. "I mean, no. Shorter, maybe, than usual."

"You could be pregnant . . . for nine weeks or more. Some bleeding, especially around the time of what would 'ave been your regular, most recent period, 'appens to a lot of women in their first trimester. Ma'am . . . Ma'am?"

"Yes." Formal now, in the face of her world folding in.

"Are you staying on New Providence with us for a while? Or 'eadin' back to the States soon? Did you want to come over? Make an appointment? S'what we recommend."

The static from Malinda's radio overtook the song. Eva wanted to curse her. Order her to adjust the damn dial. Eva could hear the song, but she couldn't hear it. Eva could hear everything else—the hum of the minibar, the weight in the hem of the curtain brushing the base of the sliding door. Eva half-heard two men exchange pleasantries in the corridor, heard their shirts brush against the other's, the press of shoes into the carpet, the skirl of a luggage cart. Eva wanted to hear the song on Malinda's radio.

"No," Eva said. "But thanks. I'll see a doctor at home."

"Best wishes to you, then."

No awestruck belly-touching.

No Scotch-sipping.

There was the getting dressed, and the dodging of the gospel brunch.

Eva didn't reach for her sundress or her newest lambskin purse with the ostrich-skin pockets. Instead she grabbed her passport, flipped through it, and then stuffed shorts and tees in her Nike pack, slipped into a bathing suit and a stretchy yellow lace skirt she considered as all-purpose as dungarees. Grabbed her woven bag, toothbrush, and the coconut oil. It was a typical gift from Sunny—FedExed from someplace far, customer service calling to correct the transposed address, or the zip code, only thing intact being Eva's name and her cell number and what Eva liked to believe was the sweet spirit in which it was sent. The present was Philippine virgin coconut oil with "miraculous" fats, the label said, like the fats in breast milk. The printed label made to seem casually handwritten, as if a cheery Filipina, after a walk through her garden, had pressed the oil herself and passed it corked in green glass to a deserving friend.

Eva walked back into her bathroom. She had to pee. Again. Still on the toilet, she wrapped the pregnancy test stick in tissue and placed it in the lined wastebasket.

I am pregnant. Again. I've always known what to do. I always go to the clinic. Go to sleep. Wake up free. Solo.

Get up. Go.

Eva placed her bags near her on the bed. She looked hard at her portable disc player and earbuds and CDs. She had enough music in her head. She thought of Malinda's radio and wished she could beam over to the Nassau Family Planning Association if only to twist the dial, make things clear. Eva hated noisy half-sounds, the itch between stations. Just remembering Malinda's calming, half-congratulatory voice made Eva pick up the phone and put her thoughts into action.

She dialed Dart. To him, and to her reflection in her vanity's oval mirror, Eva said, "We going? Or what?"

The plan was to meet Sunny, get her to the gospel brunch, then to get to Cat Island.

Eva walked in the open door to Sunny's suite. She and her brother were arguing. Dart had a nylon do-rag tied around his head. Hanes white Beefy-T and long denim shorts.

"Don't DRINK," Dart bellowed. "Unless it's tea, Sun." He looked at Eva. "Hullo. Doing what you said. No alcohol. See me doing it."

"I drink too much now?" Sunny looked at Eva. "This is the type of conversation you and him have?"

"Not that you drink too much," Eva said soothingly. "Just that it's not cool for you. On singing days. That's all. And you have to do 'Lift Every Voice' at the brunch."

Sunny drained her pillar. Then she used it in the small bar like a shovel for more ice chips.

"Let's keep it movin'," Eva said to Sunny. "We came down here for a reason." *The conventioneers distrust you.* "Every director from every urban station is still here." *They think you treat fans and radio as after-thoughts. They feel taken for granted. They didn't invite you here. I cajoled them.* "They love you already. Especially after last night." *I wined people on two coasts,* and *in the boring-ass middle of this country. I lied about how you love them. Apologized for shit you don't know you did, and for shit you did and reveled in. Told them fictitious sad stories about your childhood.* "So, it'll be an easy crowd today." *I told some you were mid-breakdown, told others that you were on the comeback from one. Turned you into an infant so they'd feel like devils if they chose not to embrace you.*

"Then why do I have to do it?" Sunny poured cola and rum into her glass.

Because what else are you going to do? These people know the game. They are the game. They know how and why I lie. And they don't give a shit. By coming to the showcase last night, and to the brunch today, they're paying me back for my effort. They're paying me back for the wine.

"BECAUSE," Dart said. His eyes looked bigger and set deeper, his jawbones sharp and burned. Sunny and Eva paid him no mind.

"Because the album's in eleven weeks," Eva said. "These people need to hear you sing about marching on until victory is won."

"Three months. And I'm only doing the one song."

With her nip, Sunny flounced to her bedroom. From behind the almost-closed door she said, "I heard you can get real goosefoot down here. Amaranth, and lemongrass. From the rainforests. Supposed to be good for the voice. The whole body. I want some before you all do whatever it is you're about to do. 'Cause I know you ain't going to this brunch."

"Sun—" Eva started.

"That's in BELIZE," Dart said, geographic homeopathy being his strong suit. "Goosefoot is in *Belize*. We're in the BAHAMAS. NORTH of the equator. In the ATLANTIC Ocean." It was like he was saying *south of HELL. In the ATROCIOUS Ocean.* "They DON'T HAVE rainforests here."

Sunny looked from the door of her room, pissed. "As a matter of fact, I'll get to the brunch with Vic."

"Sun, you have to—"

"Take Dart, please. I'm going to the shit no makeup, my own hair. So I'm fine. Go on."

Any other time, Eva would have babysat. But she and Dart had places to go. They walked from the suite, picked up their bags from where they'd dropped them in the hall, and jogged to the elevator.

———

We could go to a bar. No. Doesn't strike me as a drinker. Eva knew what was better than food, or a natural gas ride: a crisp, swanky spot to lay your head. So after the 1994 Innovative Music for Innovators festival in Monterey, Eva's assistant had quickly booked rooms for Eva, Sunny, and D'Artagnan at a sprawling golfers' hotel in Carmel, just up the road from Monterey. Eva'd ditched Hakeem. Said they'd meet him for dinner, had no intention of showing. Eva suggested the three of them go to a movie, but Sun looked at the big bed and big bath and big fireplace and told Eva and Dart to go on ahead, she'd see them in the morning.

Eva drove Dart slowly down Carmel's main strip. The Pacific bordered it, but all else in Carmel's four-block downtown was Lilliputian and neat. Between mute bistros and bars, there were jewelers' displays bare but for blue velvet cases. A petite public library rose from squared bramble. Galleries featured green granite dolphins, Dali prints, and big blank-eyed black figurines playing saxophones and wearing jazzy suspenders—art that spoke to Eva about introspection and aspiration.

She parked. Eva and Dart walked a bit, then paused before Realtors locked in full flower. Eva was mesmerized.

FANTASTIC VALUE SET IN THE OAKS. BREATHTAKING MOUNTAIN, VALLEY & GOLF COURSE VIEWS. CASUAL OPEN STYLE & ELEGANT OVERTONES. CATHEDRAL CEILINGS & LOTS OF SKYLIGHTS. WINDOWS & FRENCH DOORS INVITE THE OUTDOORS IN. TASTEFUL NEW LANDSCAPING ADD TO THE PRIVACY OF THIS FINE HOME. $850,000.

This written in hurried, leaning blocks, as if announcing a noon bargain of monkfish, not typed in IBM Selectric, like

```
FILTERED OCEAN VIEWS FROM NEW "FRENCH" COUNTRY
CHATEAU. CROWNED W/SLATE ROOF & WRAPPED IN
TINTED STUCCO W/STONE TRIM. HIGH-TECH LIGHTING.
FORMAL DINING ROOM. KITCHEN BOASTS GRANITE
COUNTERS, HARDWOOD FLOORS, VIKING STOVE.
BREAKFAST NOOK OVERLOOKS GARDENS W/PATIO &
OUTDOOR STONE FIREPLACE. WARMED BY A STONE-
TRIMMED FIREPLACE & GLEAMING HARDWOOD FLOORS,
LIVING ROOM OPENS TO TILED OCEAN-VIEW DECK.
MASTER SUITE W/FIREPLACE, W/ANTIQUE FRENCH
MARBLE MANTLE ADJACENT TO WINDOW SEAT W/OCEAN
VIEW. MASTER BATH OFFERS SPA W/SPACIOUS SHOWER,
JETTED TUB & LIMESTONE VANITY W/DOUBLE SINKS.
TWO ADDITIONAL BEDROOMS & BATH. OFFICE &
EXERCISE ROOM. $1,998,000.
```

This suggested a kindly, old-fashioned manner or at least an older way of doing business, suggested a moment in time at which the agent had been on top of all things modern, but had peaked there in Selectricville, happily and retired from newfangledness to quiet, rich Carmel.

Eva read and reread the ad until Dart gently pulled her, but then she stopped in front of a tiny Saks Fifth Avenue, its windows alive with headless ivory mannequins. Eva coveted their creamy satchels. Even before she had money, Eva'd been a brand loyalist. Commercials for places like T.J. Maxx made sense to her: why buy no-class, no-name clothes, when you could just search around a bit and get brand names for less? Eva paused before Saks a long moment, fondling clunky buckles in her brain, visualizing the pride in ownership.

She and Dart sat on a bench on the parklike lane divider. An island-oasis flanked by pristine asphalt rivers. SUVs chugged by sporadically, and Eva thought of L.L. Cool J's "Boomin' System"—*Twelve o'clock at night with your windows down*—but the trucks were silent as sentries.

Her cell rang. She flipped it, saw it was Hakeem, flipped it closed.

Big wheels keep on turnin'. That slow part of Tina Turner's version is what her mind played then.

Sunny's brother was plump. Puffy like he'd been beaten from within and swollen up. "Don't feel like a movie," he said. "Dark enough without going in a darker room." He sat three feet away from her.

Eva slipped from her shoes, put her soles on the cool cement. It seemed an earthy thing to do, and she thought Dart was one who'd respond well to earthiness. To her surprise, it felt good.

"Tell me about you," Dart said. "I can tell Sun likes you."

"Tell me about you."

"I'm not a musketeer, if that's what you think."

"Maybe you are." She looked at his bloated, grim face, thought how cute he'd be if he lost weight and put on at least a better brand of knockoffs. It was a skill of Eva's, to envision After through the depths of Before.

Her cell rang again. Eva flipped it, glanced at the caller ID, saw it was Ron, flipped it closed. "You sing, too?"

"Used to, sometimes, with Sun. But I don't like singing in front of people. Get too worked up. Over the top."

"Like in church?" Eva was thinking, *That could work. Like James Brown? Eddie Levert? Solomon Burke. We could take it black to the future.*

"Wears me out. Either kills me or has me on a weird, fake high. For days afterward."

Eva was silent, still looking for the downside. *Brother-sister acts are corny. Who, besides the Carpenters? BeBe & CeCe Winans. The Wilkinsons? That's father-daughter-son. And bluegrass.*

"So you're a person who can sign her to a record deal," Dart said. "How do you get that job?"

"By being a slave first," Eva said, pleased to discuss herself and her experience. She felt solid and smart when she talked about the record business, liked the sound of her words spilling boldly, lush with lingo and knowledge of the real deal. "And answering other people's phones," she said. "Eavesdropping. Finagling. Figuring out a way one thing about one act could be done better, then finding a master or mistress who's lame enough not to take successfully credit for it. Then you either work really hard and have a few more successes, so people realize you need your own slaves, your own budget. Or you work really hard on your game, your ability to talk yourself up as a winner, as an executioner, and then people not only give you your own everything, they kiss your ring as they do it."

"Which did you do?"

"Both." *And I never lost one minute of sleeping / Worrying 'bout the way things might have been.*

"But you *like* music." He was earnest, reaching for common ground.

"Oh, everything," Eva said in an airy sweep. "Billie Holiday, 'Singin' in the Rain,' Sinatra, Ella, Tina"—Eva slipped Turner in midway, so as not to give away how the song was slicing her brain, the same few lyrics, like serrated knives—"the Temptations, Stevie, the Emotions, Earth, Wind & Fire." She took a giddy breath and exhaled with a blissful smile. "The Police," Eva went on, names erupting from her in shaky rhythm, altogether a love poem, a jamming song itself. "Michael Jackson, and of course the Jackson Five. I love L.T.D. and WAR and ELO. Run-D.M.C. and N.W.A. I love the Eagles and the Clash and Hall and Oates. Rob Base and Keith Murray and K-Solo and Special Ed. MC Breed, MC Hammer, Doug E. Fresh. Who else? A Tribe Called Quest. Digital Underground and Tupac. Tupac! Gang Starr, Mary J. Blige, Jodeci, Heavy D. Public Enemy. I love music. Of course." *How do I sound. Like a teenager.* Eva wondered if it was manipulation if you were telling the truth.

Her cell rang again. She flipped it, saw it was Hakeem. Pressed the off button.

Dart's face loosened. Lips relaxed into a peaceful pout.

Points, Eva thought. *And by accident.*

"Why do you love it?" he wanted to know.

"Dude! I just do."

What a question.

Answer honestly.

"I like to *dance*," Eva said, and a small sway took over her upper body. "Get my groove on. Music sends me from plain happiness to pure ecstasy. *Loud* music, the way it infiltrates my body, the way I can feel the bass in me, taking over my heartbeat. When I sing along, and my voice melds with Whitney's or DJ Quik's. My voice and their voice like the same. I'm singing what they're singing, meaning what they're meaning."

He is totally feeling my energy.

"And you liked Sunny today."

"I really did." Eva'd felt Sunny's groove through her entire being. "She's double brand-new."

Is this real? Am I real, Eva thought, *or Memorex?*

Eva got in the record business to do what she loved. It's what was said and said and said and said: *You will be lucky if you can do for a living what you love to do anyway.* It's the road to happiness.

I am telling the truth right now. To this boy, Dart, I'm saying exact honest truth.

In a gig where you use your passion and love to fuel a business that gambles on the passion and love of people trying to get past broken hearts, trying to put symbols to experiences, and trying to dance until breakfast, people wanting to sit home and play A so they can feel or stop feeling B—you need your damn feelings, your real ones. Because at work it was:

We got to make a song people want to have sex to.

We got to make a song people will have babies by.

The artists were real, but the people who made people into artists were more real. This is what Eva believed.

People can sing and bang drums all they want, but if no one puts shit together, if no one organizes and markets and distributes and promotes the love and the passion, then an artist might as well be your cousin Mariah, second alto in the goddamn choir.

"But," Dart said hopefully, "Sun's like from like another time."

Mmmhmmm. "Yeah," Eva said, "She reminds me of somebody."

"Another singer?" Dart was brightening. "Carmen McRae, sometimes. Or Dinah Washington."

This was what she loved. How could music be work? It was how her life was archived, the key to her pining soul. Sitting there next to D'Artagnan, all sides of Eva were alive, ringing, singing. She thought, *There's nothing new under the sun. A twist on that would be a good album title. His sister has a great name. All kinds of meanings. She sings like she loves it, like she's desperate to do it. It's why first albums are always the best, why there are so many one-hit wonders, so many returns to the top after drug-ridden slumps, why so many addicts make great music. What will make this guy like me? He's a weirdo chubbo with a sad face and idealistic notions. He's not coming on to me. He loves his sister. His sister loves him. I do like Sunny's voice. Her look needs to be cleaned up, but she's pretty and in shape. I need to sign her. Need to do it without Hakeem. And Ron can kiss my ass. People think I'm falling off. I am a little bit. The stuff people bring me doesn't move me, and the stuff I find on my own is not good enough. I want a star who's not a rapper. I want to take myself to the next level. I win Dart, I win Sunny. Any fool can see that. Sunny doesn't sound like anyone but herself. I need to do something. I need Dart to feel something. To feel me.*

She slid her feet back into her shoes, looked at him directly. "I like all this." Tina's knives had done their work. Eva was herself, cubed. She knew the subliminal game. Eva knew all the games. She could speak in tongues, if she had to.

"Carmel-by-the-Sea, you mean."

"The whole thing today," Eva said with a pinch of wistfulness. "Monterey, the water, Sunny's name, the whole nine." Her strategy was hazy, but when she had a clear goal, Eva trusted herself to say and do the things that would get her what she wanted. She gladly, easily followed her own lead. This was what confidence felt like.

"Everything's just . . . coalesced," Dart said.

"I lived just south of here," Eva said, "for a while when I was growing up. It wasn't like this—" She waved her arm in the direction of the Saks.

"So you're home."

"Kind of. It was just a few years, but they were good years—with my mom."

"You and your mom are close."

"She died when I was thirteen." Eva touched her dime-store bangles.

"Wow. So when Sun was singing 'Imagination,' that part about 'The torture is when you see / Something you wish would happen is never gonna be,' you had to be feeling that. How'd your mom die?"

Eva paused. "The thing is, she killed herself."

"Damn." Dart placed his palm near Eva's thigh, then pulled himself over and erased the distance between them. *"Why?"*

"Nobody really knows. Not my dad, or anyone. She left me something, just a trinket. But it didn't explain anything." Eva was inspired.

"You still have it, what she left you?"

"A bracelet. I lost it. Had, like, this . . . tiny plaque on just a tin chain. There was a raindrop . . . a sun, a red leaf, and a snowflake. For the four seasons of life, I guess."

"A sun. Huh. You were a kid. Don't stay mad at stuff you can't control. It's a slippery slope."

"You know about that?"

"I know about slippery slopes." His face closed again. Eva put a hand on his wrist.

Time for a change of venue. Eva said, "I want a drink."

Within a half hour, in a miniature bar on a side street, Eva and Dart were two of the last four customers. Eva drank Scotch. Saw Dart looking at her with grave interest. With pity. He drank cranberry-grapefruit juice, no ice. He drank three glasses of tap water. Eva was irritated with herself for unwinding at the dark table in his odd, quiet company. His nosy sincerity made her feel half-dressed, and delicate.

When Dart stood up, like, *I'm ready,* she got up, too, found someone to give money to. On the television above the bar, the Yankees appeared to be playing the Orioles. From near the coatrack at the door, Eva watched until the game went hazy.

Keep your eye, she told herself, *on the ball. Keep your mind in the game.*

Through the last outs of the last inning, Dart's hands rested lightly, from behind, on Eva's hips. *Like he knows he needn't hold me close. Knows I'll stay. For right now.*

More in her head than with her body, Eva pressed back toward him.

With the same, almost imagined weight, Dart's fingertips pressed on her hips.

Eva pictured his hand inside her. As the Yankees or the Orioles won, as some of the players appeared to shake hands like good sports, as an elfin busboy stripped tables, as Eva waited on change from her c-note, what Eva wanted was to be entirely naked, on her back, Dart neatly licking her. She imagined his tongue dry as sand, smoothing off layers of deadness.

In Eva's suite overlooking the golf course, a pine fire had been started. Standing near the foot of the bed, Dart grabbed her in a gawky embrace. In her shoes, she was almost as tall as him, so her throat smashed into his pillow of shoulder. Eva wouldn't have been able to speak, even if she'd known what to say.

When Dart squeezed even more tightly, Eva wriggled free. He peeled off his clothes, faced her in his too-snug briefs, and stared like it was a critical moment in a child's magical game. But Eva wasn't enough spellbound to take her turn. The room smelled like Christmas, and Eva stood so close to the fireplace her sweater roasted, smelled like Boer goats on some New Mexican afternoon. Eva had lived there for a short while, when she was in junior high school. This was when hip hop still sounded electronically funky and created by robots. She'd enjoyed her time on Planet Rock. Eva thought back then that she was one to let (as Afrika Bambaataa had advised) her soul lead the way. She ate *carne adovada* all the time, and anise-seed cookies. Break-danced in front of Mexican boys in dented cowboy hats. They barely moved.

Dart turned to put his stuff on a dresser, and Eva saw that his back was treacherous with red pimples and craters and holes that looked like tiny worms had dug in. There were thick, raised calluses and patches shiny with oil. Colorless, cracked paths crossed over his shoulder blades. She wondered if his back spoke of neglect, or if he was somehow ill.

"It's my fault," D'Artagnan said like he was reciting a poem. He plopped down in the deep window seat and faced Eva. "Never rubbed anything back there. I mean, I get clean. But one of those brushes on a stick, I never have one. Guys don't get that kind of stuff, until they get a real girlfriend." The back of Dart's head, his padded shoulder blades, on down to the top of his ass—all faded into the dazzling dark night. He seemed flimsy as a sewing pattern, a glowing outline of something real.

"So, you're trying to bone," Eva said. *Just don't turn around on me again, please. I can't look at your back.*

"That's how you say it?" His eyes resigned as a griever's.

"How should I?"

"Your lips are puffy."

"My lips always look like this."

Eva made up her mind that she was going to play and make him beggy and sweet and a little mad. But Dart was eager. The kind who says, "I'm not gonna come until you tell me to come," and since he was pounding like a maniac, like he hadn't fucked in two months or two years, Eva said, "You're about to come," and he did, like a switch had been flipped. And when he started up again, and Eva was sore and exhilarated and rubbed raw, she put her tongue in his ear, in a way she thought was devilish.

"You want to come right *now*?"

Dart climaxed again. His cries like a kitten's. Dart closed his eyes tight and for longer, Eva thought, than a man needed to.

"What are you doing?" Eva said.

"Paying attention to what's in my head. The actual, physical ecstasy. I haven't had it like this in a while."

"Like what?"

He opened his eyes, rolled off of her, and lay on his side. "Been sick," he said. "Medication has my body sometimes." He caught her mute alarm. "Not sick like that."

"What do you mean, 'has your body'?" *Maybe his back is a reaction to whatever medication—*

"Meds that sharpen the mind and blur the . . ."

"Dick." *Oh. Those kinda meds.*

"Yeah. Lithium."

Dart said "lithium," and Eva thought "Lithuania," which brought to her mind the initials USSR, and notions of an "Iron Curtain," and torture, and people being kept in a place against their will, and revolutionaries being sent to Siberia, and being lobotomized and left to mumble nonsense while peering blankly through dusty venetian blinds of a mental ward. Eva's thoughts followed no logical course.

So he's a little crazy.

"I feel good, though," Dart said. "Today. Weaning myself off the 'scripts. Started this herbal therapy. I try to memorize good feelings so when I go under, I can try to force myself to focus on when I felt good." He fell back and spoke to the ceiling. "Sometimes I can do it. Sometimes I have no control, no consciousness of good feeling, of anything good, or even knowing how under it I am. I can't explain . . . everything's exaggerated. What sounds like a tinkling bell normally, sounds like a bomb. What looks like a light going on to you, it's blinding."

'So you get sad, still. Even with the . . . herbs."

"When I'm feeling like I do today, I know the herbs are about the power of suggestion more than them changing the chemicals in my brain. I like being at least in charge of the *suggesting.* I don't like my brain being balanced. To whose specification? Who's the calibrator?"

She curled next to him for a while, until he shifted so his jaw was across her ribs, his arm across her, and his long fingers tucked tightly under her arm. The jumpy rhythm of Dart's breathing settled, and the sound of it sent her to an easy sleep.

She slipped out as light was breaking, had coffee and toast in the hotel's quiet restaurant. *We used condoms and everything, but he was all up every*where. *Aside from his back, he's got nice hands and he filled me up. His voice. Loud even when it's soft. The things he said.* Stay with me. That's right. Please look at me. Look at my face. *Why was I so into it?*

I guess because so little is at stake. Except for with Sunny. But she likes me. Already. She even likes me for her brother.

Eva finished her breakfast. On the way back to her room, she figured a way to get Dart out of it, with minimal drama.

But Dart was already gone.

In his spindly graffiti, and with a swordlike flourish under his name, the note read

MEET US BY THE WATER. SUN WANTS TO TALK.
D'ARTAGNAN

T*he water.*

A graveled path toward it gave Eva time to think. She zipped her hoodie to the neck. The wind off the ocean was carrying mist.

She found Dart and Sunny at a picnic table on an oval of manicured grass. They had clear plastic cups of juice with straws.

Eva said, "You guys eat?" She slid onto the bench on Dart's side of the table, but as far from him as possible. Eva was directly across from Sunny, balanced on the edge of California.

"It's all right I got room service?" Sunny asked, like she was certain it was all right. Dart looked sheepish, and Sunny added, "He ate some of mine. Dart says you used to live out this way."

Okay. Interview me. Cool. "I wish. We were a little south of here."

"I guess you know," Sunny said, already bored with details, "we're from San Diego."

"Dad in the service?"

Dart said, "Mom."

"She started calling you Sunny?"

"Mom did," Dart said, looking at his sister and then at Eva.

"Dart started it. I don't know why he hates to claim his part. We were babies. He couldn't say 'Deirdre,' and Mom hated 'Dee Dee.'"

"Mom said you had a sun face."

Sunny smiled at that. "Plus there's the Addison," she said. "Addi-Sun."

There was a pause. Eva let it hang. She had the feeling Sunny was one to fill silences, and wondered what she would choose. Platitudes, gratitude, questions? Sunny's choice would give her personality away quickly. Besides, Eva didn't use inane getting-to-know-all-about-you chat. She didn't chase people when they could see her coming.

"Thanks for the rooms and all," Sunny said without thankfulness. "We've been Motel Six-ing it."

"Camping sometimes," Dart said, like he missed it already.

"Your job pays for this, right?" Sun said it like she might catch Eva in a lie. "Not like it's out of your pocket."

Break me down. Feel like you're breaking me down. I love it. "Road-show pays, yeah. They trust me to spend like I should."

"So I'm how you should." Sunny tapped her empty cup on the dewy table. "Why?"

Eva had no hesitation before the truth. "Your voice, for one. It's beautiful. Rich but raspy. Real . . . strong. And I like your songs—the fact that you write them. I like your act, too, with the yoga and everything—"

"It's not an act," Sunny said. "It's what I'm about."

"Figure of speech, Sun."

"Usually it's a while before anyone calls me Sun."

"Time's the only criterion?"

"Time and trust."

Okay, cool. "Sunny it is, then." *Feel like you've put me in my place. Act like you're not loving the love.*

The pause hung powerfully again, and again Eva let it.

"Don't be finished, though," Sunny said. "I wanna hear more what you thought."

Bingo. "Everything was *right* yesterday," Eva said, her eyes like beams on Sunny and then, finally, on D'Artagnan. "I was in the right place hearing the right artist singing the right songs. You ripped that shit. Maybe it's personal, though, too. The fact I'm from this area. My mom's buried not too far." *It's all true,* Eva thought, *in its way.*

Dart looked at her with kindness.

"Your mom died?" Sunny said. "How long ago? I'm sorry."

"Oh no, it's cool. When I was seven."

Dart's voice was quiet and probing. "How old? How'd she die?" He was suspicious.

Eva's blood rushed. She felt it pound in her cheeks and neck. "She, um, it was suicide."

"Why? And you were seven? Or a teenager?" Dart leaned toward Eva.

"Don't ask that, Dart." Then Sunny turned to Eva and said, "Don't pay him any attention."

"All I can say is she was sad," Eva said, relieved. "That's what I remember." Eva didn't want to answer any more questions about her mother. She wanted to get down to brass tacks. "What I was trying to say before was that maybe yesterday was . . . serendipitous. Your voice, the songs, the place."

"The memories for you," Sunny said, the tiniest bit pensive.

Dart said, "It could be a sign."

Sunny blurted, "I want to make an album so bad."

"How many songs you got?"

"I got binders full."

"Your brother manages you?"

Sunny looked at her brother and nodded. "I have a lawyer, though." She added the last hastily enough that Eva took it to be untrue.

Dart was still fascinated. "Who found her?"

And Sunny, too, looked to Eva for an answer, for grounds other than business that might connect them all. A serendipitous story might mean that music was art and art was mysterious and crossed boundaries of life and death and time.

Eva was uneasy, but she said, "My dad did. She left a note."

"You read it?"

Eva's left hand twitched at the index and thumb. Hair stood curved and trembling on her forearms. She put her hands on the bench at her sides, and then sat on them.

"Let's change the subject," Sunny said, on the line between sympathy and her desire to get to the deal. Eva took in the bright roundness of Sunny's face, the damp hair in beige phone-cord ringlets, the shadow of real sun across her curved jaw. There was desperation at the corners of Sunny's mouth.

"I'm just thinking about this . . . bracelet she left me." *Play it right,* Eva thought. *This whole thing could go either way.* Eva put her hands back on the table.

"One of the ones you're wearing?" Dart wanted to know.

"No."

Dart said, "You don't wear it?" He was appalled.

"I told you I lost it." *Lost almost everything she ever touched a long time ago.*

"But I mean, that's the reason you liked my show?" Sunny said. "Tied up with your mom?"

Eva moved a bit closer to Dart and was able to look Sunny directly in her face. "Your voice and your performance and your songs—they make anyone in a ten-mile radius remember the loves and the pain of their lives. When you reach for the richest, longest notes, they reach with you. I know I did, and I've been in this game a while. Yes, my mother came to mind today, but everybody's lost somebody, loved somebody, misses somebody. Everyone feels lost and unloved. Yesterday on the pier, you brought each person closer to who they are. You did more than entertain them—though you did that, too. You transformed a tiny part of the universe. Made it safe and warm. Sunny Addison made it warm enough for people to feel things, to remember, to dream, to be who they are and not ashamed of who they are. You're going to change people. Help people. You're gonna fucking blow people's minds."

Dart touched Eva's hand under the table. Eva acknowledged him with a quick brush of her pinkie and maintained eye contact with Sunny.

"People'll get all that," Sunny wanted to know, "from a CD?"

"If we produce it right," Eva said. "No fake instruments. Keep it all very real. Let the voice speak for itself. Put it out there, like, *bam!* Like Roadshow isn't building a star. *No!* Roadshow is giving you *the Sun.*"

Sunny nodded her head slowly. "And my money would be like what?"

"Good money. We can talk about all that. Then I'll get with your lawyer—"

"I don't have one," Sunny said matter-of-factly. "Or I should say I don't like the one I have. She's not . . . I don't know if she has the experience—"

"I can recommend someone who works with the biggies."

Sunny nodded again, even more slowly. Eva saw the stun set in. She let the silence deepen until the *rasp-snap* of a gardener's shears was loud and rhythmic enough to rap a verse over. *Deeper than Atlantis / Deeper than the sea floor traveled by the mantis.* X-Clan, Eva's mind yelled. *"Grand Verbalizer, What Time Is It?" from the album, To the East, Blackwards. Nineteen ninety.*

Dart said, "So this is all true?"

"Best if you all come to New York." It was time to paint a picture with tangibles and logistics. "Meet Sebastian and everybody. Stay here another night, though, enjoy yourselves. I'll have tickets sent over, car will pick you up tomorrow, take you to the airport in San Francisco. We'll put you up someplace fly in Manhattan, near the office."

Sunny was suddenly humble before Eva's poise, the confidence with which Eva put things into motion. "I'm glad for some reason that this is happening with a girl," Sunny said. "A woman. I talked to other people, but it's like, maybe you get me. Maybe you see who I am."

Eva reached her hand out to Sunny's and covered it. "It's gonna happen just the way you want it."

"We have to do something," Sunny said dumbly, "with our car."

Her hand still over Sunny's, Eva looked at Dart. "You got that, right?"

She took his bland look as a yes, and Eva stood. Deal about done, she wanted to get away from the memories of Carmel. She wanted to leave Sunny and Dart pondering the possibilities of success. "So no worries," Eva said. "I'll see you guys in New York in a couple of days."

Dart ran to catch Eva on the path back to the hotel lobby. "I can't believe all this is going to just happen. Tickets will show up. Hotel rooms in New York will be booked."

"Believe it," Eva said easily. *I feel it.*

"That sun is what freaks me out," he said grimly. "The one on the bracelet . . . from your mother. The sun for summer. It's like . . . the universe has taken us into consideration."

A cell phone rang, and Eva heard Sun slyly answer it. Eva's experience shouted at her to make moves.

"You know what?" She grabbed Dart's hand and he squeezed it. "Get your sis together. I'm going to make a few calls. I'll drive us to L.A. We'll take care of the business part of this there and get Sun in the studio right away. Sebastian'll meet us."

Sunny was right there. She took in Eva and Dart holding hands, Eva bright-eyed and focused, Dart looking at Eva with hope and calmness. "I'd rather make an album in Los Angeles," Sunny said, "anyway."

This is about to happen, Eva's mind screamed at her triumphantly. *This is so fucking about to happen.*

I n the lobby of the Lost City, Dart ran to the men's room.

Eva had to call Roadshow. There'd be no going AWOL.

That's not how I roll.

"Seb, it's Eva."

"Ah. She rises. Miss Bahamas 1998. Good people have called, saying good things."

Yeah. Fuck you, too. "It was good. Sun blew it up. And in light of that, I'm gonna take a few days—"

"Few days? Eva, no." It wasn't so much a decree as feigned disappointment in her judgment. Sebastian feigned everything except his love of being perceived as the biggest boss. "Now's not the moment," he said. "We have this drive now, this thrust—"

"I'll be back in a week."

There was a pause. "*Oye.* A lot can happen in a week."

"Like someone can start a new label? Yep. All kinda moves can be made."

He was quiet. But Eva was familiar with his strategies.

"So a week then," Eva said. "I'll call—"

"Everything's not what it seems, *mi chica pequeña.* Everything's not what it looks like from where you are."

"It'll look right from where I'm 'bout to go."

"And where's that? Tell me so I can meet you in this place where everything looks all right. You've been on the road too long."

"What road?" Sebastian said "road" like it was a turbulent, mythical place where people forgot the destination of their original journey. It irritated Eva, though, because she felt he might be right. "I'm working. That's why you're jerking me?"

"How are you speaking? To me."

"That's why I'm taking the week," Eva said dryly. "I don't even know what I'm saying."

"Usted debe saber lo que usted hace." Sebastian's way of being strict with Eva was to get personal. His code for being personal was to be condescending in Spanish. To speak with her as he had in crisp hotel beds, on midnight flights. Sebastian knew Eva respected money being made, lived for the show going on. He valued that. He also knew how Eva's face contorted when she had an orgasm, and nursed the scorn some men have for that flattering, fleeting, unreliable image. Sebastian wanted Eva back in the office so he could see how she stood, what she wore, how she spoke and breathed and reacted to unpleasant news. His want for her back in New York had to do with Sunny's momentum. It also had to do with Eva's will and how Sebastian liked for her to fly only as far and for as long as he let her.

You better know what you're doing, he'd said.

Eva was familiar with how Sebastian's lilt could slice through gut to spine. She didn't miss a beat.

"Si lo voy a saber, señor," Eva said in her best southwestern Español. Sebastian used to like to hear her Spanish when he lost it, surrendered, sleepily mumbled, "Feed me," sucked her breasts. *"Usted puede creer eso."*

Oh, I will know what I'm doing. Sir. Soon. You can believe that.

She pressed OFF with Sebastian, and pressed ON as Ron's number came up on her screen.

"Where you at?" he said.

"Right here." As if he could know where that was.

"Why aren't you at his brunch? If I gotta be here, I know you do."

"I'm not—"

"You're not coming down here? Why?" Harsh as he sounded, Ron wasn't pissed. He was curious.

"I'm getting out of here." Eva sounded uncertain.

"What's that mean? To New York? What happened? Seb pull your leash?"

"Not New York. Dude, I'm getting off the phone." Eva was exasperated, light-headed. Her leash hadn't been pulled. Her collar had been tightened. Since Showcase Savoir Faire, her collar had been tighter and tighter.

"What's wrong with you?" Ron said. "Seemed like something was wrong with you last night."

"Where'd you get the bracelet you gave me?" Eva worked to not yell at him. She'd stayed on her game with Sebastian, though, and it had worn her out.

"Why you so concerned with that bracelet? You got Sun down here with nothing but a stylist. Myra's wondering where you are. I found it. Found the damn bracelet and knew it was some gypsy shit you'd actually like. I found it on a doorknob."

"So that's what I am. If it don't cost a grip, I don't want it. I'm fake like that."

"Listen to me. Jesus! I'm saying the *opposite*."

"You're not saying shit."

"Why you so . . . emotional? You on your period?" He paused. "You pregnant?"

"I'm not emotional." She didn't sound emotional. She could chew through his furniture, though. Shit in his shoes.

"You're pregnant. You're pregnant. It's in your voice." He paused. "Not by me, I know."

Eva continued tersely. It was the same transparent tone she'd used with Piper. "Why'd you act like you got it for me, like it was something—"

"Say you're not pregnant. You can't. Goddamn."

"I'm not pregnant." Weakly, like she was lying to an officer of an important court. Slowly, like her reply would determine whether she got the needle.

"You're a liar," he snapped out. "By the way you said it. You running to get it taken care of?" Before she could answer, Ron switched to cajoling. "You can't come down here, represent, behind this? Or call room service, tell 'em to bring you some Pepto or something, some tea. I'll come up."

Represent what? Represent who? What is this voice he has on right now? "I gotta go," she said.

"Who's gonna go with you?" he said, back to snapping. "Ain't like you got no real girls. Maybe Sun? Or you're gonna round up Giada?"

"I'm cool, Ron."

"I know." He did think Eva was "cool" about most things. It was what made him want her when he wanted her, and dodge her when he dodged her. "What you want me to tell people? They're asking for you here. You're sick?"

"As far as anyone is concerned," Eva said, "you haven't talked to me." *You haven't talked to me.*

"You're taking punk Dart with you. That's what it is."

"Actually," she said in her very regular Eva voice, "he's taking me with him."

Dead air. From his side.

What's changed?

Did I know a little bit?

Yesterday?

They should make it hurt more. It should cause a year of concentrated physical and psychological pain. People can't be counted on to have regret. So maybe this is payback.

It was the kind of posttraumatic arrest Eva had never believed in. The kind of crisis she'd leaped over. But now Eva didn't know if she'd been tough all along, or if the abortions had made her tough. She did know, though, that she wasn't as tough as she or Ron or Dart or Sunny thought she was. And she wasn't as tough, anymore, as she needed to be. A mass was encroaching. Cold shame. Weakness. Fear. Her collar wasn't tight enough to kill her, but it was tight enough to remind her what life is. She fought it. She used discipline, and steered her mind.

It's time to go.

Eva roused herself by thinking she'd made Ron angry enough to hang up the phone in her face. She roused herself further by thinking of the glorious sunsets and sunrises there'd be on Dart's Out Islands. She reached into what she considered the normal part of her brain, glad, after dealing with Dart, for the ability. She thought that wherever Cat Island was, there'd be a chance for peace for the both of them. And for her, in sad moments, there'd be the thin-skinned berry pout of Dart's bottom lip.

*See it ain't nothin' wrong with
dreamin' / Boy don't get me wrong.*
— "NEXT LIFETIME,"
words and music by Erykah Badu

T he man's voice called out, quizzing tardy messengers on
the status of deliveries. Syllables soared, dove, Haitian style. *Words as
birds.* The vessel bobbed heavily with crates of flour and fruit, canned
milk, mail and vegetables.

"Édouard, miss," he said, holding out a huge, hard hand to Eva as
she stepped onboard. "Here for you." Édouard's voice was luxuriant
and ceremonial.

"I'm Eva," she said, trying to match him in tone and inflection.
"Nice boat."

Giant intestines haphazardly stuffed with warm lumpy fat—that's
what Édouard's upper arms were like. He reminded Eva of huge
brothers from Philly, and Brooklyn and West L.A, too. Nearsighted
nerds with ill nicknames. Cats wearing Vans and slouching like skaters.
Boys who wrote twisted, iron-fisted rhymes. Boys with no muscle
tone, who intimidated with their weirdness, their bulk, or on the
strength, on the *fact* of their blackness alone. This amused and an-
gered them, sent them to arty white girls or beatnik black or brown
girls for compassion, and then back to their clubrooms to get blunted
and beery, to peruse deliciously sick comics, brutal graphic novels,
and the newest porn.

Édouard's eyes avoided her body. She warmed to him in the faintly formal fashion he'd initiated.

Hypocrites always want to make it seem like good intent / Never want to face it when it's time for punishment. Lauryn Hill leaked from Édouard's headphones, a totally different drum line under the lyrics, and some high-pitched bells. Hill was cursing a former lover, but it sounded to Eva like Hill was cursing her. So Eva concentrated on the boom-boom beneath the words, abstractions she could qualify and quantify in terms of work. *This Édouard probably cut the mix himself.*

Dart clomped on board behind her and dramatically lost his balance as immediately as Eva found hers. She sat down on a bench along the low rail. On the boat was just her, Dart, the skipper, who looked like Paul Winfield in *Sounder*, and Édouard.

Dart sat his pack down next to Eva. "This is aft," Dart said, "I'm going fore."

"I'm just gonna sit here," Eva said. Thinking she was sitting at the stern of the red-hulled workboat, and he was going to the bow. She'd lived right off the Pacific, had been on her share of boats big and small.

"There's some food in the zip pocket," Dart said, "if you're hungry." Then he stomped up front with awkward enthusiasm.

As soon as he said it, Eva was starved. She reached in through damp folds, found waxed paper wrapped around a piece of bread hard enough to be days old. She bit into the twist of sourdough, slipped feet from her sandals, placed them on the deck. *Hot. Warm wet wood under soles.* Eva gnawed as the boat with its peeling cabin chugged out to sea.

They hadn't been out fifteen minutes when she saw Dart's long arms gesticulating passionately, crowding the cabin's doorway. Édouard moved his bulk gracefully away from him.

"Miss Eva." Édouard peeled a green apple with a small curved knife. Handle like a polished pinkie bone. "Your friend. He should relax." On the thumb of the hand with the knife was a gob of peanut butter.

"What's he saying?"

"Let him tell you. Skip's patience is wearing. You have people on Cat? Friends?"

"No. Dart just wants to go."

Édouard nodded his head, sliced a crescent from the now creamy apple, neatly bit peanut butter from his thumb. "Have a good time, then. Get your sun and your relaxation. He's not your husband. He's still looking."

Eva'd rarely thought of being Dart's wife or girlfriend, but the thought of him "still looking" narrowed her eyes.

"Your friend wants a remedy. A key," Édouard snorted, "to an enchanted door."

"You have those on Cat?" Eva liked referring to the island as he did, like she knew about it.

"No. And so your . . . Bart?"

"D'Artagnan, actually."

Édouard opened his mouth around a mocking, titanic laugh. "He'll be mad when he gets there."

And if you don't change then the rain soon come . . . More Lauryn Hill leaking. Then the Temptations, something from before Norman Whitfield starting producing the group. A song from the Tempts' early, pretty era.

Édouard licked the last butter from his hand, and then pushed his teeth into the now egg-shaped apple. Slid headphones back to his ears, attended to some ropy business past the cabin. Eva let her eyes climb a ladder of clouds.

That morning, she and Dart had walked through the lobby of the Royal Towers, Eva glancing around like a fugitive, though anyone they knew was either asleep or at the gospel brunch, where hair-of-the-dog was free and flowing. They stepped from the conditioned air of the hotel into heat unframed by a view of the sea, heat unreflected by bluish oval pools. Sunlight slapped the ground like long curse, and Eva baked sorely for the first time since arriving in the Bahamas. She palmed $10 on a doorman. Checked her bag for her passport as sweat rolled from her armpit to her waist.

Pimpy as Billy Dee's Louis MacKay, as Fishburne's Bumpy in *The Cotton Club*, a doorman installed Eva and Dart in a gleaming gray 1980 Monte Carlo, a cab driven by a perfectly pleated woman who looked like she was on her way from church, looked like Pearl Bailey ready for three choruses of "If They Could See Me Now," looked like her hat was where her pin money had gone, and like whatever she'd spent had been worth it.

Without a dot of sweat on him in the heat, the doorman gave a little salute, a hard hint at his brow saying, *I'm down for whatever,* and at the second of Eva's realization that the doorman was the bartender of the coco water, and the gardener of the acrid can, Dart made a booming request to be taken "INTO NASSAU, PLEASE," and the Pearl woman cruised, one hand on her wheel, over the new bridge from Paradise Island, then along a two-lane road lined with short buildings, sherbet-colored houses and shacks selling legal advice or sardines 'n' grits or hairstyles.

This place is like an extension of Miami.

They passed half-built minimalls, the British Colonial Hilton, Esso and Texaco gas stations, a McDonald's, a Hertz Rent-A-Car, and any number of conch spots. A fort with shiny black cannons. Scrubbed, cornrowed kids with fake Louis Vuitton backpacks. Everywhere the passenger cars were small and newish, the Mack trucks huge and churning cement for the new hotels and new time-share communities, everywhere there were signs for Pepsi, Heineken, and Kalik Gold. As advised by a barrage of municipal signs, Eva put on her seat belt.

Finally trapped on a packed Nassau avenue. Dart jerked and moved. Perspiration puddled at the roots of his mustache. Eyes under crunched brows, he hunted a clear route. A pod of cruise ships idled nearby, snow-white and belittled with garlands. Two horse-drawn carriages idled just in front of the car. At Dart's jab, he and Eva hopped from the sleek old taxi. Eva thrust two twenties at the polka-dotted driver. Dart was halfway down the block. No price had been discussed, but the Pearl lady, unmoved, slid the bills into a pouch attached to the dash. She'd carried a thousand couples—glowingly furtive in their own minds—on a Sunday to sweltering downtown Nassau and points beyond.

Eva caught up to Dart, and they trotted down Bay Street with its cabarets of crystal statuettes and diamond rings, timepieces and chokers. From the tide of church traffic and tourist traffic and trolleys and small buses and cars of kids with trunk speakers bumping DMX and Puffy and old Buju Banton, the Queen's Staircase rose, a limestone flight to a colonialist's idea of heaven. Sixty-five steps, Eva counted, and each representing a year of Victoria's reign, she overheard a winded old man say.

"Enough slacking," Dart snapped, and they rushed down the queen's stairs, in the direction of the cruise ships, hand in hand, hustling, Dart seemingly in the know about transportation and destination, Eva glad for the wild guidance, for something to move toward other than Sunny and work. Eva was thinking about her last period and how normal it had or hadn't been, and that she might be nine or ten weeks along, which left no time, really, for decision making, left her thinking that if she was going to go with it for the whole forty weeks, and so go with it for the rest of her life, she needed to get her ass to some prenatal care, get herself someplace where a professional would recite rules to which Eva'd never graduated, rules about what to eat and not eat, what vitamins to take, what books might prove helpful, and what-all alcohol she needed to leave alone. Eva thought of Malinda, and her radio, what had been "recommended," and that the static-filled song on her radio had gone *You make me feel like an itty-bitty girl, what you do to me.*

At the dock, Dart frantically negotiated with Mr. *Sounder.* The boat belonged to him, and he smiled and took Eva's money like it was a formality he wished he could overlook. To Eva, though, especially as she watched him move boat-type things around, the pudgy, strong little vessel belonged to Édouard.

Dart walked toward Eva, grabbing at the rail like a toddler. They were out to sea, with only low contours of islands in the distance.

"These guys aren't helpful," he said. Dart's eyes were dark and hyperalert. "I'm asking about finding an Obeahman or an Obeahwoman, and they look at me like I'm being nosy. Or like I'm dumb."

Or like, Eva thought, *you're being an asshole.* "Why not just get there, see what happens. Island's only so big, right?" Eva kept her eyes on vast blueness.

"Only twenty-five hundred people on the whole thing." He hurled the fact out like it was an insult.

"Well then."

"I can find what I need," Dark said, his words burned at the edges. "But I want a hint."

That Dart thought he could glean from people he'd never met information about a religion that by its nature was uncommon and based in secrecy and a belief system of which he clearly had only the most rudimentary and desperately found knowledge was beyond Eva. *Who does he think he is?* There was innocence and arrogance in Dart's desire for help, in his blustery nosing about. Arrogance was to be expected—from Dart because he tended to fall back on his bellowing status as Sunny's moneyed Lewis and Clark, from Dart because even as he denied it, he reveled in being an ambassador from the enchanting land of hip hop and neo-soul. It had been only three years since Sun came up, but it had been three years of the kind of favor and fawning and abundance and truly high stakes that change people forever—even after a month. The DNA evidence of Dart's arrogance—*Or maybe*, Eva thought, *his mania*—was his idea of himself unaffected. Dart's sister was a "diva," a superstar. She was One to Watch, the Penthouse Suite, cover material, a Very Special Guest. The hottest of the hot were honored by her appearance. No doubt Dart had come by his arrogance honestly. Fine. But innocence? Who wanted to deal with, or even see any kind of, innocence in a grown man?

This must be the craziness.

Light spray kissed up from the ocean, a gift.

She wondered if she could tell Dart she was pregnant.

He'll tell me to have it. He'll tell me that this is the new millennium, and that for all we know the baby I carry will save the world.

"Eva," Dart said, flailing around and grabbing for the rail again. "You know I don't take money from Sun."

"You take it off the books," Eva said absently. She was watching sapphire sheets fall back away from the boat. *What kind of Midnight-Train-to-Georgia journey am I on? Going to a "simpler place." And I don't even have the Pips urging me on. "I'll be with him," wails Gladys, and the Pips pipe in "I know you will," as if there's* no *question that she's doing the right thing. Like, of course she'll go, even after the guy's "pawned all his hopes." The Pips don't* encourage *Gladys. They* chastise *her. To the Pips, Gladys's allegiance is a given. The song was originally called "Midnight Train to Houston," anyway. Which means the place doesn't even matter.*

"Just money to live on," Dart was saying. He spoke quickly and with white spit on his lips. His words were far behind his thoughts, and he was frustrated. "Just a per diem."

She faced him. "A per diem for every day of your life for the last almost three years is money." *Why are we having this conversation?*

"Only money for food, basically. And incidentals."

"So rent is an incidental," Eva said slowly. She had no patience for Dart's words running together. "CDs are incidental, a three-hundred-dollar disc player is incidental."

"When we're 'home,' which is never, I usually stay with Sunny," Dart said. He stood, but then almost fell. He half-stumbled back onto the bench, but farther away from Eva. "I take money for clothes—clothes good for the weather wherever we're going. I used to take money to pay for . . . the doctor, and meds."

"Okay, so." Eva faced the water again, faced from where they'd come.

"So if we're rolling on what I've got, we'll drive around until we find a family that takes in guests."

"Like a B and B." *Whatever. Relax.*

"A family that lets an extra room. I talked to the skipper about it."

"And we don't know them, the people with the room."

"Wouldn't know the owners of a proper B and B, either."

"True." She didn't look his way. She wanted him to stop talking. *I'm here, right? Where you wanted me to be.*

"Cool," he said, and then bitterness slid out. "'Cause I know how you like to live."

How I live? Eva was pissed with Dart for exasperating her. *Fucking up my little gaze-at-the-water tranquillity.* She called herself shallow, then reneged. *It's sick. My sense of entitlement—to not have babies already created. I can rationalize. Say, life is complicated. Maybe it is. Maybe I'm hard on myself. But I don't think so. I've become vain. And too dreamy. It's unbecoming, unwise, and unproductive. Dreaminess is for teenagers. And I don't remember being dreamy then. Sitting here, staring at the water. Ridiculous. The fuck am I doing right now with all this introspection but doodling my name on a goddamned napkin.*

She turned to Dart. "Everywhere I go," Eva said, a TV lawyer stating facts already in evidence, "you're right down the hall. Every restaurant I eat in, you're at the next table. The clothes you—"

"I just said, Sunny buys clothes for—"

"My point, exactly."

"I work for the things I—"

"We all work, Dart." *He can be,* she thought, *such an idiot.*

"I DON'T WANT MONEY," he said at full volume. She hated when he roared. It was an unfair advantage, the strength of his box. Édouard looked over, but stayed where he was.

Eva chose to keep her own voice to just above the rumble of the motor. "Sun should stand on a sand dune and sing for free."

"She SHOULD! She was HAPPIER then!" He gestured widely. It would be easy for him to fall into the ocean.

"That happiness came from being twenty." *Fool!* "From not knowing anything. Not from being broke. Your sister was always trying to make money, get known."

"It was better before Roadshow. She sang for herself. Out of love." His sentences seemed popped from a slingshot. His eyes were ahead of his words. He could not catch up with himself.

Eva found herself not only unafraid, but unmoved. "And now?"

"She's a monkey," he said in a voice so low and rumbling it could've been a part of the engine. "And you grind the organ."

"Yet," Eva sang, like it was a most appropriate carol, "we're your favorite girls in the world."

Eva didn't want Dart to be mad at her or himself, didn't want him to get all worked up. She didn't want to bring him over to her side, or make him see himself for the hypocrite she believed him to be. Their tiff turned her thoughts to what she was going to do about Sun. Eva

wanted to glean some information from Dart about that. Wanted Sebastian to make whatever moves he was going to make, without her
there for him to use as a clue. Eva wanted Sunny to feel her absence.
And even if Ron and Seb were planning something with Sun, and
Sun's loyalty to Eva waned, Sun would take her brother into consideration. Eva might be an organ-grinder, but to Dart she was the lesser
of at least half a dozen evils. Eva was certain Sun wouldn't push her
brother over whatever edge he was standing on.

Dart moved away from her when she reached into his backpack
and pulled out his Discman and headphones. She clamped them on
her ears and was lambasted by early Ice-T., some N.W.A, Nice &
Smooth, Granddaddy I.U, MC Breed, and Too Short. It was a call to
her steeliness—the bass and the bragging. Eva liked being tested by
hardest hip hop artists, the most profane and woman-hating. They
couldn't hurt her. They could shout all they wanted. For a few moments, she was strong enough to think about talking to her baby's father about the committments she didn't want, the input she neither
required nor desired, and the many ways she was not about to become
someone who makes decisions based on what she *should* do for the
sake of anyone or anything.

The boat slowed, approached a port. SMITH BAY, a sign read. Eva
had lost track of time, again.

I'm thinking in weeks. That's how I'm counting.

"Feels good, huh."

"Yeah, Édouard. Does." She liked saying his name the way he pro-
nounced it. *Ed-oo-ar.*

"D'Artagnan is a handful for you. And for us. I tried to tell him
there'd be no rental cars ready, on such notice. He says there will be.
There are bikes, though. You have no luggage." Édouard handed her
a stamp-size scrap of paper scrawled with a first name and a business's name.

"Making friends, I see," Dart said, lumbering up as the boat
docked. His shirt soaked with sea spray and sweat.

Édouard put his headphones back on.

Dart picked up his pack. Eva picked up hers and stepped off

the boat with him. They took long steps toward a row of stores with neat blue trim. Their vivid fronts were open to the water and tinkled with chimes. Mobiles with tin dolphins and real scallop shells. Crest-stamped white shirts dangled near long skirts—red, mustard, lime, turquoise—that fluttered in the warm wind.

Dart quickened his pace, moved toward two ladies with empty cloth bags. The women changed their path by a step, so as not to be on a collision course.

At the gangplank, Édouard held a crate of battered peaches, and Eva thought of her breasts in his hands. Dart paid her no mind as she turned and walked back to the boat.

"What's your nickname?" Eva said.

Édouard balanced the crate on a pole with one hand. "People afraid to use it."

"So I'm supposed to guess?"

"It's Porc de Mer, then. My sister gave it to me. When I get my own boat, it has a name."

"The Sea Pig?"

"For a sea pig. Miss Eva. I like the way you say it."

I like the way you say it.

No double entendre. No leer.

He don't know me, is what it is.

I usually hate guys like him. Not hate them, but feel sorry for them for having a simple desire and going for it. Édouard will probably get his boat and be happy. He'd come to a convention of music professionals who want their marketing to take over the world—he'd arrive, and maybe he'd party, but he'd laugh that huge laugh.

By way of greeting, and to offer the two women an escape from Eva's man, Édouard held up three peaches in one huge hand. Eva turned to the sound of Dart's voice. He spoke too quickly and too loudly to the women. One was confused. The older one, harassed. She locked looks with her sea pig of a grocer, angry he'd brought nuisance to an isle too tiny and isolated for foolishness.

Dart's voice rang out like mike feedback. And so Eva ran after, ready to adjust the levels.

va was onstage. There were no rising tiers of seats in the small amphitheater. Not so much as a concrete step or anyplace to sit, except for a few rusted folding chairs. The venue's walls were an olden mix of sand, burned lime, and ash, and seemed to have grown, blotched and flaking, from the ground.

Might've been contests here in ancient times, Eva thought. *This is Italy. Not Rome, but still. Who knows what Rome's boundaries were back then. Could've been races here, or third-rate gladiators battling starved lions.*

"You don't see this many stars from the city," said Eva's guide. Her name was Giada, she was from Sardinia, and she was an assistant from the label's London office. Giada with short dark hair bobby-pinned behind her ears. Giada in jeans and a plain blouse and plain watch. Giada with her acrylic clipboard, plainly honored, with Madonna's new *Erotica* blasting from the van's stereo, to squire Eva and her groups around.

Eva worked for an indie label that had just been purchased by a conglomerate. Her coworkers complained about the "product" being watered down, and about the new corporate dogma, but Eva'd been promoted to senior product manager, her salary raised by half, so she didn't grumble at all. Hampered with only minor, typical, girlie doubts about her clothes and hair and her ability to say precisely what she meant in the moment she meant it, Eva was 90 percent certain she could make happen whatever she put her mind to.

"Sweets," Eva said to Giada with a smirk. "The stars came out for me."

Eva had been at the venue for six hours, but it seemed like six minutes. Hours went by like handclaps to a backstage babel of Italian, Italian-accented English, Spanish-Spanish, English-English, and American English. Finally, the audience bounced loosely into the open place that still smelled of night blooms and cigarette smoke and Euro beer.

In a micro denim skirt, a California Angels T-shirt, and loose-laced work boots, Eva moved shoulders-first through the thickening crowd of crew onstage, and then through artists and rambunctious entourages backstage. Giada at her side, she ducked under rickety scaffolding, stepped nimbly over cables and toolbox-size batteries on her way to check in on her rap girl group (Lo-Note, Hi-Note, and Coda were "establishing an international base") and her boy duo, Imperial Court (they were midlist rap idols already). Sectioned off by a dirty canvas drape, Eva's three girls sprawled on the cement floor with stuffed totes under their heads. The group was called Trix, they were from Dallas, and they had passports for the first time in their lives.

"These people ain't gonna appreciate us," said Hi-Note.

"They already do," Eva said, soothing and silencing. "Or they wouldn't have come out."

"Shut up, Hillary," Lois said as Eva looked on approvingly. "Eva handles hers. Radio's been playing our shit every day out here."

Hi-Note/Hillary rolled her eyes toward Coda. They were equally bored with Lois's sincere pursuit of success.

Eva felt large. She'd walked her groups through convoluted office politics, and now she was walking them through a country she'd already been through twice. Trix and Imperial Court were billed right beneath headliners PeaceLove&War. PL&W were a thriving, unpretentious New York trio recently become an even more successful duo due to the specter of a dead DJ for all to invoke and pray to.

"Peace and Love are playing themselves," Lois said. "Since War shot himself."

Eva nodded. *War would want them to go on like this. Make money while there's money to be made. Who knows how long this rap shit is gonna last? Staying paid, blowing up even bigger, that's the respect.*

Boyz II Men's woeful "End of the Road" trickled from the head-set around Eva's neck, followed by Stereo MCs' frantic "Step It Up." The contrast freaked Eva's mind. *The mix.* She listened to the local station wherever she traveled, so as to be up on trends, bubbles in airplay, and disc jockeys with influence. Eva crept back onstage, this time with a path cut for her by Giada's Italian. The Italian radio station played MC Hammer's "Let's Get It Started," and whenever she heard that song, Eva also heard in her head Hammer's "Ring 'Em" galloping 120 beats per minute over frantic cowbells. Every hip hop song took Eva to another song, then another. She stayed fascinated by the links between songs and artists and what about them made certain melodies or loops or phrases stick to her brain. Eva was fired up by Hammer. Her head nodded to the bells. Eva wanted to dance.

But she was working, so she took the temperature of the room.

The promoter had obviously oversold the event.

On the floor, bodies pressed against other bodies cloaked in coats too huge for the weather and in pants too big for the wearer. It was hard to tell who was wiry or husky, who was boy or girl, who was buddy or bandit.

Clothes could camouflage weapons, too, but Eva didn't think about fear enough to acknowledge that she didn't have it. She'd been moving up in the music business for four years and was certain she knew the secret order in the disorder. When her stepmother asked her about the "violence" at hip hop shows, Eva told her that hip hop was a culture where you always might get your ass beat.

From her tiptoes on the stage, Eva saw PeaceLove&War's manager knocking through the audience like a mallet. The guy had a partner trailing him valet style, cradling a shoebox.

"Lil' John gets it *done*," Eva admiringly said to Giada. *He steps it up. Gets it started.*

Lil' John didn't have his usual bodyguards. Since War's death, whenever Eva'd seen Lil' John in the States, he always had two burly brothers clocking the room, daring fools to step up. Wearing that bodyguard face, eyes like soldiers' eyes, set at ten paces. Face that says I'm not *just a friend*, I'm not *crew* or *posse*. I'm not some nigga from the neighborhood—the Neighborhood meaning any neighborhood where pickings are slim and escape chutes as real as Scotty's transporter—*not* a nigga just happy to be put on. I'm not bonded, or licensed to carry, but I'm carrying anyway, and word is bond: I'm watching you, and don't think—*please* don't think—that because I'm black and because you're black or Puerto Rican or whatever form of not-white you are, that I won't keep this white boy safe as gold bars. Safe like he's a baby. I have his back. The pussy I get is always free, and always new. Rent is paid. I act unafraid. Step *up*, fool. Step the fuck up if you think you got it like that.

Lil' John didn't need those bodyguards in Europe. It was mostly in L.A. and New York that a fatwa had been sown and grown, the thorny act of War's suicide trimmed down to White Man Is Responsible for Black Man and Black Man Is Now Dead. Forget the fact that Love had gone on record—BET and MTV—to say with pragmatic sadness that War had "issues," that he had problems "outside the industry," and that War had loved Lil' John, that in fact they all did. Lil' John had shown them "mad respect," always, Peace said, and had seen them through "mad drama."

On MTV, Peace said, "It was like, for my boy War, him just ponderin' that"—he'd stopped short of the words *killing himself*—"it wasn't enough." Lil' John had been beaten and stomped soon after, and he wore his beatdown like the dented badge of honor it was in hip hop, all the while pimping the ghost of War with the composure of an old-school player.

Eva had known War. He was Trent McAllister, who used to spin at parties under the unavoidable nickname of T-Mack. He had two daughters by Min-Hee, a Korean girl with hair she could sit on. Every-

body called her Minnie, which evolved over time to Money, and, finally, to Money Min (*You know, War's gangsta Chinese chick*). War was
a crate-troll too kidlike for kids and the tragedies and to-do lists of
family life. Too gutted by glory and a gory adolescence to do much of
anything but keep his vinyl dusted, keep his turntable case plastered
with promotional stickers from groups and record labels from around
the world and from back in time. His case was an atlas of hip hop—
coded colors, ideals for living up to, neighborhood notions, and
names heavy with history and irony and in-jokes and pun.

ARRESTED DEVELOPMENT.
WILD PITCH. PAID IN FULL. COLD CHILLIN'. RUTHLESS.
RAP-A-LOT. RAP SHEET. RELATIVITY. RHYME PAYS.
J.J. FADD. JIVE. THE BOMB.
75 GIRLS. YOU DOWN WIT' O.P.P.? HOT.
LET'S GET BUTT-NAKED AND FUCK. COME, BABY, COME.
FREESTYLE FELLOWSHIP. LYTE AS A ROCK.
INDUSTRY RULE NO. 4080/RECORD COMPANY PEOPLE ARE SHADY.
TOMMY BOY. B-BOY. GETO BOYS. GANGSTA BITCH.
PRIORITY. STETSASONIC. FIRST PRIORITY. SOLAAR.
GANG STARR. KILL AT WILL. CYPRESS HILL.
STREET KNOWLEDGE. DEF JAM. BUST-IT! BEATDOWN.
MO' WAX. SOULS OF MISCHIEF. SLEEPING BAG.
CHRYSALIS. DANGEROUS. RIGHT ON!
DOOWHUTCHYALIKE. LOUD. ENJOY.
YOUNG BLACK TEENAGERS. FEAR OF A BLACK PLANET. WHO'S
    HOUSE? RUFFHOUSE.
NEXT PLATEAU. UPTOWN. ADVENTURES ON THE WHEELS OF STEEL.
    COMPTON. 4TH AND BROADWAY. BOOGIE DOWN. BROOKLYN
    QUEENS.

War didn't know the difference between North Korea and South
Korea. Didn't know there was a North Korea and a South Korea. Loved
his daughters, though, learned to like soy paste stew and shrimp chips,
and though Money Min supposedly came up with his new name—Min
hated "T-Mack" because it was so common and obvious and high

school—it became a point of contention later, when suits were filed and counterfiled. Lil' John said he'd come up with Peace, Love, *and* War, and that the group would have never been a group without his introductions and direction.

"Little John is a dick," Giada said in an official tone that made her opinion seem fact. "He plays with fans' emotions, treats War as a commodity. War was the soul. They should have put down their microphones, out of respect."

Leetle John. Eva tried to keep a smile from her face. Giada made him sound like a cockroach.

"Eva!"

Trix needed massaging. Eva looked to Giada to administer because the opening act, local boys with an Ethiopian front man, stepped onstage to the mikes and turntables. No one to master the ceremonies, so no emcee to announce the MCs. The room was chockablock with cats in gray and black and deep green, all stamped with swooshes and stripes and pumas. The crowd was pumped until the DJ stumbled, chose two wrong records to warm up with, then chose two more, worse. Homeboy was rushing, dropping sleeves, flustered. Eva thought the DJ was a disgrace.

Trix and Imperial Court stood in what passed for the wings. Peace and Love stood opposite. When it was their turn, they'd play a DAT of War's work. They'd roll down a bedsheet-size poster of War mixing and scratching, fingers light on an LP, head cocked low to the right, fat mug of a headphone between shoulder and ear. Eva saw Money Min in the wings, too. Broad cheeks like raw pancakes, her hair matted like she was still mourning. A ruby-eyed Buddha rested on her shallow cleavage, and WAR 4 LYFE was blackly tatted under her left collarbone.

Eva didn't see Lil' John. He and Money Min kept space between them—unless, as they'd been many times in the months since War's suicide, the two of them were floodlit in tribute.

They say your party wasn't pumpin' and your DJ was weak. MC Hammer lyrics licked her brain again. People hated on him, but Eva believed Hammer to be a showman extraordinaire. She loved a pop hit.

Eva loved a winner. *I know Hammer's DJ wouldn't be dropping records at some no-pressure show in Italy, I know that much.*

There was no consistent music, so the crowd began to meld. In a seemingly choreographed way Eva'd seen many times, fools pressed toward the center of the room and flailed forward.

And the flygirls who came with the beat in mind, they all up against the wall like a welfare line.

Arms thrashed. Snails were sucked down and stomped. The crowd heaved, juiced with desire to confront what had failed them.

The opening act bolted. There were grunts and yells. Equipment toppled.

Eva climbed nearby scaffolding until her view was clear. The orangey metal rods were shaky, but Eva was above the churn. She saw the tour's Mutt & Jeff main roadies, Vic and Swan. She spotted Imperial Court. They were hyped by the massive energy, pissed at the possibility of not rapping after having flown, under the scrutiny of first-class stewardesses, all the way to the outskirts of a city in another country where you have to ride bucket in a Peugeot for thirty minutes to find a McDonald's.

When a knife finally materialized, Eva was relieved. The show couldn't continue until that pin had been pulled, until everyone got stoned on the steep, life-affirming sensations that surge right before someone not you was hurt or killed.

The knife was up high.

Let's get it started.

"Man up! You ain't supposed to pull out your shit unless you gon' use it. Fucking man up! Use it! Or you shoulda stayed your ass at home. Let Lil' John know he shoulda come with security. He shoulda been rolling deep. Fuck! Don't y'all got some shit to be mad at?" It was Money Min screeching from the wings. She'd pawed her way up onto some guy's shoulders and was ranting. "Man *up*." The usually droll hybrid of *be a man* and *grow up*, Min hurled at the audience like a fiery superball. She kept them hot in her pocket. Had hit War with them, people said, dead in his face. There was no feminine counterpart for "man up." Then the thought crossed Eva's mind: *Maybe it was a one-time thing for girls—Ah, so you got your first period.*

The knife reminded Eva of a potato peeler. It careened down into packed, padded bodies, and the audience imploded. Oval within oval of jumping in on, swinging and grabbing. A few girls screamed. Some guys formed an outer oval and lackadaisically pulled fighters by their coats from the continuous collapse inward. Lil' John was looking at Min, but Min scrambled from her perch, and then Eva couldn't see her anymore.

She teetered on the scaffolding, looking for Min, and took again the temperature of the room. Legs steady, Eva saw Imperial Court scuffling with their own security, wanting or wanting to seem like they had to be a part of the melee. On the relaxed fringes, Lil' John made a beeline for the harangued promoter.

Going to get his money, Eva thought. *Smart.*

For all his hard girth and know-how, there was an ugly anxiety about John. It froze his eyebrows, and sometimes forced a crooked set of his mouth. Even when Lil' John smiled his hundred-toothed smile, when his thick arms hung from short-sleeved shirts and his ring-heavy hands hung loosely curled and he had on the right sneakers with the right laces and the right jeans with the perfect amount of sag and drag, even when his goose-gray eyes were focused and unblinking, even then Lil' John looked awkward where he stood. He thought he was at peace about what was all right to have taken in the course, as a matter of the fact of doing business, but depending on his company, and on his blood alcohol level, John was either pompous, mortified, or defiant about where he was from and by what he'd gained, by what he'd created, and by what he secretly worried he stole.

Brothers were known for loving Lil' John and bigging him up, known for using him, guilting and taunting him with *You a white boy in this, John, baby,* and for trying to take what they felt Lil' John had— money, juice, white-boy keys to white-boy doors—but more than that, take what was equated with his manhood. More than one brother had been known to say that somebody needed to fuck John in the ass, show John who he was in this hip hop shit.

He can't be him without us being us.

That's what was said.

Fuck that cracker.

We started this shit.

Lil' John looked up, all around. He saw Eva, raised his eyebrows in approval, then walked over and stood directly under her and ogled her panties.

Men in uniform showed up. *"Diffusione! Vada a casa! Nessun rimborse!"* Disburse. Go home. No refunds.

Eva didn't know if they were cops or military. And still she had no fear. Police were starring characters in hip hop. Their presence neither added nor relived tension. That somebody might get arrested or shot was a given. That there'd be fury if that happened was a given. Everybody had a part, and everybody fell into character—a tragedy staged so many times already, every movement was reflex.

Whistles screamed. One boy stumbled, his palm in a tight crescent, clutching at where his kidney lived. A few people jogged toward doors and vanished.

Where's Money Min?

The stumbler finally straightened, gingerly unzipped his coat, and looked at his torso. Whistles shrieked again. Lil' John shook Eva's scaffolding with his hands and she had to clamber. She was scared for the first time that night, and looked down at John with a scowling question on her face. *What, motherfucker?* she mouthed. He didn't look bothered. He shook the scaffolding again.

A uniform snatched the injured boy by the arm and the boy's face twisted tight, then opened up slack and wet. Eva looked for blood on the injured kid, in the dirt, on his boots. There wasn't enough light. The uniform walked the boy out while another officer tried to corral people toward doors. Only a few exited. Eva heard music.

It was Public Enemy: *Here come the drums.*

Money Min was on the wheels of steel. Changing the course of the night. Giving it a different, dancing ending. People started to move again, together, to PE's "Can't Truss It." To jump up, up, and down.

Min flipped through the Italian DJ's abandoned records, fishing for a mix. She found House of Pain. Two Irish-Americans and a Latvian type, rapping over terse base and a roiling drum loop. Left fingers on the fader, right fingers slow-twirling the LPs, Min wore her dead husband's headphones like a thinking cap. Public Enemy's horns thundered like elephants charging into House of Pain's "Jump Around." The song had sirens like Public Enemy was famous for, so the mix sang on multiple levels. Eva rode each current, her knees bent and locked like behind a woolly mammoth's flapping ears.

Jump up / Jump up jump up and get down.

Jump.

Jump.

Jump.

Min was rocking. The sound was hypnotic. Eva didn't have the space in her head to wish she were jumping on the floor. All she was aware of was the mix, the beats, the wave of kids jumping beneath her, rising up and down, a riptide she could joyously dive into. On the shaky scaffolding, Eva bounced.

Jump.

Jump.

Jump.

It was like War had given Min the skills when he was alive or had sent them to her from wherever he was because she was leaned over the tables like her name was DJ Jazzy Jeff, and she was a gifted boy from Philly whose name would always be, to hard-core hip hop heads, ahead of the Fresh Prince's for a reason.

Jump.

Jump.

Jump.

I'll serve your ass like John McEnroe.

The amphitheater's ancient walls seemed to shudder in the moonlight.

Then Min went to Kriss Kross's "Jump."

Eva gripped the horizontal pole in front of her, braced her feet, and shook her ass to beat the beat. "Jump"—from thirteen-year-old Atlanta rappers who wore their clothes backward and rhymed over the Jackson 5's "I Want You Back"—had come out a few months before "Jump Around." *Nineteen seventy. Motown, post Holland-Dozier-Holland.* In her soul, Eva felt Michael Jackson's mute *Now. That. I. See. You. In his arms. I want you back* over *The Mac Dad'll make you / Jump / Jump.* She felt the chimes and harmonies of Motown, the immortality of a number one hit, the glory of two number one hits within the same song. Eva shook the scaffolding harder than Lil John had. *These shits were number one for a reason.*

"That's your song?" John called it up at her, and Eva could barely hear him over the music, so she incorporated a nod into her dance as her mind shouted at him, *How can you not just* see *that it's my song? Can't you feel it?* And that thought took her straight to the Jacksons' 1980 "Can You Feel It?" and the whole amphitheater scene connected and worked on too many levels to count. *Every breath you take / Is someone's death in another place.* The song made Eva think of a 1981 night with her father at the Forum in Los Angeles, the Jacksons' Triumph Tour. Thirty-nine U.S. cities, began in Memphis, ended with four sold-out nights at L.A.'s Fabulous Forum. Michael, Marlon, Tito, Randy, and Jackie came out to *Can. You. FEEL. IT???* At the Forum, in the rafters with her dad, Eva had *jumped / jumped.* On the Italian scaffolding even she tried to *jump / jump.* Eva was in a world. She was every place she had ever been, hearing every song she had ever loved. *Yes,* her body's every twist and pop said. *Yes, I can feel it. This is my fuckin' song.*

Lil' John shook the scaffolding again, and when Eva looked down at him, he held out his arms like he'd catch her if she fell.

He looks strong enough. I should let him be my angel.

Lil' John put his hands on the poles again, smiling. The crowd around him bubbled and whooped.

It doesn't count if the person makes you fall so they can have you in their clutches.

John climbed the lower level of the creaky scaffolding. He said something to his valet, who passed Lil' John the shoebox, and then ran off toward the stage, toward Money Min.

From the shoebox, John passed Eva a stack of glossy flyers and a handful of cassettes. Boys in the audience bounced and pointed to the sky as if it were the origin of the beat. The valet jumped on the stage.

Eva reached down and took the flyers. Saw that the cassettes were the remix of a new single from Peace&Love, with "lost" tracks from War, and a bonus debut track from "DJ Money Min." Just then, at the hands of the valet, a poster of War unfurled, heavy as a dictator's, or one from The Gap. It was a new poster, this time of War with arms raised in victory, Peace and Love beside him, saluting their DJ with homely scepters of microphone. War with the look of wanting to fly away, of having been pressed into a service he was built for, but had been used against him.

The crowd was out of hand. The uniforms by the doors with their stern faces and long guns were trivial and small. There was nothing in the dirt bowl to tear up, or it would have been wrecked. People were starting to stomp and get stomped again.

Can't truss it.

Public Enemy number one! ONE one ONE one!

Money Min had gone back to PE. Lil' John hit at Eva's boot, but she knew what she was in a great position to do. She tossed the flyers up, and they fluttered down like giant confetti.

I drop jewels like paraphernalia / I'm infallible, not into failure. Eva tossed shrink-wrapped cassingles into the air one by one, then by the twos, and people grabbed for them and snatched them from each other, and picked up flyers to retoss them or stuff them into pockets. *Not into failure.* Eva loved that line. *Gang Starr featuring Nice & Smooth. From Smooth B's verse. The hot shit from Chrysalis right now.* "Dwyck," the hottest shit out, period.

"¡Sopra qui!"

"Over here!"

"¡Mas aqui!"

Lil' John handed Eva more and she threw them up and out, and she was ecstatic. He gazed at her like she was a half a mile from heaven. When Eva looked down again, Lil' John gave her a thumbs up, and then twirled his index fingers around each other as if to say, *Wrap it up, enough. Don't want to give away too much.* Then he pointed his thumb at himself, at Eva, and over his shoulder, saying they should leave.

She pointed at her groups, and then held up her own index to say, *One minute.*

Lil' John pointed across the stage to the promoter, and nodded, like he needed the same minute. This mute exchange gave them both the feeling that they'd much in common, and that the road to sex and mutual respect would be easy.

Trix was beneath her, scared and ready to go. Giada stood there, too, disappointed. The crowd hooted for more prizes, but Eva climbed down.

"You coulda fell," Lo-Note/Lois said.

Eva frowned at her. "That's the kinda shit goes through your mind?"

She and Lil' John's individual minutes turned into an hour, but when Eva got back to her hotel later, tired and needing to pack for the drive south to Ravenna, Lil' John was at the bar on his third lemon liqueur and soda. He saw her, pulled a wad of lire from his pocket, looked at it for a second like he might attempt to figure out the exchange rate, then placed all the money on the counter, walked over to Eva at the elevator, and stepped on with her. She pushed a button, and he didn't.

"Imperial Court," Lil' John said, "didn't even go on."

"Neither did Trix."

"You don't care?"

The doors opened with a *ping*, and Eva stepped off.

"I care," she said, looking at him from the quiet hallway. "But shit happens."

He took this as a summation of her personality and as such, an invitation. Lil' John stepped from the elevator. "That attitude'll get you far," he said as they walked.

It's gotten me this far. "You don't know what my attitude is." Eva unlocked her door. He followed her in.

"I think I do," he said, plopping down on a chair. "You're glad I came up here."

"You're glad you came up here."

"Sit by me." He flushed pink, but didn't look bashful.

"You got that chair," Eva said, "pretty well filled out."

Lil' John stood, paused, and then sat on the bed. "Then I guess I'll move over here."

She sat next to him. "You're smooth as hell," Eva said dryly, feeling nice and smooth herself.

"First time you had somebody up here?"

Guys. Always checking their place in line. "I've been here one night."

"So I'm asking."

They were talking toward the television cabinet. Their shoulders were touching, and if they faced each other, they'd be kissing. Eva thought for a second about the last person she'd had sex with, Imperial Court's manager. Brother called Fred Truth, after Hampton and Sojourner. He couldn't make the trip. Jacked his back up in a minor car accident, plus his girl was about to have their second baby. *Truth was all up in mine, though, like he loved it.*

"You think you're fly," Lil' John said, and tugged a bit of her hair.

He's corny. "I am fly."

"Kiss me, then."

"Kiss you."

"Yeah. Think you can condescend," John said, "to that?"

CHAPTER

12

PeaceLove&Money
The All-World
United Tour, 1992

va had to wipe her mouth after each kiss. Wipe her chin and even the tip of her nose.

He's the most slimy kisser in the world. I like the way he handles me, though. I hate a tentative toucher.

The sex was over.

So fun. Sex twice with two condoms. Sex all flirty and fancy. Oh, and with liquor. So no shyness. I had on my Big Bad attitude. All nasty and daring.

John pulled on his drawers, grabbed his jeans and undershirt, and went to the bath.

The way he looked, sitting against the headboard. Way I stood up and dropped my skirt to the floor—smooth. Lifted my shirt over my head and I was unhooking my bra and walking toward him and climbed on top. Yeah. Feeling good, feeling high, feeling like I wanted my body touched. Not thinking, Does he like me? Does he respect me? Should I be with him? Am I doing too much? Too soon? Too nastily? YUCK. Never that.

Was more like, Homeboy looked fine as fuck, and he was confident even with his gut a bit too thick. He's got that sexy scar on his chin, looks not that pasty, straight clean teeth, a grown-out buzz cut, girl lashes, top and bottom . . . Gray eyes—I think they're gray. Him looking at my lips, checking the boobs, stretching out glances, feeding me drinks. White boy. White boy from Strong Island trying to represent! I wanna just close my eyes, replay the sex in my head . . . Have I ever been so nasty with any man? Have I ever been so . . . free?

Yeah, I have, if I'm honest. But with Lil' John, goddamn. It don't seem like role-playing. The shit seems real.

He stepped back in smelling like soap, toothpaste, and Eva's body. She was naked still, except for her boots. Lil' John fell onto her. She bit his lips, he sucked on hers. Eva used her forearm to mop her face and he didn't remark on it.

Both wanted to lie in bed and talk and kiss and have more sex. Neither knew how to communicate that without seeming needy and already too infatuated. Eva shifted clumsily, reached for her panties and shirt. John hopped up and pulled on his hoodie.

"I'll see you on the road, though," he said, like she'd mentioned something that would make seeing him on the road difficult, when she'd said nothing at all. "At Ravenna or wherever."

"I might not make that stop. They got this chick from the London office. She'll deal with Trix and I.C. I got shit to do back in—"

"You make me laugh," John said.

"That what I do." She said it hoping she'd not betrayed herself with a rise in her voice on the *do*. She thought, too, that while he was talking shit, Lil' John was extending, even if it was just for moments, his stay in her room.

"Not in a bad way, but you take yourself crazily serious."

"I am crazy," Eva said, "and I am serious."

"Especially," John said, "for a girl."

Black girl? Or white girl? Wise girl? Or wild girl? "I'll wake up tomorrow with a new attitude. Promise. Just for you."

"You should have a new one now. After how you were just acting."

"You mean how *you* were acting?" *White boy!* she thought, *please. It was good, but please.*

"I know what you're thinking."

"Tell me." Eva liked this game.

"Thinking, 'White boy, please.'"

She smiled a little. "You're familiar with that sentiment, then." A dis, an endearment. A two-word stooping-down-to, a welcome. *Like "nigga,"* Eva thought, *but without slavery and Jim Crow and red-zoning and separate water fountains and shit behind it.*

"It's come up before," John said smugly.

"And what's your usual response?"

"My response is, that's not what you was saying an hour ago. 'White boy, please.' Ain't gonna get into all that moaning you were doing. Way you were bouncing. My thumb all in your mouth."

She felt fucked with. He was fucking with her. But this is what she liked—a skilled bluff-caller.

"Why just the thumb?" he wanted to know. "You don't like it? Head? Or you don't give head to white boys?"

"I don't give head to white boys." She hadn't. She'd had sex with two or three, but to suck a white boy's dick was further than she wanted to go. To go down on a white boy was too generous. Seemed enough of a treat for a white guy to be in the bed with her. *And he gets head, too? From this mouth? Nah.*

"You have. And if you haven't, you will."

Future tense. Caught it. "I love a dreamer," Eva said, daring to toss out "love," as he'd dared to speak of tomorrow. His eyes stared into hers, and then plainly at her breasts, and then back in her eyes. Eva liked John's nerve.

"You'll do it in Ravenna," he said.

"Dude. Make no assumptions—"

"I'm not your 'dude,' dude. And you know damn well you're going to Ravenna, and to Bologna, and every other place on the tour."

"You been tested?" She asked it quick, like it didn't matter.

Took him a second. "Yeah."

"Why?" *I know this fool isn't in a high-risk group.*

"Because I fucked a lot of people."

A lot of women.

"A lot of females," he said. "If we were home, I'd show you the test slip."

She looked at him for some proof that he was virus free. For proof that he'd find her again, so they could have sex and get to know each other better, even if it was just for the tour.

"You're gonna do it," Lil' John said, back on topic. "You're gonna go down on me."

"You didn't ask me. If I was tested."

"You're tested. Because you asked me if I was."

"That's your method? Real scientific. I hope you're careful."

"I was just careful with you."

Careful with me. Eva's insides surged in his direction. Because she wanted badly for him to come back to bed, and she didn't want him to have that power over her, she exercised discipline: "It's time for you to go, Lil' John."

"You know my name's Ron Littlejohn."

Of course she knew. Ron Littlejohn's father had negotiated on behalf of too many Motown artists to name. Big Lil' John (called that as hip hop began to dominate, and as his son rose in the business) had untangled publishing rights behind the Philadelphia Sound and worked for charting black stars whether the charts were top-heavy with disco or Duran Duran, whether the hit songs were about being born in the USA, about girls named Mandy, dogs named Brandy, or hot fun in the summertime.

The Littlejohn mystique ran deep. Ron's grandfather was rumored to have been the man next to the man who booked Billie Holiday when Holiday was with Basie. Some said Ron's grandfather cooked mendacious books for Decca in the 1930s and '40s. Some thought the biggest Littlejohn had pimped Louis Armstrong for almost all Armstrong's early money. But the truth was that in the forties, Ron's father's father had sold heroin at Harlem spots to jazz drummers and blues singers, was run out of town for reasons both played down and overblown, and ended up on the scandalous team that launched California's biggest jazz festival.

So Ron's Long Island family had for three generations made money, one way or another, mostly off black music and had had for those sixty years the kind of comfort level around blacks that white people in the American South tend to have—the kind that comes from exploiting, but comes also from being in close quarters with (and believing that close quarters lead to an understanding of) the negro.

Some extremely tight relationships had existed between the Littlejohns and their clientele. There'd even been love. Ron's uncle, also a lawyer, was still married to a Dominican woman who'd been one-third of a girl group in the early sixties. Ron's mother had taken a three-year leave of absence from his father and spent it with a burly seventies soul singer. Eva wondered how any feeling between the Littlejohns and their black associates could have been real. How could any partnership, friendship, or love affair escape the ill dynamic of whites paying to see blacks interpret joys and pain? Of blacks interpreting for and selling grief to those whose father's father's fathers shaped and honed or stomached it?

Us allowing it. Participating. Us fighting it, and mostly losing.

Where's the goddamn purity? Right there in the Italian hotel room. Eva's mind swirled. *Their dominance, just their sheer numbers make me sick sometimes. Always at the head of everything in this business. Behind this, above that. The few of us that rise up as owners or CEOs or chairpersons, why do we all seem like puppets? Does it* seem *like that, or is it really, actually* like *that? I can work within it. Shit, I win within it, but no one can claim a black-white relationship in which race isn't a factor, if not the factor. A relationship in which the dope sold, the spot booked, the record made, the song marketed, the hire made, the drunkenness shared, the addictions managed, the love made ain't shot through with who did what to whom when and who allowed what to go down because. Who could come to the table, let alone a relationship, with hands unmuddied or unbloodied?*

Eva shook her head at her rhyme.

No one.

On bad days, she thought there was nothing worse than a white person who was rich due to rap, and who walked like he or she'd earned a right to be in hip hop. But on worse days, when Eva dealt with dilettantes of any color, she appreciated any person who had some experience, however skewed, with creative people not used to being loved by the masses, or to having money. Eva knew who Ron was. She knew what Rons were. Eva had known the deal when she saw Ronald Littlejohn in the amphitheater. And she'd thought he was sexy as hell.

"You know who I am," Ron said, "and you like me, so let's be back in the bed."

"Go on, Ron Lil' John. I'm going out. Me and Giada."

"Giada is a snake," Ron said before he stepped out, but before the door closed he walked back in, gently pushed Eva flat, drench-kissed her, and then spoke directly to her mouth. "Gonna put my dick right here," he said.

"Dream about it."

"Already have," he said with a hitch-up of his jeans. Then Ron wiped her chin and mouth with his palm, and he was gone.

Showered and scented, Eva stood on the sidewalk in front of the small lobby. It was a little after 1:00 a.m. Lois from Trix stood by. All the taxicabs were Benzes. Giada flagged one.

"Where's your crew?" Eva asked Lois.

"About theirs."

"Why you ain't about yours?"

The cab pulled up and they got in the back. "I'm trying to be," Lois said. She surprised Eva by naming a club to the driver, and as he pulled off, Lois said, "I didn't know you and Lil' John were down like that."

"He's all right."

"You don't work for that white boy, yet you threw that stuff up, fools went crazy. More fights could've happened. Already two dummies hurt. You get blinded by the hype. I thought that's what we artists were supposed to do."

Giada watched the driver.

Eva felt reprimanded. "They got hurt before I threw those flyers out."

"Whatever," Lois said. "Just more money for Lil' John and Min."

Giada looked at Lois and said, "Does the money come out of your purse?"

Eva was glad the cab came to a stop. Once in the cavernous club,

Giada located tall chairs for Eva and Lois, walked away, and then brought three cups of wine.

"Don't like red," Lois said.

"G.'s off the clock, Lois. And she wasn't your slave when she was on it." *She was mine.*

Giada motioned like she needed the ladies' room, and Eva followed her. Once in the minuscule booth. Giada pulled out a cigarette, slit the paper with her thumbnail, and emptied the tobacco into a small plastic bag with weed crumbs and coke dust in one corner. Giada shook her mixture around, and then poured some of it into her own paper. Giada used the cigarette filter—hooked up the cavvy completely, then lit it with a lighter old and heavy enough to have belonged to an ancestor. Flame blazed up three inches.

They smoked.

Giada said, "Your lips are making me happy."

"Why?" Eva blew smoke. She tilted her head a bit. She knew what came next.

"I just like. The shape."

Someone knocked on the door.

"Glad you approve," Eva said. She waved back the cavvy, done.

Giada leaned a few inches. There was another knock on the door. *Giada smells good. This bathroom smells clean like bleach.*

"I heard," Giada said, "you were . . . out there. Down for . . . whatever."

"Finish what you started, if that's how you're feeling."

Someone knocked again, louder and longer. Neither girl was bothered.

"In this situation, I'd rather the other person . . . begin."

"So, what? So there's no confusion later about you having pressured me? What are you, a dude? It's not that deep, Giada. You brought me back here."

"To smoke."

"Bullshit," Eva said, smiling. She was happy. She'd just been with Ron, she was a little high, she was in a random, cool Italian club, and now homegirl was in her face. "What, you just want to frustrate me?"

"Lucky Eva. With your teasing. Her new friend Giada is all that frustrates her."

"Oh we're friends now." Eva did like Giada's personality.

"I guess. So we might as well dance."

Lois was pouting at the table when they returned. She was snapping, "Where *were* you guys?" when they pulled her onto the strobe-lit dance floor.

Giada, Lois, and Eva danced together like they were friends, like there was no crack-of-dawn wake-up call pending, like the DJ's every mix was hypersonic. *She got Bette Davis eyes* and *Cel-e-brate good times* and *She's just a girl who claims that I am the one* and finally, right before the DJ yelled, *Va la sede ed ha sesso, ibridi*, it was *Let's sway through the crowd to an empty space.*

Go home and have sex, mongrels. The three girls were a sweaty mess. They held hands on the street in fast friendship, each high and happy, each one's heart still on gallop from the music and movement, each elated with her swiftly rising rank in the music business, each with the belief that she was special, culled from the masses for service in a flawed but righteous battle for world supremacy. The three girls stood closely in the last darkness, starving for food and sleep, until another Benz scooped them and dropped them at the hotel.

"So you gonna go on up to your room," Lois said, "let Lil' John smack it up and flip it. Rub it down."

Eva laughed.

"After the tour," Lois said with real worry, "he'll see you and he'll be very Hi and Bye."

"And I'll be what? Crying? Stalking his ass?" Eva laughed more, kissed Lois on the lips, and Giada, too, and went up to shower again, and to push her stuff in her new Louis Vuitton duffel. The room seemed bigger, was balmy, and smelled like sweat and his 'n' hers colognes. The room and everything in it was discrete from her, already monument to a significant event.

Over the rest of the tour, and for years afterward, Giada never said anything to Eva about Eva's relationship with Lil' John. Giada's

silence on the subject, and her remote loyalty to Eva, cemented a sporadic, long-distance acquaintance that would last until Giada got in the
middle of some shit that was not her business, and changed Eva's life
in a way Eva had been terrified to imagine.

––––––––––

NIGHT TWO

Eva lay belly down across a Ravenna hotel bed in a striped thong,
wondering how her ass cheeks looked from behind. Wondering if
the strip of transparent ivory bra across her back made her electro-
magnetic. Eva pulled her knees up under her hips. Ron stood behind
her, still in layers of clothes and the mingled scents of his day.

Why you nekkid?

Trying to get fucked?

Trying to get into trouble?

What's on your mind, today?

Belt unbuckled. His pants hung right above the knees. Ron
pulled her by where femurs fit hip bones, pulled her ass to where he
could push in and a little bit up. Her shoulders on unironed sheets.
Right jaw down. Lips relaxed, soft, slightly twisted, seemed as exaggerated as her cheeks in the air. Plumper. Accessible. She pictured
herself an invitation, a warm, tight party of his dreams. *Of course the
power shit gets played out—consciously and subconsciously. Who does
anyone think we are except 1992 man and woman, black and white,
and American all over? Of course the power games appeal and most
times satisfy. Of course I'm defensive, here in my own mind, never to
anyone else. Of course I worry if I'm getting all exoticized and objecti-
fied and all the shit I should worry about. And I know the field isn't
level, but I worry, if I exoticize him. His being a cool-ass white boy
floats my boat. But isn't that what sex is, anyway? What's your freaki-
ness? Who's on top?*

They fucked, then napped, and then fucked until the wake-up
call.

NIGHT THREE

Frankie, didn't I tell you, The lion would come in for a kill /
Frankie, didn't I say, It had power over your sweet skill.
—"FRANKIE'S FIRST AFFAIR," music by Sade Adu and
Stuart Matthewman, lyrics by by Sade Adu

Eva had her nose near Ron's armpit. They were in Florence. FIRENZE, the signs all said.

What white boy smells like sandalwood gambler's soap and Murray &
Lanman Florida Water? So damn Puerto Rican. So damn Caribbean.
Jesus, he wants to be black.

They both had the off-hours of the artists, usually from one to about eight in the morning. This morning, Eva and Ron had until noon, and they lingered over red orange juice and yogurt and sweet bread. They listened to music from saucer-size speakers Ron attached to his Walkman. Eva felt inhaled by him, intoxicated by his intoxication with her. She felt soft and like her flesh might burst through her skin, like her sleepiness was her sexiness. Like her sexiness was her strength.

"No one is that perfect person," Eva said, under cover of stale quilts and orangey darkness. "Everyone melts down to who they are."

"Truuue."

"No one stays new, or infatuated or infatuating," she said close to his ear. "No one stays awake twenty-five hours a day being wonderful and smelling like tea tree oil."

"I can smell like tea tree, bay rum, Vandi Kananga, Hoyt's, whatever you need, twenty-four seven, three-sixty-five." His fingertips were on her rib cage. He moved them up to her breast, pinched her nipple to right before it hurt.

She bit his earlobe—"Listen"—to right before it hurt. *I can resist this fool. He don't have me like that.* Eva spoke so her lips brushed his auricle with every word. "No man is unintimidated by real conversation from a woman."

Ron tensed but didn't move his ear away.

"Especially if she's a girl who really works—"

"Get out my ear." But he didn't move.

Eva clutched his dick tightly. Ron crunched his eyes shut. His dick had been in her hand all along.

"—and takes care of her*self,* a girl who's strong *and* weak." *Everyone melts down, and some, to nothing. I melt down to a clenched belly and wet eyes and they run. Cosign on that, baby boy.*

"No one's the sun the moon the stars the sky," he said. "I get that. Not so hard, baby. Let him go so he can do his thing."

Eva squeezed harder, kissed his ear so sweet.

"Let go," Ron said, from some raw place between ache and elation.

"No one's rock-solid—"

"You think you run this? *That's* what it is. You think you run this." He smiled hysterically at the pain. He choked out little laughs.

"—and emotional at the same time."

"No one," Ron said, "but me." His turn to get in her ear. "So spread your legs and put daddy's dick where it belongs. You like holding it so much, put it where it fucking goes."

They never walked together like lovers. She adored this understanding between them. Eva and Ron operated super-separately—to make phone calls, deal with venues, handle their groups. They traveled with their own, both of them easily managing the daily detachment from the other, both busy, both certain that those who cared to know, knew and shut up, at least around them. Eva and Ron didn't speak of the sex, or whatever feeling they had, with anyone on the European continent. They were both self-consciously and randomly attentive, but Eva and Ron acted like the colleagues they were.

In the Firenze room, Ron said into Eva's hair, "Why do you let me have sex with you without a condom?"

It was such a valid question, she blanked for a second. "Why are you doing it?"

"It's . . . warmer," he said. "More real."

"Consequences are more real."

"I know," he said gravely, like he'd considered the penalties and was puzzled. "I'm trying to figure out, though, why I don't feel careless."

Before they got lost in it, Eva pulled his face back by his hair, "Negro," she said to him, "you need to put a condom on." She said it so that at a future date, she'd be able to say she'd been wiser than he.

"I'm your negro now?" He was pleased and tried mightily not to seem so. Ron jerked his hair from her grip and kept on stroking.

"You need to—"

"I'm not gonna come in you." He wanted her to shut up, to feel him, to let him feel her and what she'd said.

After, they fell in and out of sleep with the music on low. *I can't go a day without my sunshine* and the Five Blind Boys of Alabama and *I only want to see you walking in the purple rain.* Right before they had to go to work, Ron was too tired for more sex and Eva was too sore, so they made elaborate bargains, negotiated who was going to do what sexual trick to whom the next time, and for how long. They tested each other with threats of exposure to their tour mates, threats never to be made good on, threats to check that the casually silly reaction of the other hadn't changed.

Night Eight

In Modena, after a tense, sold-out show at Parco Novi Sad, and an after-party at which they'd both baldly flirted with other people, Ron and Eva were both about four drinks in, and they were exhausted. What had become the PeaceLove&Money spectacular was a success. More people, more press, more fights than they'd anticipated. Lois's Trix upped their profile to the tenth power. Imperial Court was as they always were—fanatically received, but barely gold even after the international dates and bitter about it. Peace and Love kept to themselves when they weren't thrilling crowds. They explored vineyards and *museos*, chapels and ancient clock towers. Peace and Love spent hours talking to their lawyers back in the States. Money Min had hooked up with a writer from *Blues & Soul* magazine.

The tour was almost over. Ron and Eva were in Eva's room at the Holiday Inn.

"How old are you, anyway?"

"Twenty-six," Eva said. *If it's your business.*

"I'm twenty-eight."

"And?"

"I wanted to know." Ron loved Eva's lips and ass and legs and the way she dressed to show it all off, and he hated that other people wanted to have her, talk to her, make deals with her. They knew she'd fuck them, too, with barely a preamble. Eva was loose as a goose, but he liked her personality and her work ethic. He thought she was smark and slick. He liked the way she touched his face, the way she sucked his dick like she liked it, not like it was an afterthought or a chore. So he felt stupid and was furious in her room at the Holiday Inn, but drunk enough to try and explain himself, and to press her for anything that would make him feel smarter.

Silence and drinking and facing each other on a tiny balcony.

"You ever give in?"

"To what?" she said.

"Anything. Anybody, I mean."

"I give in to you." With an angry, sexy smile. *Fuck you and the eager Italian witches with their wack-ass singing group and their halter-tops they don't even have the boobs for.*

"No."

"I do."

"You let me do what I want to you," said Ron Lil' John.

"Let you do what you want with me."

Ron was supposed to be someone to have had sex with, to have stopped having sex with, someone to think about with small sadness when it was over. And when it was over, Eva figured she'd wonder, like she usually did about men that lasted more than a week, why it hadn't evolved into a relationship, and then she'd decide that it had to be because in her heart of hearts she didn't want a relationship, because she felt that if she did want one, she'd have it.

"I'm talking about, like, show your secrets," Ron said. "Act your real fuckin' self."

"You know my secrets." *As if. So you could do what you want with them—my mom. Dad. Other boys. The clinics? No.*

"Listen to me!" Drunk.

"Keep talking that loud," Eva said. "See how far you get."

"Listen to me. Sometimes, I feel like I could—"

"Could what?"

"Submit to you," he said.

"Submit? For what? Sexually?" Eva was slurring her words.

"Whatever, just make it like you were important. Like you were worthy."

"Nigga, I am worthy." *I am. I am. Yes I am. Yes I am. Yes I am.*

"Comebacks. That's all you have. Never give in."

"So I give in, then you do." *That's the game suddenly? I've played it. Lost. Learned. It ain't my tourney, white boy.*

"Tit for tat. That's what you play."

"Give to get. Tit for tat. It's not a game. It's the game." *And so don't hate the player, sweetheart. Do not hate me 'cause I play as good as you.*

DAY ELEVEN

"There were cute guys there, right, Ron? And cute girls?" Eva was talking about the party celebrating the last tour date. They'd held hands in public. Had sex in an anteroom while the guys from Imperial Court banged on the door, yelling drunkenly for Eva and Ron to open up. "You niggas ain't shit," they said. "We can hear you!"

There in a room at Milan's Hotel Principe, Ron nodded dumbly. Purple candles had melted into tonguelike shapes. Eva was sitting on his chest in a blue bra and nothing else, and he was on his back in gray boxers and nothing else, and they hadn't had sex, but he'd held her and hugged her and gone down on her twice, and no, she hadn't had an orgasm, but all that was right there for the morning when they had to make things happen quick because there were flights to catch back to the States. Between them, he and Eva had had three bottles of champagne and various other cocktails.

"Cute girls and cute guys, right, Lil' John?" *He's looking at me like I'm the pretty one, and he's the lucky one.*

"Yes, I said. Some of both." Ron indulged today's game, amazed at himself. Wondered if he'd found a girl he could respect. A girl he could attempt faithfulness with. A girl who'd leave him if he acted an ass too many times in a row. One who wouldn't give him a pass on his lies because of the money he was starting to make. For Ron, Eva was the distillation of every Vanity 6 desire, every swollen bass loop, every pretty black girl who'd played him to the left wth an eye roll, every beautiful black girl who'd laughed at his jokes because she felt sorry for his corny ass at the bar, every aromatic, graceful, wild sister his dad had as mistress while Ron was a kid.

"And they didn't matter, did they?" Eva was literally bouncing with glee.

"Nah," Ron said. "They didn't matter at all."

And then the messy kisses were dewy as the Mediterranean air, apple tangy and long. His lips were slim pillows kissing her forehead and then sucking her tongue softly—not like he was trying to take it from her, not with any noise, not with one sound at all. But he pulled on it with a sure suction that made Eva spin into the warm belief that his arms were okay arms to lean into for a minute.

He's the best kisser in the world, Eva thought drunkenly. *But this is all a dream.*

Seven hours later, Ronald Littlejohn and Eva Glenn talked about love at Heathrow Airport. Her layover was four hours; his, one hour. Ron was going to Los Angeles International via Boston's Logan, Eva direct to John F. Kennedy. They were seated in British Airways' tidy first-class lounge. Eva was back on Giada's turf, and Giada had Trix and Imperial Court doing some in-stores in Brixton that Eva wouldn't be bothered with. Ronald hadn't told Eva that he loved her; he told her that he could.

"You could," she said. "Ain't I the lucky one." *Ain't I the Lucky One*. Sounded to Eva's ears like the B-side of a Stax 45.

"I'm saying that if we were . . . real people, with everyday lives—"

"Then what?" But Eva understood what he meant. She'd already begun to feel like her life wasn't quite real. She made more dollars per year, at twenty-six, than her dad had made in any three years of his life. She'd been to twenty states, three continents, and six countries. She shopped with confidence and freedom. She had an assistant. Eva went, with decent seats as well as backstage passes, to the Grammys and other nationally televised award shows and concerts. This was her everyday. She knew celebrities like other people knew their coworkers or neighbors—closely and without intimacy. The thing most people did with celebrities—wonder about them—Eva'd stopped doing two or three years ago. They were as usual to her as were sacks of coffee beans or patients to grocers and doctors.

"I might," Ron said, "think about trying to make it happen with you."

His ambiguity was irritating and, Eva thought, plain lame. "Make what happen?" There was a crunched question mark on her face, like the idea of her allowing anything to *happen* with him was ludicrous, like he was bigheaded for even imagining it. Her frown was reflex.

"We could have, like, a sex house," Ron said. "All the perfect shit for sex."

A sex house? Eva wasn't thinking marriage, but . . . a sex house? *That's trifling.* She felt disappointment—that was her ego. And a tiny bit of relief because she was back on familiar ground. Eva knew the rules of on-tour hookups. "Um, no, Ron. We're road dogs," she said without sadness. "And the tour's over."

"But that's who really should be, if you think about it, together." Ron was having a real revelation. "We roll well, don't get on each other's nerves. You understand my life as an executive. Watch when I get back. How shit goes down. Watch your boy as he blows up the whole spot. Flips the crazy corporate cheese. Watch."

Eva felt she'd be watching. She thought, *White boy or no, he's a nigga like any other.* In this case, Eva thought "nigga" to mean a man acting in a way that disappointed her, a way in which she expected, though she'd hoped for at least the option of the opposite.

British Airways called his flight.

"You got all my numbers, right?" Ron held her hand tight, and looked in her eyes.

Eva was unmoved. "Yep, sure do." She sounded overly bright, wanted him to suspect she was faking brightness so he'd suspect she was overcompensating for true nonchalance about their situation.

Ron, though, took her words to mean what they meant. He hadn't asked for her numbers. Not like Ron couldn't find her easily. But in Eva's mind, he hadn't asked her for anything, really, but that first blow job.

"So when you're in Cali," Ron said, using the abbreviation for California that Eva hated because it was used to mean L.A., like L.A. was the only city in California, "buzz me up. We'll hang out."

Buzz you up? The hell is that? "If I get out there, I sure will." *Suck my dick.*

They called his flight again. Last call.

"You will," he said, walking toward the other stragglers. Men ruddy-cheeked and focused. Money Min with three shoulder straps and a half gallon of Evian. "I know how you do, Eva. You'll be all at the Nikko Hotel, flossin'."

"Flossin' for sure." *Why is he stretching this out? We know what this is. Must these people be privy to our tired-ass good-byes?* Eva thought to say, *I stay at the Mondrian when I'm in L.A.* But she didn't. "Safe travels" is what she did call out.

"Call me." Ron's hand was in a hang-loose sign. He put it to the side of his face, pinkie at his mouth, thumb at his ear.

As if I would ever call. He doesn't know yet that I'm not that girl.

Eva didn't call Ron. Not until she felt she owed him, at the very least, the courtesy of a conversation.

CHAPTER

13

Cat Island

They stood under a long wooden sign that read SMITH BAY.

"Miss, we are looking for a place to rent a car," Dart said in loud, clipped tones.

The woman, harassed, pointed a finger curved as a question mark. "Down there."

"Down where?" Dart moved into her space.

"There," she said, taking a step back. "Not far."

"Not far," Dart said earnestly. He moved toward her again. "Be more exact than that."

But the two women walked away from Dart and Eva, and toward Édouard and his boxes of peaches and condensed milk.

"WAIT," Dart yelled after them. "Tell me."

They stopped, and turned to him from about ten feet away.

"I'm looking for an Obeahwoman," he shouted. "Or a man. I want to experience it."

They looked at each other, and then back at him.

"You don't have to give me a NAME." Dart was suffering. "You can just POINT, like you did for the car."

Édouard looked at Eva. She walked past the two women, and

over to Dart. "Dude. Let's settle in," Eva said, soothing and silencing. "Then we can ask around." Eva turned to the women, hoping for a nod that included her in their sensibility. None came.

He has no finesse. Eva wanted to apologize for Dart, but sensed the futility. She wanted to provide him with a more articulate energy, but knew the desire was her trip, and was vain, as well.

"The only way you can find out things," Dart said to Eva, already ahead of her on the road, "is to ask."

"That's working real well for you about now." Eva stopped walking. "Do you have your pills?"

"They're not pills," he said, still stepping. "They're herbs."

"Do you have them?"

"They don't work like that," he said, not even over his shoulder. "If you wanted a brother on meds, you missed that window."

They walked, Eva behind Dart. The woman had pointed to a small white cottage with a closed door and an open service window. There was no lot.

"HELLO? Hello!" Dart yelled. "Anybody work here? HELLO?"

Eva, her mind made up to let Dart be Dart, slowly brought up the rear. Then Dart pounded a bell on the ledge three times.

"What the—"

"It's why the bell's here," Dart said to her.

From behind the cottage a man in neat slacks and a thin shirt emerged. "I can help you?"

"Yes, sir. How are you? We need a car," Eva said quickly, wanting to beat Dart.

"Your name? You reserved a car?"

"No," Eva said, "we didn't. Are there any?"

Dart stood next to her. Taking short, heaving breaths.

"I'm sorry. No car today. Maybe the day after tomorrow." The man, unfazed by the yelling and the bell-banging, spoke to Eva, and looked at Dart.

"Where are the cars?" Dart was accusatory. "Where do you keep them?" Dart marched toward the rear of the cottage while the man watched and made no move to stop him.

"Where are you staying?" the man asked Eva.

He's at least fifty. And he looks good. Eva sat in a metal chair and stretched out her legs, now that she could connect with someone minus Dart's histrionics. "We're trying to figure that out now," she said.

Eva reached in her bag for her cell, pressed ON, and watched the screen come to life. The notice flashed up: ELEVEN MESSAGES. Eva stared at it. Picked up the scrap of paper next to her phone.

"Can you tell me where is . . . Hermitage?"

"On the mountain?"

"Car-rental place? Maybe? Hotel?"

"You are at Hermitage Transport right now."

"Are you Ben?"

"I'm Benjamin. So you did call and reserve."

"Édouard gave me your name."

The password finally uttered, Benjamin laughed. "Eddie is my brother-in-law. What he promise with my name?"

"Nothing, really. He just gave it to me."

Benjamin took a drag from his cigarette, dropped it, and pressed his sandaled foot over it. "Well then," he said. "I guess that means you can ask of me anything."

"A car?"

"There are no cars. I don't lie. If I had one I would provide. It's my business."

Eva's phone rang.

From out of sight, Dart yelled, "Don't answer it."

"It's Eva," she said into the phone.

"Where are you? Tell me Dart's with you."

"Yeah, Sun. He is."

"What's going on?" Sun was as nosy as she was worried. "He's all right? Eva, you know Dart is supposed to be on . . . his stuff, and he stopped taking it, and . . . you see how he's been acting. Not crazy, but like—" Sun paused. "Where *are* you?"

Eva glanced around. Fishing boats with rods outsticking like hairpins, up-pointing like steeples. Every beige catamaran and blue dinghy with a number-stamped hull, every *Pure Visions* and *Kokanee* and *Carpe Diem* noosed by soaking lines but still nodding smugly with the secret of its ability to float.

"On the Out Islands," Eva said, like she could be on six hundred of them at the same time.

"That's what it's called? They have a spa? I should come there?"

"For what? We're fine."

Benjamin lit another cigarette.

"I knew you'd be good for him right now. After he told me he got that bracelet and everything, acting like he'd gotten you a square-cut diamond. It was so important to him and I was worried, but then I saw you had it on, but you were talking about Ron, so I just didn't know."

Yeah, yeah, whatever. "Where are *you?*"

"At the airport, about to fly to Miami. Went to the gospel brunch." Sunny added the last like a spoonful of honey.

"With who?" The question was in regards to all three statements.

There was a short pause. "Vic and Swan are with me," Sunny said. "Hawk's talking about getting on our flight. And Myra. Piper's coming down, to meet us at South Beach, to help me out, since Dart's . . . away."

Eva was silent.

"Ask, Eva. Ask."

"Kiss my ass."

"Ron's got a bungalow, at the Delano. And some guy from the Heat's got both penthouses, having some supposed-to-be-chill parties or whatever. So—"

"I gotta go," Eva said. She thought of the Delano with its airy lobby and billowing drapes. Thought of its back courtyard with the rows of coiffed palms and the chess set with pieces the size of boot boxes next to fluffy daybeds on a lawn so green and tight you could bowl balls on it straight into the pale blue pool. Eva thought of the Delano, and she wanted to be there with people she could predict. In a lofty duplex bungalow with a flagrant view of the Atlantic and a mini-bar with Glenfiddich and Perrier and Orangina and Famous Amos. The hotel suddenly held for her all the tenderness of an adored home.

"Car's coming to pick me up," Eva said sharply. "I'm out."

Benjamin smiled a bit to himself.

"Just gonna stay in Miami for a day or two, Eva. And don't go getting mad at Piper. She loves you. You and Dart come, to the Delano. Tell me now, so we can get suites big enough—"

"I'll call you." Eva pressed OFF. *So Piper's crying to Sunny, now.*

"Who was it?" Dart sidled up. He was disheveled and damp, as usual. And like he'd been walking through shrubbery. Standing next to Benjamin, who was neat and cool in the ninety-degree heat, Dart was anxious, and seemed, as he could sometime, half-embarrassed to be alive.

"Just work," Eva said. "I turned it off." Suddenly she was tired and hungry. A breeze came up, fluttered the skirts in the distance, and cleared for the moment the smog from Eva's head. She leaned her head against the cottage and closed her eyes. Thought of hotel room after hotel room, and Ron Lil' John in each one.

"You want a ride, you two?"

"Yes, *please*," Eva said. She looked at Benjamin like he'd offered up Dart's cure. "To anywhere."

———

Cat Island, from what Eva could tell, was shaped like a curved Band-Aid.

There were a half-dozen homegrown hotels, mostly clusters of tidy cottages. The Greenwood, and the Bridge Inn (both NO VACANCY), whose cottages were appointed with periwinkle columns, in no way qualified for the enormity of experience "resort" implied. Cat was all but untouched by commercialism or development.

Eva had no idea where they were going. Dart lolled in the backseat, dropping in and out of sleep. She kept turning to check on him, felt like his head might bounce too hard against the car window. As they rode along the main way in Benjamin's air-conditioned four-door, Eva saw a few intent people on bikes, but not a soul walking or driving.

Water here's so blue it looks chemically created, like a melted tropical Bomb Pop they sell off ice cream trucks in Manhattan.

Benjamin turned onto a narrow unpaved road. There were stone bungalows with thatched roofs. People sat talking on porches. Motor scooters leaned against yellow walls and whitewashed outdoor ovens. Gray satellite dishes mushroomed along Benjamin's route, huge and familiar and big enough, Eva thought, to sleep in.

Benjamin stopped at a house that would be considered small in most U.S. cities, but next to the others, it loomed like a manor. Dart scrambled from the backseat. In front of the big house with the shingled roof, Eva got out as Benjamin did. There was an asphalt path leading to the front door. The knocker was a marlin green with patina. In the near distance, blue-green sea lapped pink sand. Eva saw a smaller house off to the left. Clothes hung heavily there on a line.

"A nice place," Benjamin said, and he could have been talking about either house or both of them, or Cat Island itself.

"Real nice," Eva said. "And quiet." *Damn near the sound of silence.*

Dart walked to the front door and opened it without touching the marlin. Eva caught Benjamin's almost imperceptible frown, but she was too tired to apologize. They followed Dart in.

"How much is it?" Dart asked, like he was paying. He dropped his pack on the couch. The room was plainly furnished, and immaculate.

To Eva, Benjamin said, "Come see the patio."

Once outside, Dart bounded off to the shore. The patio was the same beige stone of the house. There was a lounge, a small table, and a few chairs. Brown-and-white striped cushions neatly stacked under a plank shelter.

"What's your name?"

"I'm sorry. It's Eva."

"You're from?"

"All over. But from the U.S."

"Yes, Eva, I guessed that."

The sun was setting. Eva looked at the unnaturally blue stretch of surf. Dart, with his shirt still on, walked purposefully out into the water, deeper and deeper. *He's fine. He's a grown man. Been around the damn world.* Dart's discordant self was rubbing off on her, though. She felt inadequate and muzzy.

"He's not your husband."

"No."

"Your boyfriend."

"Kind of," Eva said. And then she didn't like the casual way it sounded. She didn't want to be on a blasé encounter. Not on Cat Island, where Édouard's brother-in-law was being so gracious and comfortingly brusque. "I'm—"

"My wife and I," Benjamin said, "take care of this property. That's our house—" he waved toward the clothesline. "You can stay here tonight. No one is expected. Then tomorrow, when you and . . ."

"Dart," Eva said.

"—have rested, we'll see about a car. You can find a good place on Fernandez, or in Bight."

Wherever that is. "You're sure?" Eva was relieved as Benjamin nodded. "Thank you." The sun raged, the sky hot plum as Benjamin's shirt. His rounded forehead was lustrous enough in the light to make him seem wise, and his hair sat back on his head like a yarmulke. The Delano's blowy, sterile ambience seemed second-rate to her suddenly, and remote.

"Keep things neat," he said bluntly. "My wife will bring you something by. Her name is Audrey. Call me Ben."

"I can't put you through any more trouble."

"No trouble."

"You must like Édouard," Eva said, clumsily falling back on her wide, flirty smile.

"Eddie is Audrey's brother. I told you." Benjamin showed Eva the linens, and the restroom, and then left her.

In the first room she saw with a bed, Eva plugged in her cell phone and then lay down on the bare mattress. Tired as she was, she couldn't sleep.

She looked at the bracelet both Ron and Dart had given her, and her mind went straight to late 1977. *A banner year for pop music.*

Eva was in seventh heaven. Right outside Carmel, California, in a snug living room that doubled as Eva's bedroom. Her family lived in a rented caretaker's bungalow behind an estate inhabited only during the summer. Eva'd never seen the owners, but liked them for providing such an excellent stereo. At eleven years old, Eva was slim as a Siamese cat. Dark hair parted down the middle and pulled into a severe ponytail, she was in jeans and Kinney tennis shoes and a *Good Times* T-shirt. She wore, as was her habit, a tangle of self-braided yarn and lanyard bracelets and flea-market bangles on both wrists.

Because her parents moved a lot, and what was breakable, broke, her parents held onto only a few Stevie Wonder albums, some other Motown artists, and some jazz vocalists. Eva was a radio junkie. By holding her cassette recorder next to the speaker in the living room, she could tape all her faves. At eleven, there was much to be fascinated by—what had before sounded like grown folks' pleading conversations, or like *tinkle-ring-snap* for her to bounce around to in the car, now sounded big and pure and directed toward her. The Jackson 5's 1970 *ABC* was the only album Eva considered "hers," and as "ABC" was the song the album was named for, she figured it to be the most important, and had begun to listen to it endlessly for all the bells and the rises and the short silent spaces, for Jackie's part, Jermaine's part, and Michael's main part. All the boy's voices fit the other's perfectly, like rushing liquid puzzle pieces.

Ow! Eva shivered to Michael's ad libs and to drums gone for a second and then drums back in a rush. Thrilled by the Jacksons' urgency and rhyme, Eva was wowed to find out from her mother that "do-re-me" were musical notes, and that there was a song from a movie (titled, perfectly, Eva thought, *The Sound of Music*) called "Do-Re-Mi." Everything came together—*Me, a name I call myself* was woven tightly in Eva's mind to Michael's breathtaking *Come on come on come on lemme show you what it's all about.*

Whenever she was near a radio, Eva listened to the stories in and about songs, searched for meanings and connections between them. In the evenings, when Eva's homework was done and her parents were tense or out or one of them was alone in the bedroom with *Little House on the Prairie* on blast, she twisted open a three-pack of fresh, blank TDK (high bias!) ninety-minute tapes. And on the ruled, folded slip TDK provided, Eva neatly penned the song titles and artists and other pertinent info (culled mostly from disc jockeys, her mother's *Ebony*, her father's *Rolling Stone*, and her own *Right On!*). Eva even taped index cards to the folded slip, so as to have more room for her own liner notes. By writing and rereading the info, Eva felt organized and thorough, and like she could get a better handle on why a song made her feel happy, or sad, or like dancing. Eva lived for the feeling of music, but had a taste for the art and science of it as well.

With her GE cassette recorder/player (black with a wood veneer) aligned perpendicular to the speaker (it was the best way, Eva'd found, after experimenting), and sitting so she could press the record and play buttons, as well as reach the volume and tuner on the receiver, Eva silently cursed the radio DJ for talking over the first bars of the Emotions' "Best of My Love." The beginning notes of the song—all zip and anticipation—was what Eva had been angling to get on tape for weeks. Eva loved the Emotions for their straightforward name, and for the romance of gospel siblings Wanda, Sheila, and Jeanette, previously known as the Sunbeams, fighting their way to the Top Forty with selfless aid from the valiant Maurice White, leader of her heroes, Earth, Wind & Fire.

Eva turned the dial with precision, knowing exactly the distance between her desired stations, looking for her song. Eva could tell by looking at the amount of tape left on the cassette that there was just enough room on Side B for "Best of My Love." This tape was crucial, and almost done. A perfect collage, Eva thought, of how people felt about life and love in 1977.

"Ain't Gonna Bump No More (With No Big Fat Woman)": **Joe Tex,** used to write words for songs for James Brown. Can't believe he said the woman is fat. Mean, but a good song.

"Rich Girl": **Daryl Hall and John Oates,** white, but sound like they are black. Number 1 in the Top 40. Says BITCH in it!

"Just the Way You Are": **Billy Joel.** Cute. Short. Sunglasses. Better than Barry Manilow, but kind of the same as B. Manilow. Both sound very real and like they mean it.

"Lovely Day": **Bill Withers,** born on Independence Day. This is the best song of happiness. He has other good songs from before this.

"High School Dance": **The Sylvers.** Foster is fine and he can sing. Trying to be Jackson-like and doing it so good. Best song. Best! Best! Best!

"More Than A Woman": **Tavares.** Hate the name of this group. Good idea from lead singer to be *more* than woman to a boyfriend. A wife, a friend. Also: A BeeGees song?

"Gloria": **Enchantment.** Nothing is better except Stevie Wonder and also Enchantment has "It's You that I Need," which is number one in my soul. "Gloria" was also Number 1 in the Top 40.

"Sir Duke": **Stevie Wonder,** but also made me learn about other people. Dad's favorite.

"Looks Like We Made It": **Barry Manilow.** Number 1 in the Top 40. Like it because it seems happy from the title, but when you pay attention, it's sad.

"I Wanna Get Next to You": Best song ever. Hate name of group: **Rose Royce.** Mom says it's a car.

"Keep Me Cryin'": **Al Green.** Only for Dad.

"Peg": **Steely Dan.** Neither man in group is named Dan. The song is not steely. Dad told me what blueprint blue is. Love this song. The voices.

"Short People": **Randy Newman.** I can't believe someone made a song like this. Saying the things said. I love this song.

"Christine 16": Rocks! **KISS!** No age rhymes with Eva or Evey.

"Boogie Nights": **Heatwave.** Their name paints a picture of who they are and what song is like.

"Don't it Make My Brown Eyes Blue": **Crystal Gayle.** Number 2 in the Top 40. Blue is sad, not the color. Mom explained.

"Evey. Baby."

"Hmm?" Still on the floor, twirling the knob from station to station, Eva heard her mother come in the back door.

"I'm here, but Mommy's gotta go." Eva's mother's name was Elaine, and at thirty-one, in this new town, she'd stopped introducing herself as Lanie.

"Where to?" Eva asked absently. "I'm going?" She didn't want to miss another chance at the Emotions.

"Mommy's gonna be gone for a lil' while." Elaine sounded stressed, but that was standard.

So Eva paid her no attention.

"A little *while*, Evey. It's bad. Mommy's packing a bag."

"Why?" The word was a placeholder.

"I told you. Evey." Elaine stood in the door between the bedroom and the living room. She'd been crying for weeks, and had cried right before she came back to the bungalow. Elaine had imagined this scene a hundred times—how seeing Eva would confuse her, how grueling it would be to stay on course for departure. Eva seemed unnaturally vivid to Elaine—hair black as soot, red shirt too tight and wanting to burst into flames. The music was erratic and ghostly, and Eva's fine future emanated from her in a glow. All this was excruciating. But Elaine was braced, and had been coached by her new man. Elaine wore justification and fatigue over her eyes like shades. "You know you're my baby girl, right? My smart pretty lady."

"Yeah." Eva was intent on the stereo.

Elaine made her teary voice playful. "Play Mommy her songs, then."

Eva sighed, irritated. "Mom, I'm trying to—"

"Play me some Temptations, Evey. I know you have them on one of those tapes. 'My Girl,' or something. Nothing from after they kicked Ruffin out. Play it for me while I'm packing."

"I don't have 'My Girl.'" Eva did, but she hated it. Radio still played it relentlessly, and she was sick of it. "I have that rain song."

"Play that, then," Elaine said, her smile strong and fake. "And come talk to me."

Eva went through her orderly Tupperware bin of tapes and found MOM'S FAVES VOL. 1. She slipped the unfinished 1977 compilation from the player, put her mom's in, fast-forwarded to "I Wish It Would Rain," pressed PLAY, and carried her cassette player by its handle into the bedroom. The closet was torn through.

"What are you doing?" Eva had sensed a building-up, but thought, when she thought about it, that the buildup was toward another move for the three of them, like usual. But this wasn't how a move usually went down. "What are you looking for?"

"I had to get my stuff, Evey."

Eva stood there with the chunky player dangling from her hand. Her mother's voice—*Sad?* Eva thought. *Mad?*—seemed to be holding a lot of things. Elaine was placing folded clothes in a green army duffel Eva'd never seen before, but even moving slowly and precisely, she seemed hysterical. Eva didn't know enough to sense guilt and vacillation. "So I'll get my stuff," Eva said, not moving, still clutching the tape player, and hearing raindrops and seamless harmonies and thinking that she was already away from the radio now, anyway, so she wouldn't be getting the Emotions. Eva began to twist the tape player nervously. The music playing was distorted. "For how many days?" Eva said. She accidentally bit a hole inside her bottom lip and almost yelped. "How many underwears?" Eva was shaking.

"Underwear. Mommy's gonna give you this note for your dad," Elaine said. "For when he comes home."

"Where will you be?" Eva saw her mom leaving. Eva realized this was no like-usual, Mom's-mad, overnight trip. But Eva couldn't comprehend that her mother would leave for a long time, without saying where, and without taking her. Tears started down Eva's cheeks.

"Evey, Mommy's sorry." Elaine was struggling, but she'd added everything up—hatred of her husband, a hard-core and hopeless puzzlement about herself, a skewed, bitter respect for her husband, and a chance to be with a daring man who oiled her hard feet and encouraged her coldnesses. Eva, Elaine told herself, would be better off without a mother who always needed a new man who looked at her with fresh eyes. She knew it was cowardly and that it was the path of least resistance, but still to leave, and to return when Eva was old enough to listen to an explanation and an apology with a woman's ears—it was what had to be done, Elaine felt, or she might damage Eva, or physically hurt Ned, or herself.

Eva was abruptly tired of "Evey," and she wished, for a reason she couldn't put her finger on, that her mother would say "I," instead of "Mommy."

"How are you getting there?" Eva, in her father's manner, went straight to logistics as things became incomprehensible. "Dad's got the car." Eva heard Foreigner on the radio from the living room. *You're as cold as ice / Willing to sacrifice my love.*

The radio's off. The song's in my head. Eva couldn't hear her mother's rain song anymore.

"Mom!" Eva screeched it.

"Evey." The word was half of a whisper.

"I thought you *wanted to hear the Temptations.*"

Elaine moved into the living room, crammed duffel bag dragging. She looked around, and then went to the kitchen and opened the refrigerator. It let out a gasp of ripe cantaloupe and spoiling milk. "There's lots in here." Elaine was blinking and blinking. She wouldn't look at Eva, who was standing by the stereo. The rain song had faded into the raucousness of "Ain't Too Proud to Beg."

Eva couldn't hear it, because her mind was clicking. *There's a song for everything.* "Go Your Own Way" by Fleetwood Mac, "Just a Song Before I Go" by whoever, I can't remember, "Don't Leave Me This Way" by Thelma Houston, "The First Cut Is the Deepest" by Rod Stewart, "Say You'll Stay Until Tomorrow" by Tom Jones, "She's Not There" by Santana. There is a song that describes every single thing. They're in my head. I could make a tape I could make a tape.*

"When are you coming home!" Eva was demanding now. "What am I going to say when Dad asks!"

"Evey, Mommy's gonna go." Elaine walked to the door and took a quick look around. But she had all she was taking.

"Take the Tempts, Mom. It's a lot of good songs on here other than the rain song. 'My Girl' is on here."

"Mommy just needs a break, baby. You keep your tape. You keep it for me." She touched Eva's wrist, tugged her bracelets, and Eva hated her.

A break from me? "Elaine!" Eva was frantic. She tasted blood in her mouth. "What day are you coming back!"

Elaine looked at her daughter and told her the truth. "Soon as I can, Evey. Might be a little while, though. You're gonna be good. Such a good girl. I'll come back as soon as it's okay."

What's changed. That's what Eva wanted to know. *I'm here on some weird island, but what's changed?*

She heard Benjamin's car start and the radio.

You make my heart beat.

You make me feel so real.

Eva thought she heard Dart trudge in right before she fell asleep.

———————

E va woke to the odor of sweating onion. She'd no idea where she was. In her next breath, she took in Dart's musky spoiled apricot smell and her stomach flipped with nausea and hunger.

Dart. Cat Island. Out Islands. Pregnant. Dart. Édouard and Benjamin. No Sun. Ron.

She resisted the impulse to go knock on Benjamin's door, ask if dinner was coming now.

This is not a hotel. Eva got up, grabbed her cell, walked outside, and dialed Ron's number. It was night.

He answered the phone, puffing. "You better had called."

"I better had? For what?" Eva almost smiled a tight smile.

"Where are you?"

"What're you all doing in Miami?"

"Living," he said. "Handling business."

"Stay out of Sun's head."

"If you were here, you wouldn't have to worry about all that. If you were smart, you'd let me think you had everything under control. But you're not smart right now." He paused, but Eva didn't say anything. "Why you dial my number then? Need rescue from the crazy house? Where'd Sun say you were . . . Out Island? What the fuck is that? Rehab? For your boy?"

He's not on drugs. He's off them. "What's Piper doing?"

"Up under Sunny. Why do you worry about stupid shit? Sun wants you. She needs you to run point for her. You got her on lock, yet you're holed up with homeboy like your life's over because you're pregnant."

"Stop saying that!" The thought of anyone from her real life knowing about her pregnancy and making chess moves based on what Eva felt was a chink in her armor made her panicky. "Who're you standing by?"

"Calm down. Get to Miami. I brought your shit."

"What?" This wasn't something Eva expected.

"It was handled. Lost City packed you up. You were checked out. Your stuff's here."

So happy about his gesture, she acted the exact opposite. "What if I needed my things?"

"What if you said, 'Thank you, Ron. Thank you for thinking of my runaway ass.'"

"I barely brought anything over here." *What if you said, I'm coming to get you, Eva. Coming to read your mind and do everything that will make you happy.*

"Your stuff's in the hotel lockup. Here. So you need to ask yourself what that means for your plans. Have you taken care of what you're so anxious to take care of?"

Eva was silent.

Ron said hotly, "Hello?"

"No."

"Have you told the father? Have you asked the father?"

"I'm not talking about the father."

"I know you know who he is."

She was silent.

"Stop," he said, "with the quiet shit."

"I'm getting off the phone."

"It isn't me, Eva."

She was silent.

"Confirm that," Ron said. "Before you get off the phone. Confirm it."

She pictured his paw around his cell. Big, dull fingers, nails round and flat as nickels.

"Playing bullshit games," he said. "I hope your ass finds a life over there. I'm done." And hung up his phone.

Eva stood there, phone in hand. She felt a presence, flinched. A small woman was behind her. "Have some tuna and some grits for you," the woman said. Her voice was keen as Édouard's apple blade. Her skin as creamy brown as ganache.

"You're Audrey?" *Tuna and grits? Together?*

"*M'rele* Audrey," she said, squinting in the moonlight. "Wife of Benjamin. Sister of Édouard. You, Eva, have met everyone but me."

I guess. "Thanks for the food." She opened the door to the house. "Dart's asleep."

"He should be hungry, too, after that swim." Audrey slid two broad tins on the table. Her eyes were heartbroken and mean. Her earlobes dangled in halves. Audrey was younger than Eva by three years and looked ten years older. "I have dessert. Later. Everything you need."

"You saw him."

"All of him. No towel 'round himself walking to the house. I laughed."

Laughed at what? And if you did, why are you telling me? Rude. "Your husband said he'd help us find a car," Eva said. "So we could find a real place to stay for tomorrow. We'll be out of your hair."

"My hair is fine. You have money?"

"Yeah," Eva said easily.

Audrey's head sat back on her neck. "Then this a real place to stay." Her eyes went colder than they were to begin with, but Eva was looking at Audrey's hands as she peeled foil back from the tins, then at chunks of fish in there with cooked-down tomato and green pepper. Eva wanted to grab it with her fingers, steaming grits and all. Wanted to tell somebody she was pregnant, and that whether it had to do with the baby or not, she was so hungry, she was light-headed.

"You can go to the store in the morning," Audrey continued tersely, "so you have snacks in the box. You can eat supper at our house tomorrow."

Eva was surprised at the invitation. "That's all right?" *Leave please, so I can eat.*

"You have money, it's okay with me." Audrey stood in the doorway. "So it will be okay with Benjamin. What the Rowes don't know doesn't hurt them. They come in the summer months, when it's so hot they melt. Sit inside all day, with the fans. All the way here from . . . Pennsylvania for what."

Eva assumed the Rowes to be the owners of the stone house. *Let me at least try to be friendly.* As Audrey walked back toward her place, Eva called out, "I guess it's a good thing we were on Édouard's boat."

"Eddie wishes that was his boat," she answered without turning back to face Eva. A bun of braids rested on her neck like a turtle's shell. "But it's his birthday tomorrow, so who knows." And Audrey was gone.

Eva shut the screen and settled into the food like a hound. Dart woke up and joined her. They ate from the tins with found plastic spoons.

"You swam naked." She was chewing and angry at his freedom. He was buoyant and without responsibility for anyone but himself.

"Earlier? Yep. You missed out. We'll do it tomorrow. You're gonna be glad you came here."

Eva nodded. *Just say it.* She wanted to give him something to deal with. Wanted to come clean—be the pregnant woman who would either have the baby and get the tummy-rub accolades or have the abortion and get the pitying or disgusted looks. Eva wanted to state her truth on tiny Cat Island where she was far away from everything and almost everyone that mattered. "I hope you know," she said, "I'm pregnant."

"No way."

"How about 'congratulations'? Or, 'How far along are you'?"

"You can't be too far along." He ladled more food in his mouth. "Are you having it?"

"I need to." The everydayness about the way he was responding relaxed her. *Your boy's moods swing.* She heard Ron's voice in her head.

"Well then, congratulations. It's a blessing."

"I've been pregnant three times before."

He put his spoon down. "Damn." His face was full of pity and curiosity.

"It's my problem."

"I get it now," Dart said, like long-standing questions had been answered. "Why you came over here."

"Not to be felt sorry for."

"You're the one acting like somebody died." He stopped. Started again, slowly. "Some people, a female in your situation might make the announcement, even to me, the man you're over here with, the man who's not even the father, with some happiness. I'm saying the reason you came over here is because the baby made up your mind for you. And maybe for me. This could be perfect. This could be the culmination of a dream neither of us dared to have. This, us all here—this could be the baby's dream."

"Dart, you're not the father."

"I just said that. I know that." He scooted back a bit from the table. "Have I been?"

"No."

"So maybe this one . . . is supposed to be spiritually ours. Maybe he wants us to be here. The three of us, together."

Eva was stunned. *He. What if it is a he? A she? Not an it.* She didn't speak.

"He'd get here, when?"

Eva knew that, or had a good idea. "May, I think. Or early June."

"A Gemini," Dart said like he was announcing a name at a commencement. "Powerful. Represented by twins. Gemini is the *communicator* of the Zodiac—you know? He's communicating with you *now*, already! And 1999 will be the year of the Rabbit, I think, or the Cat. In Chinese, I mean."

Twins. "I haven't thought about that kind of stuff—"

"Eva, look *around* here. What better place to be? Can't you see yourself, getting round, being healthy, sitting in the water here, bringing our boy into the world in a place like this? This is a chance to be taken."

There were footsteps. Then Audrey tapped on the door and walked in at the same time. She had crêpes suzette in a closed tin, wrapped in a thick cloth.

Audrey stood waiting while they tasted them. Eva concentrated on the brown edges of her crêpe where the brandy—she thought it was brandy—seemed to collect. And so much butter—unsalted butter, sweet with having almost spoiled.

"These are heaven," Eva said, spinning from Dart's soliloquy, and trying again to be pleasant. "With the fresh orange juice. And the bits of zest."

"Haitian oranges," Audrey said, like to preschoolers, "are bitter for a reason."

Eva assumed Audrey was referring to the conditions of Haitian laborers. The ones who pick and peel oranges without toilets near, or washing facilities. Whose fingernails corrode from the citric acid. The ones who get paid a pittance above slave wages so people around the world can sip orange liqueur. Eva ate her crêpe, satisfied and proud she'd read about the plight.

Dart was caught up in other possibilities. "Why?" he said, mouth full of food, eyes still famished, and ready with inquiry. "Bitter, why?"

"Centuries of blood in the soil," Audrey said, more like a sage this time. "And the spirits that live among the thorny trees." Audrey, her patient eyes as clear with contempt as Dart's were with desperation, looked to Eva.

Eva flashed Audrey the kind of hot glare mothers reserve for those mean to children.

"So you know about that kind of stuff," Dart said eagerly. "About spirits and voodoo and Obeah. Me and Eva—"

"Do not *speak* of it," Audrey said to him in the same solemn tone. "You must not talk of such things. Eat your food, boy. How do you tempt such powers to notice you, when you are so blessed?"

"I'm not blessed all the way," he said. "You don't know."

Eva wanted to slap him. *How is he letting Audrey play him like this? And he just said the baby was a blessing. Even without the baby, he and me have only the problems of the blessed. This woman is enjoying herself.*

"Eat," Audrey said. "I will not stay another moment in a room so filled with recklessness. Leave the tins on the porch." She walked from the house.

Dart was thunderstruck by the melodrama. "Unbelievable," he said to Eva. "We walk right into it. Right after you tell me about the baby."

Eva followed Audrey out the door. Moonlight washed gray the patchy lawn between the two houses. "You like to tease, I see."

"How can I not?" Audrey said. "He's such a baby. Eyes so sad and wide open." Audrey's hands were free, and even her shrug was hostile.

"He's got problems." *Bitch.*

"Problems that you can't fix? He's a big good-looking boy. As you told me today—"

"What did I tell you today?"

"You're staying here," Audrey snapped, morally offended by the interruption. "Will be nice. Eddie talks nicely of Miss Eva and Mister Dart."

"Oh, *okay.* I get it now. I said we have *money.* You asked."

"I was supposed to ask."

Eva said, "Bye, Audrey," and started back toward the Rowe house. Eva was dismissive but polite. It was a knack of hers.

"Or maybe it's you? With the problems."

Eva turned. *I will curse this bitter bitch out, I swear I will do it, and sleep at whatever shack of an airport they have on this piece of shit island.* She wanted a Scotch.

"Why's your hand rest on your belly like that, Eva? Dart's already put you in a fix?" Audrey widened her eyes, in sage mode again. "You came to Cat, the island of the supernatural, to find someone to fix your problem, in the old ways." Hers were not words as birds.

"We're leaving tomorrow, Audrey." Eva wanted to rush her, rub Audrey's face in the pink sand.

"Oh no, Miss Eva. Eddie expects you at his birthday celebration."

A *chain of 700 islands, the Bahamas stretch from north of Haiti to east of Florida. The capital city is Nassau, on New Providence Island. Other principal islands are known as "out islands" or "family islands," and include Crooked Island, The Berrys, Cat Island, The Inagua Islands, Eleuthra, Andros, San Salvador, and the Biminis.*

Per capita income: $15,000 (Haiti $500, United States $35,000).

Exports: fish, lobsters, rum, salt. Main income sources: tourism and ship registration.

Population: 308,000. Many islands and cays are without population. Sixty-six percent of Bahamians live in New Providence.

Infant mortality rate is 13 per 1,000 births (Cuba 7, Haiti 79, U.S. 7). Water and electricity supplies are good. Health problems are due mostly to overconsumption. HIV/AIDS is widespread.

British colonialism competed for almost three centuries with North American influences. A majority black population, descended from slaves, was marginalized for generation upon generation, but the political (though not economic) power of the white minority was cracked during the 1960s.

English is the official language of the Bahamas. A migrant population of approximately 50,000 speaks Haitian Creole.

————————

On the sandy bedclothes. There was grit in Dart and Eva's sex. Pillows were folded in half, rolled under heads or under butts. Thin sheets and blankets wash-worn at the edges, salt-scented and stiff from drying in sea air. Dart's voice was airy, yawning, and arcane, like from a shell at Eva's ear. Then he got up to pee.

I need to dance. With people I don't know. In loose pants and a tight top with straps skinnier than my bra's. Until I'm wet with sweat I need to dance. While I'm still young. Before I'm grown and somebody's mother.

"I'm not sure I'm gonna find a voodoo priestess here," Dart said, "to exorcise demons from my soul or anything. It's the *trek* I want to be on. I don't want my trek to be running Sunny around the world, some tie to her former self. She's holding on to me, not knowing I'm barely holding on, period."

"She knows."

"I know who I am, Eva. What my strengths are and aren't."

"You're ahead of me, then," Eva said, and she meant it.

"I'm not stupid—there's probably nothing in them herb capsules but starch. But they're magic to me when I'm in the dark. A couple of times, you've been magic for me."

"But what about inflicting . . . yourself . . . on yourself?" she said, loving the idea of being magic for someone, but playing his words short because she thought herself too tainted to be wonder-working, and him too much in need of a real diagnosis and meds. "Or on . . . other people?"

"Only person I'm inflicting myself on is you."

"Why?" She really wanted the answer.

"Among other things," he said, reaching for her calf and stroking it, "because you had the bracelet on. I told you. It was meant. Why are you looking at me like that?"

"How do you know I'm looking at you? You're not even looking at me."

"I feel your stare," he said as though he were a Halloween ghoul. "It's cold."

"You're bananas."

"At last," Dart said, grabbing Eva's calf so hard, she jumped. His voice came back to its normal timbre. "She sees me."

Eva woke up just as the sun rose. She picked up a buckram-covered book from the nightstand.

> Baja mar *("shallow sea")* is the name the Spanish gave the islands. *The Lukku-cairi were the first settlers. Originally from South America, they came to the Bahamas around the ninth century A.D. Christopher Columbus wiped out most of the population of every Bahamian island in which he came into contact.*

Eva got out of bed without waking Dart. She pulled the sheet over his bare feet and left the fan twirling slowly above him. Under an overhead shower with weak pressure, Eva washed with flat, unscented, latherless soap, unwrapped from crumbling waxed paper. Then she was nude on the living room couch.

> *The islands drew pirates such as Blackbeard and Henry Morgan . . . following Britain's defeat in the American Revolutionary War, southern loyalists brought slaves to the Bahamas and cultivated cotton. During the American Civil War, [white] Bahamians grew rich running Confederate cotton to English mills and sending military equipment to Confederates . . . During Prohibition, the Bahamas were transformed into a base for rum-running.*

Everything is connected, Eva thought. *There's no paradise. Just places called that—relative to other places. There's no pure place. No pure victory, pure love, or pure crime. No pure way.*

Eva pulled on panties and a red sliplike dress and walked from the deck out to a low footbridge. She sat on it, her feet dangling over a tidal pool. The sky was warming. Eva had on the bracelet from Ron and Dart, and a plastic orange one she'd found in the medicine cabinet. It was supposed to keep away mosquitoes.

Behind Eva, a few trees were spread with yards of wet fabric dyed red, gold, and mossy green. The sand had drops of dye and wax in it. She walked over, put the book down, picked up a wax drop, and was flattening the sand-covered bean when Dart came outside. He was wide awake and moving loudly.

"I went to find Benjamin," Dart said. "His wife told me the whole thing's worked out. She's deep. Said she saw it in me that I'm on a mission."

Eva was irritated by the intrusion. "I don't know for how long it's 'worked out,'" she said.

"It's a perfect compromise," Dart said, certain. "You get to live nice. But on my budget. I talked to her about the rate." He looked at her with a gleam. "We found a family that lets a room."

"It's a house. And it's not theirs. If you don't care about money, why spend so much time thinking about how it's doled out, who's paying for what?" She tossed her sand bean at him, but he didn't flinch.

"Because you're like this . . . huge . . . measuring stick." Dart dropped his shorts and walked toward the water.

Eva sat in the sand under the dyed fabric next to neat rows of orangey-pink starfish, set on their backs to dry. *No sand flies on the beach like there were in Rio de Janeiro.* Eva had been there twice, each time to Ipanema for video shoots. What she remembered were hotel rooms. Nightclubs. A little samba, but mostly she remembered the world she and her compadres had imported. That and the sand flies. And Ron drunkenly suggesting a three-way. Eva picked up the book again.

On Cat Island, this magic is called "Obeah." The name originates from the Ashanti word "oba," for child, and "eah," to take. The name originates from the final test of the "Obeah-man," to "take" a child's soul. Some believe that in order to become an Obeahman one must have killed a child. When a child dies, it is sometimes assumed that Obeah is at work.

Eva's body tensed. She swallowed a swell of nausea. She didn't turn, but her eyes rose from the book and looked slightly to the left and right for the shadow of what was on her back.

"You like the batik," Audrey said flatly. "You'll have to buy ten from me."

"You like to walk up on people."

"You like to stare into space."

"I'm reading." *And thinking in weeks.* Eva was thinking also of her kidnapped luggage. Thinking of Ron. Thinking in weeks. Thinking of her child's soul. Her children's souls. "I may have to buy one, though, depending on how long we stay."

"Days or weeks? Months. It doesn't matter."

Weeks. Maybe until May. If I stay until then, I'm AWOL. There's a hospital on Nassau? I could do it. Dart and I can do it if he'd just be a little more normal. I could take a leave of absence. It's crazy. But Dart's crazy enough to make crazy happen.

"Come with me to the store," Audrey said. "Have to get things for *m'fré pati*."

Eva looked toward Dart. He walked waist deep through water, parallel to the shoreline. He picked his steps carefully and looked toward the bottom.

"What will he do?" Audrey said, "Drown?"

"Come on, then," Eva said. "Let's go now."

"Now I must hurry-hurry, so Eva can get back to her man. He will surely die without her for a quarter hour." Audrey pressed her fingers into the cloth, came to a conclusion Eva couldn't decipher. Then Audrey turned over a starfish, weighed it in her hand, and looked at Eva with lips tight. "Can I go for my list first? We have time for that?"

"What are the starfish for?"

"For to sell," Audrey said, like Eva was stupid. "These my wares here drying." She motioned for Eva to follow, and before Eva could protest, Audrey'd placed the rusted bars of a bike in her hands.

Eva hadn't been on a bike since college, but figured the ride was an Audrey-type down-to-earth test, and decided she'd pass it with colors.

Audrey told her that they were on the "Caribbean" side of Cat, where the water—especially of the bay called the Bight—was mostly calm. The Atlantic side, she said, was choppy and dangerous. The Rowe House and Audrey and Benjamin's were near New Bight, where there was a tiny airport. Just when Eva started feeling every dip and pebble in the road, a small green plane dove to land.

Audrey looked from the plane to Eva as if to say, *There's your proof, if you don't believe me.*

There were more signs of life on Cat than when Benjamin had driven them from Smith Bay. A man fed a kid goat with a huge bottle. A trio of girls in school uniform exchanged giggles. There was a browned blond couple on foot, with wraparound sunglasses, loudly praising a place called Tea Bay. The island, Audrey told her, was shaped like a young lady's stocking, and that Cat was in fact 130 miles from Nassau.

Thanks. For the fun facts. Eva panted and pumped. They kept at their slow ride, Eva always just far enough behind for Audrey to look at Eva like she was a slug, and for Eva to look at Audrey like Audrey was an overseer.

"Me and Eddie come from Haiti fifteen years ago now," she called out as they passed a plantation house with a sign before it announcing PIGEON BAY. It was a place collapsing in the slowest of motions. Hot wind scraped Eva's scalp like a pitchfork. She perspired. She had a worry about Dart, like he required her presence, though he'd said nothing of the kind.

Eva slowed, stopped, got off her bike, and walked it. Audrey pedaled into the distance, past walking tourists in red bathing suits, past a lone minitruck filled with fishing poles and sunburned faces. Eva had no idea whether she was right or not, but she didn't think the jolting and pumping could be good for her pregnancy. She was fiending for some rules, angry she had no experience, and was too proud to ask Audrey, or anyone, for guidance.

Up ahead, Audrey stopped near a neat cinder-block hut with a tin roof. She stood with the bike between her legs, arms stretched to the broad handlebars.

"You can ride, Eva," Audrey called out courteously. "It won't hurt the baby."

For the first time, Eva sensed in Audrey no smart-ass, no cold-ness. Eva kept walking her bike, though. *One thing I'm not going to do is hurt it by accident.*

"You and Benjamin don't have kids, Audrey?"

"I do," she said shortly, as they walked into the dank store. "Two girls. In Port-au-Prince." Audrey cradled a rice sack under her breast. "They work now. Since I've seen my daughters. Almost women."

Audrey picked up a few more things, and when they left the store, Eva got on her bike and rode. Audrey watched as Eva flew down a small hill, not knowing Eva was crying. Pedals slapped her bare feet as she recalled chances. *First babies would be in high school. Third one would be in elementary. The other one, seven years old. And this one, right here with me, speaking for its brothers — You ain't nobody's mother. Won't be anyone's mother. You could have tried. We don't even rate a grave.* Eva claimed the sacrifices she'd made and thrashed against the catch-22's that knotted her sense of self and always would. *I wish I hadn't had those abortions. My freedom's not worth those babies never coming to life. If I had it to do again, though, I'd do the same thing.* Eva swerved and scraped her leg bloody against a fence post and then crashed into a grassy mound. Eva lay flat on her back, coughing and crying. She was happy, though, to feel sad. And she had a terrifying, concrete feeling that her baby was all right.

"It's just my calf," she choked out to a panicked Audrey, who zoomed up and helped Eva to her feet. "Ain't nobody dying."

———

There was one deep, clean V-shaped cut and a distorted graph of abrasions. Eva's leg throbbed as Benjamin cleaned it with a solution that flowed bright clear red from the bottle and turned the pan of water he was using tea-brown. Dart was awestruck. They were on the Rowe House patio.

"Eddie uses this to soak his iguanas," Ben said while he washed Eva's leg. "Betadine." She braced for a sting but none came. Her blood swirled in the water and made it brighter.

Eva waved away a glass of ginger ale, and Audrey frowned at her, anxious.

"Iguanas," Dart mumbled, gazing at Benjamin's fingers. Eva was dizzy.

"Don't see the point of keeping them," Benjamin went on matter-of-factly. "Mean creatures, standoffish, picky about their space."

"Eddie doesn't keep them anymore," Audrey said. She looked at Eva, who was looking at Dart. "Keep quiet about them, Benny."

"Quiet about iguanas?" He shook his head and shrugged. "Quiet about the iguanas."

"Do you eat them?" Dart asked Audrey.

"Eat them?" Ben stopped rinsing Eva and looked at Dart like he was a child. "They bite and they swing their tails and they stare and stare—"

"Benjamin! Eva's leg needs to be wrapped." There was no more blood flowing.

Eva wanted to vomit, but she swallowed, and took the ginger ale when Audrey pushed it on her again.

Audrey handed Benjamin gauze and a roll of tape. "I guess none of the Tylenol or aspirin for you?"

Eva shook her head. She was in pain, but wanted nothing to touch the baby.

Sink your teeth right through my bones / Baby / Let's see what we can do.

She lay back on the chaise and let the sun wash over her. Eva didn't feel luxurious, but like the hot light might medicate, make the pulsing pain smaller by comparison, and seal her wounds finally. *Come on and make it hurt / Hurt so good.* It was a John Mellencamp song, from when he still was John "Cougar" Mellencamp. *From the* American *Fool album. Nineteen . . . nineteen eighty-something . . .*

Benjamin folded a cushion and put it under Eva's ankle. "Sleep," he said. "If you feel like seeing Eddie tonight, you come over—"

"You rest," Audrey said, and gave Benjamin a sharp look. When she picked up the pan and started away with it, Dart looked up from his daze.

"What are you going to do with that?" He asked Audrey.

"Bathe in it," Audrey said angrily. "And boil what's left up for soup."

Eva was asleep for four hours. When she woke, Dart was showering sand from his body. She washed up and fashioned a dress from a piece of green cloth Audrey'd left her. Eva tightened but didn't change her bandage.

"You're sure you want to go."

"Of course we're going," Eva said. "It's for Édouard." Like she'd known him for years.

Leaning on Dart's arm, Eva limped barefoot over to the smaller house. Her leg burned, and she thought it might be leaking behind the bandage.

"You okay?"

Eva pressed her molars together. "No."

Dart picked her up and carried her into Audrey and Benjamin's spotless, light-trimmed house, just as guests were starting to arrive for Eddie's party.

Her mind was blown clean. Eva was in the air, helpless and being helped. As Dart sat her on a low couch, and pushed a footstool under her injured leg, there was no doubt for Eva that she'd come to the right place.

This ain't no record industry after-party.
There was Édouard and Ben and Audrey. A youngish guy with a crunchy natural Ben introduced as his helper from down at Hermitage Rental. Another man old enough, and looking like Ben enough, to be Ben's father. Ben introduced him as Jeeter. Jeeter was slightly bent over, in ragged canvas slip-ons and neat, creased slacks that had been cut off at the knees and hemmed with a cuff. His palms were amber, and in the place of three fingernails were pinched black scars. Dart was transfixed by Jeeter. Shook his hand solemnly, spoke in an awed murmur. Jeeter was impressed to meet such a polite American boy.

"You like that man," Eva said when Dart came over to check on her.

She enjoyed being checked on—the status of her pregnancy and her injury and the idea of being Dart's date at the party. Her leg throbbed.

"Whether I like him," Dart said, like a new jack quoting Garvey, "is beside the point. "He either knows the way, or he is the way."

A woman of about twenty walked in with a small box radio, which Édouard promptly attached to three-foot speakers. She had a deep tin of fluffed rice and pigeon peas. Had anklets and earrings and bracelets and necklaces and cornrows so tight her eyes slanted tight toward her temples. She had on a gold spandex dress over a black spandex slip, the thin straps cutting her shoulders like twine in a tri-tip, and the spandex sheaths forced flesh into smooth, tight bike tires at her waist and rigged her rump to the exact dimensions of a standard bedroom pillow. There was no jiggling. Arms wide and flanked with muscle, tough thighs in the shadow of her stride-stretched dress. Calves like small hams, her flat feet soft and slashed with scarlet polish. Silver toe rings. In a way she rarely did, Eva immediately feared comparison. The girl seemed very strong and very free.

"Miss Eva, this is Jenny. My girlfriend."

Jenny shook Eva's hand politely, smiled, and then handed Audrey the rice and peas, who set them down next to a plate of maraschinos bleeding on sliced pineapple. Édouard watched his girl with none of the reserve he had for Eva on the boat from Nassau to Cat. Plus he was being kissed by everyone, and was soon engulfed by the fuss of what turned out to be his twenty-eighth birthday.

Absently, Dart picked up pineapple with his fingers.

"First," Audrey told him, "that's what forks are for. Second, it's Eddie's day, and we'll eat when he starts."

At that, Eddie packed a plate, and a line formed behind him. After Jeeter got his food, and music was playing low and steady, and the patio was bright with moonbeams and chitchat and heart-to-hearts and complaint, Jeeter started talking, in the way spry old men do, about the trials of his day.

"Mister Bethel over to the 'ouse, carping as usual."

"For bloody's sake," said Benjamin. "And what did he have to say?"

"The normal," Jeeter said. "Stomach problems, *and* his sadness, and his stress, and his indecision about the big island."

Dart stopped eating to listen with what had become his usual fascination with anything Cat Island.

"And what did you tell him?" Audrey said, setting out fried grouper and more chicken. "That we all have those problems? That he should be glad his aren't worse than that?"

"Gave him the doctor's name in Nassau," Jeeter said. He spoke haltingly, but only because he was eating. He bundled animal bones on a strip of napkin. "Told him to kill two birds with one stone. To get the heartburn taken care of, and to stay for a few days, fill out the applications, see if he could stay, even if he wanted to."

"Bethel is undone," Benjamin said.

"Copying everyone else all the time, one day the monkey cut his throat."

"Ha!"

Jeeter continued eating. To the side of his plate sat chicken ribs like doused paper matches and bendy needles of fish bone. He tied them in a thin strip of napkin. In the quirk of a methodical man, Dart saw the gestures of a magus. Jeeter scooped the last of his rice with a plastic spoon as Dart minded the old man's marred hands and odds and ends. Monkey throats and a full moon, murdered birds, fish spines, hearts afire, and blood and stone. Eva could see it in Dart's open face. He was in the presence of wizardry and aching for a spell.

"You don't have to speak in code around me," Dart said.

Jeeter held his spoon in midair. "Pardon me?"

"It's okay," Dart said. "I see, and I understand."

Audrey looked at Eva, who looked at Dart and hated to look at him.

"Play some better music, Eddie," Benjamin said. "Play it louder."

Dart touched the bundle of bones. Then he took it from Jeeter's plate. It was a small, quick action, a theft as unusual as if he'd yanked a strand of hair from Jeeter's head.

It was Eva's turn to be transfixed.

Jeeter pulled back. "You want that?"

Like the bones were glowing, Dart dropped them back on Jeeter's plate.

Eva was grateful when more people came up the walk, wishing Eddie good luck with good cheer. Soft-cheeked women with short hair crisped yellow blond by peroxide. A graying couple both with honey-colored teeth carried a large painting of lobsters and serpents and birds and palms. They presented it to Édouard with shy pride. Eva was full of souse, and had a glass of red punch with nary a kick in it. There was laughter, and the occasional introduction that Eva participated in. People inquired about her leg, offered to get her water or punch or more food. A short man with knobby biceps that stretched a T stamped with IT's BETTER IN THE BAHAMAS smelled like sand and sea and held Eva's hand until she pulled it back. His eyes were still in a squint from his day.

Dart had made a pallet of his knees at Jeeter's feet, and though Eva couldn't hear a word that passed between them, she could see that Dart was plying the man with questions and that the man was patiently talking to him.

Who knows if Jeeter has answers? Who can answer Dart, anyway?

Jenny shimmied before the birthday boy. She had what looked like a true cocktail, and Édouard bounced like a grizzly might to "Now That We Found Love (What Are We Gonna Do with It?)." Not Third World's classic and much-maligned 1978 version, which itself was a remake of the O'Jays 1973 original depth charge, a gift also bestowed by songwriters Gamble and Huff in 1977 on Martha Reeves— but the hectic 1992 gold cut from the Overweight Lover, Heavy D. The jam lit a candle in Édouard's birthday heart. *Spread your wings / So we can fly around the world / Harmony, charm of me / Your fingertips are callin' me.* The song went faster, faster. Faster. Faster. It was an eternal question—*Now that we found love, what are we going to do with it?*—with no answer, so people keep recording it and recording it, making Gamble and Huff rightfully richer and making Dart feel it, right along with Édouard and Jenny and the others who started bouncing, bouncing, dipping on beat, dipping deeper in the pauses, smiling, happy. Eva watching, watching, she liked the song, couldn't help thinking of it in historical terms, even as she was far away from where that kind of stuff mattered most. It was the way she'd come to think of music all the time: *who produced it, when they produced it, what the promo budget was, if it could be sampled or what sample was that and how much it cost to get it cleared, how the airplay was going, was the song or the album gonna go platinum first week out*—but here it was, "Now That We Found Love," an *old*-ass song, written by two hardheaded brothers named Kenny (Gamble) and Leon (Huff) back in 1973—Picasso dying, Vietnam cease-firing, Nixon re-upping, OPEC embargoing—when they were putting together an album called *Ship Ahoy* for the O'Jays, a group whose lack of inhibition Boyz II Men could only aspire to, an album for which the title song was a reflection on the Middle Passage, an album no one thought would go over, but ended up being, along with *So Full of Love*, the O'Jays' pinnacle. And here the song was. On Cat Island in 1998. *Here it is. Here it is. And Heavy is ripping it.*

The patio, the birthday night, *so full of love.*

Heavy ripping it right up until the next song, which was one of Sunny's with a whole different beat under it, and bells around it and chimes above it, and Dart stood and searched for Eva's eyes and she looked at him to say, *Right? It sounds good, huh?* and no more than that, but Dart began to dance, and then to jog slowly around the room, but on beat so it seemed, if you wanted to give him the benefit of the doubt, like he was dancing, but if you really looked, he was getting revved, winding himself up or being wound up for something feral. And Eva thought, her not knowing how mania works, that clearly he was about to do something maniacal. When Dart's head snapped toward Jeeter, who faced his palms to the ceiling and pumped them *up, up,* like an old man trying to hang at a young man's party, which is what he was, Dart, who'd been mouthing the words to Sunny's song, began to add sound to his mouthing, to his movement, the circular motion that had to be his soul, manifest.

Dart got louder. To where he stopped moving, and in the doorway of Audrey's tiny kitchen began singing in his booming voice, and in voices he never used. The main one was like his sister's—saltant, strong, surely stronger than hers. There was no showmanship from him save vocal richness. But everyone stopped, of course, because he was singing, eyes open and unfocused, and some people looked at him with fear, like he might be crazy; others looked on with sorrow, with curiosity, like he must be in terrible pain. Dart had been damp as usual, and now sweat covered his face, it dripped from his fingertips, and spit was like milk in his mouth, but he kept singing the song as remixed by Édouard to speed up just then, to match, to buss the frantic beats per minute of Heavy's groove, and Dart stayed with it, his words completely different from Sun's record lyrics, but his sister still suddenly on the island, breaking up the party with him, freaking it.

Eva was feeling it, too. She wanted to dance to the happiness Édouard put in the beats, the pounces of sound, the pauses, the rings and snaps and slaps, the tremblings of tambourines, and Dart kept singing, singing, chanting now, he was moving again, his jog faster, and just when Eva thought he might drop to his knees because his body had loosened—his hands looked weighted, shoulders low like a boxer's—he did. Eva didn't know if it was tears or sweat or both coming down his face, and though they didn't know her, people looked to Eva because they at least knew Eva and Dart were together, at the Rowe House. They assumed that Dart was Eva's man. So Eva got up on her tingly, weak leg and walked toward him, scared and half-embarrassed as she was, but Édouard, kindly, put an arm out to block her. Then Jenny held Eva steady as she reflexively took the weight off her hurt leg.

Dart began to tweak and wrench. Eva hoped hard that it was real, that he was really crazy or being taken over by something, because if he was faking this she would hate him for having made her believe in him, even if it was just for a moment. She got to her knees gingerly, lifted Dart's head to the bed of her closed thighs. She could smell the scent of the herb he took rising from his pores. The dried apricot smell repelled her as she held him so his head couldn't slide down.

I hope, she thought, *he feels me.*

Close as she was, Eva could see Dart's tears distinct from his all-day, everyday glaze of sweat. He was still warbling in his sister-tongue, but the words were sporadic. He was blubbering, and the words that escaped were confessions or apologies or promises or requests or re-grets or entreaties or maybe all of them, and isn't that what lyrics were, anyway? Eva and Dart were on the floor by Jeeter with his mangled tips. Dart's eyes opened. He looked at Jeeter but grabbed the wrist Eva had over his chest with both his hands.

Jeeter wiped Dart's forehead with the torn yellow paper napkin. Dart looked at the napkin like it was a talisman, like he was being mopped with holy cloth. Dart lay there until Édouard sat him up. And when Jeeter handed Dart the napkin, instead of drying the rest of his face, Dart folded it, tightly and with intense attention, into a tiny, thick square. Some people stayed to watch Eva's experiment with hope, some walked closer to the shore whispering, some laughing among themselves.

Sunny's song had faded to the bossiness of the S.O.S. Band's 1981 "Take Your Time (Do It Right)," and then 1990 Ice Cube *(I don't bang / I write the good rhymes)*. All the songs were golden charms from other eras. Eva felt uncomfortable with the nostalgia. It had been thrust upon her. She wanted to toss it off, claim it too tight, too big, or, most important, not her style. It clung, though, to every curve of her con-sciousness. However itchy, it fit. And the sensation led her to think that she would not only get used to it, but that she'd find it comforting and eventually comfortable. Eva didn't feel old as much as she felt grown. She felt she'd been a part of something larger than herself and that now it was time to take on something her own size. Dart placed the napkin die in his breast pocket. Eva'd folded paper like that. She knew what it meant to take something that was so big and make it as small and hard and crucial as a crucifix.

Édouard helped Dart to his feet. Dart looked to Eva like she was his savior.

A rush of feeling made Eva woozy.

When her eyes opened, she was on the floor, lost in time. To faint is to die a little, and Eva wondered as people fanned her, as two women helped her to Audrey's couch, as the music stuck in a scratch on Eddie's CD, she wondered if she had died and woken on Cat, decided that whether she was in heaven or hell, guided by God or by idols, she would do her best to be worthy of the place, to be glad for what she'd created in her life on earth. At the thought of creation she remembered. That's how fainting is—you come back and you have to remember who you are and what your circumstances are. She sat still, knowing she would never forget or be forgiven, knowing that her last chance and her biggest fear were living and breathing inside her. Audrey brought her cold cherry punch, and Eva was as grateful as she'd ever been for anything. The drink seemed thick and sweet and like ice so cold as not to be found anyplace in the Bahamas. It hurt her teeth and coated her stomach and shocked her brain. Eva was going to follow her baby's lead. She gulped Audrey's gift like it was a potion.

Her leg hurt like a vise was being closed on it, but Eva put her hand on her belly and felt unshackled in a way she hadn't since her first visit to her first clinic. She felt worthy of assistance, which had the immediate affect of her wanting to assist someone else, and to get off Cat Island, and to partner up with Dart. It was the kind of thought that usually made her run for the hills, but now it gave her a purpose.

He needs me.

And so Eva's mind began to click—no old lyrics or album release dates—just *click-click-click.*

I'm about to make moves, and for him to make moves with me, I gotta get his mind right.

"W e're okay, Édouard," Eva said. "He's fine."

Jeeter said, "Audrey, maybe get him some of the strong punch."

"Dart doesn't drink."

"What does he do, then?" Audrey said.

"He has me."

Édouard helped Dart to his feet.

"Eddie!" Dart said. "Eva and I wish you the HAPPIEST of birthdays. Eva, who has taken this RISK with me. Beautiful, sweet EVA who is my LOVE."

Eva was mortified by his certainty, but reveled in his pride and directness. Dart's cadence was thrillingly valedictory—he'd shown them who he was and was bidding all a proud, emotional good night.

"We should get back," Eva said calmly. She was dizzy. "I'm tired."

"IS it the BABY?" It was as if Dart's ears were plugged. He spoke clearly and loudly, but was out of sync. Audrey and Édouard looked at Eva.

"YEAH," Eva said, loud as Dart, and with a smile. "It is." Eva told a roomful of people of a pregnancy. *I've been pregnant before, but this is the first time I'm going to have a baby. Whatever craziness is with Dart, it's not his fault.* He knew about the baby, and not only was he not running, he was standing up for her. So she'd stand up for him.

"Let's get you HOME," Dart said with a puffed-up affection Eva almost curled up in.

On the lawn, Eva said, "I'm not really tired. I feel fine." Her leg hurt, but she wasn't favoring it as much as earlier.

"FINE. Me, too!" His smile was unnaturally wide and dazzling. "Even after all that. Shit! I feel great! Look at this fucking place! It's OURS."

The profanity hung on Dart's mouth ugly as snot. It wasn't his way. But his eyes were alive and glassy, and Eva felt close to him for having seen his little madness.

"I shouldn't sing, huh?" He broke into a huge laugh. "I get—"

"You freak out."

"Not ALWAYS. It's when I sing with Sun, or when something else is bearing on me—it was that *guy*, Jeeter. *I know who he is.* And he's *touched me now*, Eva! WITH HIS HANDS. And I've eaten Audrey's FOOD. YOU don't believe in it, Eva, but this place is *filled with people* who KNOW things, and if you do believe in *things unseen*, things not understood, *then you benefit*, you get CALLED. *Goddamn!*" His voice rang like through tubular bells.

"That guy Jeeter's a fisherman, I think. Does tattoos on the side, Audrey said. A regular person."

"Look DEEPLY, EVA! *Open* yourself." He brushed her stomach with his fingers. "We're gonna stay here a WHILE."

Dart plopped on the couch at the Rowe House like he needed a minute. Closed his eyes like he wanted not sleep but some conscious dark. Eva opened the Rowe's medicine cabinet, and along with the box of orange mosquito bracelets and suppositories and mouthwash faded almost to water were things Eva could use. Cotton swabs and crusty tweezers. Plus rubbing alcohol that Eva sniffed and figured to be still potent.

Eva's cell rang weakly from under a towel and she ignored it. She carried the things to the bedroom, dumped them on the bed. "Dart," she called. "Shower's free."

"Yeah?" He sounded miles away and malleable. "OKAY."

He got in the shower and she went to the kitchen, put on a dented pot of water to boil, and dropped in the tweezers. Then she carried her supplies to the patio, along with the coconut oil Sunny'd given her. Eva flattened the chaise and pulled a chair and small glass-topped table beside it. She grabbed a plastic pail and walked the short distance to the shore. A few people from Édouard's party stood on dry sand with cups of strong punch and cigarettes and wilting paper plates of food. They looked her way, but Eva paid them no mind and walked directly to the damp stripe closest to the water. There was faint light from Audrey and Ben's patio, but it was the moon, even from within its halo, that lit Eva's way. On her knees, she dug the pail's lip into dense sand, and when she had what she wanted, she filled the pail to the top with seawater. The tide was dramatic and high and the water stung her leg wounds so she bit down on her tongue.

Dart's voice like mortar fire called her name as Eva walked gamely back with her prize. He stood on the patio naked. The moon washed his skin a gleaming russet, warmed his eyes amber. Quarterback shoulders, belly soft, but flat, long meaty arms and penis and legs—all lithe and peacefully primed.

"You're amazing," Eva said. *This is purity*, she thought. *Realness.* No *who did what to whom when*. Eva set down the pail. "Really . . . like, beautiful."

"Thanks. It's what happened when I got off that stuff."

"Lay down on that," Eva said, back on strategy. She pointed to the chaise and flipped on the outdoor lights. *They're weak*, she thought, *but with the moon, we'll be fine.*

He thought she wanted to have sex there, but she went back in the kitchen, put the pot of water in the sink, added enough cold until she could reach her hand in and scrape the last of the crust from the tweezers with her fingernails. Eva put a pot of clean water back on the searing orange eye.

"Evey? You all right in there?" When she got back on the patio, he was on his back, fingers laced under his chest, like a corpse in a coffin. "Full moon," he said. "Means rain."

What is he? Chief Running Bear all of a sudden? "I'm gonna do your back. Cleanse it."

"Now?" He sat up. "Full moon isn't a good time for this. Blood'll be involved. Full moon isn't a good time for a letting."

A letting? Who says that? But then Eva spoke and she couldn't believe how serious she sounded. How serious she was. Eva allowed for a minute that whether what he said was true or not, it was his truth, and so she'd deal with it like that. "It is a full moon," she said. "And I'm going to deal with your back with sand and water from the ocean. With coconut oil from the Philippines. With whatever else I've found here. If you do . . . bleed more or something, I think it's for the best. I think whatever comes out needs to come out, and should. I think you'll feel better." *I'll feel better if you're better.*

"This is you? Or Jeeter told you what to do? Or Audrey?"

"It's what I think you need. What I want to do. You have to lay down, turn over on your stomach."

"I believe in stuff," Dart said calmly. "You know that. Half the reason the herbs I'm taking work is because I believe they are. But they don't work like real drugs do, Eva. I know how I acted tonight. Know how I can act, period. You can't fix me."

"I'm not trying to fix you." *Yes, I am.*

"Don't get me wrong. I appreciate your . . . impulse. And I understand the symbolism—a cleansing, cleaning my back, my background, I guess, letting impurities from my body and spirit."

"How about your back is gross and needs care." *And I want to care. I want to do something.*

He looked at her and said nothing.

"So if magical Audrey or Jeeter had told me to do it, you'd believe."

Dart blinked in slow motion.

"Believe in me, then," Eva said. "I believed in you. I came over here." *I'm having the baby. I think I believe in you. And that's all I'm about. Me, you, the baby, Cat.*

Dart turned over on his stomach. He put one hand atop the other and put his left jaw on his knuckles. As he closed his eyes, tears came to Eva's. But she knew how to keep working, however emotional she was. She knew how to use her emotions to meet her goals.

Eva sat in the chair near him, poured a puddle of alcohol on the table, and in it set the tweezers. They looked sharper cleaned. When she dipped a thin facecloth in the pail, and rubbed it over his back, he gripped the legs of the chaise. Eva scooped sand from the bottom of the pail. It was fine and mudlike and studded with tiny pieces of shell. She placed a few mounds of it on him and rubbed it from his shoulders to the small of his back. D'Artagnan set his jaw. She moved from her chair and sat on his butt and rubbed the sand into him harder. "Taking everything off that's dead," she said.

He let go the lounge legs and let his wrists drop to the stone floor. With a small cup, Eva poured seawater over his back. Her skirt was getting wet. Her wound burned, and her bandage loosened as water streamed down her thighs and calves. Dart flinched. Bumps and pimples on his back broke open. Eva thought the water would be good for them—mineral salts and microscopic algae—she'd been to enough spas to know. She went into the kitchen, added cool water to the boiling. It still scalded her hands a bit as she dipped and wrung out a dish towel. Back on the patio, she laid it steaming on Dart's back, and he groaned so she thought he came. She repeated the process, and this time his moan was softer. When she lifted the second towel, his skin was still speckled, but more elastic and less dull, and the bumps, open or closed, had risen higher.

Eva thought, as she usually did, that his back was grotesque— ignored and left to rot, and somewhere in her there was a déjà vu of a slave whipped and of a woman trying to heal him while knowing that the back could be healed, but that the mind was out of reach.

She was determined and absorbed, alight with her own gesture. Sitting on his butt again, Eva picked up the tweezers and began a meticulous process of extraction. Alternately she pressed in with her instrument and dabbed clear welling oil or opaque oil and blood with the damp towel. His back wept rancid, teeny black-tipped snakes. Dart flinched, but he didn't yelp. The side of his face she could see was stretched and squashed into a grimace. With the slightest push, double pores sent up squiggles of whiteness. After thirty minutes of this, Dart was falling in and out of sleep.

Eva worked another forty-five minutes. She made her way down his back with patient precision. So zenned out by her chore, she heard her life's music clearly over the fading sounds of the party next door.

> *Men will cry over you.*
> *Take me to the next phase / Baby / Take me.*
> *That's not what you said last night.*
> *Watch the ball.*
> *Singularity, attitude, and panache.*
> *You said my problem is I have no cross to bear. Well,*
> *I have one now. But I turned it into wings and I'm*
> *flying away.*
> *Big bonus for you this year, Eva. Almost a quarter mil, Eva. Doscientos cincuenta mil dólares después de impuestos, negrita.*
> *It's like that / And that's the way it is.*
> *Black pussy! / Always talkin' 'bout it 'cuz I love it /*
> *Women get grown up / As soon as they let me rub it.*
> *Some women simply have a low threshold for pain.*
> *This time I'll be sweeter / Our love will run deeper.*
> *I have never seen you look this ugly.*
> *The possibility, ma'am, is that you could be more*
> *pregnant than you think.*
> *Comebacks. That's all you have.*

> *Five shots couldn't drop me / I took it and smiled.*
> *Five shots couldn't drop me / I took it and smiled.*
> *Four shots couldn't drop me / I took it and smiled.*
> *Five shots couldn't drop me / I took it and smiled.*

The sound of Tupac's voice shook Eva from her reverie. *Édouard must've set up some turntables,* she thought. *And he's playing my song.*

Eva's mind started to click. *"Hit 'Em Up," B-side to Tupac and K-Ci & JoJo's 1996 "How Do You Want It?" One of the strongest double sides in hip hop history—really the strongest unless you counted Run-D.M.C.'s*

1983 "It's Like That" b/w "Sucker MCs" or Eric B. and Rakim's "Eric B. for President" b/w "My Melody," which—as much as I adore Run, and did fuck Rakim—I don't. "Hit 'Em Up" is the most concentrated rush of fury ever recorded. Tupac daring death. Daring fools to murder him. Tupac acting like life wasn't worth it, like here on earth you only pimp or get pimped, like mother-love's triple-layered trigonometric algorithms are always reduced to coin tosses and Faustian choices. Like, as Prince put it— in 1984—on the evergreen soundtrack to his too-ripe Purple Rain: *In this life / Things are much harder than in the afterworld / In this life / You're on your own. So ruff / so tuff,* Eva thought, channeling Zapp's Roger Troutman. *Tupac so dead and us so sad and the last days of his life so filled with bitter, toxic fruit. No dad for him, barely a mom. Have to have been abandoned early on to yell out, taunting, "Five shots couldn't drop me / I took it and smiled." Almost have to have been left alone, left to die, to become a true superstar.*

Édouard backed the record over and over that lyric, wearing an even deeper groove in the vinyl. The line, as it always had, stretched Eva's wounds wide enough to halve her.

Eva startled Dart with a wash of seawater. He yelped and squirmed, and pushed himself up some with his palms.

She set the cup down, and Dart grabbed her wrist so that he almost snatched off the bracelet he'd given her.

"You're not done, are you?"

Eva was thrilled and encouraged. "Almost."

Relieved, Dart lay his head back down.

She emptied the bottle of rubbing alcohol over his back. His toes pointed immediately. His shoulders and ass tightened. He reached under himself to adjust his erection. Eva patted his back with a dry towel. He settled into light panting.

"You all right?" she said.

"I'm brand-new."

For the last of it, Eva poured a dime of coconut oil on her palm. She rubbed them together until they were shiny and thinly covered and then rubbed over the tiny new wounds and old scars, the raised hard places, the places most dry and still calloused over. Dart moaned again, faintly and insistently, and Eva knew enough to rise from her seat on his ass so he could turn over and she could sit on him and he could hold her hips and churn her in a way that could make him climax almost instantly. His stroke had her feeling high.

He could be my baby's father. He should be.

Stroke me. Love me.

This could work. This should work.

You could fuck me like this every time the baby's asleep. Make more babies. Walk in the park with a stroller and a scooter. "What a lovely family," they'll say.

I'll take care of everything. You just take care of me, like this.

He lifted her off of him right before he yelled out.

Eva sat facing him, on the lounge between his knees. "There's no worry of me getting pregnant," she said, able to be light about it for the first time.

"I know. I just . . . I don't want anything . . . impure to touch him."

"You're impure?" *Rhyme.* She wanted him to come inside her, on purpose, to seal the deal. Because of its slimy, sheer physicality, and the possibility of death and life in the same shot, the act had become to Eva a symbol of her emotional, if not actual, commitment.

"Just the imbalance."

"You're making no sense." She became aware of her leg throbbing again.

"I don't want any part of my essence to be in your body with him. His home needs to be unspoiled. I'm never having kids, Eva. I'm not passing this shit on. It was passed to me."

"But it doesn't make you impure," Eva said. "Or bad."

Dart's mood shifted quick to cold. "Well, you know I'm not passing no diseases." His nostrils flared. They were covered with shaky peas of sweat. "Only person I had sex with in the last three years is you." He was angry about it.

She believed him, but Eva said, "Unlikely." She thought Dart might like some doubt in her mind about his confession, so she left him some space in which to be big and nonchalant.

"Not on purpose. But truly. I was on that doctor dope. My sex thing was way off. Bi-fucking polar. I didn't want to climb in the bed with some chick who'd clown me."

"Good ol' me," Eva said. Now she was tart. "Service with a smile."

"With an attitude, more like. But you've understood." He pulled her to him. "You always did, in your cold-ass way. Things would be better if I could be . . . more for you."

"You're fine for me."

"Your expectations are low. I'm fine for you on Cat Island. Here, the spirits are paving our way."

———

A pink sun stalked the last lavender shadows and simmered the sea to umpteen shades of green. A breeze teased dangling petals from flowers. Eva and Dart hadn't moved from the lounge on the patio.

Dart's hand moved in her, and then touched her where she craved to be touched. Then her belly and brain clenched like a fist and opened like a star. *Light, star bright.* She saw the last few, in the brightening skies, and started crying. Her leg hurt.

Too many things are happening at the same time.

Dart was tuned into Eva enough—the fingers came out smoothly— to say, "I'm not here to hurt you."

Eva was inundated. She was wiping out.

"It's okay," Dart said. "Be louder. You're killing yourself."

It humbled her that someone could know, instinctively, or have cobbled together some psychic memory strong enough to move his finger a certain way, or say a certain thing. Eva wondered how some people knew what to do. Ron's wide face entered her mind. She pushed at it, and the effort made her face more wet, her neck and ears wet. Every morning second on the patio was Billie Holiday–Solomon Burke fierce with truth. Ringing, and wringing. She'd had orgasms of different kinds with connoisseurs who knew how to make them. But it was Dart's solemnity that encouraged a sparkly, open-sky, light feeling—mind blank, but completely stimulated, a shimmering sheet that shakes and shakes everything out.

"You did good," Dart said. Eva was ashamed that she took such comfort in his confirmation of her self.

Gold star for me.

"Your arms are so pretty."

She nodded.

"Your hands are soft like a baby's."

"Thank you."

He put salty, body-scented fingers near her mouth. His nails soft and bitten down to the quick. Then more Eva tears at the coziness and affection she hadn't felt since Italy, on the road with Imperial Court and Trix, and Ron. She thought she could smell Ron in the dawn air as Dart kissed her toes and then tried to put his face inside her. She shrieked, tried to let him in farther, and in a Ron-like move, Dart squeezed Eva's butt so hard it went beyond pain to pure loveliness to her saying stop and not meaning it.

They lay there in the sunlight, naked, heads opposite, feet near the other's face.

"Tiny," Dart said, cradling her feet like they were precious. And Eva got that ecstatic, embarrassed feeling strong women get when any part of them is made to seem delicate.

Eva's cell rang. It was a long scratch on her vinyl day, but she ran for it.

"It's Eva," she said with relief in her voice.

"Ciao! It's Pritz. Where are you?"

"Where're *you*?" Eva made herself sound enthusiastic. She had to for Giada.

"In Miami, about to come where you are. I'm fired. Paid out and happy."

"Fired. Damn, Giada." In 1998, to get fired in the record business was no big deal. If you were in urban music, and if you'd branded yourself—with an evocative nickname like Dutch Dillinger, or World Wyde, or Punch Villa—you'd be hired someplace else, even within the same conglomerate, quickly. And even without a nickname, you could misuse your expense account, set cherry bombs off in your office as part of a professional meltdown, or beat a coworker's ass, and your prospects were still passable, if not enhanced, as long as you'd kicked a rapper's or R & B singer's sales high up the charts. So there was no need for empathy from Eva. In fact, she envied Giada—now known as "Pritz," after the character of Maerose Prizzi as portrayed by Anjelica Huston in *Prizzi's Honor*—for her vacation between gigs. "I'm far," Eva lied. "I'll be in Miami probably tomorrow."

"Then we'll come back together. Tell me where you are staying."

"Are you with—"

"I saw Leetle John and Sun and Hakeem and your whole crew. Now tell me, where are you?"

"Why're you pressing me?" *We're friends, but we're not* friends.

"Why is it a secret? I know you are with Sunny's brother."

"I'm fine."

"No one said different."

"I'm on Cat Island. That's only for you to know."

"Okay. You sound bad. I will be there, probably . . . maybe by noon tomorrow.

No! "It's after noon now, Pritz. There's no way—"

"I know what time it is, Eva. I have been to the Biminis. I have been to Turks and Caicos. I know where is Cat Island, what it is to get there. Two baby planes from Miami. Easy. I will call you from their airport."

"Pritz! Don't."

"Ciao."

Eva hurried to the bathroom and threw up.

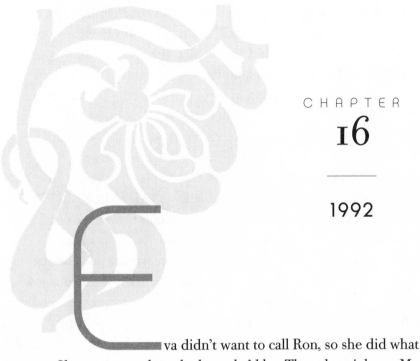

va didn't want to call Ron, so she did what was easy. She went to a place she knew he'd be: Thursday nights at Mr. Kato's, in Beverly Hills. A schmantzy Japanese place that smelled like scallion and pineapple, like just-Windexed lacquer, and colognes with names like Escape and Spellbound.

On Thursday nights, record industry people who worked urban acts flocked to Mr. Kato's to expense dinners for ten. They got rowdy and waved colleagues over. The place didn't take reservations, even for large parties—the key was to get to Kato's early enough to snag a prime, secluded-but-still-visible table, but to get there not so early that you looked like a desperado.

The place was extra hectic on this particular Thursday because so much was going on in Los Angeles. Eva was in town for two awards shows, three new-talent showcases, and a series of meetings with her Los Angeles coworkers about cross-promoting the West Coast leg of a tour for the least possible label money. She walked into Kato's at 8:45, feet free of New York socks and boots, body bare of sweaters and hats. Eva had dressed carefully. It was new for her, an attempt at what she figured to be sophistication. In addition to her new style goals was the fact that Ron had only seen her in road clothes, her hair always snatched back in a ponytail. In the few short months since Italy, Eva'd used the money and confidence that came with yet another promotion (Trix had two platinum singles; Imperial Court had gone platinum in the United Kingdom) to patronize the chic boutiques on New York's Madison Avenue. Because she'd perused oversize catalogs from boutique department stores, read them like guides to foreign countries, Eva felt briefed—if not fluent—when she walked the hospital-like, minimalist floors.

Eva was looking for a way to be. Even before Italy, she'd jocked the few black female vice presidents and senior vice presidents in the industry, and she invited them to quiet lunches. If the dining was outdoors, or in the East, or if the senior vice presidential woman had gone to Wesleyan or Brown, the woman lit a Marlboro Light (it was a Newport if the woman had gone to Hampton or Howard or tended to fall back on or take pride in formerly or diffused ghetto ways). The cig usually accompanied a shared apple tart and a third vodka gimlet, and a spiel from the woman about how people hated her for her accomplishments, and about the ongoing remodel of the place in Sag Harbor. Eva was mostly in awe of the fortyish women who went back in the music business to before hip hop started. Women who'd worked the last L.A. days of Motown, who'd been down with Prince on his ascent, who'd slaved at the labels to which powerhouses like Bootsy and Earth, Wind & Fire and Parliament Funkadelic had been signed. Once tipsy on admiration and alcohol, these rare women—some austere, some flamboyant—gladly schooled Eva in the ways of getting shit done and the clothes to wear while slogging through it. Motherless Eva soaked up their habits like a sponge.

Three months before the big night at Mr. Kato's, Eva met with Meri Heath, a woman she'd nicknamed Ms. Exception. Ms. Exception's pumps were usually French, not because French shoes were so much more expensive than Italian or Spanish, but because French shoes were so much more distinctive. *Singularity, attitude, panache— the currency of style.* That's what Ms. Exception often told Eva.

Ms. Exception was a general manager, and she managed not just the business of urban music, but the business of white music, as well—hence her moniker. Ms. Exception headed up a label Eva's competed with. She told Eva of Eva's impending promotion on their cocktail date, which was two days before Eva's promotion was announced, so Eva's perception of Ms. Exception as an all-seeing goddess among music professionals was etched in stone.

Ms. Exception talked about a lot of things that evening, and talked around alliances made long ago in boardrooms and bedrooms with men and women now in positions to keep her in her venerated position even when her profits were so off they made the business page of the *New York Times.* Ms. Exception talked about her son at the second-rate private college in Maine, talked about how spoiled her child was, and about how the spoiling was done now, and so what was the use crying about it. Ms. Exception told Eva straight-out that it was the white women in this business who needed to be watched. Ms. Exception told Eva that so many of the white women in the music business were pathological in their quest for black men, yet protective of their position with white men, that white women would fight you—secretly, while smiling in your face, while overcompliment-ing you on your hair—with the kind of bucketing intensity associated with typhoons.

Eva was pulled into these tales—especially the next ones, because they were the ones Ms. Exception told with face tight and lips thin around her Newport, her words pungent and smooth as the medicine Ms. Exception felt she was delivering:

"Negroes are the ones who'll stab you in the back soon as you turn it. They'll talk love and tell their boys how they laid you. They walk into a place of business, *my* place of business, with their basket-ball jerseys swinging like dresses around their knees. With guns in their belts, or the rumor of guns. They walk in with their knowledge of *da streets,* of what's *hot.* They swagger in, wowing the whites with a stupid, a fake, narrow, supposedly black *authenticity.* They walk in with a so-called *ear* for *what's real.*"

Ms. Exception was adamant. She stopped to sip her Scotch. To inhale some smoke, to exhale it, to tap ashes onto the constantly exchanged ashtray, to check Eva's face for signs of attention and comprehension.

"This brother," Ms. Exception continued, "comes in for the

meeting that really he's been vying for his whole life. He walks in cool and so sexy and sexual to them. And this brother's sexy to you, too. He's met you finally, right? A woman he thinks is smart and bred and who already knows about the things he craves. But he'll shake you quick after you get him his goddamned deal, after you up his goddamned budget, after you take him around to all the goddamned parties—and I'm not saying that white boys won't do the same, Eva, that they haven't done the same. They have."

"So what, then?" Eva said, sipping her drink and feeling right- eously cosmopolitan. Eva sat back gracefully while wondering from where Ms. Exception had purchased her flawless gray silk jersey dress and gray ostrich sling-backs. Eva wondered, as she sipped her drink again, if she'd ever be so unflappable and generous and sophisticated all at the same time. She imagined the sweet day when a $1,000 bag would be tucked as casually as Ms. Exception's—at her own hip. Eva wondered if she'd ever truly run things.

"Eva," Ms. Exception said, like Eva had been running her mouth. "Little Sister. Listen more. Talk less. And get yourself some decent jewelry. Start with earrings. Good diamonds. Pay the fifteen grand— you'll have them for life, and men'll know what you expect."

Little Sister is what Ms. Exception often called Eva. Eva felt the love in the words, had yet to put her finger on the grandiosity. "I'm saying I expect—*I used to expect*—more from a brother. I never ex- pected shit from a white man, was raised never to expect shit from him. So when a white man acts right, looks out for me, it stands out extra tall. Because in my mind, white boys start from under zero, any- way. When a brother dogs me—in this business, in life, *and the two are the same thing, Eva, make no mistake*—it stands out cold and short. So, for real, Little Sister, it's about you." Ms. Exception smiled then, and put out her cigarette. She put her bag on the table, placed her ciga- rettes and her sterling lighter in it, pulled out her coat check and tapped the tablecloth with it. "It's about being wise. You don't need to let people know who your allies are or who they aren't. I see it in you, Eva. You're motivated. You don't talk from the side of your mouth. You're a winner."

So thrilled was she to be sitting across from her future, Eva didn't pluck the shinola from the shit. She'd been around, but not enough to know Ms. Exception had, when the Commodores were still a band, been married to Eva's friend Hakeem. Didn't know that the spoiled child of which Ms. Exception spoke was by a white executive with whom Ms. Exception had carried on an affair for nineteen years before he finally left his Kingston-born/Bryn Mawr–educated wife and married Ms. Exception at a small ceremony on a cloud-dotted Nevis afternoon. Eva, who picked up the bill for the cocktails and conversation, reeled in what she considered to be Ms. Exception's hard-core truth. Eva did wonder, but only fleetingly, where other black women fit into Ms. Exception's philosophies—white men and women and black men having been broken down at length. It was years before Eva realized that black women belonged across a slender table from Ms. Exception. But more truly at her feet.

———

"Chill" gained popularity as a term meaning "to relax, calm down," in the 1980s. It comes from Black English slang, which has been a source of informal words in Standard English, often through the medium of various African-American musical styles, including hip hop. The word "chill" has had many lives both in-side and outside Black English. Since the late 1920s "chill" has been used to mean "to crush" and even "to murder." The recent use of "to chill" in the sense of "to calm down" is another example of slang's ingeniousness: English has used variations of "cool" to refer to tranquillity since before America's colonial era. Though "chill" is a new way of saying "cool down," the evolution of "chill" continues: the new sense of "to relax" has recently been ex-tended to mean "to laze among friends, to mingle." Chill is a model of how language evolves in ways unforeseeable yet instan-taneously graspable.

—*THE NEW AMERICAN DICTIONARY*
OF THE ENGLISH LANGUAGE

I t was with freshly tousled, oil-sheened curls and with dangling high-heeled sandals (a British designer's, Eva's stab at distinction) that Eva chilled at Kato's bar. Her dress had a cinched waist and a filmy skirt, a snug bodice, and a deep, square neckline—the very definition of panache. Eva didn't want a table at Kato's. She knew Ron would soon be there to hold court as a new executive vice president of urban music at a label he was charged with resuscitating. Eva'd seen Ron's promotion announced *in Billboard,* but she'd made her plans based on what she'd heard from her friend Hakeem, who knew everybody and everything.

Hakeem's data was on point.

"Eva," Ron said. "I thought you might be out here." He was surprised, she could tell, but as unruffled as she'd ever seen him. Especially as he wasn't wearing his usual promotional T-shirt and jeans and sneakers. Ron, in black pants and a light sweater, was a part of a long tradition—a white guy in charge of black music—so Eva hadn't given him a Mr. Nickname. People Eva knew had begun to call him Ron more than Lil' John.

"Duty calls," she said. Eva's plan had been to be beautiful, and to assault him with straightforwardness. She wanted to say, *I came here tonight because I knew you'd be here. I have something to tell you, but here's not the place.*

"Wish you woulda called me," he said. "Today, I mean. I got a table, but I got this girl coming by. She's not *my* girl, she's this rapper, outta Tampa, and she's expecting my—"

"Attention."

"You know the game."

"My friend Hawk's gonna be here," Eva said brightly, "so—"

"Hawk? Somebody's friend? That's new."

"You like Hakeem." Eva knew this to be true.

"I keep him close." Ron glanced up at the bar. No bartender. "Why are we acting, though," Ron said, moving closer to Eva, "like we don't know each other's secrets?" He was sweet about it. Ron's face fell into the startle-eyed, slight smile he could have when something other than new money and fresh triumph pleased him.

"'Cause we don't."

His face lifted back to false mellowness. The bartender had returned, and stood framed by neat rows of bottles. Bars had begun to
seem glamorous and twinkly to Eva, havens lined with labels promis-
ing escape to Monte Cristo, Bombay, Belvedere, and Calvados. The
bottles stamped JAMESON'S WHISKEY SIX YEARS OLD or GLENMORANGIE
SINGLE HIGHLAND MALT stood out zaftig among bones. Eva identified
with Ron's hard gaze at them.

"So you sitting with Hawk?" Ron said. He got the barkeep's attention with a glance. "Or with me?" Whether he was the issuer or the receiver, whether it was business or it was personal, Ron wasn't one
to hesitate before an ultimatum.

Eva stood. She relaxed one shoulder, challenged him a little with
her chin.

Ron was charmed by what he perceived as her confidence, by what
he considered only a slight style transformation. He was worried, as he
tended to be around Eva, about his utter appreciation of her beauty.
It made him raw.

"Sit with me," he said, and when she continued staring at him, he
added, with a twinge of awkwardness, "please."

When a man appreciated Eva's looks, and the effort she put into
enhancing them, Eva heard her father's voice, and knew he'd been
right about everything. The bartender brought Ron a Scotch, and
after a quick scissorslike gesture of Ron's fingers, poured one for Eva.

She sat across from Ron at a table for eight. The Tampa rapper
showed up in jeans and a too-big bomber jacket. Her predeal clothes
made her uncomfortable and made Eva feel superior, especially when
the girl, who was cute if a little rough around the edges, mumbled
hellos to the industry luminaries and hangers-on at Ron's table. The
girl looked at Ron searchingly and then turned abruptly toward the
door with her pink-haired manager. Ron jumped up and walked them
from Kato's, and the dialogue Eva imagined was one she'd have in the
same situation—all assurances and affection and promises that when
the rapper blew up, she'd walk into Kato's and everyone would kiss her
feet. That someone else told the tales she did was as much a comfort to
Eva as her hazel iris of Scotch.

Ron got back to the table, didn't sit, and said, "I'm out." Then he added, "No worries," and it was understood that the bill was taken care of. To Eva, Ron reached out his hand and said, "Let's roll."

She was happy and confirmed by this—as she always was by public displays, however vague and abbreviated. Eva kept her attitude, scooted with assurance from the table. She and Ron got in his spotless car. He wanted to show her the house in Malibu he'd just purchased.

They inched onto crowded Sunset Boulevard, and Eva saw the Mondrian, the hotel at which she used to stay when in Los Angeles. *Limousines to hide the stars,* went the disco tune in Eva's head, *tinted windows to hide the scars.* Then to *And in the city it's a pity 'cause we just can't hide—tinted windows don't mean nuthin', they know who's inside.* She was usually mesmerized by the Strip's brutal billboards, had partied on its lamp-thawed plazas, grubbed at 3:00 a.m. at the pristine restaurants, overseen artists' visits to the florid record stores. *Donna Summer,* Eva tagged her thoughts. *And Run-D.M.C.*

Ron and Eva rode along quietly. The Tampa rapper's voice rhymed away through the speakers. *Ron'll never clear the Steely Dan sample* is what Eva thought. *So it doesn't even matter that the shit sounds good. And if Ron does get it cleared, it'll be a zillion dollars.*

Ron sped through the part of Sunset lined with memorial parks and tall hedges hiding golf-worthy lawns and mansions with columns Eva connected with plantation houses of the South. Then through Brentwood and Bel-Air, the foothills of the Santa Monica Mountains, and a garden shrine housing the ashes of Mahatma Ghandi. Eva knew Malibu, and it seemed closer to Hollywood than usual. She was nervous as they rode north on the Pacific Coast Highway a short stretch, then turned away from the ocean and up a steep street lined with the garage doors of homes whose fronts mocked the tide with astonished faces. *Drink Scotch whiskey all night long, and die behind the wheel.* That was the line, the unclearable snatch of song.

Ron pulled into a garage under what seemed a small house for the neighborhood. He switched off his car.

Eva did what she did in business meetings when she had bad news to pass on. She took a deep breath, tried to speak as if her news was rosy, prepared to tell as much of the truth as she could while pretending to tell the full and exact truth.

Eva said, "I don't know if you want to know this." *Spineless,* she chided herself. *Get to it.*

"Not a good way to start a conversation between two people who've had sex like us."

"Not that."

"I didn't think so. But still." He paused. "You're not pregnant." Ron's chest was still up near the steering wheel, fingers on the key in the ignition.

"No."

"What, then? Damn. Work? Fired?"

"I was pregnant."

"By me."

"Yeah." Eva's hands had sweated a circle on her skirt.

Ron sat back in his seat. The keys dangled with a tinkle.

"You had an—"

"Mm-hm." Eva nodded. *Dewar's,* she thought. *Bushmills, Jamesons.* The warmth of the one drink at Kato's had faded. She wanted its hollow heat.

"You didn't feel," he said, "like I should be in on it."

"In on it to say what."

"You coulda had it?" It was the first time Eva'd heard Ron sound actually unsure. He could make himself sound unsure. He could make himself sound almost any way that served his strategy or justified his end. But she'd never heard an unintentional waver in his voice. It made him sound fragile, and so to Eva, sincere.

"I'm nobody's baby's mama." *They got a name for the winners of the world. I want a name when I lose.* Eva could shake the Tampa rapper's voice. But Steely Dan was forever.

Ron switched on the car, buzzed open the moon roof. Rafters and a concrete ceiling above them.

"I know you're not judging me." Eva's own heat kicked in where the liquor would have.

"You judged me," he said. "When you didn't call to say what was going on. You judged me in Europe. At the airport. Shit, before the air-port." He was looking straight ahead.

"You were talking about a sex house," Eva said. "Are we sitting under it now?"

"You're the one—"

She sat up, ready. "One what?" She stopped before she called him a *motherfucker*, since this time it was literal.

"The one that was carrying my baby and aborted it." The word *aborted* was a fart from his mouth. He wouldn't look at her. "That's the one you are."

Eva reached onto the floor, picked up her shiny pocketbook. Held tight to what was hers—lipstick, phone, passport—and to what the $800 bag meant, to the security it stood for. "I don't owe you jack, really," she said.

"Owe? How could you owe? You gotta take something to owe. At least accept something. What could *you* owe *me*?"

Speak the truth, white boy, she thought. *You know it like I know it. I couldn't owe you a goddamned thing. Under any circumstance.* She patted door leather for the handle and opened the car. Eva stepped onto the spotless floor, walked through the open garage door and into the moonlight. She teetered a bit. The heels of her sandals felt like ballpoint pens.

She thought of Ron with loathing. She didn't see him as one of those cartoonish white-boy gangstas from Idaho. She didn't think of him as a caricature of a caricature. She didn't go that far. She al-lowed, as she usually did, that Ron at least tried to have something of his own.

But what is it to be white? To have that, as your base? And on top of it to be all up in me. All up in my business.

These are the things she thought, because she was angry at her-self, and guilty. She had been in the studio, with A Tribe Called Quest. Q-Tip, the lead MC, recording his part of a new song called "Award Tour." She'd been there, just hanging, because she loved the trio and because she'd dated the DJ, Ali, for a while. There was a line . . . *You can be white and cool but don't prep the role.* Or it was *You can be white and blue but don't crap the roll.* Eva wanted to know the exact words of the song right then. She scraped her mind for Q-Tip's exact words, his phrasing, his cadence, everything.

This night, the night she told Ron about her abortion, the night she was feeling as low-down as she'd felt strapped to the gurney, she thought of Ron like she thought on any given day of most white males in hip hop: that down to his drawers and up to his buzzed haircut, Ron was a biter. *All of him one big bite of black people—not of what we created, even, but of what we actually are. What we in hip hop have become. Ron and his wack-ass compadres take big bites of our evolution. Not even chewed and regurgitated! They slap us still bloody and dripping on their sorry selves.* This is where her mind went. She counted his faults. She was aware of what she was doing, and thought, *That's what they do. They get mad at themselves and they count the stereotypes. So, cool. But really I don't even need that justification. I don't need justification for anything I do or don't do in terms of this or any white boy. He's thinking black girl right now. He's thinking nigga that killed the baby with no remorse.*

Ron and Eva were both quiet.

White boy, Eva thought.

Got your fucking nerve.

You didn't build no city on rock 'n' roll.

You ain't built shit.

Then Ron laid on his horn. It ripped through the silent enclave. "You climbing down this mountain in those heels, Eva? Where you going?" He leaned on the horn again, for five long seconds. Rested. He honked again. And rested. Eva didn't move. He opened his door, put one foot out, and called to her. "Get in the car," he said, half-command, half-plea. "I'll take you where you need to go."

Trying to tell me about myself. Trying to tell me anything.

She got in his car. Every curve in his face puffed and pissed off. She thought he was going to peel out like a maniac, but he backed out like he was on his way to work, and early enough to beat the traffic.

"I'm not saying we were in love, Eva." Matter-of-factly. "I'm trying to talk to you."

"Talk, then." *Who's to say that I'm in love with you? But who's to say that I'm not?* Eva's mind sang and tagged. *Janet Jackson, "Miss You Much," 1989.* Tagged and sang.

"If you could just chill for—"

Chill? "Fuck you." She looked at him and she wanted to spit on him. He'd said *chill* a thousand times to her, around her. Right then she hated the way he sounded saying *chill. Chuck Chill-Out,* went Eva's brain, *New York City radio DJ, veteran, been on air since 1982. Groove B-Chill from* House Party. *Chill Will of the Get Fresh Crew.*

"Chill" belongs to me. *I could never,* Eva thought, *owe you shit.*

Ron glanced at her. "How are you looking at me? I'm your white boy now? That's it? Me being a brother right now, though, I could say what I wanted."

"Don't mention brothers to me." *What right do you have to mention a black man, even a hypothetical one, to me?*

He turned up the radio. A talk radio host introduced callers.

—We're back and still discussing the continuing effects of the Los Angeles uprising. Tomorrow night we have a special guest, Sister Souljah on Bill Clinton and on Ice-T's "Cop Killer." On the line right now we have Linda, from West L.A.

—It was stupid we tore up our own neighborhoods, yes! But were people *thinking?* NO! People are enraged! Can you understand the words, *long simmering resentment?* Can you understand that video? Can you understand the last three hundred years? Where do you think that goes? Nowhere but up in flames on the right day.

—Linda, appreciate your passionate response. Gonna go straight to Brad, now, from Rancho Cucamonga.

—I'm LAPD. I'm a white cop. Blacks hate us. They can say that. We can't say how we feel about them, even the criminals. If we do, we're racist assholes.

—Brad, good to hear from you, but we've got to go to Paul from Venice.

—I'm homeboy to my heart—straight-up second-generation

Mexicano, and you know what? I can't be racist. Blacks can't be racist. I don't know what to say about the Koreans, but it's not about the color. It's about the power. Why can't white people understand that. My wife's a white girl, and I ask her that all the time. It's a willful ignorance, that's what I tell her. Sometimes she agrees with me.

From the steering wheel, Ron switched the station. He found a Sade song. This was a consolation to Eva. Ron knew it.

When she was in college, Eva thought Sade held the map for heartbreak. Eva buzzed down the window.

I still feel the chill as I reveal my shame to you / I wear it like a tattoo.
She let Sade wash over her, let the sea air hit her face.

"Where're you staying?" Ron asked.

"The Peninsula."

"Aaah," Ron said. "With the big dogs."

Eva nodded her head like, *Abso-fucking-lutely.*

She didn't look Ron's way.

———

Eva kicked off her sandals. Held her purse in her lap as they cruised Wilshire, the perpetual L.A. boulevard a socialist millionaire forced the city to name for him, the sometime stomping grounds of crews like Uncle Jamm's Army. Kids used to pop-lock at Maverick's Flat on Crenshaw. Eva had roller-skated at World on Wheels on the Westside and at Flipper's in Hollywood. Flipper's was a Rite-Aid now.

This world moves fast, Eva thought. *I'm gonna be twenty-seven this year. Too young to be mulling over how things used to be.*

Eva thought about her rented car, still at Kato's. She thought about what time she had to be at soundcheck in the morning (early), about how to tell Lois from Trix that if she went with the video director of their dreams, Trix would need to go triple platinum before they ever made a dime. Eva thought about the strapless bra she needed for the next night's gig. She thought about which of her acts, recording at various places around the country, needed a call, a prompt, an apology, a something. Eva thought of the man she was dating in New York City, a Spanish guy older than Ron in this business. Eva tried not to think of the indictment on Ron's face, but it was difficult when he was right by her, suddenly and obviously taking the long way to her hotel.

For all the ire she'd expressed and hidden in Malibu, Eva had wanted, in a passing fantasy, to tell Ron she might be pregnant back when she first suspected. Eva'd wanted to call him when her period was three weeks late, but Eva thought of being pregnant as a justification for calling him that she wouldn't yield to. He'd see through the pregnancy, to her having wanted to call—the call being an expression of her missing and wanting him.

Until the moment Eva decided against having the baby—on her own, and with no advice from anyone—she weighed the idea of having it and never telling Ron. Weighed the idea of telling Ron it was his—after the baby was born. Never did she consider adoption.

Once I carry it, it'll be mine to raise.

Not giving the baby up for adoption was the only absolute Eva had when it came to pregnancy. Though logically she knew that giving it up after it got here was less ultimate than getting rid of it, the fact of her arbitrary rule made her think of herself as a person with an off-kilter morality gauge, which led her to imagine what kind of off-kilter mother she would be, which led her to think of how a baby would fit—or not fit—into her life, which led Eva to think of herself as selfish and shallow for even having had the previous thought, which led her to reflect on the kind of narcissistic, cold mother she would be, which led her to visit a female doctor on New York's Upper West Side who "performed the procedure" at a small hospital nearby. The visit confirmed for Eva (it was, technically, her third abortion and fourth child) just how about work and about self she could be. Eva had the money, after all, to raise a child in the good nanny–private school–organic veggie–music camp way that would give the kid a head start over almost everyone.

The doctor, though, was kind. The doctor didn't refer Eva to aides or techs for the ultrasounds and the blood work. "Some women prefer general anesthesia because they've had it before and liked it," said the doctor, like general anesthesia was a fruit-acid facial, a real glow-getter. "Some want it because they've experienced sexual assault or trauma, and so being unconscious will make the abortion easier. Some women simply have a low threshold for pain. Local anesthesia is fine for early term abortion, but some women have fears about pain, period, so general is an appreciated option."

Eva nodded, so the doctor continued.

"Some women want to be unconscious so they have no memory of the procedure."

It promotes amnesia. But they can't give you anesthesia, general or otherwise, for this part of it. This is the part you need it for. This, and the last ten weeks. The "so much" that was "ahead of me" is here. I have no excuse. I just don't want to have a kid.

How am I doing this? Eva asked herself. *How is this even legal?*

Eva chose general. She felt she qualified for it due to the doctor's first statement, and her last one. The woman asked no questions about Eva's marital status, or about the father. The doctor's waiting room was nonexistent, just a receptionist's desk, and then you were led to one of three examination rooms where you could ponder your and your baby's fate in private, surrounded by *Metropolitan Home* and *The New Yorker*, by framed Cape Cod shore scenes and Caribbean travel posters.

Eva thought to call Ron after the initial visit, in the week before the procedure. But she didn't because she didn't want Ron to think she needed anything—not input, or money, or emotional support. Even if she had this baby, she wouldn't ask him for a goddamn thing. Some of it was pride—Eva had that, though she also had discipline and fear.

Her desire was to have a kid some future day she couldn't picture. She mostly wanted, as she had since as long as she could remember, to be free. To be independent. To not need anything but what she could provide for herself. Free to her meant having money to do what she wanted. Free to Eva meant not being married. It meant making sacrifices (for herself) and making tough decisions. It meant being able to pick up and go when she felt like it. Freedom meant being able to do this and still put forth a face that spoke of lightheartedness and a lack of complication. This was the freedom to which Eva had aspired and acquired. She was sharp enough to get what freedom had meant to people born before hip hop. Freedom meant no more back-of-the-bus. Royalties supposedly paid fairly to artists. No more church bombings. No more trees with strange fruit. No more back-alley, wire-hanger abortions. Better jobs. Equal pay for equal work. *Oh yeah*, Eva thought. *Let freedom ring. I can get a goddamn abortion for seven hundred and fifty dollars and I can get bitch-ho lyrics played on the pop stations.*

In Eva's favorite fantasy, she would pick up her phone one sunny day and have it be Ron. She could sound breezy and busy but down to hang out. She would not be pregnant. She would seduce his body easily, and his heart eventually, and if the black-white thing didn't rear its head, they could be one of those interracial couples that seemed untouched by the effect their presence had on others, the kind that had surmounted the insurmountable issue of race, the kind that acknowledged the gulf between them as just another kind of gulf, and gulfs existed between couples all the time—cultural, sexual, emotional, regional—and people dealt with them, stayed together through them. Eva and Ron could be the kind of couple that had a nice house in a nice neighborhood, the kind that understood each other's jobs and dreams. Eva had never been in a relationship that lasted longer than eight months in row. She'd never argued about domestic issues. She'd never fought over anything except punctuality, hip hop, her job, and her right to be her. Eva felt that if she and Ron floated on the gulf between them, coped with it, got to know it, all other squabbles and temporary crises would seem like just those. Trivial and not worth the time it took to argue over them.

This wasn't the way she was thinking in Malibu, though, or on Wilshire Boulevard.

Eva didn't call Ron during the week before the procedure. She didn't call him on the day of, when she took a cab to the hospital, got herself admitted as an outpatient, stripped, and put on a backless gown and paper slippers and paper bonnet. Eva didn't think of her artists or her coworkers or her competitors as the registered nurse wheeled her in—catheter inserted and taped to her hand again. She didn't think of how she was going to con the doctor into letting her get alone into a cab when they'd asked for the name of a person who would pick her up and see her home. On the form, Eva'd written C.R. SUMMERS, a girl who'd sat next to Eva at one of her high schools, a girl Eva'd shared a cafeteria table with once or twice and who had gone off to college somewhere in the South, and whom Eva had never seen again. On the gurney, Eva's teeth chattered and her lips were dry and the only thing she really thought was *How will I look at my-self two days from now when the bleeding has tapered off and the pain pills are no longer necessary? How will I look at myself even when I pass a glass pane on the street? How will I look at myself—I'm about to count backward from ten; I know the drill, that's how low-down I am—when I wake up, and what was there is gone? What was alive, now dead.*

Think about it!

That's what Eva said to herself as hall doors snapped open automatically to receive her.

Think about it! It's the least you can do, considering the physical pain is minimal. Think! The embryo—no, the baby—will be vacuumed out. Killed. Disposed of. And you will ride away with imaginary Carleen Summers. You'll be free of what would have been your responsibility.

That's when she thought hard about Ron.

And Ron's is what she thought. His responsibility, too.

But she wouldn't have called him then, even if she could have. Her last thought before the anesthetic solution relaxed her muscles and took her into a quick coma was that this was her problem. She was the one who was pregnant. *Every boy,* Eva thought, *is not my boyfriend.*

They pulled up on the black brick drive of the Peninsula Beverly Hills. Eva got out quickly. She was almost through the glass front doors when she heard another car door shut, heard one of the white-suited valets say, "How long, sir?"

Ron answered, "Not sure." As he came around the car and walked toward her, he said, "We're not finished."

"We are."

"Not because you say so. You do owe me," he said, pushing the door for her, "the courtesy of a conversation."

They got on the elevator, and then got to her Grand Deluxe room. A Grand Deluxe room was better than a Deluxe room, though not as big or as fly as the Patio Grand Deluxe or the eleven-hundred-square-foot Executive Grand Deluxe, and not near as big as the Grand Deluxe Suite or the private, stand-alone garden Villas to which Eva aspired. Her Grand Deluxe Room did have Italian linens and French doors and her choice of domestic newspaper delivered daily and a minibar and three telephones. It was what she and Ron knew together—hotel rooms. This one was nicer then the ones they'd been in Italy. But it was the same impersonal vibe. Nothing of hers, nothing of his. Clean sheets twice a day.

He sat, and she did.

"So the way it is," Ron said, "is you come to the restaurant to tell me you had an abortion of our baby, and now you're mad at me."

Our. This gave her courage. "Why didn't you call me," Eva said, "after the tour?"

"You had an abortion because I didn't call you?"

Eva resisting blowing up, resisted saying she could never explain to him why she had the abortion, why she'd had any of them, but thought instead, *No, you asshole, it's not because you didn't call.* "I'm asking you," she said, "like a point of information."

"Rules of order. Okay. I didn't call you because when we were in Italy, you acted like it was all fun for you—fun only. And when we were at the airport—"

"And you were talking about the sex house."

"You love sex. Or you act like you do. The way we were over there, I thought I was saying some shit you wanted to hear."

Ron said, "I wasn't trying to play myself."

"If I was a white girl," Eva said, "you would've called." She didn't even know if she believed that. It was a test.

"Since it seems to matter, I haven't been with a white girl in . . . eight years." Saying it, not the fact of it, distressed him. He looked her in her eye, though, as he declared what Eva thought had to be a hatred of himself.

"Why? That's your thing?" She thought he was pitiful.

"It is what it is." Suddenly proud, and ashamed a little that he was proud, he looked down and wiped at the white quilt like there was lint on it. "It's who pulls me. I don't fight what naturally pulls me." Then he looked at her again. "It's who gets pulled to me, too."

"You have superiority in your head. Built in. So you go in on top, in your head."

"Yeah. I'm always three steps ahead of every black girl."

"And black male. Don't say it like it's impossible. Like it's some kind of urban legend."

"I know what you're trying to say, what you're saying. I know how the world is. But one, you're changing the subject—"

"This is the subject."

"You had the abortion," he said, "because I'm white?"

Eva looked at him. *I was not ready. I am not ready. I had it because I could.*

"And if anyone feels superior in this situation, *our* situation, not the world's situation or the country's situation, it's you."

Our. Eva wanted to say, *This is the third abortion I've had, the fourth baby I've gotten rid of, and this is the first time the father has been a white man.* But what she said was, "How I feel is nothing in the face of how things are."

"You don't believe that. If you did, you wouldn't have found me at Kato's. I never would have known about you being pregnant."

She hated the word *pregnant.* Like *positive,* it had equally horrible and wonderful meanings. And the first syllable sounded big and round to Eva. Full and absolute. "Do we have to keep talking about it?"

"You showed up to talk about it." He paused. "Or did you want to see me? Too. Do you feel—"

"Bad?" She nodded, felt like a freak. A dumb slut. Selfish and not worthy of anything she owned or any break in the wall of disgust by which she was surrounded.

"Can't share nothing else," Ron said, "so you decided to share the guilt."

The fact of what he said made her angry.

"Make me an accessory after the fact," he said flatly and quietly, as if agreeing with himself. "You want me—" He moved nearer to her on the bed and put his arm around her shoulder like they were chums. They sat there awkwardly. Eva finally leaned into him.

"I'm probably not one," Ron said, "for carrying in soup on a tray. But maybe I could have flown out there. Something. Did it take . . . long? I mean, did it hurt?"

Eva pressed into him closer. She wanted to hear his voice so sweet, but not the words coming from his mouth. Ron leaned her back on the bed, and she rolled onto her side. He got up, pulled a pillow from under the coverlet, pressed it against her stomach and chest. "Hold onto it," he said to her.

Ron lay behind her, his chin on her head, an arm around her waist and the pillow, his chest against her back. "Hold onto it," he said again.

Eva pressed her back into him, clutched the cushion, and felt a frantic, unearned gladness. It was good to hold onto something. Good to be held.

Ron's arm tightened around her. The mute pump of his heart sucked hers closer. His blood was awhirl, anxious to take back its living place in her body. For lists of reasons that matched in some places, both were ashamed of who they were. The ashamedness was imbedded and unacknowledged, wholly American and completely un-American: each believed they had to be who they were with no choice in the matter. And they were on their way up.

Listen to my heart beat, went the song in Eva's head. *For you.*

Eva and Ron didn't have sex. To each of them, and with a draining intensity that pulled them into a deep sleep, it felt like love.

In the morning, Eva woke first.

"Ron," she said, and shook him gently. "Lil' John. I got sound-check in ninety minutes. Way out in Universal City."

Ron's eyes opened. In his sleepy state, he looked at her with contentment. Her words seemed to hit him after a delay. He wiped his eyes. "Soundcheck," he said. "Right." He twisted, stood, and adjusted his clothes.

Eva felt better. She felt she'd done the right thing by telling Ron everything, when she hadn't told him much at all.

"That's how you're playing me," Ron said.

"Huh?"

"Not so much as a good morning. Cool. So, tonight? Dinner at the new spot on Sunset. It's where everybody's at on Fridays. Oh no, we both got the awards thing tonight, so maybe drinks after? And then we can come back up here. Order more Scotch from room service, then make it hot. Right? PeaceLove&Money tour, all over again."

"Why're looking at me like that? So evil?"

"I'm on your program." And after a quick glance in a mirror, he was out the door.

Eva saw Ron at the awards show that night, but he was far across the room talking to artists, talking to women, talking to the spruced up Tampa MC. When Eva was backstage, Ron was out front. When Eva was out front, she saw Ron busily, casually heading back-stage. Eva's pager didn't chirp with Ron's number, and Eva didn't beep Ron. Eva did go to a bar after the show, alone. Drank Glenmorangie because the name sounded dramatic and because she saw high rollers ordering it. She stretched one Scotch out for thirty minutes. Stretched another. And another.

Eva didn't hear from Ron until she'd been back in New York for over a month. He suggested she meet him in Midtown, at yet another hotel room.

"It's what we do," he said, when she'd suggested her apartment. So Eva left her office, met him at his room, and without much more than a "Hey" and a "Hey," Eva and Ron did their thing. They had sex, awash in whiskey, and it was as good as it had ever been. Eva, though, had faint bruises inside her thighs from where he pressed his fingers. Ron had bite marks on his chest, and Eva had scratched red welts over his neck and back. Laden as forensic traces, wisps of Eva's hair lay on the white sheets. Strands of it wound through the rings on Ron's right hand.

He made a point of telling Eva he was in town for four more days. "Call me," he said as tritely as he was able, "if you need anything."

She didn't call.

A few months later they were both in Reno for the International DJ Festival and neither called the other. They ran into each other at a showcase, made allusions to "complicated situations" and "crazy, needy" artists. Ron and Eva clinked glasses and kept moving.

When Eva was back in Los Angeles, for the Trix video shoot, and for a meeting about a possible new promotion, she had also a meeting in Ron's building, so she made her way by his office. They left together, and there was dinner before the sex back at the Peninsula in Eva's Grand Deluxe Suite. Twelve hundred square feet, marble bathroom with oversize tub, complimentary fruit basket, VCR, and bedside electronic panel to control the fan, lighting, and valet call buttons. Even at the Peninsula, in the Grand Deluxe Suite, they didn't discuss the last time they'd been there together in her lesser Grand Deluxe room. And they never—not in 1993, 1994, 1995, 1996, or 1997—discussed the abortion.

Instead, they kissed and licked like there was no sugar sweeter. Eva began to scratch through to blood. He pushed into her from behind until she jerked away, cursing and teasing. Eva and Ron didn't drive-by fuck. Good at each other's bodies, they settled in for opera. Eva and Ron were the most themselves with each other in bed, excavating psyches until their souls scraped.

Always they inched to their corners after, exhausted, haltingly angry, and satisfied. They dozed twitchily, each wanting to be the first awake and gone. They'd move toward the bed's center, comforted by the other's regular rasps and moist smells. Ron and Eva pressed and pawed each other unconsciously and affectionately. They nursed muddled blues.

Cat Island

Goats sniffed at conch shells and waded through Audrey's starfish crop. The sand seemed more pink than usual to Eva. It was as if red coals were buried beneath. From her frying hollow on the beach, Eva smelled fish in burning butter. It made her nauseous. Audrey walked onto the sand, offering a short glass of amber liquid.

Scotch? Eva hoped. *I wish.*

Because Eva'd caught a cold, and Pritz could hear it through the phone, and because Eva'd been progressively more evil with Pritz in each call since their first one, Eva had been able to put her off for three days. But the former Giada Biasella was to arrive on Cat Island the next afternoon, and the thought of Pritz squealing "Ciao!" in person made Eva twist a knot into the huge tank she was wearing. It was Dart's, and it came to her knees. The armholes hung to her waist, and she had a square of green batik thrown over her shins.

The Rowe House was not like the one Eva, Pritz, and two of Pritz's girlfriends had shared on Montego Bay the winter before. That palace had two stories, four bedrooms, silken sofas, a snooty cook, a thorough housecleaner, and an almond-tree-shaded pool with a view of the bay. There'd been ginger iced tea, and ackee and saltfish served on china. Star-apple salad and rum cocktails for lunch, and then whatever substances Pritz had hustled in or acquired locally to increase the relaxation level or sexual timbre or to decrease the number of sleep hours needed.

On Cat, though, Eva wasn't in a jet skiing mood or a shucked-oysters-and-all-night-at-the-casino mood or a girl-talk-with-pseudo-girlfriends mood or a flirt-with-and-maybe-fuck-the-French-business-man-on-holiday mood. On Cat, Eva wanted liquor but wasn't drinking it. She was sleeping long heavy hours and waking rested, even if stiff and congested and queasy. On Cat, Eva had yet to put on a bathing suit and walk in the ocean. Even with Dart the way he was, and maybe because of it, Eva felt ensconced in the safety and seclusion of the Rowe House and its tiny patio. She was in Gladys Knight's simpler place and time. The rush of the sea and the fact of her pregnancy was plenty.

She wanted to get back in bed with Dart and suck on some orangey benne cake. Eva wanted to smell Dart's salty apricot smell, dream about her child. Eva pictured herself and Dart and a faceless baby. Dart on real drugs and not sleeping so much and Benjamin and Audrey and Édouard and even Jenny and the Skip—her family. Eva and Dart and the son would walk on the beach and Dart would swing the child by its arms and there would be embraces and the Rowe House would be brightly lit and well-appointed and the Rowes would never return. Eva believed it was a sweet slice of hell specific to her generation to be wise to the absurdity of Hallmarkian dreams, indeed to feel superior to them—but to still dream them in Technicolor, and with a booming soundtrack. Eva wanted some Scotch with her benne cake.

"Take this," Audrey said, thrusting a small glass at Eva. She stomped her foot at the goats.

Eva shook her head. "No medicine." Eva wiped at puffed eyes, and then hacked phlegm into a napkin. She felt like she was imposing herself onto the stinging, flawless day.

"It's honey," Audrey said curtly. "Lemon."

The thought of a coat on her scratchy throat appealed, but Eva had a creepy flash about bees and their digestive enzymes and pregnancy. She believed Audrey's good intention but said, "No, thanks. Maybe just some lemon water?"

Audrey brought her eyebrows together. "If I wanted to bring you water, that's what I would have bring. It's an old tale about honey. Honey is fine for you even now."

Eva wondered from where she'd heard bad news about honey and pregnancy, and what the full story was. She wondered if girls all their lives attracted random bits of baby info to their brains like pins to a magnet. Eva wondered if she had instinct. Her current one was to lie in the sun and bake the cold from her body. Eva hadn't taken a thing for her cold except lemon juice in hot water, and her leg bled puss because she hadn't put on it so much as a dab of antique Neo-sporin from the Rowe's bathroom cabinet.

"I guess I can't complain of you sitting there," Audrey said, "a bump on a log." Then she cocked her head toward the Rowe House. "But he needs to get up."

"He gets up," Eva said with a cough.

"When I don't see him. He doesn't even swim—" Audrey knocked back the honey and lemon herself.

"I told you he has a problem." Eva scratched her nose and chin. "I can't explain it to you." Eva's skin was burned and peeling on her face, shoulders, chin, and cleavage. Her nose was raw from blowing, and she had the raised bumps of prickly heat inside her elbows. Her hair was brittle. Her finger- and toenails were hard and chipped. Dart was sullen and always sleeping, so she'd been spending every day, almost dawn to dusk, in the rays.

Audrey sat down next to Eva on the sand like it wasn't sizzling. "If you don't bring him food to the bed," she said, "I bet he won't starve to death."

Dart wasn't eating much of what Eva brought him as it was. "Dart's unhappy in this world," she said almost proudly. "Ill at ease."

Audrey was unimpressed. "He's common. The strife, lies, bias, the sickness. It's why we're all the way we are, why it's hard to bring the kids into this world. It's hard to face them. We disappoint." She gave a snorty laugh. "*Bay kou bliye, pote mak sonje.* Giver of blow forgets, bearer of scar remembers. I see the scars on you."

"Scars?" Eva coughed. Audrey winced. "Please. Don't go getting all supernatural on me."

"Supernatural? Ha. Nat-u-ral. Us that have the scars can see them. You see mine."

Audrey wasn't speaking in her forged sage voice. She was like her brother, Édouard, for a moment, utterly without fraud. Eva had an urge to loop an arm through Audrey's but repressed it, felt like she'd be rebuffed, even in what seemed a sudden sisterhood.

"You made a sacrifice in blood, no?" She laughed her stark laugh again. "It's why you came here with him, the stories they sell in Nassau about Cat? The magic herbs that do the work? Get rid of a baby?"

Eva didn't want to talk about that. Her karma, she felt, was bad enough. "Dart needs help. For his mania. He wanted a spell. A show, I guess. Something to believe in."

"*Mania.* I like that word. Like a flower it sounds. So he had his mania. Made his own spell on Eddie's night? All that foolishness. But for you?"

Eva shrugged. *Be so good to have some Scotch.* She tasted it in her mouth, thinking how nice it would be to have any whiskey when Dart took his herbs with Pepsi or whatever canned juice she'd gotten from the store on her walks with Audrey. He'd pass a few words and then sleep for fifteen hours. Eva sat with Dart in the dusky bedroom during lunchtimes, and sometimes during the evenings. He ignored her, sometimes dismissed her or feigned sleep, or put his head in her lap until he was truly snoring. Then Eva would sit on the patio, or go to Audrey and Benjamin's to watch one of the mawkish romances Ben enjoyed seeing Audrey struggle not to cry through. Mellowed toward Eva because of her brooding pregnancy, Audrey's contempt for Dart had hardened when she walked in on Eva feverishly asleep on the Rowe's narrow couch two mornings before. Eva, for her part, felt effective, and duty-bound.

She let her head fall back, closed her eyes to the sun, and sighed.

"Oh, you are so *complete*. You have everything so much you won't make one wish. Say right now what would *you* have in this world so unfit for your precious man?"

Eva looked Audrey in her face. "For everything to be even and fair and pure." Eva pushed down the snot in her throat.

"You come to . . . Cat . . . for—" Audrey sputtered. "This is where it's . . . *fair* and *pure*?" She looked like she wanted to spit on Eva and her free time and faraway home to go to. "You *like* your *everything*, anyway, *for you*."

"I never would've been here, except—"

"Except what?" Audrey had no time for wishy-washiness.

"Except Dart needs somebody." Eva wiped at her raw nose. "If it was me going crazy, he'd stay." *Of course he would.*

"You *are* going crazy." Audrey gestured forcefully toward Eva's waist, then her leg, and then her face. "And Dart is where? We're all sad, Eva. Dart makes a life of it while the rest of us work." Audrey rose and took the few steps to check her vibrant, drying cloth.

"It's chemical with him, Audrey." Eva was pleading a case, not even sure it was hers to plead. "Physical! Not laziness."

"There's medicine for this sickness?"

"Yes." Eva was weary as Audrey hit her with Eva's own argument. "He doesn't like it. He doesn't take it. He takes herbs." She thought the last would speak to Audrey's sage-y sensibilities, but it didn't.

"Ah," she said from the trodden path to the back of her house. "He has *you* for his medicine. I saw it from when you got here."

Eva didn't know why Dart's mood had turned. She didn't know if he was faking or not. She didn't know, even if he was faking it, if he didn't deserve her support. It had come out of the blue—Dart's cloud, and Eva's cold. But Eva's fever was breaking.

She gathered her things and went to the Rowe House, where Dart was silent behind a closed bedroom door. For the first time since she'd been on Cat, she picked up the house phone and was surprised and glad to hear a dial tone.

Eva got a U.S. operator and called depression hotlines in Manhattan. She tried six different numbers—all were in various states of not answering, or voice mail, or some other nonhuman, unresponsive bullshit. Eva ended up calling an 800 number for the Betty Ford Center, and a nice woman spoke to her for twenty minutes. The woman told her right away that Betty Ford didn't treat manic depression unless it was related to alcoholism, but recommended some books, and said that Dart did seem like he was going through something that he should talk to someone about. Eva got sleepy talking on the phone to the woman, who finally asked her how she was dealing with it.

"Not that well," Eva said.

She thought about all the Scotch she'd had, even knowing she was pregnant. But the Scotch had to do with Future Baby, Eva thought, and with Ron, and so Dart was not to blame for any of it. The Betty Ford woman talked about "intervention," which Eva wondered if she had the energy for. In the end, the woman sounded so absolutely sure of Dart's manic depression, Eva started to question whether she'd seen symptoms in Dart at all.

Eva went to the bedroom. Dart appeared to be asleep. She showered and then doctored some dried-out aloe vera gel and rubbed it into her peeling skin and lips. She searched for the first time since she'd been on Cat for mascara and shimmering lip gloss. The wound on her leg looked better, but still it throbbed as Eva rubbed coconut oil through her hair and looked without success for a cute, clean outfit. Dart didn't stir. Eva sat on the bed, touched his cool shoulder. A sheet was wrapped around him precisely from armpit to toe. He looked ready to be laid in a sarcophagus.

Still, Eva had hope. "Hey, now," she said. "Hungry?"

"I'm 'sleep." He kept his eyes closed.

"You know what?"

"No."

Eva was undeterred. "We have to go home at some point."

"Maybe."

"We gotta think about how different things'll be. How we can do something that lets us live a little bit like we're still here on Cat."

"And how are we living?" Dart opened his eyes. They were dewy and alert. "Here on Cat."

"More . . . free here, I guess. More relaxed." Eva took a deep breath as best she could with her clogged lungs and nose. "We could do something big together," Eva said to Dart in a charge. "Something businesswise."

"It would be difficult if not impossible," Dart said. Then he got up from the bed. He was unshowered and unshaven, but Eva took his verticality as a good sign.

"But how difficult? We could start our own thing." Eva was making it up as she went along. It felt good. "A management company. We start off with Sun as a client and everyone else will show up. People hate me, but they love you. Perfect combination."

"Who's gonna deal with the clerical stuff?"

Clerical stuff? Eva was nonplussed.

"Answering phones," Dart said, as if he had to define *clerical* for her. "The files that need to be kept." He shook his head. "It would be a lot."

No fucking way he is serious. "We could have him at work, Dart. The baby. Or I could work a lot from home." *Working from home* was a baffling concept to Eva, like *living abroad* or *having a baby* or *waiting on opportunity* or *all things being equal,* but she grasped at it. "I'd be stressed," Eva went on quickly, "but not as much as at Roadshow. We could be superselective about who we take on, and we could superserve those clients. Charge a higher percentage for stuff beyond just old ideas of management. See what I'm saying? Do a lot of crosspollination." She covered her mouth for a big cough. "Everybody wants a clothing line now, wants to make movies. We'd set that kinda shit up. I can get out from under Seb's thumb." *Maybe I'm dreaming, but I think I can have my son and have a life. I can be somebody's mother. Women do it all the time.*

"You know how to do that. Start a company." It wasn't doubt in Eva's ability that made Dart's tone so dreary and snide. It was his absolute faith in her.

"No! Of course I don't." *Of course I do. Or I will.* Eva was unfazed by his resistance. *If it's fear, okay. That can be overcome. If I need to tailor the plan more to his needs, okay.* "But I know how to find someone who knows how. Come on!" she said like she was inviting him to chase down an ice cream truck. "It'll be fun."

"This is the kind of stuff you think about. Even here."

Her leg hurt, but Eva's blood was flowing fast, she could feel oxygen in her brain and heart, and Dart was erecting dams. "It's what I'm thinking about *right now*," she said, "what I should have thought about a while ago. And we can get Pritz. Pritz'll be so down. With you and her on the international stuff—oh my God! What could we call it?"

"Call what?"

"Our company?" *Duh!*

"Call it Eva's Party," Dart dropped like a stone. "Call it Eva's Big Idea."

She was immune to his disdain. She saw a challenge. A game, a possibility of triumph. "Something better than that," Eva said, unkempt eyebrows scrunched in brainstorm mode. *Something that works on different levels. Like Sonrisa—sounds like "sunrise," means "smile." Sun was on point with hers.*

"Call it 'New,'" Dart said with even less gusto. "New Management."

"YES!" Eva screamed with the thrill of it. Then she coughed so much she had to run to the bathroom. Then she stood in the doorframe and said hoarsely, "Like, 'under new management.' Like, we're *brand-new*. New Management!"

"Works on a few different levels," he said.

Eva took his perception for collaboration, and she cleared her throat. "Gonna be *so* fly. Office in Manhattan? Or L.A.? Or do we do something crazy, like set up in Miami? Or San Francisco? Or Santa Fe?"

"Not New Mexico."

Why the fuck not? She was caught up in a dream that seemed more real to her than Uncle Benjamin and Aunt Audrey and perpetual strolls along Fernandez Bay. "I'm serious. I used to live out that way."

"I thought you used to live near Carmel." Like he was catching her in a lie. Eva saw him looking at her with hawkish curiosity, searching for faults, for weaknesses, for a place to strike.

Eva was used to that, though. Lots of men looked at her like that, threatened by her when she was enthusiastic and brainy and pretty in the same moment. So she kept on. "I lived a lot of places. Lotta creative stuff goes on in the Southwest. Good spas, too. Outside of travel, cost of doing business would be very, very low." Eva's mind was clicking. The songs in her head were her own and without words.

"Who wants to go to New Mexico to see their manager?"

"Have you heard of phone? *E-mail?* FAX? And when clients *do* have to come, they'll *want* to come. Desert's beautiful winter and summer. Be a real getaway from the melee, to come to the home offices." Eva loved the way "home offices" sounded. With her palm on her belly, she put a tissue to her nose and blew as hard as she could.

"Desert gets up to a hundred ten in the summer," Dart said. "Even at night it stays in the nineties." Like he was the Weather Channel.

What is he talking about? "No one says they have to trudge through it on foot, Dart." His disinterest had curdled to derision, and Eva could taste it. He sounded like Audrey had at the beginning, leery of Eva's self-possession. Mad at her for being her. Eva felt suddenly like she was talking too loudly, like her body and her self were lit bright and hurting his eyes.

So she turned herself down, spoke to Dart like she liked to in bed after sex—quietly, and like a sixth grader to a man. "It'll be relaxing for people sick of L.A. and New York. You might like New Mexico, Dart. Your own hours, too. Freedom." Eva was irritated, but she kept it under. "No beach, but swimming pools. Ranches."

"You should do it," Dart said.

"We're gonna." Eva's voice stretched back to enthusiasm and brightness, but the eye contact between them was iced and set. "It doesn't have to be Santa Fe, but damn, Santa Fe would just be so *extra*. Get a place with a few acres. Maybe some animals even, for the baby." *I'm tripping now, I know. Going from Abortion Queen to Farm Mom. But you gotta overshoot. You gotta imagine. It's the only way I've ever gotten anything or anyplace. Picturing it. Mapping it out. Holding the bat right. Keeping my eye on the goddamn ball.*

"You should do it," he said again, voice lowered a semitone, like a perfect flat was what he was going for.

"By myself." *I heard you the first time. I got it now. Gotchyou.*

"Everything you touch," Dart said sharply, "turns to gold."

Platinum, if you know my story, Hater. Platinum. She wanted to say those words to him in the coldest, slowest, Dart-like voice she could muster. Instead, she asked, still glaring at him, but like the question was incidental, "Is that how my life is?" Eva thought of the sound of his sotto voce in her ear when he was touching her body and it pissed her off.

"That's what I see."

"Because you don't look," Eva said, enunciating the *k* like she was trying to kill it. *I thought you saw me.*

"Maybe I'm so in my own shit, only your shiny days stand out."

Take your fucking medication. "You know goddamn well I got my other days," Eva said. *Your real medication.*

"No one sees those, though. And you're already talking about leaving Cat," he said like she was a traitor. "About *work.*"

About life. "I'm a heathen for that? I'm Evil Eva?" Her voice had graduated sixth grade and gone straight to associate general manager of Roadshow. *Nigga, I live in the real world.*

"Whatever you are, you'll land on your feet. You're built for this—shot callin', big ballin'. Music. Business. Go, Eva! Stack your chips. Start your business. Hire your nanny."

She stepped from the doorframe back into the bedroom. "Your point," Eva said slowly, "was that no one sees me on my sad days. My point is that you have. I been sad the whole time I've been here. I was sad at Vince the Voice." She coughed and wiped her nose and hated the imperfection and weakness of it.

"I spoke to that already," he said, pulling on a T-shirt. "I know that trick—calm, courteous repetition. I know it from you. Don't manage me. I don't want to fight with you."

Eva was angry now. "You don't want to do anything."

"I want to live."

"On what?" *Shit,* Eva thought. *For what?*

"How I live'll take care of itself."

What are you? Nineteen? "I thought you wanted to do this with me—"

"I'm still glad about the baby. He's a blessing of the most holy kind. But it's not like you need me. To help you do your living, I mean."

"Why would I bring all this up," Eva said, earnestly searching, "talking about 'we'?"

"You think you're talking to somebody else, I guess. Some steam-roller, empire builder."

Eva stared at him.

"I'm saying, Eva—you know me." Dart sat on the bed, and Eva took it as a softening.

She reached past her anger to her desire for change and her want for Dart to fit into her new plan. She sat next to him, picked up his hand. Eva was awkward and sincere. "But you'd be so good—"

He cut her short, his voice heartbroken and livid and low. "Was I good at managing Sun?" Dart pulled his hand from under hers. "I wasn't even managing her—I was *road* managing her. Getting her here, getting her there. *You* damn near manage Sun, and you're with the label. I book hotels. I wake her up for shows. Why you think she's got Vic and Swan around her? Why does she have Hawk on payroll? Why you think you've been able to lead her around by the nose? Because no one is really handling her BUSINESS. I love my sister, but I was in it to see the world. All the places I've been? I SAW those places, Eva. I EXPERIENCED them. It wasn't about the money. That's why I never took any. It was about the music. About Deirdre Addison. I feel blessed, when my head lets me feel blessed, to have been down for the ride. It's all I want—to feel things. To try and have my mind right, so I can. You spin gold from straw, Eva. That's your gig. You and Ron's and Hakeem's, Myra's, and even Sunny's. Me, though? D'Artagnan? I'm named for courage and loyalty, yeah, but know this, Superstar: I am not the one."

Eva heard someone at the door, and she heard her cell phone ringing. She hurried toward both, and there was Édouard handing her the cell.

"I answered it," he said apologetically. "It's a man, says he's your father."

Did you do it for love?
Did you do it for money?
Did you do it for spite?
Did you think you had to, honey?
—"THE LONG RUN," lyrics and
music by Don Henley

weetheart. Where are you?"

Eva was on the Rowe's patio. She heard faint music from down the beach, then a Miami deejay announcing cash prizes and an all-expense-paid stay at the South Beach Marriott. *Hits from the seventies, eighties, and nineties,* the hysterical jock said. *All hits, all the time.*

"I'm in the Bahamas, Dad."

"The tropics!" he said, like he was confirming an old victory. Eva's father had never been to "the tropics," and it slapped her that he was speaking as though reminiscent. "Beautiful! Work or play?"

Good question. Neither. "Work." It was what he understood best from her. "What's up?"

"That's my girl—to the point, to the point. I understand, yes I do. I need, though, for you to excuse yourself from your business associates. Find a place where you can have a personal moment."

A personal moment? Eva slid closed the glass door. "Done, Dad." The Miami deejay played a song Eva hated. *Number one pop hit for Def Jam Records,* went the computer in Eva's mind: *Montell Jordan's 1995 "This Is How We Do It."* The radio was barely audible. *You gotta get your groove on / Before you go get paid.* It bothered Eva like a mosquito.

"Your mother has died, Eva."

Stepmother. "How?" *Damn, Gayle's dead?*

"I'm not a hundred percent certain. A . . . friend of hers called, someone given my name and your name, and told to—"

Eva walked to a chair and sat on it. She put her hand on her belly in what had become, so quickly, a reflex. *Oh. My mother has died.*

"—reach out to one of us if anything happened to her. I guess the man felt it was best to call me. 'Laine'd kept up with my movements, such as they were. She kept up with yours, too."

At the sound of her mother's name, Eva coughed and tears rolled down her face. She spit snot on the ground next to her. Eva thought her father must have much more to say, so she remained silent. It was a trick she'd learned from spying on the better magazine journalists as they interviewed her artists. Just let the open space hang. Most times, the artist would fill it, and that's from where the best, most damaging quotes would be pulled. Eva almost always checked in on Sunny's interviews. She was too open with writers, too often saying or doing unsuitably revealing things.

But all her father said was "Sweetheart?" again. This was how he'd begun referring to Eva. With every upward move she made, with every thousand dollars Eva wired to the town—Laughlin, Nevada, aka Las Vegas Jr. for seniors—he and Gayle had finally settled in, her father treated her with more deference and less familiarity, with a pleased but complete bewilderment at her breezy autonomy and casual references to people whose songs were on the radio and whose bodies were (as her father put it) "two threads away from naked on the cable."

"Is there a funeral?" Eva felt her mother in her mind—taller than her mother really was with hair longer than her mother's really was, with a scent spicier than her mother ever really had—as she'd seen her last. Earth, Wind & Fire or somebody in the background. The Temptations, Eva remembered, or Bill Withers. She kept the tears from her voice. Her father was used to her composure, and she still didn't like to disappoint him.

"There was a small one," he said, "from what I understand.

This . . . man who called wasn't the most articulate person. I don't know who he was to her—"

You know. You have an idea. "When was it?" Eva was more urgent and angrier than she showed. *No funeral. No nothing.* "Please, say everything the man said."

Eva's father mistook her awkward sorrow for impatience with his having interrupted her "business" in the "tropics." "I know you're working. I hate to call you with this, but no time is a good—"

"Did the man have a message for me? Did the man say anything that came from her, to me?" *Did the man have a name? Did he sound nice? Could she have known how I used this moment before it ever happened?*

"She left the same message, the same message we have—"

"Which is what?" Eva was sharp. She thought of that message, the note her mother had given her, the one Eva'd handed to her father when he came in late and tired, the one he handed back to her like it was new policy she'd have to accept. "How old would she be, fifty-three?"

Eva's father spoke slowly now, assured of his role as messenger of importance. "The man told me that she said she was sorry. And that she saw your picture in *Ebony* and that you are pretty. That she always knew you would be as beautiful and successful as you are." He paused. "Fifty-two, she would be, by my count."

Tears rolled down Eva's face. She wiped them away. "That's not the same message." *I know the message by heart. I have the message. It's my supreme form of ID.*

"Don't grab at straws, Eva." It was her father's turn for sharpness and it was a comfort to her. Someone could be counted on for sameness.

"I'm grabbing what's there," Eva said. "Is there anything else? From the man, I mean. Did he say how she died? Did he say what she wanted?" Édouard and Dart seemed far away. *Did he say if she found it?*

"There's nothing else. From her." He paused. At first, Eva thought he might be overwhelmed. But then she hoped he was remembering who he was, and that even if he was an ass and had been an ass, he had things other than his daughter's feats to wonder at, things other than desertion to mourn. Eva also hoped he was reconsidering the ways in which he'd raised her, and that he was calculating the price of his pride. "I didn't know," her father said, "if this was going to be emotional for you or not."

"It is." Her leg throbbed.

"I can't tell with you. I never can anymore. Maybe it's the phone."

"No, it's how I am. Cold-blooded." It was Eva's turn to pause. She wanted off the phone, but she was beset again with the desire to make a gesture. Eva'd stopped believing years ago that her father was the reason her mom had gone. He'd been a fool, and mean, and often twisted, but Eva felt that at least her father had lived up to the responsibility of what he'd created. She felt her mother to be a quitter plain and simple. A flighty woman, without the demands of a career, who couldn't even handle a bossy husband and a needy little girl. "How are you with this, Dad?" she asked him formally. "Is it emotional for you?"

He grunted, surprised by the question. He said nothing.

"Hello?" Eva croaked into the phone. She was desperate.

"I will say I'm having a more difficult time with it then I would've thought." He paused. "A more difficult time than I'm showing."

"We're the same then." *There's no me forgiving her, as there is no me forgiving me.*

Then he spoke as if through a muffler. "Your mother," he said, "would have hated that."

"It's what she set up. She went *AWOL*."

"She left me, Eva. *Elaine left Ned.* It was never you."

"She should have took me with her." Eva realized how this might hurt her father, but she had too much going on. No means for strategy or tact. She reached for her leg, it hurt so bad, but she didn't touch it.

"She had no money," he said. "Or a place or—"

"She could've come back. At some point. At any point. When I was eighteen or twenty or thirty. She could have called to say she was dying. As a matter of fact—you know what? Never mind. Fuck it." *Piper.*

"This is not good. What you're saying."

"I know," Eva said tightly. She coughed. *Piper said it, told me on the phone, Your mom called.* "So let me get back to work."

"Yes, indeed," he said, relieved. "You take your time with this information, but work cures all ills. You know this. Work and time. Eva?"

"I'm right here, Dad." The Miami deejay's Spanglish burst into Eva's consciousness again. He was still tinny, but she heard him announce an old song from the Eagles.

"You know you're my girl, right?"

"Yes, Dad."

"All right then."

Eva pressed OFF. She leaned back in the chair. She heard Édouard and Dart holler something about they'd be back later.

There was no more crying. No awestruck face-holding. Just Eva, and her baby, and going back to life. She felt her leg might explode off her body.

Eva was on the couch, and awoke to the sound of Benjamin's car on the driveway. Then Ben stood in the doorway of the room with its closed curtains, said a quick hello and good-bye, and was off before Eva could sit up. Groggy, coughing, and still in clothes from the day before, Eva swished open the drapes and pushed up the windows.

Pritz stoode in the Rowe's living room in a pleated lavender silk poplin skirt, pale orange see-through tank with a form-fitting lace tank beneath, and shiny ivory sling-backs with a tiny kitten heel. Her hair was still jet but glossy now, and cut in an elfin style, with a plain black Giada-style bobby pin holding short bangs off her forehead. Pritz was moist with the late morning heat, and her neatly arched eyebrows were in a frown.

"Jesus, Eva. Ciao."

"You're here." Pritz's presence and sleek appearance made Eva feel degenerate. "Wow. Let me pull it together." Eva went to the bathroom, wiped her face and under her arms with a hot cloth, brushed her teeth, and found her stretchy yellow lace skirt, which was wrinkled and damp. She pulled on a white Nike T-shirt that she'd had drying over the shower rod and found her filthy flip-flops. Looking into the bathroom mirror, she tried her best to smooth her peeling skin with the coconut oil, but it only made her face look greasy and shocked. She wet her parched hair, pulled the front back with a red rubber band, and was glad for the diamond studs still in her ears.

I look a fucking mess. But, shit. I didn't invite her ass over here. "Tired from the trip?" Eva called from the bathroom. She let loose a long cough, and then threw up in the toilet. Her leg still leaked and ached. And she thought of her mother and mix tapes made from the radio.

"Are you all right?"

"I have a cold." Eva wiped her mouth, brushed her teeth again, and then went to the living room feeling like every blood vessel in her eyes had burst.

"You want to walk?" Eva asked. She gave Pritz a light kiss on the cheek. "To Hermitage?"

Pritz said, "Yeah," without asking what Hermitage was. In the living room, she slipped from her outfit into sneakers and comfortable shorts, and as they walked, Pritz told the tale of her last days as a senior manager of radio promotions.

Grass feathered the paved road toward Hermitage, the monastery on Mount Alvernia for which Benjamin named his car-rental place. Eva had already been there. As Audrey and Ben and Édouard had each told her, at 206 feet, Alvernia was the highest point of all the islands of the Bahamas.

Pritz and Eva turned onto a dirt road and hiked up a slope past hand-carved Stations of the Cross. Eva half-listened to Pritz until she said that after a three- or four-month sabbatical, she planned to move from London to Los Angeles to work for Hakeem for as long as her visa lasted. Then, feeling way out of the game, Eva put Pritz on complete mute.

They hiked up to the bell tower, and then stood in a chapel that could hold no more than three people. From a small window, the hushed green of North Cat lay like a eucalyptus leaf on the dark Atlantic. Eva was transfixed. In the silence, she coughed with her hand on her stomach, licked her dry lips, and made herself not think about the fact that even if Gayle had dialed the number, the message left with Piper was from her mother.

"Nothing is like the Caribbean," Pritz said, trying to draw Eva out. "The culture, the people, the ocean."

"This is the Atlantic." Eva thought that if her real mother had called, and she'd dismissed it, she wanted to drown. Deserved to drown in whatever ocean was in front of her.

"Are you sure? I would have thought—"

"It's what most people think."

Disappointed tourists poked in and out of the old stone buildings, expecting both more familiarity and more fantasy than Cat had to offer. Eva felt as connected and as disconnected to them as she felt to Pritz. The sightseers seemed like they belonged at Fernandez Bay, Cat's one resort. Or like they were booked at Lost City, on a day trip to the Out Islands for some local flavor. *Come explore the mystery and grandeur. This ancient civilization has risen up from the sea. Inspiration and adventure. Marine habitats. Imagination.*

Édouard had asked Eva on the journey over if she had "people" on Cat, and now her answer was a tentative yes. But for Dart, she would've stayed on at Lost City and then gone on to the Delano in Miami. She would have worked and partied and never thought about any of the Out or "Family" islands, let alone Cat. But for Dart, she would've gone back to Manhattan or Santa Monica and had her abortion and been back to work and planning a last-minute trip to Mo Bay again for the holidays. She'd be drinking Scotch and setting up Sun's second single and doing her best to manipulate Seb. The stuff she was good at.

My mom would still be dead, though.

And Dart doesn't want to do anything.

I'd be dodging Ron.

That's what this whole trip is? Dodging Ron? Dodging eveything. AWOL.

Eva shook it off. "So you're gonna work for Hawk?" Eva said. "Doing what?"

"What I always do. What you do. The thing that allows us this view from the top."

"I guess that's what this is." *I've been AWOL since Mix. Since Mom left.*

"It is up there, for two high-ranking, paid-ass drones. Living large. Pushing product and pushing everything else back. Making sacrifices . . . for my purse and for my freedom." Pritz brought out plane peanuts. "But what do the poets say . . . ?"

"Hip hop and it don't stop?" Eva waved the peanuts away.

"They say there is no sacrifice—only the choices we make. Everything else falls away."

She knows, Eva thought. "Say what you came to say, Pritz."

"Ron told me. That you are pregnant."

"I didn't tell him that."

"Your friend . . . Édouard, or Benajmin? He told me, too. He told me in way like he thought I knew."

Eva started back down the hill, but Pritz was on her heels.

"It is Ron's baby?"

"It's my baby," Eva said. "Leetle John got me pregnant."

"You are having it?"

Everybody's question. "Yeah." Eva huffed her way down the steep hill.

"You are glad? Why don't you sound glad? D'Artagnan?"

"Among other things, Pritz." Eva stopped at the bottom of the slope, but then started down the paved road paces ahead of her.

Pritz just spoke louder. "I think Ron misses you."

"Of course he misses me," Eva said, stopping in her tracks. "I miss him. We're sickly symbiotic. Parasitic, even."

"Simbee—?"

"A relationship between two that may or may not benefit the other. A relationship of mutual benefit or dependence."

"Ah. One thing that lives off another without killing it. That is you and Ron? It's not what he sounds like. Right now, when he discusses you."

"You talked to him?"

"You know I did."

"Where is he?"

"Leetle John thinks you are . . . getting rid of his baby. You should tell him your plans. He is going crazy."

"He should go crazy. I am."

"D'Artagnan," Pritz genuinely inquired, "rubs off on you?"

"He's not crazy."

"Sunny is worried, too."

"She hasn't called about him. She doesn't even know where her own brother is." They were on the short gravelly road that led to the Rowe House. Eva was thirsty, and she needed to sit. She took a few more steps, then leaned against a fence. "He got me here, Pritz." Eva ran a palm over her face and held her lips in her fist, then heaved a sigh through her stuffed nose. She wiped her upper lip with the back of her hand and wiped it on her skirt. "He got me away from—"

"From work, from Ron." Pritz reached in her bag and handed Eva an airline napkin. "Your responsibilities."

"By coming here, I decided to live up to the realest responsibility. You don't know how it's been, Pritz. How good this place has been for me."

"You don't look that good."

Eva was truly surprised at the fact that Pritz said it.

"You look thin in your face," she said. "A little bit . . . haggard."

"I'm going to eat more," Eva said defensively. "I've been throwing up a lot. I had a cold. You can see that."

"And your leg? What is that sore? I agree with you, this is a beautiful place. But you need to come back," Pritz said. "To Miami. Or at least to Nassau. You have more than yourself to think about."

Exactly. For the first time since, ever. "Maybe being at Roadshow isn't for me anymore," Eva said wildly. "Maybe I'm not confident enough in my vision anymore. Shit—maybe I don't have a vision. Not now—with everybody getting shot up. Tupac. Biggie. Both dead. Rap on its last legs and the best thing I can do—even for someone as dope as Sun—is make a cover album."

"That album is going to be huge. Everyone in Miami who was at the showcase says Sunny was so hot. That you were so beautiful. That you . . . get it."

You always big me up, Pritz. I swear I love you. I never see you and I love you. "Maybe I do get it, and maybe that's why I want out."

Pritz shook her head. "So you will live forever on Cat Island. Nursing Big Dart and running from Ron Leetle John."

"I'll figure something out." Her leg hurt. Eva saw her mom in her mind. Felt like she smelled sour milk. She limped heavily.

"I don't see Roadshow," Pritz said, looking at Eva with worry. "I don't know if I see Sunny. I see something new for you. *Exciting.* Plus, the baby. Have you been to a doctor?"

"I see things I should have seen a while ago." They were on a road that had become familiar to Eva. She knew the inclines and dips. A man with his goats waved at her.

"Do you see Leetle John?"

"What are you, his agent?" Eva then said the thing that came to her mind first. "Ron needs to find a white girl to settle down with, and leave me the fuck alone."

Along the way back to the Rowe House, Pritz and Eva heard music coming from a yellow, very neat shack. A few goats stood guard in front of it. Eva knew the place was Édouard's, but Eddie was at Jenny's most of the time, and so Eva was surprised to see Benjamin between the small porch and giant satellite dish, smoking, as he always seemed to be, the last of a cigarette. "My brother-in-law has a sense of humor," Benajmin said, smiling. "Your Dart, he's upbeat, too."

"Is that Eva?" Audrey called from the house excitedly.

"What, Audrey?" The music was loud, and slow like a dirge, but with what sounded like a tinkling, slow-shaking tambourine. *I can name that tune,* Eva thought, *in ten or twelve more notes.*

Dart bounded out of the house and stopped short in front of Eva. "You will never BElieve," he said loudly, "what we DID!"

Eva had no patience for Dart's voice, or this new mood swing. He was wet with sweat, his eyes were bright, and he was smiling. She said nothing to him.

"I made a SONG. WE made a song. Me and Eddie. Come look!"

Eva could hear strains of the Temptations, or what sounded like the Temptations. She put her hand over her mouth and coughed.

"I Wish It Would Rain." Nineteen sixty-eight. The rain song. My mom is straight calling me out from the afterworld.

"Eva!" Audrey called. "Come in here!"

Eva and Pritz walked into the miniature living room, which was made up as a sleeping room complete with double bed, nightstand, weak lamp, and huge television. Plus there were albums and cassettes and labeled digital audiotapes everywhere. Audrey grabbed Pritz and Eva by their wrists and pulled them into a bedroom recording studio complete with natty egg-crate foam, a dehumidifier, worn Mackie console, monitor, mixer, and speakers. Audrey, face lit up with delight and possibility, pulled the door closed behind them. With Édouard, Pritz, Eva, and herself in the room, plus the equipment, it was tight. The air had a dense, room-within-a-room, basement studio feel.

The Tempts. Produced by Norman Whitfield. The peak, really, of his first phase with them.

Eva's leg throbbed, her head throbbed.

Song was their . . . sixth, yeah sixth, number one hit in three years. Song made Dave Ruffin want the group to be billed as David Ruffin and the Temptations or the Temptations featuring David Ruffin or some such. Basically asked for what Diana and Smokey asked for and got.

She put her hand on her belly. She wanted to sit, but there was nowhere.

So the Tempts cut Ruffin, called Dennis Edwards, and went all "Cloud Nine."

"I'll start it again," Édouard said from his low bench. He looked like a beanbag chair with a proud pillow face attached.

No long lead-in for Édouard's version. The song started with a piano deeper than the original's—distorted and slightly more slow. And unlike Ruffin, Dart let go no humming moan before he sang, *Sunshine / Blue sky / Please go away.*

He sounds amazing.

There was a bass line under the piano, too, completely different from what the Motown players had done, different from what Whitfield had ever imagined.

What Eva could hear most clearly were her worlds ramming together. It wasn't until Pritz reached for her hand that Eva realized she was trembling. And the wound in her leg screamed.

Pritz looked at Édouard curiously, and he had the answer before she asked it. "No sample," he said coolly. "It is mine."

The loop was sparse and clean. Plenty of room left for Dart's burnished baritone, which, by the time he got to the words *day after day,* went deeper and scratchy where Ruffin had gone perfectly higher and scratchier. *Day after day*—Dart sang like it was more bittersweet treat than torture—*I stay locked up in my room.* Édouard had kept the tambourine sound in its original place, but it wasn't a tambourine.

Pritz looked at the song's producer again.

"Little bells," Eddie said, nodding his head up and down, completely pleased with himself. "And some bigger ones, too. Copper. Old. Lil' rake 'n' scrape for you. But you don't know nothing about all that."

Eva didn't know much about rake 'n' scrape, but she knew what sounded good. She'd heard the Temptations version a thousand times. She'd heard the other versions, too, had made it her business to find them, and to have them in her New York and her California apartments. *Recorded also by Little Caesar, by Ike and Tina, Marvin Gaye, Bobby Womack, Aretha, the Chambers Brothers. Gladys Knight and the Pips hit high with it that same damn year. That country guy in the seventies, McClinton Something. Rod Stewart, on a live album, when he was still with the Faces.*

Eva made her brain move. She forced her brain to click so her heart wouldn't stop, or break. The pain in her leg rang through her whole body as her mother's rain song boomed from the speakers *exactly the same,* Eva thought, *but totally different from the original.*

Dart was singing his own background vocals, and sounded more forlorn than ever. *Raindrops behind my teardrops* . . . and all the ooooos and oooooooooos. *Let it rain.*

The room was too small. Eva wanted to cough, but barely had room to lift her arm. She pushed her brain again. *Song written by Whitfield along with Barrett Strong—and them helped out by Roger Penzabene. He worked on the song, and then killed himself soon after, sad or mad over his wife's cheating. He never knew the song was a success, never knew it went gold, never knew it became a classic, a standard, a song, really, for all time.*

Eva pushed at Pritz. "I need to go," she said. Then Eva pushed at Audrey, too, who looked at her crazily as she opened the bedroom/studio door.

Once outside, Eva trudged back toward the Rowe House. It was her home, at least for right now, and she wanted to be in it. Her leg throbbed. She felt dizzy. She hadn't eaten anything since the day before.

Dart chased her down as she got to the Rowe patio, and Pritz was right behind him. Eva wished they both would disappear. She didn't want Dart, he didn't want her. The things they'd shared were passionate but not intimate—meaningful, but without sacrifice or risk or even hints of confession or interrogation or introspection or promises.

There's no giving in. Or faith. He and I are ports for each other. In this perfect storm.

And when it came down to it, Pritz wasn't Eva's friend. Pritz was someone she'd done business with and had known for a long time. Standing there, in the Rowe's living room, Eva was floored. She looked at the place as if for the first time. It was a vacation spot. Generic and filled with third-best furniture and knickknacks, dry, cracked bars of soap, and items that would go unmissed if the Rowe House were swept up in a hurricane. The Rowe House reminded Eva of her place on Riverside Drive, and of her place in Santa Monica.

No trace of me anywhere. Nothing to say who I am. Nothing to break. Not too much to move.

Eva suddenly hated that she'd put herself in a position where Dart and Pritz were, for watery miles around, the very best friends she had. The only thing she had now was truth. She wanted to tell it, but not to Dart or to Pritz.

But this is what I get.

Her head raged: *It's my own fault. All of it. Everything.*

Eva met her own eyes in the mirror. They were red, she was breathing hard, and she needed some water. Eva heard her people come through the sliding door.

She took a long look at herself and decided she was not about to start playing the victim now.

I am completely the same as I was before I got here, Eva thought. *Except totally different.*

D art said, "You don't look all right."

"You should sit down, Eva," Pritz said.

"Like you give a shit," she said directly to Dart. "Oh no, let me get it right—thank you in advance for your sympathy. You're so happy to give it. I'm sad now, little orphan Eva. But you can deal with that. Save me. Comfort me. Thanks. When I'm strong, though, when I got a plan, you hate me. Fuck you."

Dart looked at her evenly. "You're orphaned now? Who died?"

"My mother died."

"Stepmother."

"No."

A long pause. "But your real mother's been dead."

Pritz looked at Eva and Dart as they stared each other down. She'd no idea what was going on.

"You can do what you want," Eva said to Dart. "Because I lied." *Just us, you said. That's why I don't like "just" in a statement. It can mean "only," it can mean right or fair or deserved, but mostly it trivializes what comes after it. Just us. You lied. I lied. Nothing from nothing leaves nothing. Billy Preston, piano prodigy, songwriter, vocalist, Beatles collaborator.*

Dart left the patio.

There is a song for everything.

"This is how you act," Pritz said, "when your mother dies?" She was staggered. "Your mother is dead, now, today?"

"Yes." *Or yesterday, when my troubles seemed far away.*

Pritz needed facts straight. "Did you grieve for her when you told Dart this lie?"

"No." *I've been grieving since I was eleven.*

And then Eva thought, *Is this the kind of stuff you're supposed to say out loud? "I've been grieving for her since I was eleven?" This is why Ron runs? This is me, not "submitting"? This stuff in my head, I should say out loud. It seems weak. Self-indulgent. A bother to anyone else but me.*

"Do you need to get back?" Pritz said. "For a funeral?"

"It already happened."

This took a moment for Pritz to digest. "Do you have anything of hers?"

Fine. I'm going to say stuff out loud. Submit. Eva got up and went to her bag. Came back, limping, with her passport. From one of the clear plastic protective sleeves, she pulled a folded piece of butcher paper. It looked old, but not battered. The handwriting fat from a flying felt tip. In a hurry, Elaine had cut it at an odd angle. Unfolded, the sheet was a parallelogram.

Pritz read it. Eva didn't have to.

Ned,

It is November 2, nineteen hundred and seventy-seven. In California.

There is no reason to keep up the farce. I wish you all the luck in the world, but I have to get out. No more commitment. No more expectations—you of me or me of you. First I didn't love you anymore and now you don't love me. It seemed like I loved you a lot.

I cry and cry. Then I try to be strong and unemotional and none of it changes anything. I think you've been waiting for me to lay down this line, because you won't and I know why you won't—for Eva.

Our conversations are blank.

"Such is life," you say, about <u>heartbreaking</u> things. "Congrats in that regard."

"You would be missed," you told me last week, and I was telling you I would leave you and Evey! Missed by who? God? My friends at the café? Not, surely, by you. Evey will miss me some, but Evey understands, or she will, or I'll be her witch, something for her to face one day, and overcome.

Then you say, "I know how I feel when I don't want to be with someone and I don't feel that way about you." I should be glad of that? To be somewhat desired, and through a negative? I can only say I'm sorry one million times for the things I've done. Mostly I'm sorry for leading you to believe I was a nicer girl than I am.

In love before Evey, in love when Evey got here.

Then your moods go into overdrive.

I try to help, but you hate the help.

You crawl into your shell.

I find a man. Like usual. Call me slut all day forever. I do not care.

Maybe you need to come into yourself, recover, blossom on your own. For the sake of it, and so you don't have to ever say you had any real help. So you don't have to worry about anyone letting you down. I'm tired of theorizing. I'm so tired of you talking about the things you want to be doing like I'm the one keeping you from doing them. I haven't been keeping you from doing anything! From being anything! I believe now that <u>we just didn't work</u>. You don't like the way I dress. I don't like the way you dress. My life is too "fast" for you. You need to "be who you're gonna be when you're gonna be it." As if I ever tried to take away your little dreams. Like I haven't moved here with you, moved there. Every time you wanted to pick up, I picked up. I do wrong

things, did wrong things, but you make up stuff to bolster
your case for your hiding yourself from us.

Anthony from the café quit. I went to his ship-out, and
I'm going to go to his place up north and wait for him. You
saw this, and I lied. I know what you think: "Looking for Mr.
Goodbar." I love my Evey. I do. I'm not the bigger person.
I'm not doing what's right. I'm doing wrong. But that's me.
I was happy before I met you. You said my problem is I have
no cross to bear. Well I have one now. But I turned it into
wings and I'm flying away. I'm sorry. I'm very sorry. Not to
you but to Eva Lillian. If you make her hate me I will haunt
you. If you ever show her this letter, you deserve to die.
I'm not right. I'm not on my high horse. But I am The Mother.
I claim it and I will claim it no matter how much I won't earn
it. Eva will feel me guiding her to her own freedom and happiness and everything women can have now. The best thing about
writing this letter is that you can't tell me to shut up and
you can't shut me out. You will save this letter forever I know
you and I know you will. Remember me you broken broke-down
slave-minded son-of-a-bitch. I'm the worst mother in the
history of mothers but I love writing this down to you and
telling you what to do because I know you'll do it. I know
Mr. Responsibility will do just what I say: Raise my daughter
well. So sayeth me! Obey my command! Love forever and ever
to my babygirl Eva. She and hers will rule this world, and
they'll see a way to forgiving the weak ones like me.

Elaine Eva Sonnier Glenn

Audrey walked over with her usual tins.

Pritz didn't know what to say.

Audrey sat cracked conch and coleslaw on the patio table, and
took the paper from Pritz and read it.

"I thought you hated me, Audrey," Eva said, and she started

laughing. Eva snatched the letter back. "It's funny to me. Now that you know my mother left, you can like me." Eva shook off an embrace from Pritz and walked out onto the beach. She climbed out onto a reef, and when Pritz got up to go after her, Audrey, in her best sagelike tone, told Pritz to be still. Eva sat out there on the pointy rocks and set her mother's letter on the water. It floated quickly forward, then back farther, in and out with the waves. Eva watched it.

This is dumb, but I'm going to jump in.

Audrey and Pritz both jerked when Eva jumped into the water after the paper. More than the fact that she had lied about it, more, even, than the fact that Elaine was dead, Eva had the bile and shame and overly compensatory ways of one abandoned. Elaine had parted quickly and enigmatically, and so ruthlessly left behind a tinfoil dream of her return for Eva to chew on.

Eva had to swim out, and the note eluded her like it had a motor and mind of its own. At one point, she was underwater for what seemed to those on shore like too long a time. But she came up, took a breath, and swam toward the letter again.

This is so corny. Setting the letter out like some message, and not even in a bottle. Diving in like some kind of self-baptism.

Eva dove under the water again, felt it pressing in against her and all her passages. When she came up, Eva stood in the wet pink sand and blew what seemed the last of her cold from her nose. Coughed everything out of her chest. She put a hand to her stomach and went under the waist-deep water again, swimming strongly toward the floating paper.

In what seemed a panic, Audrey yelled for Dart, who'd emerged from the shower smelling like the starchy steam of rice. Eva wasn't there to inhale him, but the dank apricot smell was gone. Barefoot in boxers, he walked onto the beach.

"Get to her, D'Artagnan," Audrey said too breathlessly. "Hurry! She's going up and down too many times."

Dart ran to the water and was up to his knees when Eva stood in front of him, clothes dripping, hair plastered around her face, her mother's words running in indigo streams on her palm.

"I'm fine," Eva said, panting. "I got it."

"I knew you did." Dart looked at her wrist. "You lost the bracelet, though."

"Nah," Eva said. "I let it go."

Eva walked through the sand, back onto the patio.

"I thought you wanted to keep him," Audrey said, handing her a towel. "You should have let him save you, Eva."

"I know how to swim." Eva was exhausted and irritated. Her leg was stinging, but felt better. The wound was lightly foaming with salt and felt clean for the first time. "I was all right."

"We're all *all right*. But what else can he do for you?"

Eva said what she knew Audrey already knew. "Because I'm not flailing in the ocean drowning doesn't mean I don't need somebody."

Dart walked past them. "I'm out of here," he said, tramping pebble-stone and water into the Rowe House. "Peace."

Pritz had the look—worried, but completely comfortable—of a hip hop Euro-girl around a whole lot of negroes. Eva could almost see the papers flipping on Giada's old clipboard. She was putting together a plan.

"Eva," Pritz said, like she was road managing her, "you'll be fine here for a minute? I have to make a few things happen."

"Pritz. I know shit seems ridiculous right now. Do what you gotta do."

"Even with how you lie," Dart said, putting things in his pack once again, "I want you to know I think you're extremely decent."

Eva wanted off Cat Island. The sea was closing in on her.

"Really decent the way you were for a while here," he said. "The ways you've dealt with me, tried to help me, in your way. I gotta get myself back. I don't know if I'm built for the kind of stuff I asked of you."

Eva decided to say what she thought. "Why are you going?" She didn't want him to stay. She wanted his reason.

"I thought I could do it," he said. "But I feel one-down in most situations with most people, and—"

"And what?"

"I feel that way even more so when I'm with you. I'm gonna go to San Diego—to a spiritual gathering. This thing they have every first of the year."

Eva looked at him.

He said, "Stop being tough. So tough you lie about your own mother dying. Without a blink. Without a blink for three years."

"How can I seem tough when I can see myself in the mirror looking like I've had some kind of breakdown?"

"You don't let anybody help you." Then Dart grabbed Eva's hands. "I love you, though," he said. "Platonically, in the true sense of affection for someone. Virtue. Truth. I have so many high hopes for you, Eva."

"Let go of me." And she yanked her hands away. She thought of the Police's "Message in a Bottle": *Seems I'm not alone at being alone / Hundred billion castaways looking for a home.*

He said, "I'm no villain. Just like I'm no musketeer. You think I took from you? Took advantage? If I took, I only took what I needed."

"You're not supposed to take without giving back."

"You're not supposed to give with the expectation of receiving." He paused. "What all did you give, anyway?"

"I gave myself, asshole."

"I'm not capable of all what I thought."

"You're capable. You just don't want to be."

He sucked on that. Like maybe it tasted right. But "You need more" was his final answer.

"Than what?

"You know I want only the best for you. For you and for—"

"Mention this baby and I will maim you," Eva said, channeling Tupac the gangsta, half real and half fake. All wound only half healing. "I'll do my best to hurt you." *Hutch from Above The Law says, 'Cause see, once in a lifetime / Everybody did some dirt. Can't nothing change those four times. Not even this baby in me right now can change those four times. I'm never going to be all right with that. Never. That's just what the deal is. I did my dirt. I gotta live with that shit. But try to really live with it. Actually live.*

"You're going to be alone." It was as if bugles preceded Dart's statement. Like he was delivering a proclamation from some distant, shrewd king. "Even with the baby, you're always going to be by yourself and unhappy. I'll be by myself, but I'll be free."

"I've been free, dick. Free is cheap and breezy."

He took off on a bicycle, Eva guessed to the dock.

Tired of this goddamned island. Tired of being one.

The next afternoon, Pritz jumped waves in the salty blue. From the shore Eva watched her, and then watched as Audrey came out in a bulky orange one-piece and joined in. A crusty iguana stood near Audrey's starfish and Eva stared it down. Eva wanted to see Jeeter before she left Cat Island, wished he would just appear, so she could make a request, but instead Édouard walked onto the beach, Temptations music leaking from his headphones. Eva was surprised, and glad to see him. She wasn't coughing. The area around her leg wound was tender, but it didn't ache. Édouard looked at her like she had a ticket to ride.

"How come you're not on the boat?" Eva said, "You didn't take Dart to Nassau?"

"Skip took him. I came to see how you are, Miss Eva."

"Getting it together." She pushed hair back from her face. "Inch by inch."

"Yes you are."

"I liked that song. It's good."

"It can be better. Dart told me about your job, that you work with Sunny. That Sunny is his sister."

"Not like it was a secret."

"Not that you ever said it." Édouard pulled his headphones down to his neck. "Dart said you make people into stars. You know how big he said it. That you made Sunny, Sunny. Sunny is everywhere."

"Ha. I guess it's about time for me to get back to it."

"And leave your fairy-tale place."

"It's not a fairy tale to me."

"You see us, this island. We're like you here. If we're smart or fortunate, we get out. At least to Nassau."

"Édouard, if you want to leave," Eva said, "you should."

For the first time since she met him, Édouard's voice was dark. "Don't have me think different of you. Don't act like the Rowes that live here."

"Éd—"

"My sister and I—Haitian," he said ferociously. "What they say here, she and me aren't legal, shouldn't be here. Her and Ben-the-native, not married by what they call the Commonwealth. Where am I going but waiting on Skip to die so I can take over the boat and even then they won't recognize it as mine. What's Audrey for but to take care of you and the Rowes. Don't say stupid shit."

"It's not fair," Eva said and knew it sounded foolish as she said it.

Édouard loosed his mammoth laugh, and this time it was twisted and hard as the ropes he always handled. "Come over by my sister's, Miss Eva. There's a surprise for you."

Eva hadn't seen that much anger and sour desire and pity in a man's face since she'd been at Ripples pool watching a husband attend to his wife's bird hand. Eva met Édouard's gaze. Then she walked across the burning sands to Audrey and Benjamin's small patch of lawn.

"Édouard," Eva said, hesitant about imposing, but dead-set about her mission. "Can you tell me how to find Jeeter? Or I guess I could ask Audrey. I wanted to—"

You could have tipped Eva over with a feather when she saw Sunny, in overalls and sneakers, chatting with Audrey at the clothesline. And Ron beside her.

———

> *So whatcha gonna do? Feel free? Or be free?*
> —"FREE AGAIN," words and music by Soul II Soul

As Ron saw Eva, he walked toward the road, and Édouard trudged after him. Eva was overwhelmed. She was confused, and hated to hope. There were no lyrics or labels to fall back on.

She and Sunny hugged tightly, and for Eva, Sun was all the fragrance and familiarity of a home. Sun looked almost exactly like she had in Monterey, when Eva heard her for the first time. Sunny's hair was in a puffy ponytail and her face was plain and tanned and frankly concerned. Sun's speaking voice sounded like a song.

"Pritz called me," Sunny said. She had a half-dozen of Audrey's batik creations thrown over one shoulder. "So, yeah, stupid. I came over here for you." They stood there for a moment. Eva still had a hand on Sunny's arm, and Sunny put her own on top of Eva's. "I heard your mother passed."

Eva dropped her hand to her belly.

"I'm sorry for your loss. She's in a better place."

Eva thought that maybe her mother was in a better place, and that maybe she needed her mother to be truly gone—so she could stop wondering and lying. "You know I lied, Sunny."

"Negress, I felt you weren't telling the truth at the time. In Carmel. Not specifically about your mom. But the thing with the bracelet . . . I dunno. It was just—"

"Convenient."

"And Hawk and Ron had already told me—"

"That I'd do anything."

Hawk and Ron.

Ron.

"Yeah. I was new, Evey. Not dumb."

"So you signed with me, why?"

"I liked you. What you represented. I figured, the way you handled me was the way you'd handle my business. Men get points for being slick. Even get points for lying. You can't win in this business without doing that. It's a simple fact."

"I lied about everything but business."

"Go to confession or beat your own ass if you want, but I also saw in your face two things that day in Carmel. I never stopped seeing them, even to right now. You love my music, and you care about my brother."

"I don't give a shit about him right now. And what about this cover album? You hate it."

"I still hate it. But—"

"It's good for you to have done."

"I'll lie and say I never said it if you tell anyone I admitted it, but yes, it's good for me. Make us both a lot of dough. Let me live how I want for a long time. Make some more of the kind of music I want to, later. Not that you're thinking about the last part."

"I am now."

"Pritz told me you look like shit and you do."

"She told you the rest."

"Yeah."

Eva nodded slowly. Hand to her belly again.

"Ron's here."

"I see him."

"He flew over here with me."

"You hate Ron."

"Yeah. But he was calling me, calling me, about you. And then when I heard from Pritz last night, I called him, and Lil' John was like, Come on, we're going over there. He said he had to look on a goddamn map. I don't know why that won me over, but it did. Picturing him looking for you on a map of the world."

"Where'd he go?"

"Over at Audrey's?" It was weird to hear Sunny saying Audrey's name. Weird that Sunny and Ron knew Audrey. Made Eva feel like things in her life could interweave and even interlock and be all right.

"My brother needs somebody like you," Sunny said. "Dart needs a leader. You like to lead. That's what I wanted. And it wasn't my business to want anything for him. To push it. And anyway, no one said you and Ron were getting married. Jesus. But he's the father of the baby you're over here looking like you can't even carry. Your collarbones are sticking out. Your face is fading away. And aren't your boobs supposed to get *bigger* when you're pregnant?"

"I don't need Ron to be here. Not now. Some big rescue mission."

"Nobody said you need him." Sunny handed Eva her rainbow, and bent down to untie and kick off her shoes. She straightened, and then curled her toes in the pebbly grass. "But would it kill you? If you did?"

———————

Eva stood ankle deep in the ocean, thirty feet of water behind her, crystal sea before her. She walked out farther, but the water got deeper in increments so infinitesimal, she couldn't feel it. It was the way shame had encroached upon her, the way her infamy in the music business had also. From the water, Eva spied a baby gull. Then a human mother and daughter, playing Scrabble, speaking French.

Eva walked parallel with the shore, past Audrey's and farther still, until she saw anchored catamarans, and small boats blue and green. Palm trees with green hair blowing identically in the breeze.

"So I get no points on this, huh?"

Eva stood still in the water. Ron was knee deep in it. Saggy cargo pants rolled up, he was barefoot. She walked toward him and he reached out his hand. Eva reached out and shook once, then let him go. She backed up a step. And felt like her feet were sinking with every tiny lap of the sea.

"I been here since early," he said. "Sun was still in Miami, but I was in VA with . . . you don't care who with. Me and Sun are over at a hotel called Fernandez Bay, or it's on Fernandez Bay, or—"

"You came to be my knight."

"Here it comes—"

"My white knight."

"There it is. Least you ain't changed."

"I was supposed to change in a week?"

There was nothing, for a moment, either of them knew to say.

"How's the baby?"

It's his responsibility, too. Talk. "I didn't have an abortion. I'm not having one." Eva didn't know what to do with her hands. She uncurled and curled them into fists. "Feel safe about that."

"Are you glad?"

"I'm getting used to being glad about it." Eva looked directly at Ron.

"What's with Dart?" Ron hitched up his pants. His forehead was getting pink. "You and him."

"We're asking questions about other people now?"

"You were doing so good. Answer the question."

"Whatever it was, it ain't no more."

Eva sat down in the sand. The water lapped at her. The salt felt good in her wounds.

"I brought the rest of your stuff with me," Ron said.

Eva could barely remember what he could have. What selection of shorts and dresses and sandals, curling irons, tweezers, and nail polish removers.

He stepped toward her and crouched down. There was still a yard between them.

"Why are you lugging my stuff around?"

"You're carrying something of mine." Ron paused. "It is ours?"

Eva nodded. It was just that word. *Ours.*

"Can you answer me?"

"It's ours." *I need to go see Jeeter.*

"So can we get you to a doctor?"

"Yeah." Eva's hand went to her belly. "They told you my mom died."

"I heard." Ron was beside himself. He wanted to grab her. Make her feel better. He wanted to let her cry. He wanted to see her cry. He wanted her to chide him and tease him. Curse him about the Tampa MC, ask him about his points and how his money was, ask him about Hawk and Myra. He wanted her to demand that he marry her. Wanted her to take the towel from around her waist and pull him into the water. Wanted her to come back to his room at Fernandez Bay, put on one of the short dresses and a pair of the four-inch heels he'd brought over, and fuck him until he passed out. He wanted her back in NYC and L.A., plump and telling all her wack friends and jealous rivals that she was having his baby. He wanted her to feel all right about everything. He wanted them to build something together, and he was confident he could have it all just like this. He thought that their personalities matched, and that whatever happened, with work, with a kid, that they could maybe work it out. He'd been waiting on her, in his way, for a long time.

"She's never going to see the baby. Never going to see me."

"So what do you want to do?"

Eva had to think about that. It was a rare thing for her, feeling tentative. Feeling like she would ask somebody for something. It was hard for Eva to ask Ron. She made herself. For the baby's sake, and for her own. "Will you come with me to see my dad?" Then Eva Glenn braced herself.

"Where's he at?" Ron said without blinking.

"Near Vegas."

"So let's go."

Addendum

GROOVE magazine
July 2005
(cover story)

SUNNY DAYS

Celebrating her tenth year in the recording business, the legendary Sunny Addison chats with DANYEL SMITH about love and life, and finally breaks her silence about her brother, the mysteries of "The Rain Song," and her secret weapon.

SHE'S LIKE A SUN—a source of light and heat at which the world is awed at every dawn. She moves like our sun, too—slowly around her world, shining through even when the air is cold. Sunny Addison remains a mystery, a star on high sending down miraculous rays we dance in, make love in, and—when she sings about pain—we burn in. At her best, she's a place in which to find comfort from a bitter world.

Fittingly, it's a warm day in Cardiff-by-the-Sea, a shoreline community in Encinitas, California, about ninety miles south of Los Angeles, and a hop-skip-jump from Deirdre "Sunny" Addison's hometown of San Diego. The breeze is light around her oval pool, and even in

April, the view from Sunny's three-story palace overlooking the surf is like something out of a dream.

"Hell, yeah! It is a dream come true. I'm from the SD, got my true, *professional* start in Monterey, and Carmel-by-the-Sea—but it gets too cold up there for me. Cardiff is warm almost year-round. Perfect for my hot blood."

Sunny—long estranged from her father, and "in long-distance therapy," she says, with her mother, Lt. Thelma Lynn Addison (USN, Ret.)—is stretched out on a chaise ("My favorite position," she says, laughing) gulping a shot of pulverized wheatgrass. There's music on the stereo—old A Tribe Called Quest and older Full Force, Randy Crawford, some Tupac Shakur, Tamia, Carole King, Usher, Mary J. Blige, some Digital Underground. The superstar is in a bopping, sunny mood as she reflects on her tenth anniversary as a singer-songwriter. "Really, I've been writing songs since I was kid, so this whole tenth anniversary thing is hilarious to me." Her sixth album is already platinum after a month in the stores, and critics, with few exceptions, have given *On Recollection* thumbs up across the board. *Entertainment Weekly* said, "Sunny Addison remains aglow . . . is still a force to be reckoned with." *Vibe*, "Sunny is at the height of her powers . . . the only singer out there who's skill as a songwriter matches the power and soulfulness of her voice." And *Hip Hop Soul* calls *Recollection* "as mature and kick-ass as that bottle of Cristal you lifted from Puffy's '97 white linen birthday set—so tilt it back, turn it up and feel the cool sunlight."

Sun is also relaxing in the glow of being honored as Songwriter of the Year by the American Society of Composers, Authors, and Publishers (ASCAP). "Now the award *is* a big deal," she says, getting stern. "I love to sing. *Love* to sing. But to be acknowledged for my songwriting, especially after all the different kinds of albums I've done, well, it just feels important. Like folks really listen when I tell my stories."

The main hallway of Sunny's home is lined with platinum album plaques, and she has a small room off her cluttered office with cases of trophies and keys to various cities in the United States and around the world. She has guitars on stands in about every room, though she says "her" guitar is locked away "someplace safe, soaking up the world's best energy, and waiting on me to pick it up and do some writing." She has the requisite living room–size closet full of rare shoes and a breathtaking quantity of clothes. She has a boyfriend (rumored to be, over the last year, music mogul Hakeem Watkins) whose name she won't mention. "If you want to call him 'boyfriend,'" she says with a wry grin. "He's too old for that, really, and he's on the other coast so much we can't even get it together to get pregnant." She's happy, she says, that she's got money in the bank, that she's stretching herself by delving into acting, and that she has people around her that she can trust. "It's the key in this business," she says, motioning toward the kitchen for some refreshment, "knowing which bridges to burn, and which bridges to cross."

And you know the difference?

"With a little help from my friends, I do. But then, you gotta know who your friends are."

So you do know who your friends are.

"I know who my friend *is*," she says. "I'm exaggerating, but I basically have the same people around me that I always have. We have our ups and downs, but we rarely have our outs."

Addison's career has been filled with mostly ups, but has surely has its share of downs. Seven years ago, her career was in the outer stratosphere. After only two albums (her strong 1996 debut, *Poems on Various Subjects*, and the wondrous 1997 *Bliss Unknown*) she had Grammys, MTV and BET awards, and even an Oscar. "It was unreal when *Bliss* came out," she says. "Everybody was worried about the sophomore jinx, but I was confident. The spirit of Phillis Wheatley was on my side."

And it didn't hurt to have legendary hit maker Hawk Watkins on her team. "She's one of the most extraordinary people in this world," Watkins says cheerfully from his New York offices. "Sunny is that rare species—a hardworking, natural talent." It was the huge mainstream success of *Bliss* that began the murmurs. On urban radio stations around the country, jocks and programmers started complaining, on and off air, that Sunny wasn't really "black," or not black "enough."

"She was a trip for a minute," says Jimi "Go-Go" Gonzales, now program director of Los Angeles' soulful KLUV 93.1. "Right before that first cover album, *Hymn to Humanity*, came out. I was on air then, and we were playing Sun's stuff like crazy. She'd come to town, go straight to the pop stations, the big white stations, do drops for them, hang out all through their wack-ass morning shows, and not even come by here for a wazzup."

Sunny sees it differently. "I was young. I didn't want to visit *any* radio stations, or be interviewed at all, for that matter. All I wanted to do was just *be*. Record. Perform. Write. Sing. Jesus!" She sighs loudly and shakes her head. "But this is a business, and that's something I learned from Eva Glenn."

Eva Glenn, erstwhile glamorous record label executress, and now manager to the some of the most successful recording artists in the country, signed Sunny to the now defunct Roadshow Records after a fiery, early nineties bidding war. Glenn, loved and hated, is the stuff of legend herself. Often labeled as too much of a "fun" girl by her (some say jealous) colleagues and competitors, Glenn remains the marketing and managerial mini-mogul behind Sunny's astronomical sales and edgy (yet somehow still pristine) reputation.

"It's always been Eva," says Sunny, laughing. "Even when we fought like fools. And besides, she don't party like she used to. She's Mama Eva now."

Piper Gibbs, senior director of promotion and advertising for BET, was, many moons ago, personal assistant to Glenn, and sometime assistant to Sunny. "Eva was a bitch, no question. And she'd be glad to hear me say it. But she was one of the hardest-working people at Roadshow. And she tried to be honest. In this business it's hard to do that. And she wasn't scared of Sunny or any of the artists, really—like Seb [former Roadshow CEO Sebastian Turcos] was. Eva wasn't scared of younger people, either—like me. She didn't hate on us. She tried to bring us up."

And Sunny?

"Sunny and Eva were on some love-hate back then, though now I guess it's love-love. I always thought that they were more alike than not. If Sunny couldn't sing, she probably would've been an Eva. And if Eva could sing—oh my God!—she'd be bigger than Sun is right now."

Poems and *Bliss Unknown* behind her, it was Addison's third album, *Hymn to Humanity*, that pushed her into territory previously occupied by the likes of Mariah Carey, Whitney Houston, and (in terms of international success) Michael Jackson. Within two years, ten million copies of *Hymn* sold, and as of January 2005, it's up to almost eighteen million. Among the songs on the cover album: a tear-down-the-walls version of Barry Manilow's "Looks Like We Made It," a slow, acoustic twist on Bill Wither's "Lovely Day," a melodic trib-ute to Tupac Shakur's "Dear Mama" (sparked by the loop of a never-before-heard snippet from a voice-mail message from the late great MC himself), Billy Preston's "Will It Go 'Round in Circles," and a wild rendering of "Midnight Train to Georgia" that had Gladys Knight jumping to a standing ovation during Sunny's second prime-time network special, 2000's ratings blockbuster, *Sunshine on My Shoul-ders: A Prime-Time Party with Sunny Addison.*

Hymn to Humanity's last-minute lead single was a duet with Sunny's younger brother, D'Artagnan Addison.

Yes—*that* D'Artagnan, the platinum recording artist known by his evocative first name.

"And it's his *real* name," Sunny says, munching on shrimp toasts placed on the table by a discreet attendant. Then she pours herself a glass of water from a pitcher lined with slices of lime. "D'Artagnan Marlon Addison. At home, though, he's just Dart." The astonishing single, a masterful retooling of the Temptations 1968 "I Wish It Would Rain," not only anchored *Hymn* and kicked off the career of Sunny's notoriously private sibling (D'Artagnan declined to be interviewed for this story), but the song has become a fairy tale swathed in mystery wrapped in a quilt of secrets.

Tall tales and urban legends are pervasive in the word of recorded music. And they are seductive. In some cases, the tales lend earthy tangibility to the magic of music. In others, the legend just adds to the mystery and the immortality of a piece of art so perfect, it's impact goes far beyond sales and chart positions, and remains supernaturally immeasurable.

There's the myth, for example, about Phil Collins's "In the Air Tonight." No, he didn't write the song after witnessing, while unable to help, a friend of his drown. The song is Collins being aggravated about his marriage to his then wife, Andrea.

Another legend keeps up the notion that Michael Jackson's home phone number was in the UPC (bar) code of *Thriller* (No!). And the model on the cover of the Ohio Players' *Honey* is the subject of an old, macabre rumor. Supposedly, the model's skin was horribly burned by the heated (so it would drip more easily) honey at the photo shoot, and days later she came to the recording studio where the Players were working on their "Love Rollercoaster." Supposedly angry—and literally scarred—the model threatened to sue OP for every dollar they had, and so the band's manager supposedly stabbed her to death right there in the studio, her dying screams supposedly, inadvertently recorded and then included in the song. There *are* screams buried low in the mix of "Love Rollercoaster," but they aren't even a woman's. Keyboardist Billy Beck screeched for the song.

But the stories still awhirl around Sunny and Dart's version of "I Wish It Would Rain" are complicated and convoluted and have all the makings of a (Lifetime? VH-1 "Movies That Rock"?) fun film. Depression, sex, betrayal, even . . . the unexplained.

And, of course, what seems a happy ending.

Here are the particulars.

Sunny Addison "employed" her only sibling, D'Artagnan, as her manager because he was suicidal (so she kept him near). He took no (or very little) money for his work. Some say Dart never really did anything for Sunny. Some say he was devoted to her in a way that was almost unhealthy for brother and sister. Some say Sun manipulated him and he resented her. Some say he was always jealous of her success. Some say they have an extremely healthy, loving relationship that was solidified by an absent father, a strict mother, and the fact that they ran away from home together when Sunny was nineteen and Dart eighteen. They lived in their car until they had money for shifty hotels. By the time they had money enough for a raggedy apartment (one in Fresno, then one in Rosemead), they began traveling Arizona, Washington, and California's cities and back roads, Sun singing wherever she could for dollars tossed in a green glass dish that she supposedly still has in her home—now filled with floating lilies.

Eva Glenn signed Sunny when Sunny was supposedly at the end of her rope. By most accounts, Sunny'd told Dart that if she hadn't been signed to a deal by the end of that summer in central California, she was going to get a job, probably get her GED, maybe go to college, or join the service. "Dart was in the dregs back then," says Hawk Watkins, who was a part of the eventual bidding battle for Sunny. "He was very overweight, and depressed at the idea of Sunny giving up on her dream."

But then Eva signed Sunny to Roadshow.

Fast-forward.

In 1998, when Sunny and Dart were at a music industry convention in the Bahamas, Dart was supposedly upset at Sunny's success, and disappeared. "He was NOT 'upset' or depressed with my quote-unquote success," Sunny says with an eye roll. "If you knew him—and you never will—you would know that was impossible."

Sunny was torn. Does she stay at the Lost City resort and debut *Hymn to Humanity* to radio execs anxious to hate her? Or does she run all over the (seven hundred!) islands of the Bahamas looking for him?

This is where Eva Glenn comes in with a power move. Eva, repping for the scandalous Roadshow Records (in real life, Sebastian Turcos did his six months and is living fat somewhere near Marbella, Spain), and in order to keep Sunny on point for her do-or-die showcase, and also because Eva was in love with Dart (though she loved bigwig Ron

Littlejohn, too, but he wouldn't have her because his parents wouldn't accept a black woman for their son), Eva ran off to get Dart.

Eva knew Dart was into voodoo, and knew (how?) the special island on which the most intense Bahamian voodoo was practiced.

So Eva went there, found Dart, met superproducer "Giant" Eddie Innocent (who was supposedly captain of a ship!) at an open-air market. "I was not a *captain*," says Innocent, from his car. He says he's on the Williamsburg Bridge, and his music is blasting. "And my sister's name is no one's business. She loves Eva, though. Just like I do."

Eddie liked Eva, but she was in love with Dart (and Lil' John, as he used to be known back when he was down with hip hop). Eddie's sister was a voodoo priestess and put a spell on Eva, and Eva had a breakdown. Her fingernails started falling out, her hair started falling out, her legs had sores, and all kinds of craziness. All Eva wanted to do was sit and stare into the sun.

Sun. Get it?

Dart couldn't help Eva because he was kind of suicidal still, so he wanted it to rain. For some reason, he started singing "I Wish It Would Rain" to the sky, like a prayer.

Eddie heard him, and—not even knowing D'Artagnan was a multi-platinum star's brother—recorded him in his own raggedy studio, using the actual ocean breezes from the Bahamian shores for sound effects. "I did not know who was Eva, or Dart," says Innocent, who seems to be turning up the volume of his stereo as he speaks. "I thought they were a couple, running away for adventure."

Did you love Eva?

"Hahahahahaha," Eddie laughs, like I have got to the heart of something hilarious. "Hanging up now."

Did they stay at a place called the Roll House? The Roth House?

Innocent's laugh only gets bigger. "The *Rowe* House," he says. "That's it." And he hangs up.

D'Artganan has an incredible song on his debut called "Sunrise on the Rowes," which people think is a misspelling, a typo of "Sunrise on the Rose." The whole thing just gets murkier and murkier, especially when I receive a callback from a Thaddeus Rowe of Pittsburgh, Pennsylvania. On the voice mail he says, "Because you were courteous with my wife I am returning your call. I will tell you what I have told every . . . reporter who has asked: I do not know of a Sunny Addison, a D'Artagnan Addison, or an Eva Glenn. My wife and I did, at one time in the nineties, own a small home on Cat Island in the Bahamas. We had wonderful neighbors whose names I do not care to mention. Wishing you the best of luck in your quest. Please don't phone again."

Huh?

Meanwhile.

Sunny was worried. She somehow (how?) found out where Dart and Eva were, went there, and laid her background vocals in on "The Rain Song." Sunny's voice (what? crazy!) lifted the spell Eddie's sister had placed on Eva. And then the sister (Anne? Audrey? Anita? The name is never the same) put a *nice* voodoo spell on the song. Some say Anne/Audrey/Anita never existed. Some say she works in Sunny's home. Some say she cooks for Dart. Some say she lives in Haiti with her husband, surrounded by grandchildren.

They—Sunny, Eva, D'Artagnan, Eddie—came back, and Eva, back to her usual self, crashed the song onto the album, even though the masters had already been finalized.

Sunny and D'Artagnan's 1999 "I Wish It Would Rain" broke sales and radio-play records for months. Sunny and Eva left Roadshow right before the Feds shut it down. D'Artagnan (who is now managed by Eva Glenn and Ron Littlejohn) released his debut, *Kindness for Weakness*, early in 2001. The rest, as is said, is (multiplatinum) history.

On a final note, little Lanie Littlejohn, Eva and Ron's older daughter (Lanie is four, Dinah is almost two) has long been rumored to be Eva and Dart's love child.

Whew.

"Hm. I've heard all that, and it's all real cute except the part about my brother being suicidal. He talks about his depressions through his music. He never wanted to kill himself." Then Sunny gets up and pours herself a glass of merlot. "To call a kid's parentage into question is a serious thing. Lanie and Dinah are my godchildren. Ron's like my brother. Please."

As if on cue, Sunny's manager and proclaimed "best friend" walks on deck looking like the proverbial million dollars.

"Hey, miss," she warmly says to her client/friend, and gives her a huge hug. Then Glenn eyes me suspiciously. "Thought I'd pop by and see how everything's going. You have ninety minutes, right? We're at what, eighty-nine?"

"Here she is," Sunny Addison says to me while handing Glenn a glass of wine. "My secret weapon."

Eva Glenn must be forty and she looks twenty-nine. In an Italian suit probably from next spring's collections, an antique designer bag that has one-of-a-kind written all over it, Glenn's gumball of a dia-mond flashes in the sunlight. *Bling*, as the saying goes, *bling*.

Glenn's engaged to Ronald Littlejohn after seven years and two daughters. She and Littlejohn are partners in Bona Fide, a thriving music management and film production firm (their second film was the audience fave at Sundance last year, and, according to Sunny, their next film stars her) based in Los Angeles.

"I hear you out here denying rumors, Sun. You're above that. Let fools think what they want."

Sunny knocks back her wine in three gulps, and seems exasper-ated, but she wants to discuss the Rain Song. "It's always been hard for me to talk about it, because it's really Dart's. I fucking sing *back-ground* on that song."

In fact, she does, but the way the lyrics were written (by a Motown tag team), and the way Sunny sings them, the background vocals work with the main vocals as a poignant duet.

"The simple fact is," Eva pipes in coolly, "Dart and Eddie had already recorded the vocals by the time Sun got to the island."

"I didn't sing on that song until we got to *Nassau*," Sunny says. "To a better studio. Dart wasn't even there. Just me, Ron, and Eddie."

I wonder aloud where Eva Glenn was.

"Sick," she says quickly. "I was at a doctor's office. My mother had just died."

"Oh," says Sunny with a smirk. She pours herself more wine. "And your girl Pritz was there."

"Pritz? *My* girl?" Eva looks at Sunny like it's time for Sunny to shut up. "Pour me a glass of imaginary Scotch, Sun. And pass me an imaginary cigarette."

"You got jokes," Sunny says with slitty eyes. "I can talk about what I want to talk about."

"Keep fucking with me and I'll go get the imaginary wine."

Sunny smiles at me, while Eva glances at her dainty yellow gold watch. "Prizzi," says Sun, mischeviously, "gets on Eva's nerves. Eva don't like her skin to be got under. Don't like to be got over on."

"All right, Sunny," Glenn says.

"I love you," Sunny says, "too."

The villain in the story is Giada "Pritz" Biasella. She sued Sunny and D'Artagnan and Eddie Innocent and Roadshow for production credit on Dart's version of "I Wish It Would Rain," and she got it. It was a seven-figure payout, and the kind that keeps paying out. Biasella has points on the single and the *HTH* album. Reached at the recently relaunched Solaar Records, where she is general manager, Biasella seems bored with any discussion of Sunny and Dart. "I am no heavy. I don't like to comment on Sunny or Dart, or those crazy days. I got what was owed to me for setting things up, for helping produce that song. That's it. Eva, Leetle John, all of them, they know how it was."

At the Rowe House? Were you at the Rowe House?

"*Roll?* What? I don't have an idea of what you are saying."

"If you start asking me a whole bunch of stupid questions about who was where when and all that, I'm going to shut up and you can take your little recorder and pens and be out."

The sun is setting on the California coastline, but Sunny Addison is at full heat. She's talking, and while her manager had been trying to curtail her, now Eva Glenn sips at her iced water like it's a cocktail, and listens like Sun's story is new to her.

"Eva was packing to leave for the States because her mom . . . had passed. I was going to stay on Nassau for a few more days with Pritz. Eddie came up to my hotel room with a DAT and played the song for me, Pritz, and Ron. Dart was God knew where, but as soon as Eddie pressed PLAY, my brother was in the room with us."

"On the original," Glenn says evenly, "Dart was singing his own background and it sounded weird and too heavy—you know how his voice is—"

"And all Pritz said," said Sunny, "was 'it needs something different—'"

"—'a girl on the track. That would be good.' That's all the bitch said."

"*I* stepped up," Sunny says, "saying I'd sing something on it. We weren't even thinking of it being a big deal. More a present to Dart. For when we found him, to make—"

"Like a souvenir," Glenn says, "from the trip."

"Eva and Ron saw the money," says Sunny with a cackle.

"Recognized Dart's talent and potential as a superstar. He was positive. Sun is positive. It was a tough time—Tupac and Biggie had been dead a year, we were all still reeling. It was time for some old-fashioned rhythm and blues."

Then Addison gets up and leaves me with Glenn. I ask her if she's happy.

"I can't complain," she says. "And if I did, who would listen?"

"Your fiancé must listen."

"He's the only one."

Sunny rushes back out with a CD. She slides it into the system she has built into the outer wall of her pool house. The first bluesy notes of the Rain Song come streaming from the big speakers.

Sunshine, blue skies, please go away.

"Sun," Eva says sharply, "don't play that."

But Sun waves her off. Then Sunny starts singing her part, and her brother's parts. Rays of light come from her mouth. D'Artagnan can sing—his voice is undeniably lovely. But his sister got to the table first. Sunny Addison's voice is otherworldly. Strong. Full. Beyond beautiful. She has almost too much inside her. Her voice is trembly when it gets big, barely able to contain the searing love and searing pain of a sun's heart. That's what listening to Sunny is like—you're watching her, hoping she's going to keep it together, knowing, hoping she'll hit those notes, match the sweetness of the last time you heard her, touch your every sadness and happiness like she always does. Sunny makes you worry, though, because she has that little tremble in her voice—but then she hits it. Not the high note, though she hits that, too—but the emotional note, the love note the hate note the true note. And you can't take it. You have to listen and cry or laugh or dance or do whatever it is you're moved to do.

Listen, I gotta cry, 'cause crying thins the pain.

And then, right there in front of a reporter from *Groove,* Eva Glenn—power woman, executive supreme—starts weeping. Not just a tear or two, but sobs. Sunny keeps right on singing. And Glenn doesn't excuse herself, or care even that I'm there. She flips off her pumps, places her bare feet on the hot ground. With her legs un-crossed I can see a horrible, V-shaped scar on her calf. Under the V are four blue, round dots. They look like the kind of tattoo girls get in juvenile hall. Addison sings more loudly, a strong angel swaying be-fore her own cherry-orange sunset.

Raindrops will hide my teardrops, and no one will ever know.

Eva Glenn has to have heard the song hundreds, maybe thousands of times—either the Temptations' version, or Sunny and D'Artgnan's version, or the many other adaptations out there—but when Sunny Addison sings for you like maybe she used to when she brought down the sky for quarters in parks in the flatlands of San Diego, you have to cry.

Because everything seems possible.

Maybe someone can understand me. I understand her.

That's what you think.

For a few moments, there was no industry churning behind our Sun. There were no deals.

It didn't last, though. The song ended. Sun dashed off, said she had to call her brother. Eva's cell chirped out a kicky ring tone. She told me I could go in a snappish way that meant I should have been gone. She ran her hand over her tattoos, slipped back into her pumps.

But for a few verses, it was bliss. Everything came together. Nothing hurt.

It's music. Thank God for it. We all cried.

Acknowledgments

Thanks to Janelle and Reginald Jones.

Thanks also to Raquel, Parker, Hunter, and Marco Williams.

Thanks to Lottie Fields, Victoria Jones, and Brandon Wells Jones.

Thanks to Robert and Cherrie Carter.

Thanks to Nicole Jones. Thanks to Khalief, David, Maiya, and Zoe. Thanks to Amorette Brooms.

Thanks to Gail Clifton, to Robert Stoller, to Mary Fletcher and her family, and to Romaine Clifton.

Thanks to April Jones, Candi Castleberry-Singleton, and Karen Lewis Farrelly.

Thanks to Karen Renée Good for her listening ear and constant friendship. Thanks to Tamara Warren.

Thanks to Dayna Clark for her sisterhood, friendship, and for all the homemade CDs.

I would also like to thank the Millay Colony for the Arts, and the New School Writing Program, as well as agents Paula Balzer and Sarah Lazin.

Thanks to the Wilsons—Berta, Elliott Sr., Steven, and Kenny.

Thanks to my own Wilson—Elliott Jr.—for the love, and for pushing me out of my holding pattern.

Thanks again to Chris Jackson for his encouragement, expertise, and guidance.

Thanks, too, to everyone who's ever written or performed a song.

ABOUT THE AUTHOR

———————

Danyel Smith is one of the best-loved music writers of her generation. A former editor at large for Time Inc. and editor in chief of *Vibe*, she also wrote the introduction to the *New York Times* bestseller *Tupac Shakur*. Born and raised in California, she now lives in New York City. Visit Danyel at nakedcartwheels.blogspot.com.

A Note on the Type

The text of this book was set in Berthold Bodoni Old Face, a typeface designed by Günter Gerhard Lange and released by Berthold in 1983; small caps and old style figures were added in 2000. This digitized version of Bodoni is based closely on the original designs of the late eighteenth century by Giambattista Bodoni.